A MOTHER'S SECRET

An unforgettable novel by

Carolyn Haddad

FROM ISRAEL TO AMERICA ... A MOTHER'S FORTY-YEAR SEARCH FOR HER MISSING DAUGHTER

Could it be that Wanda didn't want to return Mina to Eliza? Could it be that she now thought of Mina as her own child? Eliza begged favors, put ads in the papers that were again publishing. Missing child? Was she out of her mind, everyone wanted to know. There were hundreds of thousands of children missing, most of them dead. She'd be lucky if she even found the child alive . . .

A MOTHER'S SECRET

A NOVEL

Carolyn Haddad

PAN BOOKS

First published 1989 by Judy Piatkus (Publishers) Ltd

This edition published 1990 by Pan Books
an imprint of Macmillan Publishers Ltd
25 Eccleston Place, London SW1W 9NF
Basingstoke and Oxford
Associated companies throughout the world
www.macmillan.co.uk

ISBN 0 553 17696 X

1 3 5 7 9 8 6 4 2

A CIP catalogue record for this book is available from
the British Library.

Printed and bound in Great Britain by
Mackays of Chatham plc, Chatham, Kent

For Ruth Ellen Paul Kushner

with a daughter's love

POLAND

1

MAY 1939

WANDA ZBYSZEK WAS NOT A VIRGIN WHEN THREE BOYS FROM HER village raped her that beautiful spring day in May 1939. She knew men. She had known men ever since she could distinguish between light and dark, money and poverty. Even so, she didn't see herself as fair game for whoever came along. Living in the village of Kowitz, six kilometers to the southeast of Cracow, there was order in her life, as there was order in the life of the village. These boys had violated that order when they attacked her without warning, while she gathered wildflowers for her table from the woods outside her home.

She fought. Had they expected complacency? Acceptance? Then they didn't know her well enough. They didn't understand or care about the rules by which their elders lived, by which she lived now that she was alone. Once she could have been their friend, their companion, but that ended two years ago, when Wanda was fourteen, and her mother, Magda, left her and took off for the city of Cracow. Magda made many promises to return; Wanda never saw her again. Not that she blamed her mother. Who would stay in Kowitz if there was an alternative?

Her mother had been the laundress in the village of Kowitz, which existed, with its general store and its café, to serve the farmers surrounding it. The farmers and their wives and families would come in each week for supplies, for their mail, for coffee and gossip. Then the town would come alive. Then Magda would make more than she did from washing other people's clothes and linens. Because the men came to her and she greeted them with a cheery, welcoming smile as she led them into her windowless shack at the edge of town, just short of the forest. Wanda was sent outside to wait, to freeze in the cold, listening to the night sounds, as her mother's customers came and went. When her mother left, they became her customers, part of the only life she had ever known. But they were customers, and they paid; not like these young bas-

3

tards who piled on top of her, tore open her dress, forced her legs apart and raped her.

She bit one who came too close to her teeth. He punched her in return. "I know your father," she threatened. "And yours. I'll tell. I'll tell your fathers, your mothers."

"And who will care?" one of the boys asked, laughing in her face.

Who will care, Wanda repeated woefully. God. Where was justice?

"Get off of her!" a strange, deep voice bellowed. "What do you think you're doing? Hey, you!"

Wanda, who had squeezed her eyes tight, opened them to find arms and legs swinging above her. She covered her face and felt the light spring air strike against her naked chest. The battle above her continued without her taking any part in it until she heard feet running, and then there was silence.

Wanda slowly uncovered her face and opened her eyes. Two people stood over her, staring down at her with looks of concern. They were dressed in the sort of clothes city people wore when they wanted to look as if they belonged in the country.

"Are you all right?" the woman asked. She might have been a few years older than Wanda and was as dark as Wanda was fair.

"Let us help you," the young man said. He was foreign-looking, with light brown, intensely curly hair and a strangely pensive face.

Wanda grabbed at the remnants of her clothing and sat up. The woman leaned down and helped her restore a sense of modesty. With her aid, Wanda stood. Beneath her on the forest floor were the wildflowers she had collected. Their blossoms were crushed, their stems broken. For some unfathomable reason, she began to cry.

The woman placed her arms around her and murmured some words meant to bring comfort. Wanda pushed her away. She hadn't cried since her mother left over two years ago. Then she had wondered how she would survive. But now she knew, so what was there to cry over?

"Where do you live? Let us take you home," the young man said.

Unsteadily, she led them through the forest toward her shack. They pushed tree branches aside for her and watched her carefully, afraid she might fall. "This is where I live," she said, when they came to the one-room, windowless structure that served as her home. The couple looked from Wanda to the shack. They were waiting. For what? "Would you care to come in and have something to drink?"

They looked at each other. The woman nodded.

Inside the shack were two chairs, a table, a bed, a washbasin, an iron resting in the coals. "Water? Beer? Tea?"

"Beer would be nice, if you have it," the young man said.

Wanda always had beer. The men liked it. She poured two glasses for them, none for herself. They continued to stare at her and at her surroundings. She tried to guess what they were thinking. "It's not as if I minded what happened," she explained to them. "Back there, in the forest. It's just that they tried to get something for free. Here I am paid for it."

She saw shock register on the woman's face. The man stared at her first with astonishment, then, she believed, with pity. "You must have a very hard life," he said to her.

"Sometimes it's not easy," she agreed. "In the winter my hands are raw from the laundry. Sometimes they bleed."

"You're suffering from exploitation."

She leaned forward. "Excuse me?" she said to the young man.

"Have you ever heard of socialism?" he asked her.

"Adam," the woman warned.

Wanda smiled triumphantly. "I have heard of socialism. Our priest warns us against it."

Adam gave a so-there nod at his companion. The woman seemed anxious to change the direction of the conversation. "We're from Cracow," she told Wanda.

"Yes. I thought so."

"We look like city people?"

"You don't look like you belong in the country. You, for instance," she told the woman, "your skin is much too pale. And you," she pointed to Adam, "your clothes are much too fine for a country person, unless you were a judge."

"I don't judge," the man solemnly assured her.

The woman stood. "Thank you for the beer. It was very refreshing. We should be going now."

Wanda took the glasses from them. "Thank you for saving me. No one has ever saved me from anything before."

The woman's face softened, and she looked as if she might cry. Wanda was confused. "My name is Wanda, Wanda Zbyszek. If you come this way again, you're always welcome here."

The woman smiled. "Thank you. My name is Eliza Wolf and this is my friend Adam Feuerstein. If you're ever in Cracow—"

Wanda laughed lightly. "I'll never go to the city. My life is here." It was only after the two strangers left that she realized why they had looked so foreign. By their names, she could tell they were Jews.

"Now you see why this country is in so much trouble," Adam said fiercely, when they had cleared Kowitz and were on the road to Cracow.

"What a terrible life she has to live!"

"She doesn't have to live it. That's the point. She could be as free as you and I are. If Poland would only cast off its feudal bonds and stride toward its future."

"But where does its future lie?"

He turned to look at her. "Can you doubt that socialism would free people like Wanda Zbyszek? There's so much to do, so much work, and they have me writing pamphlets. Why?"

"Maybe studying philosophy at the university doesn't make you fit for anything else?" she teased.

He looked at her and laughed. "Anyway, I hope this little jaunt frees you from your bucolic views of the countryside. From now on, may we stick to the city for our amusements?"

She smiled back at him, hooked her arm with his. "Do you ever feel—frightened?"

"Frightened? Why should I? When you know your course is right, Eliza, there's no reason to fear."

"Pompous."

"Not so. Belief is what's important. You have to believe in something in order to live. I believe that a socialistic system will serve humanity better than any other model."

"Your cousin Motti believes the same about Zionism."

"And my brother Zorik believes in God. Look where they are now. Zorik's in the yeshiva and Motti's in Palestine. Both have given up their stake in the future."

"Why?"

"Because the future is here, now, in Europe. This is where we will make our stand. This is where we will revolutionize humanity. This is where we will overthrow oppression. Why can't you have faith in our efforts, Eliza?"

"Because while you've been writing your tracts, I've been reading the newspapers."

"Oh. You want to speak about Germany again. The socialists in Germany—"

"I'm not speaking about the socialists in Germany, Adam. I'm speaking about Hitler, the Nazis. I'm speaking about Kristallnacht. I'm speaking about rumors of what they are doing to the Jews."

"When will you stop thinking of yourself as being Jewish?" he lectured.

"When everybody else does."

"Look, Hitler is a madman. Poland has her alliances to protect her. And as for what's happening in Germany to the Jews, look what has always happened here in Poland. Do you think we are loved here? The social order, as it now stands, needs a scapegoat. By tradition, by some insane birthright, we are it. When the social order changes, then we'll be free."

"Adam, let's go."

"Where?"

"To Palestine."

"Are you kidding? I wouldn't have anything to do with those Zionists. They're crazy people. Go to some desert in the middle of nowhere? Eliza? Where is your commitment? If you don't shape up, I'm going to have to drop you in favor of Hannah."

Eliza tugged on his arm and threw him off balance. "Oh, Hannah's definitely more your type. Studious, intense, yet with big enough breasts to be the sort of woman a man could dream of."

"True."

"Adam!"

"She has her good points, two of them. But you're still my female of choice."

"Thanks."

"Smile."

"I'm trying."

"Believe me, Eliza. There is a new dawn, and we will be among those who make the sun rise."

Wanda Zbyszek might have been amused to discover that she was the subject of such learned conversation. Oppression? She knew it well. It's what she felt some days when she found that the day held nothing but a new batch of laundry. She longed for change, for something new in her life. She could simply, if she wished, walk away from Kowitz. There was nothing to hold her here. And yet she was afraid. Even her mother had not run off alone, but with some man.

Jews. She smiled as she wondered what her fellow villagers would say if they knew Jews had shared a beer with her. There were no Jews in Kowitz. She knew about them only from those who traded at the South Market in Cracow. And, of course, she knew of Jews from the priest, who used to lecture the students in the church school she attended. He talked about their strange rituals, their practices, which were evil in the sight of God. He mentioned the rumors about Jews using the blood of young Polish boys to make their Passover bread. Just a rumor, he repeated with a smile, so that no one knew what to think. But when Passover came, no young Polish boy would go out alone. Or if he did something bad, his mother would threaten him with the Jews coming to get him while he slept.

These two Jews didn't seem bad, though. They didn't have horns. They were almost human. They were from the city, so she didn't know what to expect of them, but certainly they had done her a favor. If the villagers knew—But they wouldn't, because she wasn't going to tell them.

Anyway, the village had enough on its mind without knowing there had been Jews in Kowitz. Two more young men had gone away to join the army. Their mothers cried for them. Why, Wanda didn't know. If she had been a man, she might join the army just to get out of the village for a while, to try a life different from farming. And when the young men came back in their uniforms, they looked so handsome all the girls fell for them. It must be nice to be a soldier.

The men at the café occasionally talked of war, the threat that both Germany and Russia posed to Poland's fragile independence. It was like playing a game of checkers, she thought. Their conversations were filled with suppositions: If Germany does this, then England will do that. And France? And Russia?

The moves were all too complicated for her. Life just didn't change that easily. There was a constancy that nature demanded and that Kowitz fulfilled.

Oppression. Socialism. Communism. Fascism. Those were just words. What was real was getting up each morning and wondering where the day's food would come from.

2

NOVEMBER 1943

THE WAR IN POLAND HAD NOT EXACTLY PASSED THE VILLAGE OF
Kowitz by. During September of 1939, German soldiers had
marched through the village en route to Cracow. The villagers had
fled to the woods, only to return by nightfall to find some of their
buildings burned, others looted for food or what homely comforts
they could provide. Wanda Zbyszek's shack had not been touched.

Wanda knew from the gossiping villagers that the whole of Europe was being swallowed up in war, but it was strange how little
these past four years of war had affected her. In 1942 a fighter from
the Polish resistance had come to their village with some sort of
radio transmitter, but the policy of German retaliation against any
village harboring partisans was by then well known. The next village had lost twenty of its inhabitants when they took in refugees
form the Home Army, the remnant of Poland's defense forces. This
resistance fighter who dared make his way to Kowitz was quickly
turned in to the Germans by the village council and, she learned,
just as quickly executed. The people of Kowitz wanted no trouble.
The Germans gave them a quota of food and goods to produce for
the troops of Cracow. Though the measure was harsh, leaving little
to feed their own bellies, the villagers complied. Survival was important, and that meant doing what you were told to do and not
getting involved in anything else.

Sometimes German soldiers came to Kowitz, and not only to
pick up supplies and deliver new demands. The SS checked regularly to see if any suspicious strangers had shown up in Kowitz.
But after the one resistance fighter had been betrayed, Kowitz was
not troubled by patriots.

It was the ordinary German soldier whom Wanda enjoyed seeing
in Kowitz, country youths like herself who were far away from
home, from their own villages, from their friends and families. The
villagers pointed these soldiers in her direction; and she was glad
to have them, not only for the company they gave her, but also for
the chocolate, the luxuries, even jewelry that they sometimes gave

9

her. She thought that the German army must pay very well to allow its ordinary soldiers to have money to buy such fine goods. She once said that to one of them and he laughed at her as if she were a country bumpkin. She might have been from the country, but she was no longer naïve. A whore, after all, had to have a lot of guile to stay alive and fit.

"Then where do you get these beautiful things?" she had asked the laughing soldier.

"It's not important," he told her.

She gave him a teasing smile. "You don't look like a looter."

"I'm not. These people, well, they'll never need these things again."

She didn't ask anything after that. She knew that these were gifts from the dead.

The soldiers came and went; the seasons circled, unchanged by death's abundance. As summer was pleasing, winter was fierce, unbearably cold. More often than she would have wished, Wanda had to leave her shack to gather wood for her fire; her stockpile always seemed to run low.

One day she returned from wood gathering to find unknown prints in the snow around her house. These were large bootprints, but not as large as a man's. She was puzzled, because women didn't seek out her company. She dropped the wood in front of her door, picked up a stick as a weapon and entered.

Bundled against the cold and against recognition, a woman, as Wanda had guessed, sat on one of the chairs at Wanda's table. In her lap she held a child, who was somewhere between one and one and a half. The woman's clothes were unfamiliar to Wanda, as was her determined demeanor. And yet the stranger did not look exactly threatening. How could she really, with a child on her lap?

"Who are you? What do you want?" Wanda demanded.

"Wanda Zbyszek?" The voice was soft, tired.

"Yes?"

"I'm sorry. I didn't recognize you."

"I don't recognize you either," Wanda shot back.

"You wouldn't. I met you only briefly years ago, almost four and a half years ago."

Wanda, stick still in hand, came closer. The woman unwrapped the scarf muffling her face. Wanda stared at her, still not having the slightest idea who she was. "You were in the woods," the woman said. "Three boys were attacking you. My friend and I heard your cry and drove them off with a stick much like the one you're holding now."

Wanda stepped back. "I remember."

"Eliza Wolf."

"I remember."

"I have brought you my baby."

"You are a Jew?"

"Yes. This baby is mine and Adam Feuerstein's. It is no longer safe for me to take care of her."

"You don't belong in this village."

"I know. I don't belong anywhere. No place on this earth is safe for me. Do you understand?"

Wanda thought of all the pretty things the soldiers had brought her from Cracow and of the rumors she had heard. "You must leave here."

"I will, yes, immediately."

"There are soldiers—"

"Yes, I know."

"It's broad daylight!" Wanda said to the woman, as if she were mad.

"I was afraid I wouldn't find your place at night. The child's name is Mina."

"I can't keep her! Are you joking? A Jewish child in my house?"

"You must. There is no one else."

"What would I do with a child? Questions would be asked. They would think that I was—I could be killed!"

"You must have relatives somewhere else, in some city perhaps? Can't you claim that one brought this child to you for the healthier country life?"

"I will claim nothing. Why should I put myself in danger for you?"

Eliza shrugged. "If you can't find the answer within yourself, I can't give you one. Mina is a quiet child. She knows how to be quiet at night. She won't trouble you. And I will be back for her. I promise."

"Take her now. I won't keep her!"

Eliza hugged her child one last time. Wanda saw her eyes close, saw her lips moving, maybe praying. Eliza stood. "She doesn't eat much, so food should be no problem."

"She won't be eating at all if you leave her with me."

Eliza stared straight into Wanda's eyes. "When you thanked us for dragging those boys off you, you said no one had saved you before that day. No one is saving us now. Please. I'm begging. She's just a baby. How can you refuse?"

Eliza did not turn to her child again. Slowly, with determination, she walked out the door of the shack toward the forest. "If you leave her here, tonight I will put her out in the cold to freeze to death!" Wanda shouted at the woman's back.

Eliza Wolf continued walking as if she had not heard. With horror and astonishment, Wanda stood in the doorway until the figure of the woman completely disappeared. Then she turned and looked at the child, who stared quizzically up at her.

3

JUNE 29, 1945

RAPED AND RAPED AGAIN, POLAND WAS LIBERATED BY THE SOVIET army. Marshal Ivan Konev, second only to Marshal Zhukov in his military reputation, marched through Poland on his way to Berlin. On January 19, 1945, his troops retook Cracow.

Wanda Zbyszek hid the child under the bed when the Russians came to Kowitz. When the Germans came, the villagers had fled to the woods. Now that was impossible. The Germans were hiding in the woods. The villagers must stay in their houses or be shot. House by house, the Russians came, looking for Germans, looking for collaborators, looting, raping.

Two sons of the Red Army kicked open the door of Wanda's shack and tramped in. She crouched against the wall, a scarf covering her golden hair, soot covering the fairness of her face. They looked around, then toppled over her table and chairs. They came for her. She prayed they would not kill her.

The scarf was pulled from her head and her blond hair exploded around her. One of the soldiers stood close to her, his fingers moving through her hair as if it were the finest silk. They looked into one another's eyes. She saw lust; he saw fear. "Don't kill me," she begged. If he understood, he gave no sign of it. He pushed her down onto the floor and used her. But his mind seemed always on her hair, which he did not let go of. His partner was less esthetically inclined, intent only on his physical pleasure.

She lay on the floor, dirty and terrified, while they searched the room with their eyes. They moved toward the bed and she stared after them, fists tight. The one who was fascinated by her hair noticed. He raised his rifle. "No!" she screamed. "My child."

She crawled to the bed, reached underneath and brought forth the girl. She hugged her in her arms and rocked her protectively. The soldiers lifted the bed, threw the straw mattress aside. They could find nothing else. The soldier put his hand one more time through Wanda's hair. And then they left. "Mama," the little girl said, "was I quiet enough?"

Spring came again to Kowitz. For Poland, the war with Germany was over. Internally, the Poles struggled with themselves and with their new taskmaster, the Soviet Union. But Wanda had no interest in politics, as long as it didn't touch her.

News of the war came to her unbidden, stories of what had become of the Jews of Poland. Not that she should care. Hadn't they, after all, killed Christ? Still, in Oswiecim, what the Germans called Auschwitz, it was said that—but it was too impossible to believe. This was merely a political ploy on somebody's part, an effort to gain power. Because nobody could ever do that to so many human beings, certainly not those German boys who had visited her, bringing with them their gifts from the dead.

Often during the war, when they were outside working, doing the laundry or gathering wood, Wanda would watch Mina to see if the child gave any indication of being a Jew. She was dark, yes, her hair kinky and unruly, but her cheeks were rosy from the country air. After the war Wanda had heard stories of children being—well, it was better not to think about it.

Wanda had told the villagers that the child was her mother's, that her mother had come back to drop off the child because life was too harsh in Cracow. This they could well believe, and they could believe that her mother had had another child by some man or other. If they had suspicions that things might have been other than what Wanda had told them, they gave no sign. Why shouldn't the child call Wanda "Mama"? Wanda was certainly more the age of a mother than a sister, and it made for fewer complications should the Germans ask any questions. Mina was accepted, and she grew. Maybe she did not flourish, but who did in those years when there was never enough to eat, when the demands made by the armies were constant and overwhelming?

Where was Eliza Wolf? That's what Wanda wanted to know as the months passed since Cracow had been liberated. She waited, each day expecting the woman to come for her child. Not that Wanda didn't love Mina and take pleasure in her company. But a bargain was a bargain, and the woman had said she would be back for the girl.

Eliza Wölf never came.

Names became associated with numbers. Auschwitz, Treblinka, Sobibor, one million, two million, three million, four, five, six million.

Of course it was impossible. No one could have murdered so many people in so little time. The Russians had political officers who came to Kowitz now, instead of their raping, pillaging soldiers. They tried to explain how the Communist revolution was going to change the villagers' lives. She didn't pay much attention. It was just another foot on the neck of the Polish farmer. Nothing new about that. But then the officer talked about what had happened in the war and what had happened to the Jews. Good riddance was the general feeling among the villagers of Kowitz, which made Wanda hold Mina more tightly to her. Mina might have been one of those millions. Were they really gassed? Then their bodies burned?

Wanda looked into the eyes of a stranger's child. She knew that Eliza Wolf would not be coming back for Mina. Mina's survival would now be up to her. And no one was going to take the child away and do anything to her. Mina wasn't a Jew. She was just a little three-year-old girl who called Wanda "Mama."

"It's just you and me now," she told the child that night after the Russian visitors had left. Mina fell quickly to sleep. Wanda lay next to her warmth and began to think about their future. Now that she had a child to consider, she had to do something with her life. · To stay in the village, to continue to be the town whore might be all right for a few more years, but then Mina would know and what would Mina think? And yet, how wise would it be to leave the village at a time like this? In the village there was always food, no matter how harsh the demands for production were. The cities were devastated. They offered no hope. Maybe there was nothing more on earth to hope for.

The next day Wanda was off picking up the laundry at the Wieczoreks' house. Herta Wieczorek could well afford to have the laundry done for her. Her husband owned the general store. Someday, perhaps, Wanda would marry well. But certainly not in Kowitz. She was walking home, dirty laundry in hand, when a jeep pulled up next to her. "You from Kowitz?" the soldier in the jeep called to her.

Even though she was now wary of any man in a uniform, she had to admit that, yes, Kowitz was her village.

"Here." He tossed a bundle at her, put the jeep into reverse and disappeared.

The bundle had landed on the laundry. Annoyed, Wanda looked down and discovered that she had just been given the mail delivery for the entire village, not that they ever received much mail.

She walked back to her shack and placed the laundry down by her tub. If curiosity had not gotten the better of her, she would have taken the mail to Tadek Wieczorek right away for him to distribute. But what was the harm in knowing other people's business?

Nothing of interest. Letters from the cities, probably from relatives, asking for food. And then, here was something she had not seen before. It was an air letter. Maybe from Britain. She understood that many Poles had fled to Britain for the duration of the war. Would they now all be coming home? She would have stayed in Britain if she'd had the chance.

She got up from the table and took the letter to the door for a closer examination. No, not from Britain. This letter was from the United States. America! Who was the lucky recipient?

Wanda studied the address. Maria Prychek. Maria Prychek?

The woman was dead. She had died of a fever during the first years of the war. She was only a few years older than Wanda. Who would have thought that a fever could have carried such a young woman away? But what had Maria left to live for? Her husband was a soldier who had been killed defending Cracow in 1939. Her mother had died shortly before Maria. As a matter of fact, that's how Maria became sick, nursing her mother.

Could letters from America be returned?

Wanda had never had a letter from America. She had never had a letter from anywhere. She doubted whether her mother even knew how to read or write. She herself had been more fortunate, attending the church school, where she learned not only to read and write but also to do simple arithmetic. The nuns had always been pleased with her progress, and if she had been a different type of girl, maybe—well, forget the maybes, she told herself harshly.

What should she do with the letter? Maria couldn't use it. The shopkeeper would probably do something official with it. That was silly, because letters were meant to be read.

Wanda decided to keep the letter. She placed it under the mattress of her bed. Then she gathered up the rest of the mail and hurried over to Tadek Wieczorek with it. She explained about the soldier and the jeep. Tadek gave her a condescending smile and took the letters from her. She meekly returned to her work. All day she washed and hung clothes. At night she folded and then delivered them to their owners with a grateful smile for what they could give her. The butcher's wife came through with a piece of fat that might, just might, have a bit of meat on it. That night she and Mina had stew, which they soaked up with good black bread from the baker. Mina went happily to sleep with a full stomach.

Wanda reached under the mattress and withdrew the letter. She lit the candle she always kept on the table. Some men wanted to see her; others didn't care what she looked like. They preferred the dark.

Carefully, cautiously, looking about her, Wanda slit open the letter. "May 10, 1945. Dear Maria," the letter began. "You probably do not know who we are. Your mother's sister, the one who traveled to Paris, married my husband's father. Together, they came to the United States. Your mother's sister, my mother-in-law, spoke often of the village of Kowitz, so we feel we know it as well as our hometown. She was very upset when she found out from a letter you sent to relatives in Warsaw that your mother had died."

Wanda remembered Maria's mother. The woman was very bossy; the town had wondered how death got up the nerve to take her.

"This is a very awkward letter to write because we don't know each other. But my husband served in the war. He fought his way through France and Germany before he was wounded and returned home safe to me, thank God. He told me what it was like for civilians, how hard and miserable the war years have been. Now I read in the papers about all the people who have been killed in Poland and how you are still suffering. I want to do something to help, and giving to the Red Cross just doesn't seem to be enough.

"Please write me and tell me what I can do for you. Can I send you anything? What do you need to survive? Is it possible that you would like to come to the United States? I don't know how it is done, but we would be glad to serve as your sponsors.

"You are our closest relative in Poland. Whatever we can do to help you, we will. Please write soon. Our address is Peter and Doreen Novoveski, 12 Orchard Drive, Trenton, New Jersey.

"With all our love and concern, Doreen Novoveski."

Wanda sat back in her chair; an annoyed look set grimly across her features. Damn. If only she had relatives like this! Here Maria was dead and she gets the invitation to America, while Wanda is alive and well, with a child to take care of, and she gets the dirty laundry.

Well, that's the way life works, Wanda thought. You deal with what God gives you.

She blew out the candle, stood, walked over to the bed and

crawled in beside the soft, warm body of the child. Wanda's hands were raw and her back ached. She would be old before her time. Her eyes closed and she hovered near sleep.

You deal with what God gives you.

She sat up. God had given her the letter to Maria Prychek.

She got out of bed, relit the candle and reread the letter. Just as she thought. Peter and Doreen Novoveski had absolutely no idea what Maria Prychek looked like, whether she was dead or alive. They had simply written a letter; fate had sent it in her direction.

Why couldn't she be Maria Prychek?

Their age difference was not so large. Didn't she know as much about Maria as Maria knew about herself? She had grown up with Maria. Her mother knew Maria's mother. There are no secrets in a village as small as Kowitz.

But could she play the imposter? No. Certainly not if she stayed in Kowitz. How could she have anything sent to her in Maria Prychek's name? The delivery of the mail was not always going to be as fortuitous as it had been today. And even if she could get Tadek Wieczorek to go in with her on the plot, what sort of cut would she have to give him? The Novoveskis proposed to send her things from America. But who knew how regularly the packages would come?

The letter offered another opportunity. Would she like to come to America?

Too much, she thought. She was reaching for what she could never have. Freedom in America? It was a dream.

But it was everybody's dream. So why shouldn't it be hers? There was a way to get to America. Everyone in Europe was on the move, either fleeing or returning. She could be, too.

Mina. What would she do with the child?

The child had been left in her care. She couldn't abandon her. But wouldn't it be much easier for one than for two to move across Europe?

On the other hand, people responded to children, whereas a young woman alone was subject to all sorts of predicaments, as Wanda should well know from her life so far.

Yes, Wanda would take Mina with her. They would leave tomorrow. There was nothing to keep them in Kowitz. By nightfall they could be in Cracow. From there, somehow, Wanda would make her way to America.

4

CRACOW

WHEN WANDA ZBYSZEK REACHED THE CITY OF CRACOW, SHE UNderstood how lucky she was to have spent the war years in her village of Kowitz. If there was order in the universe, it did not exist after the war swept through Cracow.

"We won't stay long," she promised Mina. "Just long enough to get identification and buy tickets out of here."

Mina looked at her without comprehension. Well, what should a three-year-old child comprehend? It was all a game to her. That's how Wanda had told her to treat it. They had played a game of stuffing food underneath their clothing, of sewing what fortune they had inside the lining of Mina's coat. Mina's coat was the repository of all good things. Wanda had cut it down from a castoff of one of the neighborhood boys. Even so, there was no way it was going to be the right size. She could see Mina scratching herself every now and then, with a very sour look on her face. Poor Mina, with that slab of meat next to her body.

What a day it had been! Wanda had stayed up all night, sewing by candlelight, preparing smugglers' pockets for herself and the child. Then in the morning she had made her rounds. She had let everyone know that now that the war was over, it was only right that her mother take the child back with her. She was going to the city to find her mother. Oh, they all warned her against it, warned her of the Russian troops and the harsh conditions. But she assured them her mind was made up. Then she begged the butcher for a piece of meat to take to her mother, the dairyman for a kilo of butter, a neighbor for a few eggs. She and Mina were a walking grocery store by the time they were ready to leave. And all the guarantees she had given, all the work she would do for the donors without payment—that thought more than any drove her toward Cracow.

"By tonight," she assured Mina, as they walked purposefully down the street toward nowhere, "we will be on our way out of Poland."

18

Mina solemnly held onto Wanda's hand. The girl showed the stamina of her country living. She kept going even as Wanda felt like collapsing from all the excitement of the evening before.

The outskirts of the city of Cracow picked up her spirits and propelled Wanda forward. How magnificent it looked with the sun high upon it! Her first disappointment was that it only looked magnificent. Cracow, as it must have been, no longer existed. Now the city was just battered shells of buildings and war-weary people.

Her requests for directions led her to a government office full of people whose faces shifted between boredom and despair. She didn't like the smell of these people. There was something hopeless about them that disturbed her. Or perhaps that was the way it was when anyone dealt with the government. She didn't know. In Kowitz, so far, the government had stayed away, as if the town were not worth the effort.

With Mina in hand, Wanda snaked her way slowly to the front window. A woman in a Red Army uniform sat behind it. "I need to see someone about my identification," she said to the woman.

The woman hardly bothered looking at her. She took a white slip of paper, wrote a number on it, stamped it, and pushed the paper through the glass window to Wanda. "How long will it be?" Wanda asked.

The woman in uniform looked at her as if the question were the height of impertinence. "When your number is called," she said abruptly.

Wanda turned away and found a place for herself at the edge of a crowded bench. She doubted the eggs in her side pocket were going to make it.

She waited, Mina at her feet. The office clock ticked away on the opposite wall. A door opened. "Twenty-nine," another woman in a soldier's uniform called out. Twenty-nine gratefully stood and hurried toward the open door. Wanda looked down at her number. It was seventy-eight. Seventy-eight! They were on twenty-nine, and the day was already half over.

An hour later they called number thirty. Wanda could see herself sitting here all week. Her anxiety grew. Where was she to stay the night? How would she take care of Mina? The girl now lay across her lap, sleeping angelically.

"What a beautiful child!"

Wanda looked up sharply. A man on the bench next to her was leaning toward her, speaking of Mina. "Thank you," she said curtly. She returned her attention to the floor.

"So well behaved."

He obviously intended to start a conversation with her. She looked up again at him. He was older than she was by a good ten years; his fingers were yellow from where he constantly held a cigarette between them. His eyes looked haggard; his face was scarred. "What number are you?" he asked.

"Seventy-eight."

"Ah. You have a good two days left. May I take you out for some tea?"

She didn't want any tea. She didn't even want to speak to this man. But if she had a good two days to spend here, maybe he had a place to stay. She had to be practical.

Wanda nodded. The man smiled, stood and lifted Mina from Wanda's lap. The child woke and fell back to sleep just as easily, resting against the man's shoulder.

They were out in the hall before the man spoke again. "You're from the country, aren't you?"

"Yes."

"I thought so. You look healthy. There are not many of us in Cracow who look as well as you do."

What was he asking for, Wanda wondered.

"What brought you to the city?"

"I must travel, and I have no ID."

"I thought even villagers had to have ID."

"Mine was issued by the Germans. When they left, I burned the papers. Now I have nothing."

He looked at her and smiled. "Really."

She didn't like his smile. She knew he didn't believe her.

"Do you have a birth certificate for you and the child?"

"No," she admitted.

"Baptismal certificates then?"

"No. None for the child either. But I have a letter. Addressed to me," she said defensively.

"Ah." As if he understood. "You will not get your ID on the basis of that. Surely not from the government."

And she had thought it was all going to be so easy. Should she believe what this man was telling her?

"There are other sources of paper. If you have the money."

"I have no money," she lied. She had money, saved up from the men she slept with, but there was no reason why she should tell him that.

"Your child is very bulky in strange places."

Wanda smiled. "It's not gold."

"Pork is gold when people are hungry."

Wanda now knew this man wasn't buying; he was selling. "I need ID good enough to get me and my child into Austria."

"Take my advice. Do it in stages. Buy your ticket for Bratislava. Much less interest in people going to Bratislava. From there make your way to Austria. Now what can you pay me?"

"The meat."

"And?"

"Tell me how much the papers usually cost in money. I'll tell you how much I'll give you."

He smiled. "Follow me."

His apartment was full of people. There was one very old woman, two couples, seven small children, and a woman who came to greet him. She must have been either his wife or girlfriend. "Business," he said to her. The people parted for him, and he took Wanda to a small room, which looked like an enlarged closet. By this time, Mina was fully awake. "Why don't you let her play with the others," he suggested.

Wanda carefully took Mina's coat from her before she would allow the child to leave her. The man smiled. He seemed very understanding. "Now what can I do for you?" he said.

"How do I know that your papers are any good?" she asked.

"They were good enough for the resistance." He nodded toward the other room. "Go ask some of the people out there how they managed to travel during the German occupation. Believe me, my papers are gold."

He could say it, but should she believe it? She supposed, in the end, the scars on his face convinced her. She was about to take the letter from America out of her pocket to show him how she wanted her name, but she held back. What if he read the letter? What if one of the people in the other room decided she would make a better Maria Prychek than Wanda? "I want my name to be Maria Prychek." He wrote it down and showed it to her. "Yes."

"How old?"

He looked up at her and waited. She was now twenty-two. But Maria had been three years older than Wanda. The Novoveskis in America might know when Maria was born. Better play it safe, though she didn't relish being older than she actually was. "Twenty-five," she decided, with regret.

"Do you know your birth date? The one you want on your papers?"

So. He didn't believe Maria Prychek was her name. When had Maria been born? She had absolutely no idea. "Make it March 10, 1920."

"Very well. Now. Will you be needing a baptismal certificate, too?"

"What for?"

He shrugged. "Sometimes it's easier to move around if one is not thought to be Jewish."

"Do I look Jewish?"

"The choice is yours."

She considered it. "How much extra?"

"What do you have besides the pork and the eggs?"

"I never told you about the eggs. Besides, I need money for the train."

"Money. Not eggs."

"Does this mean you operate your own monetary exchange, too?"

He smiled. "I do what I have to survive. The baptismal certificate?"

"Yes. Go ahead."

"And your daughter?"

"She's—yes, my daughter." The man stared at her, the first hint of worry coming to his eyes. "My daughter will also need identification papers and a baptismal certificate."

"And what is her name?"

What would Maria call her daughter?

"It's better to leave a child that age with the name she's used to," he suggested. "It's very hard for them to be deceitful at such a young age."

"She's had plenty of practice," Wanda said, almost to herself. "Mina. Her name is Mina Prychek."

"And her date of birth?"

Good lord! Wanda had no idea how old the child was. She was about one when Eliza Wolf brought her to Wanda, maybe one and a half. "February 14, 1942," Wanda said, taking a guess.

"Fine."

"How long is this going to take?"

"Not long. Please, go into the living room. My wife will bring you a glass of tea."

"I want to leave Cracow tonight."

"To Bratislava?"

"Yes. If you say it's best."

"Yes." He stood up and escorted her into the living room, where Mina was scampering around with the other children. It made her realize how isolated she and Mina had been in the village, whether by their own choice or that of the villagers.

Room was made for Wanda and she sat down. The forger was whispering suspiciously to one of the young men in the apartment. The other man put on his coat and went out the door. Wanda could only wonder what would happen to her now. Who was the other man going to get?

What could she do? Run away? Go back to the government office and wait a few days? Trust the man?

The forger's wife brought her a glass of tea and a slice of bread. Wanda thought longingly of the butter she had stuffed inside her blouse. It would melt if she didn't take off her coat. But if she did take off her coat, everyone would see it. No one seemed to notice anything unusual about her. Maybe after the war, nothing was unusual.

She sat on the couch while life went on about her. The other man came back into the apartment alone a few hours after he left. Maybe he had set up an ambush for her just outside the apartment building. But why? They could just as easily attack her in the apartment. He went to the back room to speak to the forger. She waited. Mina slept on her lap once again, then was up and playing with her new friends. Wanda was tempted to return to the safety of Kowitz, where she knew exactly what was going to happen to her.

The forger came out of the back room. He sat down next to her on the couch and showed her the papers he had created for her. "They look used," she told him. Should she pay for what were obviously secondhand documents?

"They must look used," he explained. "New papers would be very suspicious for someone who is twenty-five years of age. Even the child's papers have to look worn. Papers are demanded for everything. Now the baptismal certificates, you will note, are fresher, especially the child's. That's because you would keep them in a safe, sacred place. They are very special. For many, baptismal papers meant life or death."

With a stab of guilt, Wanda thought of Eliza Wolf. And Mina. "You are sure that these will do?" she demanded to know.

"Trust him," his wife said. "His work has saved many lives."

Wanda nodded grimly. What could she do but trust him?

"Now I would like payment. The meat. The eggs. I would like the butter, too."

"How do you know I have butter?"

"I can smell it. It will turn rancid if you leave it there much longer."

"I told you I need money for the train tickets."

"Jan," the man called.

The other man, Jan, the one who had left the apartment, came to them. He took two tickets out of his pocket. "For the night train to Bratislava."

Wanda looked from one man to the other. For the first time, she smiled. She got up and took the tickets from Jan. Then she said, "You will let me do this in the kitchen?"

"Certainly," the man said.

His wife followed Wanda into the kitchen. Together they unstitched Mina's coat and freed the meat. Then Wanda took the eggs out of the inside pockets of her coat. Unbuttoning her blouse, she took out the butter. It was in very soggy shape, but the woman didn't mind. "Tonight we will eat," she said happily. "And you?" She looked at Wanda with concern. "Do you have anything for the journey?"

"I have some bread and cheese, which your husband did not nose out."

The woman laughed. "Good luck to you. Your child is so sweet, so huggable."

"Thank you. Yes. She is a good girl."

Wanda returned to the living room and called Mina to her. Together they made a final trip to the bathroom before Wanda tucked Mina once more into the safety of her coat. She thanked the man. She hoped she had reason to. Then she and Mina were back on the street, heading toward the train station. They were on their way. They had moved one step closer to America.

5

J O U R N E Y   W E S T

THE TRAIN STATION AT CRACOW WAS FILLED WITH GHOSTS. WANDA stopped in front of the sign that directed passengers to the train for Auschwitz. By then there was no doubt about what had happened to the Jews of Poland. She looked down at Mina to see if the child felt a shiver of recognition. But Mina, with her thumb in her mouth, was just gazing casually at the passing stream of giant adults. If she had an intimation that her real mother might have taken her last

train ride from this station, she gave no sign of it. Perhaps God was
kind after all.

"Come, Mina," Wanda said. She pulled the girl in the direction
of the train for Bratislava. Together with Wanda's small valise, they
hiked themselves aboard, then squeezed into a compartment that
was already overflowing with people.

Wanda stood and gazed at two men reading the paper. They did
their best to avoid her, but her stare was continuous. They both
looked up almost simultaneously, then shifted their bodies, barely
giving her enough room to fit in. She put the valise between her
legs, after which she drew Mina up on her lap, hugging her tightly.
Then she closed her eyes and leaned back, resting her head.

It was so crowded, so stuffy in this compartment, she felt as if
she were going to faint. She remembered what she had heard in the
village—how the Jews, piled one on top of the other, had been
stuffed into freight cars, mothers, children, babies, so that by the
time they arrived at Auschwitz many had already died.

Her heart began to beat irregularly. She felt faint and sweaty, as
if she had a fever. It was too close, too close.

She must leave the train carriage; she must be free.

But it was toward freedom that she was headed, she reminded
herself. And even if she could live out her life in Kowitz, how could
Mina bear it?

Control yourself, Wanda warned. Forget the Jews. It's not the
Jews who are bothering you, or their ghosts. This is your first train
ride. Naturally, you are nervous. You've just bought forged papers
from a man you don't know; you're traveling across borders with
those forged papers. It's enough to make anyone ill.

She smiled. She had never before had an active imagination. She
never saw shadows in the woods; no fortunes danced in the fire.
Perseverance was what she needed now.

The train pulled out of the station. Slowly the city of Cracow
receded, maybe forever. Wanda breathed deeply, then swallowed
hard. She was safe. She would make it.

The conductor came by for tickets. He was a bored little man
who looked as if he were asleep on his feet. Wanda handed him
their tickets. Her first thought was that these tickets might be as
forged as her papers. But if they were, the conductor didn't care.
He punched them and handed them back.

Wanda was feeling better with every click of the wheels. Safety,
safety, safety, they spun out to her.

The train stopped. There was no looking out the window; the

shades had been drawn. More people? How could they fit more people on this train?

As the train started up again, she heard men call down the corridor, "Passports! Papers! Passports! Papers!"

She felt sick again. This wouldn't do. If she was sick, they would take her off the train, maybe ask her a lot of questions that she couldn't answer. Where was her strength?

But what was she? Just a country whore who had never been on a train? No. She wasn't Wanda Zbyszek anymore. She was Maria Prychek. As Wanda remembered, Maria had thought she was the princess of the village.

The door to the train compartment flew open. Two men in two different customs uniforms stood waiting, one Polish, the other Czech. Everyone in the compartment was fumbling with his or her papers, preparing them for inspection. Wanda held hers as casually as possible in her hand, waiting her turn.

One of the customs inspectors took her papers and Mina's, smiled at the child, gave the papers a cursory look, and handed them back to Wanda.

Like a criminal released from prison, Wanda sank back into her seat and held Mina to her. Yes, it had been very smart, very, very smart to bring along the child.

The rest of the night passed in a blur. She slept; Mina slept. Mina woke. Wanda gave her some bread and cheese. Then they both bumped along, dozing, until the graying dawn woke them.

The clicking of the train wheels slowed. "Bratislava!" the conductor cried, as he made his way from one car to the next.

Bratislava, Wanda thought happily. We're here.

As soon as Wanda left the train, she joined the line of those buying tickets to Vienna, Austria. Austria is where the Americans were. Once she saw the Americans, she knew she would be safe.

With Mina in one hand and her valise in the other, Wanda slowly inched forward in the line, silently cursing those in front of her for taking so much time. The station in Bratislava was crawling with soldiers, especially those of the Red Army. Soldiers made her nervous. You never knew what they were going to do, but whatever it was, it usually wasn't good for the civilians.

The hour-long wait for her turn at the ticket window over, the money withdrawn from its secret pouch and held carefully in her hand, Wanda said to the clerk, "Two tickets to Vienna, please."

"State your business in Vienna."

Wanda fumbled. Her business in Vienna was to get out of Europe, but how could she possibly tell the clerk that? "What business is my business of yours?" she belatedly shot back.

The clerk looked up at her. "Haven't you been reading the papers?" he asked.

"No. I just arrived." Had war broken out again?

"Only those with official business may buy tickets to Vienna."

"But why?"

"Those are our orders. If you want to go on a sightseeing tour, it will have to wait."

"I've just come from Cracow," she protested.

"Congratulations."

So near and now this stumbling block. She started crying, tears of frustration, tears of exhaustion. "My husband. Two years ago, my husband, he was taken by the Germans, forced labor, taken along by their army. We just got word that he is alive and in a hospital near Vienna."

The clerk softened. "Can you prove it? Do you have the telegram or the letter?"

Wanda shook her head. More tears fell. "It's with his mother. She wanted to keep it, to have something to reassure her he was really alive."

The clerk looked doubtful. He shook his head.

"Please," Wanda begged. "How can I go back without her son? What shall I tell her?"

"I'm not supposed to—"

Wanda covered her eyes with her hand. "I know. But what am I to do?"

The clerk bit his lower lip. He asked, "Can the child sit on your lap?"

"Yes."

He took out two tickets and stamped them. "Say you are going to join your husband, who is an officer in Vienna."

"Thank you, sir. God bless you."

Wanda turned away from the ticket window, feeling weak in the knees. She found a bench and sat down. Mina followed her and touched her hand. "Mama, are you all right?"

Wanda looked at the child. Then she looked up at the departure board. The train to Vienna would leave in an hour. They would have time for some tea, a chance to use the restroom. But first, "What is my name, Mina?"

"Mama."

Wanda smiled down at the dark-haired girl. Mina had called her Mama since the morning after Eliza Wolf left her. The child had wanted to know where her mama had gone. Wanda had said to her, "I'm your mama now."

"Do you know me by any other name?" she asked the girl.

"Wanda."

Wanda shook her head. "No."

"No?"

"This is very important, Mina, so listen closely. From now on my name is Maria. Can you say that?"

"Maria," the child repeated.

"Maria Prychek."

"Maria Prychek."

"And you are Mina Prychek."

"Why can't I have a new name, too?"

"Shh," the woman hushed her. "Maria and Mina Prychek. Don't they sound like pretty names together? Come, let's go get some tea. Would you like some tea, Mina?"

"Yes, Maria. But can I call you Mama?"

"You must call me Mama all the time," the woman said. The little girl looked very confused. "Tea with milk will put you right," Maria told her.

Forty-five minutes later Maria and Mina Prychek were boarding the train for Vienna.

6

D P   C A M P

FROM THE MOMENT MARIA PRYCHEK FIRST MET THEM, SHE LOVED Americans. How could God make a people so good? They had no secrets. Perhaps that was it. They were open and friendly. Without questioning, they knew right from wrong, good from evil. After arriving in Vienna, she was glad she had made certain to reach the American sector. There, the Red Cross directed her to a displaced persons' camp run by American soldiers.

Not that there weren't the usual lines to stand in. She and Mina had to be registered. They had to have tickets for their food rations. They needed requisition slips to get blankets. They had to be assigned to a tent to live in temporarily.

It seemed to Maria that half of Europe was displaced, living right here in this one camp. There were so many nationalities. Her story to the ticket seller in Bratislava had not been far from the mark. Many of the people in the camps were slave laborers, forced laborers of the Germans, who were too sick, too weak, too weary to make their way home again. However, there were no Jews in these DP camps. The Jews had once again been segregated into camps of their own. Perhaps it was better for the rest of them not to bear witness to the full horror of the war against the Jews.

Maria was surprised to find there were many Poles in the camp, fleeing the Russians. That was the advice one woman gave her. Tell the Americans you are afraid of Communist persecution. Fine. Maria would say that if she needed to. But her ticket to freedom wasn't fear of persecution; it was the letter she carried with her always.

On her fifth day in the camp, she was called for an interview with a Captain Waring, who looked quite forbidding. She had heard nothing about him through the camp grapevine, so he could be new here. Maybe later she would be able to trade information about him for something more substantial, like extra food from the camp's black marketeers.

Captain Waring did not speak Polish. Her English was confined to hello, good-bye, thank you. A soldier, a corporal, sat next to Captain Waring. "Maria Prychek?" he asked.

"Yes." She took out her and Mina's papers and placed them on the table in front of her. Captain Waring took them into his hands. He was not an old man, nor was he young. It was hard to tell his age. He simply looked tired, as if other people's lives had become too much for him. The captain glanced from her to Mina, back again to her. Then he said something to the young corporal.

The corporal said to her in Polish, "My name is Corporal Gorbonski. I'm going to be translating for Captain Waring."

She smiled broadly at him. "You speak Polish?"

He smiled back at her. "Yes."

"You are from Poland?" It would be helpful if he were a countryman.

"My parents. The captain wishes to know if you would rather your child stood outside?"

Maria put her arm protectively around Mina. "I am afraid. She might get lost. How would she find me?"

Corporal Gorbonski explained that to the captain. Captain Waring nodded and spoke again in English.

"The captain wants to know why you are here in camp and why you want to go to the United States?"

The moment Maria had been waiting for had arrived. Out of her blouse, she pulled the letter from Peter and Doreen Novoveski. She unfolded it carefully and placed it before Captain Waring. Here in black and white was her invitation to America. She wanted the captain to know that, unlike many in the camp, she had a place to go to, people to welcome her. She would not be a burden to anyone.

Captain Waring had the corporal translate the letter, then consulted once again with Corporal Gorbonski. "The captain wants to know if you've written to these people to let them know you are here?"

"No. I didn't know how to do it. I thought—"

"After this interview, I'll see to it that you get paper and pen. We'll send your letter out with the military mail. If everything else stacks up, you should get priority."

Maria smiled with relief. She gave Mina a little hug. "Thank you. Thank you," she said to Captain Waring. There was no returning smile, and she could only wonder what was going through his mind.

"I have to ask you what you did during the war," Corporal Gorbonski said to her.

"During the war? I lived in the village of Kowitz. Do you know it?"

"No."

"It is right outside Cracow, not close enough to be a suburb but close enough so that we used to supply Cracow with food."

"And during the war?"

"During the war the Germans took our food. Like all villages, we were given a quota we had to meet. If we failed to meet it— well, you know what the Germans are like."

He nodded sadly. "Was there any resistance in your village?"

Maria thought of the resistance radio operator who was turned in to the Germans and taken away. "Once. But the Germans got him. This may not sound brave, Corporal, but we had heard of the reprisals taken against villages that did not cooperate with the Germans. The Germans would roll into the village, line its people up, and shoot them down. It may have been unpatriotic, but we wanted to live."

Corporal Gorbonski translated all this for the captain. The captain responded with another question. "Captain Waring asks if you know where your husband is?"

Maria shook her head. "He was a member of the Polish army in

1939 when the Germans invaded. The last I heard from him was
when his unit had to retreat from Cracow. Not a word since. Six
years.''

"You assume he's dead then?''

"Yes.'' Maria dropped her eyes. She noted that Mina was looking soulfully at the captain, who stared back at her.

The captain said something for Corporal Gorbonski to translate.
"Your child is younger than six.''

Maria blanched. She almost panicked. Lying was not going to
be as easy as she had thought. "She's not my child,'' she blurted
out.

"Not your—''

"Oh, God. Oh, I'm sorry. I meant—'' She covered her face with
her hands. What did she mean? And she must be quick about it!
"My husband isn't the—the war—I was—''

"Oh,'' Corporal Gorbonski said, his voice very low.

She heard him conversing with the captain. She was almost afraid
to raise her eyes, but when she did, she found the captain staring
at her with sad understanding.

"It's all right,'' Corporal Gorbonski tried to assure her. "But
why didn't you stay in Kowitz?''

"I probably would have if I had not gotten this letter,'' she confessed. "But with the German invasion, and now the Soviet invasion, we would never be left in peace. There is no more independent
Poland. For myself, I am used to it. But for my daughter I wanted
freedom.''

The corporal translated her statements to the captain, who had
one last question. "Did you know about Auschwitz?''

Maria was troubled. Would the guilt for Auschwitz be laid at her
feet? Should she confess that Mina was the child of a Jewess? What
should she say? Yes? And no?

"We heard rumors. Yes, we heard rumors. When the men of the
village gathered together some food we had saved from the Germans, they would take it to Cracow to sell on the black market.
That's how we got our news of the war. We heard of the reprisals
the Germans were taking against civilians. We knew they were
rounding up civilians and marching them to the west to forced labor
camps. We heard reports of what was happening to the Jews in
Auschwitz. We heard of Plaschau, which was even closer to us.''
She turned and looked directly at the captain. "But who could
believe it?''

Captain Waring stared straight at her while Corporal Gorbonski translated. There was absolutely no change in his expression at all. If she protested her innocence, would she protest too much?

Corporal Gorbonski stood. He took her outside. "Was it all right?" she had to ask him.

He smiled. "Sometimes I think it will never be all right again." He led her to an office in a real building, not a tent. There he gave her paper and pen.

"I must write it in Polish," she said to him.

"Their letter to you was in Polish."

"I know. But what if they had it translated for them?"

"Then that same person will translate your letter."

Maria looked doubtful. "I'll write a PS on it," he said. "Okay?"

"Okay." There was another English word she was learning to use. She wrote her letter to the Novoveskis. She told them she had received their letter and had made her way to this Austrian displaced persons' camp. Now she would appreciate another letter from them, assuring her that they would sponsor her and her daughter as potential American citizens. She showed the letter to Corporal Gorbonski to see if it was all right. He nodded. So she signed it, "With great affection, Maria Prychek." She handed the letter to him, and he wrote something down at the end of it. "What does that say?" she asked.

"It says that the sooner we hear from them, the sooner you will be able to continue your journey. It says conditions in the camp are not easy and you have a little girl with you."

She smiled. "Thank you. Thank you," she repeated in English.

The weeks added up to months. Maria Prychek began to fear that the letter from America had been a hoax. The Novoveskis had not expected her to respond. The Novoveskis had expected her to be dead, or to stay where she was, in Kowitz. Now what was she to do? Who would take her in?

Many had already left the camp. She had heard from the rumor mill that the Jews, whom no one would take before the war, were being admitted into Canada, Australia, South Africa. Small groups, she understood, were even being smuggled into Palestine, to create a new Jewish state. Much better to have one's own state. Much better not to be stateless, as she and Mina now were. What were her options? To return to Poland? To wait until some country said they had room for her?

In the camp there was a forger, who worked overtime. He created papers for those who no longer wished to wait, for those who would leave the camp to make their own way in the cities of Europe. But how could she make her own way with Mina? Could she abandon the child now?

Winter was coming. The rains inundated the camp, flooding the very ground they had to walk on and turning it into mud. She and Mina both came down with colds and a fever. They went to the infirmary, but what could the doctor do but issue them another blanket? There were refugees for whom a cold meant death, not just days of discomfort.

They sat huddled together on the cot inside their tent, blankets wrapped around them, listening to the rain tumble down. The weather was as bleak as their future.

Through their flap came a helmet in an army poncho. "Maria and Mina Prychek?"

Maria perked up. "Here!"

"Gather your things and come with me, please."

She sorted out the words in her mind. At least living in the camp so long had taught her some English. Gather her things. She had only the small valise she came with and the blankets. She couldn't forget the blankets.

The soldier in the poncho was waiting. She and Mina wrapped their blankets tightly around them and followed him out into the rain. It was hard to keep up with him; he was moving so fast.

He led them to a truck and helped them on board. There were others in the back of the truck, waiting, talking softly to each other. "Where are we going?" she asked them.

"Maybe someplace," one of them responded wanly. A big help.

More people boarded the truck, until it was filled. Then it lurched off.

To Maria's disappointment, it simply took them to another camp, to other lines. Despairing, she stood and waited.

A murmur started at the top of the line and tumbled down to the end of it. There was only one word, repeated over and over again: "America."

But what did it mean? What could she hope for?

Her turn. "Name?"

"Maria and Mina Prychek."

The clerk's fingers moved swiftly down the list until he came to their names. He checked them off, then handed her a bundle of papers. "Do not lose these," he ordered her slowly. "These are your tickets to the United States."

She smiled, such a glorious smile that he had to give her an answering one. The smile stayed in her heart throughout the train ride to Italy, and during the crossing of the Atlantic in winter, no matter how seasick she and Mina got, no matter how little they ate. Because, at the end of their journey, waiting for them in New York Harbor, was the Statue of Liberty. And she knew that once they passed by it, they would be free forevermore.

ISRAEL:
ALL IS
HISTORY

7

CRACOW OVERRUN

SEPTEMBER 1, 1939, GERMANY ATTACKED POLAND. BY SEPTEMber 6, 1939, Cracow was in German hands.

Eliza Wolf remembered the hoarding that had gone on, the grabbing for food, clothes, blankets—anything that could help the citizenry of Cracow survive. When the Germans came, she had been with her family: her mother, her father, her older sister and her sister's husband, their two children. Through the socialist underground, she had heard rumors of Dachau, of the rounding up of Jews. She had repeated the rumors to her family before the German army came, but after Cracow was occupied, what was the point? Their fate had already been sealed in the book of life.

Adam and Eliza had immediately joined the resistance. They were both members of the same socialist cell. Although their cell was all Jewish, they made contact with socialists who were not Jews. That was their pipeline into what the Germans had in mind for Cracow, and especially for Cracow's Jews.

Neither she nor Adam ever told their families what they did during the day, or during the night. First of all, their families were apolitical. Second, it wouldn't be healthy for any of them to know too much. There was enough hardship to go around without finding out one's children were working with the resistance.

The worst blow to both families came when they received orders to give up the homes that had been in their families for many generations and to move into the ghetto. Eliza remembered her mother asking the rather useless question, "Who will take care of my things for me?"

For a while, living in the ghetto had little effect on either Adam or Eliza. With their work permits, they could still make their way in and out of the ghetto, still work, still scrounge for what was needed to survive. They felt a kinship with their Polish brothers. All were feeling the harshness of the German yoke, except the collaborators, and action would be taken against them when the time was right.

Early in 1940, they heard rumors of something happening in the town of Oswiecim, or Auschwitz, just to the west of Cracow. All through the year they kept in touch with the situation at Auschwitz, as conditions in Cracow for the Jews and for all Poles grew more untenable. It was becoming impossible to walk on the street for fear of looking too healthy, too able to be snatched up and forced westward to work as slave labor in Germany's war factories.

It was deplorable, Eliza had thought at that time, how people could delude themselves, how they could act as if everything were normal when nothing was. Marriages, births, deaths, the cycle of life continued with little forethought. She and Adam hid their cynicism as well as possible while their families accepted step by step the restrictions imposed upon them. She had only once lost her temper: when her sister Lina proudly displayed her son's report card, telling everyone who would listen to her how little Mendel would grow up to be the finest doctor the world had ever seen. What farce was her family acting out? Her mother had come to Eliza after the shouting died down, put her arms around her, as if Eliza were still a child, and said, "There is no life without hope."

The trouble was, there was no hope.

In September 1941, they heard a rumor that no Jews would be allowed out of the ghetto, not even to work. She and Adam met that evening in the alleyway outside her family's apartment. He looked at her severely as he placed his hands on her shoulders. "The game is over," he told her.

"What game?"

"The game of resistance we've been playing."

"It hasn't been a game."

"What have we been doing? Getting food, stealing medicine, sending messages."

"All vital."

"Vital? Yes. We surreptitiously take off the Star of David we are forced to wear. We pretend we are like anyone else when we leave the ghetto. But now, what if it's true? What if we are never allowed to leave the ghetto again? The Germans have already deported 60,000 of us."

"But that was to other cities, Adam."

"Yes. Other cities, other ghettos." He stood back from her. "Do you know what Auschwitz is?"

She hesitated. "It's a work camp."

He shook his head. "It's a death camp. It's for us. We have to decide now what we're going to do."

She didn't understand him. "We fight," she answered.

"With what?"

"With whatever we have."

"Do you remember the walks we used to take in the woods?"

"Our hikes, you mean?" She smiled. "I can remember you were never fond of them."

"It's time we took to the woods, Eliza."

"Leave Cracow?" she asked in disbelief. "Leave our families?"

"Cracow is a death trap."

She shook her head. "We have friends; we can get papers. There are always ways to slip in and out."

"And when the noose tightens and there is no way? What if you're on the street when they come for you? What if there is no escape?" He grabbed her tightly by the arms. "What would I do without you?"

She looked into his eyes and was almost swept away. But she resisted. "I say we depend on our friends."

"Friends aren't friends anymore when the Gestapo gets hold of them; neighbors aren't neighbors. And frankly, my dear, we look Jewish."

She smiled. "That's never bothered you before."

He didn't return her smile. "Two days ago, three members of our sister cell slipped away to the woods north of here. We all have an invitation to join them. We're leaving tonight."

"No."

"Eliza!"

"Listen to me. You can't expect me to leave my family—my mother, my father, Lina, the children. Our friends."

"You idiotic—" She raised her hand to him and he gritted his teeth. "Remember two years ago when you chided me for not following my cousin to Palestine?"

No. She couldn't remember.

"You were right," he told her. "If we had—but we didn't. We could have been safe. But we're not. Next time we won't have two years to reflect on our mistake. You're coming with me because I won't leave you to die in Cracow."

"And our families? You'll leave them?"

"Would they come with us if I asked them? Do they believe us even now when we tell them about the concentration camps? They—my father thinks it's all part of a political game I'm playing. My brother can't believe the worst about anybody. But I, Eliza, I can believe. And so can you. So what do we do? Stay here where there's no chance? Or go into the forest and fight?"

Eliza looked away from him. "I can't desert my family. Not now when they'll need me."

"If I could wave some magic wand and save them, I would. But I can only save me, and I can only save you. I'll wait down here in the alley. I'll give you ten minutes. Go upstairs. Grab what's yours and come. If you're not down in ten minutes, I'm coming up to get you; and no one's going to stop me from dragging you off."

She went upstairs. The electricity had been cut. By candlelight, Mendel was doing his homework, her father was reading his philosophy, her brother-in-law was playing a game of solitaire. Both her mother and Lina were sewing fresh Stars of David onto the outer garments the family would wear. Her mother looked up. She held out a star and said, "Look, I've cut out a nice new one for you."

Eliza wanted to vomit. Instead she went into the room she now shared with Lina's two little ones and grabbed the clothes and jewelry that were hers. She came out and stood in the middle of the room, studying the tableau. "Listen, everyone," she said. They all looked up. "Adam and I are leaving Cracow." Neither her father nor her mother uttered a word of protest. "If you can, leave also. Head for the woods, the forest. Lina"—she looked at her sister—"take the children and hide them away in the forest. Please," she begged. "Auschwitz is a death camp the Germans are building for us. They are going to exterminate us there."

"Propaganda," Lina's husband, Hershel, said. "Auschwitz is a work camp. You know how the Germans are desperate for a labor force. They're conscripting anyone they can catch on the street, anyone who looks healthy."

"How long are you going to believe these lies?" Eliza flung out at him. "What comfort are you going to take when the Germans drag you away and kill you—you and your children and your wife?"

"Eliza," Lina pleaded. She didn't know why her sister didn't try to get along with Hershel.

"Mama, please," Eliza begged her mother.

"Where would I run to?" her mother asked. "Live in the forest? How?"

The knock on the door was followed by its quick opening. Adam stood there. "Eliza," he said.

Her mother and father rose. Her father said, "Whatever happens—I'm glad you will be taking care of her, Adam."

They shook hands. Eliza held her father, then embraced her mother, feeling the softness of the woman who had spent a lifetime comforting her. She kissed Lina, the children, shook hands with Hershel. "We'll be waiting for your return," Hershel said to her.

She looked one more time at all of them, drinking them in. Then, without saying good-bye, she left them.

8

THE FOREST

BRANEK WEISS WAS THEIR LEADER. WHETHER IT WAS BECAUSE HE was a bull of a man or quick-witted enough to plan their forays, Eliza never did decide. He was just there when she and Adam arrived, and he remained a constant all their years in the forest.

Their group of partisans never consisted of more than fifty people. Even fifty was too large a number for quick movements. There was always the chance of discovery, always the fear of being wiped out. This was especially true at the beginning, when no one knew who was a friend, who was an enemy. It hadn't been this way in Cracow, at least not in the socialist cells; but out here in the forest, everyone quickly learned there were two kinds of partisans—Jewish and Polish—and most of the Poles were just as intent on exterminating the Jews as the Germans were. It doubled the Jewish partisans' terror of being caught.

And they were such clumsy woodsmen. All the members of Branek's group could remember vividly their picnics in the woods, but then they had brought the food from Cracow and would return to the city for dinner. Now it was a matter of foraging for food, of building protection from the elements. That first winter so many died needlessly, from simple inexperience. They were not tough yet; they were not fighters; they were simply survivors.

Adam and Eliza became lovers that first winter in the forest. All those years in Cracow they had known they were in love, but they had limited their physical relationship to kisses and smiles and tentative caresses. Now, in the woods, there were no familial sanctions, no rights or wrongs, except to stay alive, to cherish the life each brought to the other.

Still, it was awkward the first time; it was cold. Some people could claim a corner in a shelter and make love. But she and Adam were virgins. At least she was. She assumed he was, too. He took her away from the fire, into the forest. He had brought a blanket with him, so she knew what was going to happen. He was doing it so matter-of-factly, as if now was the time, the place. There was really no romance. She had to ask him to tell her he loved her. "You are me; I am you," was all he said.

It was a credit to his masculine desires that he could perform at all that night. She was huddled under his body, grasping him for warmth, but he was totally exposed, and freezing his backside, as he kept telling her. They laughed about it later, when they lost their inhibitions and would gladly kick someone out of a shelter for half an hour to enjoy each other. But it had really not been amusing, not a gentle breaking into the art of love. They had not had a gentle breaking into the art of life either. There was no gentleness in a world gone mad.

She was glad that she had Adam and he had her. There were other women in the camp, but not many. The men outnumbered them a good ten to one. When men fought, it provoked other passions as well. Some women found it a game. Eliza knew it was not a game she would enjoy.

It took their unit until spring to become an organized fighting force. And by spring they had plenty of reason to fight. The Germans' effort to make the world free of Jews had begun with the Jews of Poland. Auschwitz, Chelmno, Treblinka, Sobibor, Belsec—all existed to annihilate. Wherever they could, the partisans took their revenge: against isolated German troops, against taverns that served Germans, against German vehicles, German-requisitioned food, German fuel, against anything that would impede Germany's war efforts. For this they paid a terrible price. Many of them were wounded and died of their wounds, since there was no adequate medical treatment. Some were captured. It was then that one base camp was deserted and another established. But the partisans knew that the civilian population bore the main brunt of their actions. It was they who were rounded up and shot down in response to partisan tactics. Not just the men, but women, children, sometimes whole villages were destroyed by German fury.

Branek justified their actions. "The world is going up in flames," he said. And so it seemed, as their ranks became filled less with escapees from the ghettos and more with escapees from the work camps, the death camps of the Germans. When they told their fellow Jews what was happening, there was no holding Branek's army back. It wasn't just the world; it was their families going up in flames.

By the beginning of 1942, Eliza knew she was pregnant. She had missed her period, but that wasn't unusual for women in the forest. Even that part of life was not normal anymore. It was just that she believed there was life inside her. She didn't tell Adam until she felt the first kick. That was in March of 1942. She didn't tell him because by this time she was pretty good with a rifle herself. Branek called her his best sniper. And she wasn't willing to give it up to sit making stew out of grass. But when the baby kicked, she felt Adam had a right to know, to understand that their lives were going to extend beyond themselves.

Adam, the fool, had a man-to-man talk with Branek, who then had a man-to-man talk with her. "Do you really want to quit going out with us?" he asked.

"Of course not," she said.

"It's just that Adam feels—"

"Adam and I aren't married."

"Hmm. Not legally I suppose. Still, I don't want any trouble in camp."

"So when hasn't there been any trouble in camp?" She had him there. There always seemed to be seventeen different opinions for every action taken.

He smiled. "I don't want there to be any trouble between me and Adam," he said. "You straighten things out with him."

Eliza never really bothered. When Adam was off in one direction, she would go off with a different band in another direction. She stopped only when she became so obviously pregnant that no one, not even Branek, wanted to take her along.

Her baby was born in July, in one of their lean-tos, with three women acting as midwives. She thought it was a difficult birth, but maybe it was normal. If her mother—but she would not allow herself to think backward or forward. Today was all that mattered.

The child had lots of dark hair all over her head. Adam insisted that she looked exactly like his side of the family. Eliza was too weak to argue. They called her Mina, Mina Feuerstein. They clung to her as if she were their salvation.

So Adam made war, while she nursed their child and helped the women in the camp. It was an uneasy life but satisfying in its own way. She worried all the time about Adam. Sitting in camp, she worried more than when she had been out on the raids herself. But seeing her daughter grow, knowing that she and Adam had created Mina, gave her more pleasure than she had ever known in this world.

A fool's paradise. Fantasies of spun sugar.

She could no longer make war with the men, but she was still good with a rifle, good enough to hunt for their dinner. She would place Mina on her back, hushing the child, praying Mina would not make a sound, as she stalked the night's stew meat. Mina learned very early that stillness was of deadly importance.

Then, one day, Eliza managed to bring down two birds and a squirrel. The squirrel's fur would serve to patch someone's coat. She grimaced. Oh, how she longed to be able to go into a store and buy what she needed, especially for Mina's sake.

She was headed back toward camp when she noticed the smoke. Not that they didn't have fires, but not such a fire and not in the middle of August.

She hesitated. It could be nothing. But it never was. She turned around and went back into the forest. She took off the sling she used to carry Mina with her and sat the child on a bed of moss under a tree. Placing her finger to her lips in a sign for silence, Eliza left her year-old daughter and made her way toward the base camp.

The smoke was from the cooking grease one of the women had managed to dump onto the fire before she and her young son were gunned down. Stalking around the camp now was a platoon of German soldiers, who seemed very sure that no one was coming back to disturb them. And they were right about one thing. None of the women and children was left alive to raise a hand to them.

Eliza's first temptation was to lift her rifle and fire at the unsuspecting Germans. She could get one, two, maybe three or four. But she knew that she wouldn't get all fourteen before they got her. And there was Mina to consider.

She withdrew into the woods. Mina was busily mashing a beetle with her palm when Eliza reached her. Eliza grabbed the child and hurried farther into the forest.

Where to now? She knew the location of Branek's latest target. It was a small farming village where the Germans were set to collect their quota of meat and grain. A perfect opportunity for Branek and his men. But she now had the feeling that it was too perfect. A setup maybe? Whom could one trust? That was the question they always had to ask themselves. It usually turned out to be nobody.

Still, what if the raid had gone well? It might have been just chance that the soldiers had stumbled onto their base. The men must be warned.

Eliza changed direction and headed for the path she suspected Branek would use for the village. She made her way quickly and silently through the trees, stopping every twenty paces or so to listen to what the forest would be telling her. Nothing. It was still safe. Birds flew, animals burrowed in the leaves. Eliza moved on, Mina bouncing lightly on her back.

The alarm, when it came, was the single pop of a rifle, then the rattle of machine guns. Theirs? Or the Germans'? They were coming in her direction, and fast. She found a clump of bushes that allowed her shelter and maneuverability at the same time. There she would wait; she would see who was fighting whom.

The first appearance was made by members of her own partisan band. They barely paid attention to the rifles in their hands. Some were simply running; others were dragging wounded friends with them. "Stop!" she stood to cry out. She almost got herself shot for her effort. "There's nothing to go back to." She had to let them know. "The Germans are there."

They lay down on the forest floor as she had done and waited. More gunfire, and the second wave of her fellows appeared, running in a mad effort to escape. They also received the news that there was nowhere to escape to. "Olsza's Creek," one suggested. Yes. It would do. It was higher up, where fresh water could be harnessed to run a wheel, which had ground the grain in earlier days. No one was there now. One had to hope.

The wounded and those who aided them left for Olsza's Creek. The rest stayed and waited.

The third wave of the retreat carried Branek and the rest of the men. By this time, those who had come before had organized themselves in a wedge formation. The Germans followed seconds after Branek, right into the wedge. The crossfire got a good number of them. Eliza herself knew she had brought down five before the Germans turned back and threw themselves into a defensive position.

There was a problem with fighting the Germans. They had an army. The partisans had limited men, limited supplies. More troops would be called up by the German in charge of this operation. Branek had no more troops. He called for a retreat.

They slipped away singly and in pairs. All the time, those remaining kept firing to signal a strong, determined offense. Eliza waited her turn to retreat, then made her way toward Olsza's Creek with Yoseph, who had been wounded in the arm and bled all over her.

9

THE ASSAULT

NIGHT CAME. THE SOUND OF WATER FALLING RAPIDLY THROUGH the sluice could have been the sound of their tears. Yesterday they had been a band of fifty. Tonight twenty of them remained.

Eliza sat by herself, holding Mina loosely, as if she were a dead doll. Sophie came up to her and kicked her hard on the sole of her boot. "You're not the only one who has lost someone today," the woman snarled at her.

"Go to hell," Eliza said numbly.

Morris was sitting not too far from them, staring up at the moon. "What is war but a celebration of death," he pronounced.

If Adam had been here, he and Morris would have examined that statement in detail, all its implications. Morris had been a philosophy student in Warsaw, Adam in Cracow. How they loved to talk and talk and talk. But Adam would not be talking anymore.

When Branek told her, she had simply asked, "Are you sure he's dead?"

"Quite sure," Branek said. "He was next to me. I saw him get hit; I saw him fall. The bullet caught him in the face. He was dead before he hit the ground."

"Good."

Good, yes, because if he had only been wounded, if Branek had not been able to get him away and the Germans had got hold of him—

They had talked about death only rarely. Adam would say, "If one of us should die, then the other would have to continue. Sort of like a living memorial. Because otherwise we are nothing."

She had always believed that death would come to neither of them. They were too special.

Now she sat in the darkness—they were too afraid to light a fire—and all she could remember about Adam was his smile. And his eyes. Those sweet, gentle, fierce, loving eyes.

"There's work to be done," Sophie said.

Oh, God. She could not go on.

"The wounded," Sophie reminded her harshly.

Eliza's mouth hung open and she wanted desperately to cry, but no tears would come. Was her life past crying?

"Mama, hungry," Mina said.

It was Morris who heard the child, Morris who gave Mina a piece of stale crusty bread he carried with him in his pocket. Always, he had a piece of bread in his pocket. "Bread is worth its weight in gold," he would tell anyone who would listen. Morris had escaped from Belsec. Bread was life.

Eliza lay Mina down and left her lying there, sucking on the bread Morris had given her. She went to Sophie and asked what had to be done. "Just look around you," Sophie snapped back at her.

She and Sophie were the only women left, Mina the only child. Of the men, seven were wounded; two looked like they would not make it through the night.

Branek sat by himself, brooding. Eliza barely noticed him as she went zombielike about her tasks, accomplishing what she could, which wasn't much. All their medical supplies had been lost when the Germans destroyed their base. "There are thousands of us dying daily," Branek said, almost to himself.

"So?" she responded. "It doesn't make our deaths easier."

He looked at her, that raging lion's look that made him the leader, or at least made them followers. "We're not dead yet."

"Adam is."

"Parts of our body have been cut off, but we still breathe."

"Not all of us are breathing too well tonight," Sophie reminded him.

"The Germans are."

"Nothing stops the Germans."

"It was that kid, the tavern-keeper's son."

"What are you talking about?" Sophie asked.

"The one who betrayed us. The one Romuald sent us because his partisans would be busy in the north."

"The one Romuald brought into our camp?"

"Yes. The one who so obligingly gave us all the information about when the Germans would be in his village to pick up their quota."

"You don't know," Eliza said. "It could have been anyone. It could have been a member of Romuald's group."

"I'm voting for the kid."

"So vote."

Branek finally got up from his self-imposed exile and made his way to their packs in the middle of the encampment. He checked them out. "There are enough hand grenades in here to blow up a tavern."

"Who's going to blow up a tavern?" Sophie asked, bitterly casting her arms about her.

"Besides, we have to go foraging for supplies," Eliza said. "We can't exist on thin air."

Sophie saw that Branek was still considering the possibilities. "All of a sudden you're a dreamer?"

"Ten of us. We can make our way back to the village, get what we need, and make our way out again."

"Would you be surprised if the Germans were still hanging around there?" she asked. "I wouldn't."

"We didn't kill enough of them today. Not for what they did to us."

"So we should lose more men trying to get even?" Sophie stared hard at him. "Branek, you're an idiot."

"I see it this way. Ten men. There'll be a curfew in town. We take out the perimeter guards. We get our supplies where we can. Then we get the Germans."

Sophie knelt down beside him, her jacket grazing the earth. "Why the need for vengeance? Do you think you're invincible? Let's lick our wounds. We'll fight another day."

"Look at us," he told her. They both looked around the camp. "Does it look like we'll fight another day? If we don't do something now, we'll lose our nerve."

"If we do something now, we'll lose our men."

Eliza went over to them. She hesitated to intrude on Sophie and Branek, because arguing was their one means of communication, aside from fucking each other. "I'm with Branek," she said.

"She with her child has spoken," Sophie replied.

"Mina's asleep. She'll sleep through the night. Adam's dead. I don't think it's wrong to want vengeance."

"It's not wrong to want it, but can you get it without hurting yourself?"

"I'm willing to try."

"And if you don't succeed, you expect me to take care of your child?"

Eliza supposed that was why Sophie finally decided to go along with Branek. Motherhood was not the role she wanted to play. Soldiering was definitely more appealing.

Branek asked for volunteers. Everyone who wasn't wounded surrounded him. He left three behind who were whole to watch the wounded. The ten who were going cleaned their rifles and got ready.

It was eerie making their way through the killing ground of the afternoon. They could almost point out where each of their members had fallen.

Contrary to what Branek had supposed, the perimeter of the village was not guarded. However, the Germans had not left the scene of their victory. The tavern was well lit, and German vehicles were parked around it.

As Branek had suspected, there was a curfew in town. No one was out on the street. In front of the tavern were three guards. They were humped together, and it would be hell to take them out without creating a commotion.

Eliza received a poke in the ribs. It was Morris, directing her attention away from the tavern. Against a side wall, all too clear in the moonlight, lay a pile of bodies. That morning they were alive and fighting. Those who had not been killed outright, the way Adam had died, had been captured and later shot.

It made the ten of them all the more determined to right certain wrongs. But the problem still remained: How were they to get rid of the three sentries? After all, no one had a good enough aim to be able to lob the grenades over the sentries' heads and into the doorway. What if they missed? They could all visualize the Germans pouring out of the tavern, then placing ten more partisans up against the wall.

"The windows," someone pointed out to Branek.

"I want some supplies from this, too," he said.

"Maybe you can't have everything," Sophie whispered.

"Then at least let's destroy the tavern," he conceded.

The tavern had windows on only one side, because it adjoined another building, which served as the town store. But it had both a front and a back door. Eliza was sent around to the back door with Meyer. He had the strong throwing arm; she had the eye of a sharp-shooter.

Branek said he would give everyone five minutes. Meyer began counting. When he pulled the pin off the first grenade, Eliza got ready. Before he even threw the first grenade, he pulled the pin on the second.

He ran. He kicked in the back door of the tavern and tossed in the first grenade, and socked in the second. Then he dove for safety, granting himself only a second. The explosion sprayed a shower of splinters all over him. Eliza silently urged him to get up, as she waited for any German to dare make his appearance.

To the side of her, from beyond, she heard the sound of further explosions as the others relieved themselves of their grenades. Out the back door came two staggering forms. Eliza fired and brought them down. The only trouble was that one was a soldier; the other was a woman as young as herself. Life was definitely cheap.

Meyer pulled her away. He was right to. They were in the most exposed position, open from behind. A retreat was in order. They circled around to the side and kept firing as Germans tried to escape the flames and dust that cycloned within the tavern. The partisan band hit as many as they could, until Branek gave the order to melt away.

Melt away they did before the Germans could get organized, before they could follow, before they could wipe out the rest of them.

All ten of them made it back to camp. For some reason, Eliza felt no better than when she had left.

10

SANCTUARY

"I'M LEAVING."

"You're leaving here?" Branek asked Eliza.

"I can't see the point anymore. We're not accomplishing anything."

"What did you want to do, win the war single-handedly?"

"Maybe. Anyway, it's not safe here for Mina."

"Where is it safe for Mina?"

"I must find a place for her."

"Eliza, don't go. It's like committing suicide to leave us."

She looked at him and saw that he was sincere. He really did care what happened to her. Well, she had been with him now for over two years. But it had been nearly three months since Adam died, and nothing was the same. They raided; they harassed; they resupplied themselves, regrouped, contacted Romuald, and got some of his overflow fighters. They were building strength. But what for? Another catastrophe?

Her nightmares haunted her days. She saw Adam dead. She saw

his body with his face blown away. And she saw herself lying next to him in some mass grave for all the Jews.

A living memorial? Mina was their only memorial. Was she to be sacrificed, too?

Despite Branek's pleadings and Sophie's ridicule, she packed up her things and left camp. Winter was coming. She must find a safe haven for Mina.

It seemed to her that all of Poland was pockmarked by disaster. So where could she take Mina where the bombs would not fall? Into the city? She knew what was happening in the cities, how the Jews were being rounded up, transported to the death camps. Leave her with some Christian in the city? The only Christians she knew belonged to the socialist underground. Were they in any less danger than she was?

No. The cities were out.

The country, then. She and Adam used to love the country. They dreamily talked about retreating to a village, enjoying a simpler life, where they would grow grain, make bread, weave cloth. Villages were a safe place to be. Yes, safe if the inhabitants did whatever the Germans asked of them, if they weren't used for reprisals against the acts of the partisans. The only trouble was, she knew no one in a village. She was a child of the city. Besides, who in the village would take in her child? For what reason? Eliza had nothing to offer them—no money, no bonds of blood, kinship, friendship. "Oh, Mina, what shall we do?" she asked, nuzzling into the warmth of her daughter's neck. Maybe Branek was right. Maybe it was best to return to him.

She got up, lifted Mina onto her hip, and walked. There was no terror in the forest for her now, only safety. Perhaps she and Mina alone could—but she remembered the harshness of the last winter, Mina's cough, her pale eyes, runny nose. Would illness do what the Germans had not managed to do so far?

Who was safe? Men, women, children—all were at risk. If not according to sex or age, then according to type. What type of person was safe? She had heard that in the camps the safe ones were people who could do something, like tailors, laundresses, nurses, carpenters. Outside, the same thing: farmers, taverners, whores. The Germans loved their whores, whether they were women, young boys, or young girls.

But Eliza didn't know any whores. She had obviously never been allowed to associate with the right type of person, certainly not for this situation.

But wait! She did know a prostitute. That girl in the village of

Kowitz, the one who had claimed she didn't mind what was done to her as long as she was paid for it.

Eliza looked down at her daughter. Could she chance leaving her daughter with such a person? She reminded herself to focus on the objective: her daughter's survival. Her morals she would worry about later, after the war. If there ever was any "after the war."

Eliza came to the village of Kowitz much as she and Adam had approached it the first time, through the forest. It had been so many years ago; she couldn't really recall if that dirty hut she saw before her was the prostitute's shack or not. It was midday, and Mina had had very little to eat. But the child did not complain. She crouched down next to her mother. Oh, what a great stalker Mina would make when she was old enough. She waited as Eliza waited.

A blond woman returned to the shack from the center of the village. She had a basket of laundry with her. She put the basket of laundry down by the tub and went inside the shack. She came out, alone. Was there no husband then? No children yet?

Methodically Wanda Zbyszek washed the clothes, hung them to dry, even though the wind was stiff and they might freeze on the line. Then she rolled down the sleeves of her jacket, put the laundry basket inside, and came out with a cloth sling.

Eliza thought she would be discovered for sure now, as Wanda entered the forest to collect wood. But the woman walked almost right by Eliza without seeing her. This was a good sign. It must mean there was nothing to be afraid of in the village of Kowitz.

When they were alone again, Eliza picked up Mina and walked swiftly toward the shack. Inside, there was warmth and safety.

The hut was exactly as Eliza had remembered it. Still wrapped against the cold, she sat down at the table and held Mina in her lap. "Mina," she said. Her child looked up at her with warm, brown, trusting eyes. "Do you know how much I love you?"

Mina smiled. "I love you" was a phrase she often heard and repeated. It made everything all right.

"Mama will always love you. Papa loved you. Mama loves you enough to leave you here. Do you understand?"

No, of course she didn't. How could she possibly?

"Another woman will be your mama until I can come back for you." She smiled brightly. "Isn't that nice? You'll have two mamas," she cooed.

Mina was having none of it. She looked puzzled and doubtful. She circled a finger in her dark hair and tugged at it.

"You'll have food and warmth. Most important," Eliza said to herself, "you will not die."

Mina brought a hand up to her mother's cheek. Sadness was catching.

There was bread on the table. Eliza was sorely tempted. Mina also stared covetously at the dark oval. Cautiously, Eliza broke off a piece. She handed it to her daughter, who gobbled it down. Conspiratorially, they smiled at each other.

Eliza heard footsteps approaching; then they stopped. Wood fell into a haphazard pile. Sensing that on the other side of the wooden door stood Wanda Zbyszek, Eliza understood that in a few seconds she would have to summon up the words that would save her daughter's life.

Afterwards, when she had left the shack and walked back into the forest, Eliza could barely remember what had passed between her and Wanda. She only remembered the warmth of her child as she had hugged her good-bye and, yes, Wanda's threat to put Mina out into the cold that night.

Eliza stopped in the woods, sheltered from sight, and looked back toward the shack. She saw and heard nothing. Mina had not been kicked out; Wanda was not rushing into Kowitz proper to let them know there was a Jew in the forest nearby. Had Eliza achieved her goal? Would Mina be safe after all?

Count on nothing. Depend on nobody but yourself. Hadn't she learned that much over the past few years? Yet sometime somewhere someone has to trust. She had to trust Wanda with her child. And there was the promise she had made to Wanda. She would return to Kowitz and reclaim Mina after—

Eliza smiled grimly while she fought against the tears struggling to appear in her eyes. For her would there ever be an after?

Mina was alive.

And so was she. There were things to do. Wanda had threatened to put Mina out in the cold that night. Night was a good ways off. Meanwhile, Cracow was only six kilometers. Eliza had time. She would go to the city of her childhood and hope, despite all she knew, all she had heard, to fall into the arms of her own family. But in the evening she would be back. Mina would be safe or Eliza would kill Wanda Zbyszek with her own hands.

11

CRACOW

WHY HAD SHE RETURNED TO THE CITY OF HER BIRTH? THERE WAS nothing, there was nobody to return to. Eliza dared not even approach the ghetto, in case her tears gave her away. But from a distance she could see the destruction, almost hear the wailing of her people.

"Have you food to sell?" A passerby stopped her.

"What do you mean?"

"Have you sold it all then?"

"I don't understand you."

"Don't be coy," the passerby warned. "You're from the country; I can tell. No one here looks so wholesome. So you've sold what you had on the black market. I'm not going to report you. I just want to know when you're next coming to Cracow. Can we make some arrangement? What can you bring me?"

Eliza smiled. Something finally amused her. So she looked like a country lass? Well and good. It was healthy to be just a peasant. Now she had to decide if she should turn this man away or assure him that there was hope, that she could get something for him. If she turned him away, might he not complain to the ever-present authorities? "Where can I meet you next week?" she asked.

"Here. At this corner. By the monument."

"Seven-thirty?"

"Fine. Don't be late."

"Don't worry."

Satisfied, the stranger walked away, and Eliza was left once again with her fatal temptation. She wanted to get as close as she could to where she had left her family, and yet she knew it would be suicide. Instead, she chose a middle path. She headed for the apartment of Tadeusz Dlugosz, who had been the leader of the socialist cell in this area of the city when she left Cracow two years ago.

The door to his apartment house was open. She climbed up three flights of stairs and could smell cabbage being cooked. It reminded her of home. She knocked on the door, ready to make a quick retreat, ready to admit to a mistake.

The woman who answered was old enough to be Tadeusz's mother. But whether she was or not, Eliza had no idea. "Yes?" she said.

"Oh!" Eliza feigned surprise. "I'm sorry. I must have the wrong apartment."

"Whom are you looking for?"

"A family used to live here. A young man with—"

"Tadeusz?"

"Yes. I believe that was his name."

The woman looked her over. "What do you want with him?"

"I'm an old friend."

"An old friend who doesn't even remember his name?"

"It might not be healthy to remember," Eliza took a chance saying.

The woman stared at her, then grimaced. She nodded. "Come in." She called a small boy to her and whispered something in his ear. He raced out of the apartment. "I can give you tea with no milk, no sugar," the woman said.

Eliza stood by the door. "Where is the boy going?"

"You wanted to meet with Tadeusz, didn't you?"

Distrust outweighed Eliza's desire for tea. She opened the door and hurried down the steps while the woman called, "Wait!" above her. Outside, Eliza felt the cold wind nip at her. She thought of Mina, how well protected she should now be from this frigid weather.

Eliza turned the corner. The bus stop was still there; people were waiting. She was safe in the crowd. Every now and then she would peek around the corner to see who was coming, Tadeusz or the Germans. In the end it was neither. It was Luba. The young boy was hurrying her on. Eliza streaked around the corner before Luba could approach the apartment. She knocked into her as if she was a pedestrian misjudging distance. "Sorry," she said. "Pardon me."

Luba looked at her, her eyes widening. "Eliza," she said, as if she had seen a ghost. And moments before Eliza had been a simple, rustic peasant. "Go," Luba said to the boy. "Tell your grandmother it's okay." Luba continued walking. "Follow me," she said.

Eliza followed her five or so paces behind, as Luba made her way through the streets of Cracow in a businesslike fashion. Down the steps to the cellar of one apartment building they went, then up and out the back way, across the street to another. In this one, they climbed two flights. Luba took a key out of her pocket and let Eliza in. The apartment was extremely cozy, perhaps because it housed so many people. One of them was sitting before a transmitter. "Yes," Luba said. "Our base of operations." Then she threw her arms around Eliza and hugged her tight. "Have you eaten?"

"Not for a long time."

"Tea with milk? A little bread?"

"Anything."

Luba smiled. Room was made for Eliza at a table. She sat, gratefully dunked the stale bread in the tea that was poured for her, and ate.

"Now," Luba said, when the edge had been taken off Eliza's hunger, "what are you doing here?"

"I had an errand nearby. I couldn't resist coming to see what has happened."

Luba shook her head. "Nothing good."

The door to the apartment opened and Tadeusz Dlugosz stood in its frame. The war had slimmed him down but had in no way affected his height or his recognizable red hair. He should have dyed it, Eliza immediately thought. "Eliza?"

"Your hair is still red."

"In keeping with my politics. You're alive."

"And you."

"There have been many times when I wasn't so sure I would be. You know, Cracow is not a place of safety."

"She was nearby," Luba explained. "She wants to know what's been happening."

He sat down at the table with them. "What's been happening? Have you been living on another planet? How's Adam?"

"Dead."

Luba sucked in her breath.

"A raid. We were betrayed. We lost three-fifths of our force."

"I'm sorry," Tadeusz said.

"Every day is a gift. Or a burden."

"You joined Branek's group, didn't you?"

"Yes."

"And is he still alive?"

"Yes."

"Do you know how to reach him?"

"Of course." She became suspicious. "Why do you ask?"

Tadeusz looked across to Luba. But he didn't answer Eliza's question.

Eliza was not offended that they had secrets to keep from her.

Keeping secrets meant staying alive. She said, "I really came here because I wanted to know about—"

"You don't want to ask," he told her.

"We have among us those who have escaped from the camps," Eliza informed him.

"Then you know. The Jews of Cracow no longer exist."

"At first they were gathered piecemeal. The Germans would raid the ghetto, grabbing the healthier-looking ones for the work camps. But then, it seems, the Germans have quotas to meet. The old, women and children, the sick were taken away by train to Auschwitz," Luba explained. "We don't know how many are left in the ghetto. We only know that there are very, very few. They are desperate, starved. There's been some resistance. At times we've been able to get some food in to them. But for the most part, we haven't been able to lift a finger to help them."

"In the beginning we occasionally got working papers to them," Tadeusz corrected her. "But the Germans came after us, too. We're always on the move."

"We all have to be registered," Luba explained, "where we live, where we work. But we never sleep where we're registered. Almost every night all of Cracow swaps apartments. It cuts down on German efficiency. They never seem to learn, you see. They consistently go to the apartment where we are registered. It gives us an alert about whom they are looking for." She smiled weakly.

"Do you—have you—did you ever see my family?" Eliza had to ask.

"There were so many families," Luba said. "Mothers with babies and young children, grandfathers." She shrugged. She placed her hand on top of Eliza's. "Don't hope for much," she warned.

"Don't hope for anything," Tadeusz corrected her. "What is it like for you partisans?"

Eliza sighed. "We also move constantly. Unfortunately, there are no apartments. We raid; we harass; we sabotage. We do what we can and still try to survive. Sometimes we are more successful than others."

"I hear there is fighting between the various groups."

"Yes. Some of us cooperate. But many of the Polish partisans are as anti-Semitic as the Germans. They take as much pleasure in hunting us down as they do in fighting the real enemy."

"You look rustic," Luba told her.

Eliza smiled. "One of Cracow's citizens took me for a peasant trying to sell food on the black market."

"I wish you were," Tadeusz said. "We could use the food. When are you going back to Branek?"

"Why do you ask?" She wasn't willing as yet to admit that she was unsure where she was going.

"Because there are people who need the safety of the forest," Luba said.

"People who will be killed if they are spotted on the streets," Tadeusz added.

"Two of them are Jews," Luba said. "We've been hiding them for six months now, but no papers can disguise their looks."

"It makes no difference to me whether they are Jews or not," Eliza said. "As long as they can fight."

"They haven't had the opportunity, but I don't think anyone's a pacifist anymore," Tadeusz said.

"I also have no papers," Eliza told them. "So the sooner I leave the city, the better. Matter of fact, I want to be out of here by tonight."

"Tonight?" Luba asked.

"Before it's dark. Surely it's cold enough so your refugees can wear scarves around their faces during daylight."

Luba looked at Tadeusz. "Luba will put you on a bus for the South Market. Three men will get off at the same stop as you. They'll follow you out of the city. I should warn you; they have nowhere near your robust health."

Eliza smiled. "They soon will, if they survive."

12

THE HIKE BACK

ELIZA WALKED AS IF SHE WERE ALONE. BEHIND HER WERE THREE men. One of them had separated himself from the other two, who held onto each other for support. It was a bad situation, but it could have been worse. The road could have been less crowded. But now it was filled with farmers returning to their villages from the South Market. So if Eliza and her trio walked steadily onward and no one faltered, they should survive passing inspection from German army vehicles that swept up and down the road.

Eliza turned around when she heard someone drop. She knew it had to be one of those two men. Unfortunately, she was right. The one who had had a coughing fit every few steps since they left the bus was down on the ground. Her instinct for survival told her to keep on moving. But she was bound to these men by Tadeusz and his commitment to them. She turned back. His friend was helping him up. He had the look of death about him already.

Eliza took a chance. She stopped a farmer and his wife with their cart. "Please," she begged them, "my cousins have nearly died in the city. I'm taking them home to recover. Can they ride on the back of your cart for a while? Please?"

The farmer and his wife looked at the two men doubtfully while the third man walked on ahead. "What disease do they have?" the farmer asked.

"No disease, I promise you. They are simply tired and starved."

"No," the farmer's wife said.

That decided the farmer. "Yes. They can climb up. But they better not get sick inside the wagon."

Eliza smiled gratefully. She helped the two men onto the cart. Through their coats she could feel the lack of flesh. Were they from the ghetto? Perhaps they would know what had happened to her family.

She trailed along behind the cart, keeping an eye on the two men, in case one should fall out. The third man had stopped by the roadside to examine nothing in particular until the cart and Eliza passed him. Then he rejoined the procession. Six kilometers down the road, the cart showed every sign of veering off in the direction of Streswicim, a small village on a side spur of the main road. Eliza stopped the farmer, told him they were going in the opposite direction, and thanked him profusely. The wife looked sourly back at her. Well, it would give the couple something to argue about tonight. Eliza was sure, after farming, that was their main occupation.

The quartet did not stay on the road for long. The sun was beginning to set, and the road at night was no place to be if you wanted to live. She guided the men off into the fields, now giving her shoulder to the weakest among them. "Do you know where you're going?" the third man asked.

"What's your name?"

"Anton."

"Anton, we're cutting through these fields and heading for the forest. By dark we should be where I came out into the fields this morning. I've left something there I have to pick up."

"Fine. As long as you know where you're going."

"My name is Aaron," the one with the cough introduced himself. "Is it true, as Tadeusz says, that you are a Jew, one of us?"

"Yes."

He had another coughing fit. Like the farmer's wife, she, too, was hoping it was not contagious. "It's a miracle," he told her. "You are so strong."

"You will be as strong as I am soon."

"As long as I die free. That's what matters."

"I'm Simon," the other Jew told her. He smiled and nodded politely. She returned his smile. He also looked weak and sick. But at least he wasn't coughing convulsively.

By dark, as she'd promised, they were in the forest. The moon was almost entirely obstructed by clouds, so they could not see as clearly as they would have wished. What had become second nature to her, stomping around the forest, was to them frightening.

"Animals?" Simon asked.

"None as bad as the Germans," she assured him.

"Do you know where you're going?" Anton wanted to make sure. "All these trees look the same to me."

"Just follow me." She took them far enough into the forest so that there would be no intrusions, so that this space would be their own. Then she told them it was time to sit, to eat. "I'll be back for you," she promised.

Anton grabbed her hand as she was turning away. "What do you mean you'll be back for us? Where are you going?"

"I told you, I have to retrieve what I've left."

"What have you left?" Simon asked.

"My rifle."

He looked amazed. "Your rifle?"

She smiled. "Yes."

"How do we know you'll come back for us?" Anton asked.

"I'll be back because I promised you I would. You'll have to trust me."

"Why should we?"

"For the same reason that I've trusted you. It would've been easy at any time to have lost the three of you. Why should I bring you into the woods to desert you? Use your senses."

"Our senses have fortunately deserted us," Simon said. "Otherwise we'd be crazy."

She smiled at him. "I'll be back. Eat. But save me something."

She turned away. It was true she was going to retrieve her rifle. She had left it close to the edge of the forest, near where Wanda

Zbyszek lived. It was buried under a pile of leaves she had hastily pushed together, and it remained there waiting for her, somewhat the worse for wear. She rubbed it down with her shirt, took it apart, cleaned it, making it ready for use. Then she crept to the edge of the forest.

She sat on her haunches staring out at the lamp-lit cabin of Wanda Zbyszek until her eyes became totally adjusted to the area. She wondered if near her somewhere in the forest sat her child Mina, hungry and freezing. Had Wanda made good on her threat to turn Mina out into the cold? Or perhaps the Germans had come through. Wanda could have turned the child over to them. Eliza sat and worried.

If Mina were not in the cabin with Wanda, Eliza soon would be, forcing Wanda to tell what she had done with the child. And then Eliza would kill the Polish woman, shoot her or stab her, whatever suited her at the moment. If Wanda had no humanity, Eliza would have none either.

She waited. She thought that, if Mina were outside, she would be wandering about the village, only to come back to Wanda's to see if she could get in out of the cold. But Mina was nowhere to be seen.

Finally, Eliza gave up waiting. With her rifle in hand, she walked silently toward the shack. It was about as sturdy as some of the partisans' thrown-together affairs, and it looked like a good wind would blow it over; but it had survived over the years, so perhaps there was safety inside it. Still, why didn't it have any windows?

Eliza reached the door and once again crouched down, facing outward, watching to make sure no one from the village was around. Then she listened. Inside she could hear movements, chairs scraping, objects being placed on the table, maybe. But no voices.

Finally. "Don't you like food?" It was Wanda Zbyszek's voice. "I should think that your mother would have taught you to eat what is offered to you."

Your mother? Then it was Mina, still inside, being fed by Wanda?

"Mina?" the voice continued. "Is it the pork fat? Is that what you don't like on the bread? I know you Jews don't eat pork, but, Mina, you must never tell anyone you are Jewish. They would kill you. They would kill me. I'm not going to die for you." A pause, and then, as if the woman were muttering to herself, "What am I saying? You can barely speak. You certainly couldn't tell them about your religion. Tomorrow we'll go into the village. You'll meet other people. I'll tell them you're my mother's child." She laughed sourly. "They'll believe anything about my mother. But you must eat.

Come on. Open your mouth. Yes! That's a good girl. Yes. See how good food tastes? You should be thankful. There are so many people who don't have any bread at all tonight. I know, I know. You're missing your mother. I know. I miss my mother too, someone to take care of me. But you know, Mina, in this world you've got to learn to take care of yourself. Well, you're a little young for that yet, but you'll learn. Tonight I'll let you sleep in the same bed with me. We'll keep nice and warm together. And tomorrow will be another day. Things will look brighter then. I tell myself that each night before I go to bed. You'll learn to do that, too. It's the only way to survive.''

Eliza smiled. As silently as she'd come into the clearing, she left. Mina was safe. As safe as she would be anywhere. Certainly, she was much safer than she would be with the partisans. Eliza entered the forest, sure she had done the right thing. What else could she tell herself?

The men were waiting for her, silent and accusing. ''I'm back,'' she told them. ''What more do you want?''

She ate, then moved them out. For the next two hours they traveled farther into the forest, deep into its sanctuary. Then she had them gather wood for a fire, not a large one, just big enough to ensure they wouldn't freeze to death. ''We'll take turns sleeping,'' she told them. ''I'll take first watch.''

When it was his turn, she woke Anton. He wanted her rifle to keep watch with. ''This weapon is mine,'' she informed him.

''But if someone comes?''

''Wake me.''

He grimaced, but she lay down with the rifle held to her as if it were a lover. There was nothing he could do.

Morning came. She opened her eyes to a ceiling of branches, her own special canopy. Before she sat up, she looked around. She was displeased to find she was the only one awake. She turned over on her belly, her gun drawn into firing position. If they were being watched, there was no sign of it.

Eliza stood and moved into the forest to make use of its facilities. Then she returned to where her companions were sleeping. ''Whose watch was it?'' she asked in a normal voice.

They didn't stir.

She went around and kicked each of them gently with her toe. ''Whose watch?'' she wanted to know, as they rubbed the sleep out of their eyes. Simon looked at Aaron, who was caught up convulsively in his coughing. She shook her head. ''Get ready to go,'' she told them.

They moved clumsily into the woods and back again. Meanwhile, Eliza sat by the embers of the fire, poking them with a stick, removing the potatoes they had put in while the blaze was dying last night. Carefully, with her knife, she cut a potato in half and gave a half to Aaron, one to Simon. The next she divided between herself and Anton. Breakfast was hot, which made it filling.

It took them three days to reach Branek's camp. It should have taken them two. But they never made the distance they had made on the first day. The men were not used to walking long stretches; their muscles were sore. Aaron grew weaker with each trudging mile. "Leave me," he begged. "I am happy now."

Eliza could see that Anton would like nothing better than to leave him, but first she and then Simon supported Aaron, bringing him along step by step. There were better ways to die than just lying down and waiting for it.

By the third day the men were hungry and ragged, and unappreciative of the small animals she killed so they could have food. She couldn't blame them. When she first came into the forest with Adam, she, too, preferred her meat from a butcher shop.

On the third night they complained as she drove them on while the sun fell. "Time to make camp, to gather wood for the fire," Simon said. Aaron looked pleadingly at her. She marched implacably forward.

Darkness came, and Anton doubted she knew where she was going. She traveled on, and they had no choice but to go with her or be abandoned. She couldn't tell them that Branek's camp was within reach, because she wasn't sure. It had been just over a week since she'd left. In the circumstances of war, she couldn't be certain Branek or his camp still existed.

"Halt!"

The three men shuddered into each other. Only Eliza stood free.

"Firelight." Eliza gave the password as it had been.

"That was last week's," the voice from the branches said.

Eliza shrugged. "I haven't been here this week. It's me, Eliza."

"Eliza? And the others?"

"Refugees from Cracow."

"Are they armed?"

"No."

"Shit. You mean you're only coming back with the rifle you left with?"

"Sorry."

"All right. Walk slowly on, single file, so I can keep an eye on your friends."

"One is weak and needs support," Eliza explained.

"Just get going."

Eliza looked back reassuringly at the three men and then led them the last few steps into Branek's camp. All the partisans came out to look at her, some puzzled, some with smiles. Branek was there too, with Sophie.

"I bet him one potato you'd be back," Sophie said. "I'll get fat on you."

"I knew you'd be back," Branek said. "But I didn't know you'd bring such riffraff with you."

"From Cracow," Eliza explained.

Those were the magic words. Anton, Aaron, and Simon were surrounded by the partisans, who wanted news of what was happening to their city, their relatives, their friends. Eliza, relieved of her burden, walked silently away. Branek went up to her and put his arm around her. "We missed you."

"Thanks."

"Where's Mina?" Sophie asked.

"Where she will be safe."

"In Cracow? Are you crazy!"

"She's not in Cracow."

"Where?"

"Where only I know." Eliza stared at Sophie and saw the woman was really troubled. "Don't worry. She's in no danger, nor will she be. If I die now, I know that she will live."

13

WINTER 1945

THE WAR WAS OVER. ELIZA LOOKED AS IF SHE ALMOST HADN'T survived it. Typhoid. Of all the injustices on the earth, to have come down with typhoid, when neither bullets nor hardships had killed her, was the most criminal. Even now she could barely move. She looked like an old woman, a dead old woman.

It was joining up with the Red Army that did it. The army took the partisans to places they had never thought of going. And it also wiped many of them out, when disease struck. Now there were no more partisans, and the Red Army was in control of Poland. Branek's group dispersed, each traveling a different path back into life.

Branek got on so well with the Red Army colonel they had joined with that Eliza was sure he would become an officer in that army himself. In actuality, the Russians had tried to coerce him into the army. But, as Branek told her, he had decided that from now on, he was going to fight only for himself. He and Sophie had made contact with a Zionist from Palestine. Even now a route was being set up for them to make their way through Europe to ships that waited to take them to what would be their new state when they got through fighting for it. "You come, too," Sophie insisted.

It didn't sound like a bad idea. A new life in a new land, a land where she could be free and still be a Jew. Yes, Eliza would give it thought. She knew that whatever happened she could not stay in Poland. During their march toward liberation she had seen the camps; she had worked in them, trying to help; she had seen what had been done to her people while no one gave a damn, no one lifted a finger. She would not live among those people no matter how far she had to run.

But before running, she had commitments. Her daughter was waiting for her. She had recovered health enough to reclaim Mina without fear of passing on the typhoid to her. And then she must go to Cracow. She must find out what had become of her family, even if the truth was something she wouldn't want to hear.

The village of Kowitz was untouched by the war. Or so it seemed. Even in the winter it looked like a golden sanctuary. Was it only two years ago that she'd left her child, her Mina here for safekeeping? And now Mina would be a three-year-old, walking, talking, laughing. It would be so good to hear a child laugh, her child.

She walked through the town of Kowitz aware that people were watching her. What would they do, come out of their houses with their ax handles and finish the job the Germans and the typhoid had started? She wished she still carried her rifle. But they were all civilized once again.

The shack stood where it had always stood, waiting for her. Her heart beat faster; then, it did not seem to beat at all as she approached. She knocked on the door. There was no answer. Of course. Wanda would be out with Mina, gathering wood, getting food, doing chores.

"Whom are you looking for?"

Eliza turned around to face a woman as old as her mother would be, if her mother had lived. "Wanda Zbyszek," Eliza answered.

"She's not here."

"I see that. Do you know when she'll be back?"

The woman shrugged. "She's left Kowitz."

"Left Kowitz!"

The woman stared at her suspiciously, not about to give out further information.

"I know Wanda. I knew her from before the war," Eliza said. "Please. I must find her. Did she marry? Did she run off? What has become of her?"

The woman shrugged again. "Months ago, after the Russians had come and gone, she said she was going to Cracow to look for her mother. She never came back. Of course, her mother never came back either, so maybe she found her."

Eliza held her breath. "Did Wanda have a little girl with her?"

"Yes. Her mother's child. Did you know her mother, too?"

"Yes. Yes, I did."

"Then you should be able to find Wanda."

"How was the girl? What did she look like?"

"Dark."

"But happy? Was she happy and well fed?"

"Happy? All children are happy, aren't they? And she ate as well as the rest of us."

Eliza came forward to take the woman's hand in gratitude, but the woman backed away. No, all children are not happy, Eliza wanted to tell her. But the woman wouldn't want to hear. Eliza walked out of the village of Kowitz and toward Cracow. Her child was in her old city. Maybe even now Mina was with Eliza's family, playing happily in their old house, singing and dancing and—

Oh, Eliza, expect nothing, she warned herself.

Nothing was what she got. Cracow was not a city to come back to. The city of her childhood had been pulverized, the ghetto and the people in it destroyed. Like ghosts, she and other Jews returning to the city trailed through its streets and its buildings trying to conjure up a past that no longer existed and could barely be remembered without pain. She thought of Aaron and Simon, how she had brought them out of Cracow two years ago. Fate. Aaron, with his cough, lived; Simon died. There was no sense to life at all.

Crisscrossing the streets of the ghetto, she ran into Hershel, her sister Lina's husband. She didn't recognize him; he didn't recognize her. And yet there was something that brought their eyes back to each other. "Hershel?" she questioned tentatively.

"Eliza?" He looked at her. "You too? They got you, too?"

She understood. She shook her head. "Typhoid. After liberation," she explained. "Lina?"

He shook his head.

"Tell me," she insisted.

He shrugged. "What's there to tell? If you know what happened at Auschwitz, then you know what happened to Lina and my babies." He sank down onto his knees.

"Tell me anyway," she insisted. "I have to know."

He looked up at her. "When our time came, we were marched to the railway station. All of us—me, Lina, the children, your mother and father. From there the train took us to Auschwitz. Your father died in the car, heart attack, if he was lucky. Many smothered to death. I think it was a good way to die, compared to the others. At the entrance to the camp, when we got out of the rail cars, we were all lined up. Lina held onto Mendel's hand; I was holding Yaacov. Your mother was standing next to Lina. We made our way toward the camp. People were whispering to us from all sides, "Let go of the children." I thought they were crazy. We got closer. A German soldier came up to me and ripped Yaacov from my hands, placed him with Lina. I didn't know what was happening. The night. It was so confusing. All of a sudden, I was going in one direction, and Lina, the children, and your mother were going in another. And that was it."

"They were immediately sent to be gassed?"

He shook. He pleaded. "I didn't know. They had to explain it to me over and over again because I couldn't understand."

She placed a hand on his shoulder. "Oh, Eliza, forgive me," he begged tearfully.

"Forgive you?" she said to him. "You're not guilty. We're not guilty. We didn't do anything but exist."

"And now existence is too much."

"And Adam's family?"

"I don't know," Hershel confessed. "I think his brother might have lived. I don't know. He was taken away before we were, but to what camp?" Hershel shrugged. "Adam? Is he with you?"

"He's dead, Hershel. He died fighting the Germans."

"Good. I'm glad he died fighting."

"We had a child."

He looked up at her. "And the child?"

Eliza raised her shoulders and dropped them. "I don't know. I'm trying to find her. I left her with a Polish girl I knew. The child was alive a few months ago. That's for sure. But they left the village and came here. Now I'm searching for her."

Trying and trying. How does anyone find one person in a city of lost souls? Eliza went through the Russian bureaucracy, but they could tell her nothing. She found Tadeusz and Luba, both of whom had survived the war, and enlisted their aid. They gave their help, even though both were very busy as potential stalwarts of the new state. Luba finally came up with a death certificate for Wanda's mother, but no Wanda, no child.

Eliza traveled back to Kowitz, letting the village know that Wanda Zbyszek's mother was dead. It didn't seem to have much effect on them. And Wanda had still not returned.

Now what was Eliza to do? "Give it up," Tadeusz suggested. "Wherever this Wanda Zbyszek is, if she doesn't want to be found, she won't be."

If she doesn't want to be found? Could it be that Wanda didn't want to return Mina to Eliza? Could it be that she now thought of Mina as her own child? Eliza begged favors, put ads in the papers that were again publishing. Missing child? Was she out of her mind, everyone wanted to know. There were hundreds of thousands of children missing, most of them dead. She should be grateful she knew the child was at least alive.

Eliza believed that she could not begin to live again until she found her child. But month after fruitless month of searching wore her down, especially because her searching meant contact over and over again with death in all the many forms the Germans had served it.

She was exhausted when she returned to the room in the ghetto that she called home. One evening, a man waited outside the room for her. Another ghost looking for the lost? In a way, she doubted it. This one looked too young, too strong to have survived any war in Europe. He stared at her as she approached. She knew she was nothing to look at. Although her bout with typhoid was over, the search for her child had drained her so much that she continued to look like one of the walking dead. "Eliza." He spoke her name.

She looked at him. She didn't know him from Adam. Adam? Freudian slip? Or *did* she know him? Could this be Adam's cousin? "Motti? Motti Feuerstein?"

He smiled. "Motti Gever now," he said. "A new country, a new name."

She continued to look at him in amazement. "You—why aren't you in Palestine?"

"Because."

"Hmm—because what?"

"We wanted to save the remnant."

"I'm not an idealist anymore. You can tell me the truth."

"There's a war coming and we need fighters. I met a friend of yours in Italy. Branek Weiss. And his wife, Sophie."

"So they finally got married?" She smiled broadly for the first time in months.

"He said you'd be here."

"Don't tell me you came to Cracow to look for *me*. I'm not that good a fighter."

"Sniper, I understand. No. The *Yishuv* knew I had lived in Cracow and sent me here."

"Have you seen Zorik, Adam's brother? Has he survived?"

"Yes. He's in a transit camp, waiting for the first opportunity to reach Palestine. And you?"

She hesitated.

"I understand the problem," he assured her. "And you must realize that you may never find her. Leave word with your friends in the government. Let them keep an eye out. This Polish girl has to get papers sometime. When she does, they'll locate your daughter. Until then, start to live again. You owe that to all those who died. You owe that to Adam."

Adam. We would each be the other's living memorial, they had promised. And yet she still walked around this city of the dead. The child was not lost. The child lived. If she held onto that one thought, perhaps she could begin to live again, too.

14

PALESTINE

ELIZA DID NOT SEE THE SHORE OF PALESTINE COME INTO VIEW. She stood on the deck and watched, but the night was so dark she did not know whether she was looking toward land or out to sea. She was anxious. All during the war she had not realized how lucky she was. She had been free in the forest, fighting with the partisans, even if death, disease and starvation were their constant companions. Ever since she had taken Motti's advice to go to Palestine, she had been a prisoner. How long ago was that? Over a year. It was a year in which she had been shunted from one camp for displaced persons to another, all the time trying to evade the British embargo on Jews entering Palestine. Many times, she wanted to give up the struggle, go someplace else, like Canada or Australia, especially when she saw others, even relative newcomers to the camps, leave before she did. But she held out for the dream of living in a country of her own. Still, there was a system she was missing out on. And when she complained to the Zionist bureaucracy who had infiltrated the camp, she was told that those whose skills were needed were being sent first.

In early October 1947, she was once again being moved, from Austria into Italy, near the sea. And then one night, just as she had finished eating some rather spicy bean soup, she was told to grab her things and come. Come where, no one specified.

The ship, if one could dignify it with the name, was called *HaGiborim*, the *Brave Ones*. That's what its passengers were told, though on the side of the ship it said the *Hermes*, registered in Greece. It was captained by a renegade Briton named Ronnie, who had become disgusted with his own country's actions toward the remaining Jews of Europe. There were thirty passengers taken on board that night, including Nehemiah, an officer in the army of the Jews, the *Palmach*. On their trip over, he was to train them in the art of war. In actuality, the people on board *HaGiborim* were excess baggage. What was important was the cargo: weapons and ammunition needed to fight the coming war that everyone expected.

It was while on board the ship that Eliza heard of the UN vote for partition. The British mandate for Palestine would be divided between the Arabs and the Jews. The Jews would have their own state, Israel. Nehemiah was ecstatic. Eliza was just relieved. Now all those poor souls who waited in the DP camps in Europe would have a place to call "home" once again.

"Unlikely," Nehemiah told her.

"What do you mean?"

"The UN vote doesn't come into effect immediately. We have six months left with the British. Believe me, the British will spend those six months doing everything possible to help the Arabs wipe us out, including limiting, by any means possible, the number of Jews entering the country."

In other words, if they were to get into Palestine, they would have to do it by stealth.

HaGiborim was not a quiet ship. It was obnoxiously loud. But Ronnie aimed it for Lebanon, sailing, when they reached that area, a course parallel to Palestine's coast. Until night came.

"The British can't be everywhere," Nehemiah said, as words of encouragement. "But do you all know how to swim?"

The groan that went up proved to Nehemiah that swimming was not high on their list of skills. "We're not pulling in to the shore," he warned them. "Because we are not going into port. Launches will come out to collect the cargo. The cargo is what's important. Please try to remember that. So if there's trouble, the one way to reach shore is to swim for it. Otherwise, if the British catch you, it's back to the camps."

Eliza considered whether risking her life using her doggy paddle was better than being sent back. She decided it probably was.

When she heard Ronnie call, "Drop anchor," she knew she was as close to Palestine as she was likely to get in *HaGiborim*. No sooner had the tub of a ship ground to a halt than they were boarded by tough-looking men, all carrying guns. These were followed by others, who went down into the hold and began unloading the cargo into launches surrounding the ship.

Eliza stood by, hearing curses in a hundred languages, including her own. She smiled. Something stirred in her. Understanding grew as she realized that all these men were Jews, alive, strong, fighting, not about to be rounded up and marched to the slaughter. Her own country lay within reach. She had never been a Zionist. She had always believed that socialism could cure the ills of nations. Nations maybe, but socialism was a system, not a belief. It could not alter prejudice or change the tribal instincts of a millennium. Here, finally, she would be safe from the madness of Europe. If she made it to the shore alive.

"Get ready," Nehemiah said to his group of thirty. "They are sending two boats back for you."

"No swimming for it then," one of the men said.

"No. Tonight was quiet. For a change."

The boats did come back. One by one, refugees made their way down the rope ladder and into the launches. Some fell into the water first, which Eliza was sure would happen to her when it was her turn. "Are you coming?" she asked Nehemiah when there were only two people ahead of her.

He shook his head. "Ronnie and I have many more trips to make."

"Good luck."

"You too, Eliza. Don't worry. There's someone on the beach who'll know where to take you."

She climbed down the rope ladder, fearful of even the gentle rolling of the water beneath her. But someone grabbed her when she got to the end of the ladder, and she plopped down safely into the boat. She looked back only once at *HaGiborim*. Then she gazed steadily at the approaching shore.

The launch was beached, and everyone moved forward to the prow in order to step onto sand, not into the water. When Eliza first felt the earth of Palestine beneath her, she was half in the water, half on the sand. "Move, move!" someone urged her. But this could not be rushed. She leaned down and took up a handful of water-packed sand and held it to her. She smelled it, then let it fall through her fingers. She was home.

"If you're not planning to live on the beach, you better move your rear," someone said to her in Yiddish.

Eliza headed farther inland. It still seemed like beach. It was all sand, hills of it, with a little bit of brush here and there. Behind her men were working to obliterate all signs of the night's activities, so the British, she thought, would not know who or what had come ashore the night before.

The refugees were again left standing and waiting, while the more precious cargo was taken care of, packed onto trucks, jeeps, whatever was available. Then it was the humans' turn. Her name was called: "Eliza Wolf." She strode quickly up to where the roll was being called, and waited. Someone grabbed her arm and pulled her toward a jeep. Then she was pushed into the seat as if she were a child. The jeep started, and she left the darkness of the beach behind her.

"Where are we going?" she asked the driver in Polish—not that she would know even if he told her, but she wanted to make conversation with this new breed of Jew.

He looked at her and shook his head.

She tried her sentence in Yiddish, which she was not very good at. Again, he didn't understand her. *"Evrit,"* he said to her, which she took to mean Hebrew. She started to laugh, and he stared at her as if she were crazy. She couldn't believe that people were actually using Hebrew to communicate, not just for prayer. "English," he suggested.

"Hello, good-bye, okay, thank you," she said. She had picked up a little bit more in the DP camps, along with French, German, even a little Russian. But they were all just words.

"Soon," he said to her.

Soon. She knew that word. When would she be going to Palestine, she had asked over and over again. Soon. Always that promise. When would life start again? Soon. And now, all of a sudden, soon was here.

15

KFAR HANNAH

"GUARD THE CHICKENS," DVORA ORDERED HER.

"Guard the chickens?" Eliza repeated. "From whom?"

"From the soldiers."

"From the Arab soldiers?"

"No! From our soldiers." Dvora, big and broad, looked at Eliza as if she were the most stupid person alive. She was about to walk off. Then she turned to come back and explain. "They're stealing our chickens to eat. So we won't have any eggs. We won't have any baby chicks. We won't have anything. Guard those chickens. Use force if you have to." This time she did leave.

"Use force if you have to." Fine for Dvora to say, but what was Eliza to use as a weapon? She was given no rifle, no knife. And how does one fight one's own soldiers? She sighed. The first day of her new life, and all was confusion.

Last night she had been driven into what she had assumed was a military compound. There was a watchtower, and barbed wire had to be drawn back before the jeep could enter. As soon as they entered, the barbed wire was put back into place. The people in the compound busily began emptying the jeep of its cargo. Absolutely no one paid attention to her. Not that she expected parades or a marching band; but for someone to say to her, "Welcome," well, that would have made a difference. Instead she was left standing in the middle of nowhere, until, as an afterthought, someone came by to ask her if she would like something to eat. She would very much like something, if only a glass of cool water. She was given coffee, a piece of bread, a minuscule piece of cheese and an apple. She was stuffed by the time she finished eating. Then a woman, who'd waited impatiently for her, led her to a barracks, where she was given a sheet and a pillow. In the barracks were six beds, two of them empty. Although she had lost all modesty fighting with the partisans, in this new country and strange surroundings, Eliza was glad to see that all four in the barracks were women.

She put her pillow down on one of the iron cots and fell quickly and even peacefully asleep under the sheet.

The sun did not wake her the next morning, nor did the other women in the barracks. She slept and slept. When she finally opened her eyes, she found she was alone. Nervously she threw off her cover and rose. She was still in the ragged clothes she had worn since she left Poland. Once outdoors, she knew they were no longer going to be serviceable. Even in November, it was just too hot.

Very few people were in sight, and those who passed by seemed to have no time for her. Eliza finally decided to go to a small building that stood apart from the others and looked like an office. She had come to recognize official buildings from her months in DP camps. She knocked respectfully and opened the door. Stepping inside, she said good morning. The woman, who later introduced herself as Dvora, looked up at her sharply. "You've missed breakfast," she said accusingly.

"I'm sorry, I—"

"We get up early here. This is a farming village. Of course, if this doesn't suit you—"

"No. It's fine. I love it here already. I just—I was so tired from the journey that I simply didn't wake up."

Dvora looked at her as if that explanation were totally unsatisfactory. "I suppose I can find you a tomato and some bread. Do you like onions? We have lots of onions here."

"Onions are fine," Eliza said agreeably.

"You'll have to stop speaking Yiddish, you know. We can't have that sort of thing around here."

Eliza was deciding whether to be angry or tearful as Dvora got up and led her out of the office. She would have been glad to stop speaking Yiddish if there had been an alternative.

Once both were inside the communal kitchen, Dvora arranged for her to have bread, tea and a tomato. The tomato was ripe and juicy. It refreshed her and made it possible to face Dvora again, to ask her if there was anywhere she could shower.

"Shower?" Dvora repeated, as if Eliza had asked if she could murder someone. "We shower on Tuesdays and Fridays for Shabbat. Water is like gold here, you know."

Well, no, she didn't know, not really, certainly not yet.

Dvora studied her, then wrinkled her nose. "However, a shower might be a good idea. Where are the rest of your clothes?"

"This is it," Eliza explained. "I have a few underpants, but I have to wash them. The journey—"

"Yes, yes. Come." The imperious Dvora led her to the laundry room, where three women were hard at work, particularly under Dvora's watchful eye. Dvora grabbed some clothes from a shelf. "These are old, but they should fit you. After you take your shower—a quick one, with no lollygagging—bring your dirty clothes back here. Then report to me."

There was a communal shower at Kfar Hannah, as there was a communal everything else. Outside the shower door, she had to place a cork plaque with a picture of a woman on it, so that any man would know enough not to come in, or so she hoped. There was no roof to cover the shower stalls. They simply stood open to the elements, which that day were bright and sunny. But the area where Eliza was to leave her clothes was covered.

She ran to the shower and found soap already in the dish. She quickly pulled on a chain and let water cascade over—even she would have to admit it—her stinking body. Then she let go of the chain and lathered every bit of herself, including her hair. She guiltily pulled the chain again and let the lather spill off and down the drain, along with the water it took to cleanse her. She felt so good, so clean, so refreshed that she simply stood there under the spigot and looked up at the sun, smiling as the warmth caressed her body. How long was it since she had even remembered that her body existed as an entity with sensitivities of its own?

Lollygagging. She must have been lollygagging, because she barely had to dry herself at all. She looked through the clothes Dvora had given her and found a stiff cotton bra and a pair of cotton underpants, good sturdy farmer's clothes. Then she put on the shirt, which was khaki and long-sleeved. She rolled up the sleeves. Next she picked up the—shorts! What happened to the legs? There had to be some mistake. She peeked outside the shower to see if there was any woman she could call to. No one. Well. She would put on the shorts and make a dash for the laundry to see what else was available.

Eliza felt naked as she sprinted for the laundry. One of the women took her dirty clothes from her, even as Eliza protested that she knew how to wash her own clothes. The woman didn't seem to understand her. She just kept saying "Dvora" over and over again, while Eliza tried to explain that she needed a pair of pants.

It seemed there was no hope of making herself understood. So she cautiously made her way back to the small office. When she let herself in, Dvora was with a man. Eliza didn't remembered blushing in a long time, but she did now, as the man turned and looked at her legs. Since Adam's death, she had thought of herself as a fighter, not a woman. But now, with her body so revealed, the balance had swung to the side of femininity.

Dvora introduced her to Amnon, who was the *maskir* of Kfar Hannah, which Eliza later learned meant the boss. "I'll be right with you," Dvora told her. Eliza waited, trying in some way to move her legs so they would not be quite so visible. Dvora kept staring at her as if she were a little girl who had to pee.

After Amnon left, Eliza blurted out her problem. "These shorts don't cover my legs."

"Are you religious?" Dvora asked.

"What?"

"*Dati*? Religious?"

"No."

"Then why are you worried about your legs? Do you think they're the most marvelous pair in the world?"

"No, but—"

"Listen, what's your name?"

"Eliza."

"Listen, Eliza, here we do what's practical. When the sun's out, it's more practical to wear shorts. When it's raining, we wear pants. When it's cold, we put on a jacket. When it's hot, we take it off. Life is very simple here. All right?"

Eliza was not ready to commit herself. That fact didn't seem to bother Dvora at all. She got out of her chair—she was wearing pants—and led Eliza through Kfar Hannah to the chicken house. Then the order: Guard the chickens.

16

THIEF!

ELIZA HAD VAGUE RECOLLECTIONS OF CHICKEN STEALING. BEFORE Izzy, a member of Branek's group, had been killed, he used to believe that war wasn't a reason not to celebrate Shabbat. If they were near a village, or if he knew how to get to a village, he and a few friends would go grab a chicken. Even now she could smell the soup they made from the bird, soup with potatoes and onions. Those were the feast days. Until this moment she had never considered how the villager must have felt when he discovered he had one less chicken.

She had decided, after a few hours among the chickens, scattering feed and standing guard, that she really didn't like the birds. They had a propensity for fighting, and they didn't seen to realize she was not an object for pecking. She patrolled, but at a distance.

This quiet time, except for the clucking, gave her an opportunity to observe her new surroundings. Kfar Hannah didn't look like much to her, just a little bit more developed than the base camps Branek had built, the buildings a bit more permanent. Most of the buildings on Kfar Hannah were sun-washed and communal, although there were scatterings of individual huts, which probably housed married couples. All of the village was surrounded by barbed wire, with the watchtower near the entrance she had come through last night and another watertower marking the other half-circle of Kfar Hannah.

Kfar Hannah was mainly dust, which suited the chickens. Here and there gardens had been planted, stones laid for sidewalks. Their color only served as a contrast to the dullness of the dust that nature had provided. Beyond the barbed wire lay fields and orchards. This must be where the men of Kfar Hannah spent their time, unless they were all off fighting.

She was at a loss as to where Kfar Hannah was located. Was it in the south of Israel, near Jerusalem, or in the north, near Haifa? Where had she landed? Was it only last night?

The chickens squawked. She turned. She caught a glimpse of a man dressed in khaki. He had grabbed a chicken by its feet and was now running away. While she had been daydreaming, the thief had come.

Eliza couldn't fail at the first task she had been given in her new country. She yelled, "Stop, thief!" which only served to spur the man on.

She wouldn't allow him to escape. Dashing through the chickens, she chased after him. She was helped by the fact that neither of them could hit his stride, since there were no open spaces within the perimeter of the village. Further, she had righteousness on her side, whereas the thief was hampered by having to dodge the villagers her alarm had alerted.

Suddenly, she saw how he had entered. There was an opening in the fence near the motor pool. He was now racing toward it. If he succeeded in reaching it, he would have nothing but open fields to run through; and she would lose him. With one last burst of energy, she took a flying leap, tackling him at the knees.

Down went the thief. To save himself, he let go of the chicken, which cackled in outrage. Eliza pounded on the man's back, and was about to stand up and kick him, when he quickly turned over and captured her hands. She fell flat on top of him. Aware of the precariousness of her position, she struggled to free herself. Then she looked at his face. She was surprised to find the thief laughing. *"Motec,"* he said to her.

She didn't know what the word meant, but she knew enough about men. From that look in the thief's eyes, the sooner she removed her body from his, the better. She pulled away, and he released her. She stood. He remained seated in the dust, looking up at her, at her bare legs and heaving chest. She was flushed, and not only from the exertion and the heat of the day.

Dvora saved her. She came at the young man shouting torrents of Hebrew, which Eliza understood not at all. Instead of being embarrassed about his act of criminal outrage, the young man sounded as if he were defending himself. Finally, without shame, he allowed himself to be escorted off Kfar Hannah, with a "Good riddance" from Dvora.

"Well done," Dvora allowed her. "Now get this chicken back where it belongs."

Months passed, during which Eliza increased her knowledge a hundredfold. First, she now knew where she was: up north, in the Galilee, above Safad. And she knew the threat Kfar Hannah faced, because the Arabs considered the Galilee theirs. Now, whenever the men of Kfar Hannah went out to plow their fields, they went with rifles. No one ever knew when an attack would take place. Everyone had to be a fighter, because the war was brought home to them every day. But this was a situation she was used to, and it did not make her feel uneasy.

What did make her uneasy was when Dvora, moving her from one job to another, put her in the children's house. There were only twenty children on Kfar Hannah, but every single one of the twenty was a reminder of what she had lost. It wasn't so much Mina, her own child, who was alive somewhere, she believed. No, it was her sister's children and all the other children of the ghetto. All dead. All never to live, to play, to learn, to laugh, as these children could, even in the shadow of war. It was unfair of her, Eliza understood, but she was jealous. She could not see such normality without suffering a combination of rage and despair, which made her totally unresponsive in the children's house. Children were not stupid. They could quickly sense when someone was not reacting to them in the normal fashion. They stayed out of Eliza's way.

After two days of suffering, Eliza gave up. She marched into Dvora's office and told her she could not work with the children. "Nonsense," was Dvora's response.

Eliza was more explicit. "I *won't* work with the children then."

"Why not?" Dvora demanded.

Eliza remained tight-lipped, and something in Dvora softened. "The laundry then," she ordered.

At Kfar Hannah they never asked Eliza what had happened to her during the war. She thought it was because they didn't want to know. Being a Jew in Europe during the war was, in a way, something to be ashamed of. The villagers could feel this way, Eliza believed, because they would never understand, didn't have a glimmer of what it was like in Europe, of how quickly the German menace fell upon the Jews of Poland. And Eliza also thought it was because the Jews of the Yishuv were used to fighting, against each other, against the Arabs, and now for a state of their own, her own. So they couldn't understand docility in anyone.

She didn't remain in any job for long, not the laundry or the kitchen or the dining room, until they discovered her real skill during a debate one night in the communal hall, which served for meeting, eating, and every other social occasion. Men were in short supply. Those who weren't out in the fields were with the Palmach, fending off Arab attacks on the settlements of the Galilee. But there was always one man within the perimeter of the village itself, on the watchtower, to give the alert and, if necessary, to hold off any Arab band that might try to attack Kfar Hannah during daylight, when the village was essentially defenseless. Still, the army considered this a waste of a man.

Eliza had been learning Hebrew, as she had been learning a lot of things, such as how to wear shorts with some grace and ease. She understood what they were talking about now, so she rose to speak.

No one noticed her, or chose to notice her, for the longest time. Then finally Dvora said, "You don't need permission to go to the bathroom."

Eliza sighed loudly, but at least she'd drawn their attention. She began carefully in Hebrew. "In the war I fought with the partisans. I took my share of the watch. I was the best sniper. I will serve on the watchtower."

They didn't believe a word she said. All the women on Kfar Hannah knew how to use a rifle, but they didn't. And here she was telling them she was an expert marksman. The next morning they tested her. The men put several targets in a field. They had her climb up the watchtower. Amnon said, "If you can't hit them with one bullet each, don't try again. We can't waste the ammo."

It was simple, a game she could win. She hit each target. From that day forward, she was "the woman in the watchtower." It felt good, in a way, to be back with what she knew so well; and it gave her a measure of respect in Kfar Hannah that she hadn't felt before. But being in the watchtower, she also missed talking to the other women, learning to be more proficient in Hebrew. How was she to know that very soon she would have a more expert teacher?

17

MAY 14, 1948

THE CHICKENS OF KFAR HANNAH WERE DOOMED. NOT ALL OF them, of course. But many would not make it through the day. May 14, 1948, the State of Israel was reborn. It was time to celebrate.

No one was fooled. There would be war with the Arabs. But thanks to the tactics of Yigal Allon, much of the Galilee was free of any immediate military threat. They would be able to savor this day of all days, this day of magnificent independence.

Dvora and Amnon had decided to invite a unit of the Palmach to Kfar Hannah to celebrate with the villagers, despite the fact that the army had not stopped its raids against the village food supplies. But now was a time to be generous. These boys were putting their lives on the line for the settlements of the Galilee, and their lives included their stomachs. Why not allow them to enjoy one night in Kfar Hannah without the danger of being attacked and condemned for their waywardness?

Eliza wore a dress for the occasion. It wasn't a new dress. It was one that Dvora had outgrown with her third pregnancy. But it was the first dress Eliza had worn since before the war, when she and Adam used to go to parties at the university all the time, parties where there was food and laughter and talk, such talk as to make the head spin and the heart believe they were the only people who knew anything on the face of the earth. Now she looked in the mirror and understood that she knew nothing.

She was twenty-seven years old, an old maid by prewar standards. She had neither husband nor child, none that she could point to and say: "These are mine; we belong together." She didn't look as bad as she had when she first arrived at Kfar Hannah. Eliza had to give herself credit for that. She was no longer skeletal or worn. In fact, her face was glowing from the effects of such a healthy life. Who could have believed what a difference these months had made? And yet, as happy as she was, as satisfied as she felt at choosing to start life over in a new country, a reborn state, she knew there was an emptiness that only love could fill, the love she felt for Adam, for Mina, for her family, for all that was missing, vanished, dead. She dared not even hope she would ever capture that love again.

And yet love is no respecter of persons. It goes where it wants, when it wants, and no one knows when he or she will be struck by it. As Eliza prepared herself for the feast, she had no idea that, at an army base very near her, someone was also looking into the mirror, wondering if he, too, would ever find anyone to share the joy of the moment with, to share a life with. Loss is too common, too universal, but, thank God, so is love.

Eliza's task for the evening was to set up the dining hall for the party. That meant plates and silverware and a *kolboinek* in the middle of the table for the chicken bones. Just the thought of chicken on bones excited her. The village authorities didn't really know exactly how many men from the army base were coming, but Dvora was sure the invitation to dinner would bring as many as could possibly make it. So Eliza put the place settings close together. Even the children were joining them for this most historic of occasions.

Just as she finished the place settings, Ronit joined her, to put tomatoes and peppers and onions on the table in big bowls, so that everyone could cut what was needed to make salad. The feast was about to begin. Way before the hour of seven struck, the soldiers had begun to arrive.

At first they were very polite, even shy about entering the dining room of Kfar Hannah, whose food had been a constant source of delight for them over the months, but when Dvora shouted, "If you want to eat, you better sit," they found their way to the benches quickly enough.

"Can you join me?" a voice behind Eliza asked. She didn't think anyone would be speaking to her, so she continued to search for a seat. Someone tapped on her shoulder. She turned around. "Thief!" she said, this time in Hebrew.

"I'm flattered you remember," he had the nerve to answer. "May I have the pleasure of sitting near you on this festive occasion?"

He was teasing. She looked doubtful.

"That dress becomes you," he added. Now she knew he was teasing her. "Though I preferred the shorts."

She stared grimly at him. "Are you committed elsewhere?" he asked.

"No," she admitted.

He took her by the arm, as if he owned her, and led her to a bench. Then he watched closely as she swung her legs over the bench to sit. If she weren't so determined to be firm with him, she would have blushed.

The chickens were brought to the table, potatoes and okra and carrots accompanying them. The smell of the food almost made them swoon with anticipation. Her escort expertly speared her an entire leg and placed it on her plate. She looked guiltily around her. This was definitely too much meat. "I can't eat all this," she whispered to him. She saw that he had a hefty chunk of breast on his plate.

"Let's try," he whispered back, his breath coming hot against her neck.

She found that the chicken went down effortlessly, and the salad, and the vegetables. But did she really taste them? No. She was more intent on the conversation of this man who seemed to be pretending only he and she existed in this room.

His name, she discovered, was Yehuda Barak. He was a some-time commander of this unit of the Palmach. At other times he retired to his home in Tiberias, where he worked with his father, who had a small grocery store. "Not that that's what I plan to do after the war," he told her. "After the war, I'm investing in the future. There's a pension on the outskirts of town I have my eye on. The springs of Tiberias are known for their health-giving properties. The city overlooks the Kinneret, the Sea of Galilee to the Christians. Capernaum is right there, and also the river Jordan falls from the lake. I believe Tiberias is going to be one of the centers of tourism in Israel. Israel! Isn't it wonderful to be able to call our home Israel again? And you? What are you going to do after the war?"

"I don't make plans for after the war," she said carefully. "I tried that once before."

He looked at her arms. "No number?"

"No." She cursed him for his indelicacy, but she couldn't hold it against him. It was an Israeli trait. "I was with the partisans during the war."

"Where?"

"In Poland."

"Ah. Then you must be the girl in the watchtower. I've heard of you. I didn't know it was the same woman who pummeled me so brutally months ago."

She smiled. "Does your family look forward to running a hotel? It can be a lot of work."

"Oh, I'll have to hire help in the beginning. My father certainly isn't giving up his grocery store. My mother helps him out. And my sister is busy with her own life."

"What about your wife?"

"I have no wife." But the way he said it made her believe that sometime, somewhere, there had been someone.

After they ate, they went outside, where a bonfire was blazing. Solemnly, everyone stood at attention and sang "HaTikva," the national anthem of their new country. And then the party began. One of the men of the village brought out his accordion. People began singing, requesting their favorite songs, dancing the hora around the bonfire.

Yehuda asked Eliza to dance. "I haven't danced in years," she confessed.

"Tonight everyone must dance," he told her.

She knew the hora from watching. But the steps to the other folk songs were strange to her. Dodi Li, My Beloved, was the name of the next dance. Yehuda took her into the circle and led her through the softness of it, as if they were dancing in a dream. She felt his hand on her waist, each finger pressing into the flesh over her ribs. It was the first time she had responded to a man since Adam. There had been other offers, from other men in Branek's camp. But she had been dead inside to everything except survival. Now there was something more.

Yehuda held her eyes to his. She felt the sweet moistness of his palm in hers, the strength of his shoulders as he circled her around. It was intoxicating. She broke away and left the circle of light.

He followed her. "What is it?" he asked.

"I feel something I haven't felt in a long time," she admitted.

"A certain sexual urge?" he said, hopefully.

She laughed. "No. Sorry. I think it's life."

"That sounds like a sexual urge to me."

She looked at him. He wasn't spectacularly attractive. Thin, like most men living on rations, weathered by the sun, muscular. His eyes could change from sweet to intense, but they were always kind. His lips parted slightly, tempting her. She moved closer and touched his lips with hers. He grabbed her, held her head, and forced his lips hard against hers, his tongue into her mouth. She pushed him away. "No!"

He turned his back on her and stood shaking. It was sex he wanted, someone to sleep with, someone to fuck. And as she stared at him, she realized she wanted it, too.

She surprised him by taking his hand. He turned to look at her. She beckoned him backward, away from the fire, the singing and dancing, the people. "I know a place," she promised him.

She fantasized he was Adam come back to her. She felt his lips on her face, his hands desperately deciding whether they should be on her breasts, her thighs, inside of her where she anxiously awaited him. She held his face in her hands and kissed him over and over again. Then she moved her hands downward, unbuckled his belt, unbuttoned his pants, pulled loose and caressed what she hadn't realized she had been longing for. He pulled off her underpants and lifted her legs to encircle him. When she felt him inside her, she came, his thrusts adding to her elation. She felt his wetness within her and felt pleasure at the heaviness of his body upon hers, his lips now so gentle against her cheek.

Afterward, they didn't speak. Yehuda helped her dress. They brushed each other off, so it wouldn't look as if they had been tumbling on the ground. "You better go first," he suggested.

She went back into the light of the fire and tried not to notice when he reappeared. For the rest of the evening, they kept away from each other. She danced, and she took her turn serving. He talked to others of the village, to the men in the unit. Only when the party was over did he come back to her. "Thank you," he said softly to her.

"It was my pleasure," she responded just as politely.

He left without any promises that they would see each other again.

18

LETTERS

"WAR IS NOT A HEALTHY THING FOR THE ECONOMY," DVORA EXplained.

Eliza silently sighed. This was news? She had seen what war had done to Poland, to Austria and Italy. Now Israel. Was war following her, or was she following war?

She was in the second group of women to whom Dvora was speaking. The first group had already received their lecture and now were out doing something about it. But Eliza didn't need Dvora to tell her the problem. The men were gone. A farm without men to do the heavy work can be a very trying place. Especially when the women had to not only continue farming but also, should it come to that, defend the fields against Arab attack.

Eliza avidly read and listened to reports of Arab preparations for war. She knew all too well that both Iraq and Syria were moving toward Kfar Hannah's part of Israel. If she were fighting the war, she would simply cut their lines of supply. But those were the tactics of a guerrilla, and the Israeli army wasn't a guerrilla force. Well, perhaps that wasn't entirely correct. It was still made up of various groups with different uniforms, but they were all fighting for the same cause, the survival of Israel.

Tanks bothered her. She didn't like them, and that's what the Syrians, who were set on invading the Galilee, had. She had seen what tanks could do when the Germans used them. But the partisans had had weapons to fight with. Here in Israel there were few weapons and little ammunition for the weapons they did have. Dvora asked her advice. All of a sudden, Eliza had become useful. She taught the women how to make Molotov cocktails and homemade bombs. Then she set up a duty roster for their defense. Defense wasn't her specialty, but at least she had seen action, which most of the women on Kfar Hannah had not, so they deferred to her.

Tiberias was in Jewish hands, as was Safad. Those were the two main centers of Jewish population in the Galilee, along with Haifa, which was also held by the Jews. Still, the settlements of the Galilee were wide open to attack. Many of their fields lay adjacent to Arab fields. There was always the danger of mines, of sniper fire.

Mishmar Hayarden had been overrun by the Syrians. Malkiya and Kadesh were under attack but holding their own. They needed to be resupplied, but there was nothing to supply them with. The kibbutzim to the south of the Kinneret were holding on as well.

The women on Kfar Hannah talked about their men. Eliza had no man to fear for, but she wondered about Yehuda. Where was he? Against whom was he fighting? The Syrians? The Iraqis? Did he ever think of her?

Oh, you are so stupid, Eliza, she warned herself. In the middle of a war, why would he think about you? And she had more important things to do than concentrate on him. The defenses of Kfar Hannah were now her responsibility.

By the beginning of June, there were smiles on the faces of the women of Kfar Hannah. The Galilee had been defended. The threat of massive Arab invasion, while always real, no longer seemed imminent. Although the situation in the south, near Tel Aviv and, especially, near Jerusalem, was precarious, the men of Kfar Hannah began to return home.

One of the men, Udi, stopped by Eliza's table as she was eating dinner one day. She looked up at him and smiled. "Welcome back."

Udi almost managed a smile in return. He looked exhausted. He reached into his pocket and pulled out a wad of paper. "Sorry it got so messed up," he apologized. "I've been carrying it around with me for over a week."

She took the paper from him. It was actually an envelope, almost yellow with age. Her name, Eliza Wolf, was written on the front of it. She looked up inquiringly at Udi, but he had already turned away to get another cup of coffee.

"Who is it from?" Tzippi asked.

"I have no idea," Eliza replied. She liked Tzippi, but the girl was ten years younger than she was, and they remained close only because they shared the women's barracks together.

"I thought you said you didn't know anyone in Israel."

Well, that wasn't exactly true. She imagined that somewhere in Israel she could find Branek and Sophie, maybe others from her days in the forest, even others from the DP camps she had spent time in after the war. But did any of them know where she was? And if they did, why would they write to her? And in Hebrew, which she could now speak well enough, but couldn't read with much proficiency.

"Well?" Tzippi waited.

"Well what?"

"Open it."

"Mail is private."

"Not on Kfar Hannah, it isn't," Tzippi corrected her.

Eliza made a face and put the letter into her pocket. If it had waited a week, it could wait a little longer. She left the dining room to do her chores; then, she retired to the village library, a room off the dining hall that held a Hebrew dictionary. There she carefully withdrew the letter from her pocket and unsealed it. The paper inside was small and thin; the handwriting slanted downward.

"Dear Eliza, I hope you can read this. I never asked if you could read Hebrew and my pencil point is dull and the writing smudged. So, maybe it's just the idea that counts.

"I think of you so I do not have to think about war. I hope that doesn't offend you. Before our second meeting, my war was in Tiberias, where my home is. There we fought through the streets to secure our city. Now it's the wide-open spaces. As I write you, we are winning. I must be happy about this. But the cost is great. Many of my men are dead or wounded. I wonder if it is because of my orders. Yesterday we overran an Iraqi position. Not much of a victory. Their soldiers had been chained to their guns so they could not run away. But maybe you have seen worse sights.

"Can I see you again? I know you can't answer directly, because you don't know how to reach me. And mail service leaves something to be desired. But if you want to write me, you can send it to me in care of my parents: Barak, c/o Mendelsohn, Rehov Bialik, Tiberias. If there is no letter, shall I assume the mail didn't get through? Yehuda."

From the children's house, Eliza borrowed a piece of paper with lines. It was unfair of Yehuda to expect her to be able to write to him. First, for her, writing in Hebrew was so unnatural. Second, how would her letter ever reach Tiberias? Men never changed. They were always impossible. "Dear Yehuda, I got your letter." Now what could she say so he wouldn't think her too forward? "I also wonder about you. I hope you are all right. I am still here at Kfar Hannah and going nowhere. Please come. If you can. Eliza."

Well, it was short. But she hoped he would consider the effort she'd put into it. Her tenses were probably all wrong. His parents better not read it. They would think she was an idiot.

She gave her letter to an officer in the Palmach who was making a tour of the settlements. He couldn't promise anything, of course, but he would try to see that it got to Tiberias.

Eliza was worried. After she sent the letter, she learned that soldiers no longer needed in the Galilee were being sent south to Jerusalem to join their former commander, Yigal Allon. Jerusalem was cut off from the rest of Palestine by the Arabs, its population starving. So where was Yehuda now?

"There's going to be a truce," Tzippi sped by and announced.

"What?"

"A truce. Amnon say it's because we're winning, and the Arabs want time to regroup. He thinks it's a bad idea, but Udi says it's a good idea, because we don't have any supplies and our men are exhausted. So each side gets a month's breather."

"Starting now?"

"No. June 11. Jerusalem is supposed to be allowed one month's food and water supply."

"And then they go back to starving?"

Tzippi shrugged. "My father's coming home."

Eliza smiled. "I'm glad, Tzippi."

On June 10, Amnon called Eliza out of the laundry, where she was picking up her clothes. "The army wants you," he told her.

"Me?"

"They're bringing in fresh troops from the DP camps."

"I thought that was forbidden under the truce agreement."

"Listen, Eliza, if we paid attention to all the agreements, we'd never have a state. Do you think we're willing to let the Arabs take it away from us now?"

"I guess not."

"These people are straight off the boat. The army wants you to help train them to use a weapon."

Well, at least it was something she knew how to do. "Fine," she agreed.

"The camp's right outside Haifa. We're landing the immigrants there and taking them straight to the camp."

"Right."

"So."

"So?"

"So get your stuff together. They're picking you up in an hour."

Eliza hesitated.

"Yes?" Amnon said.

"If anyone comes looking for me, will you tell that person where I am?"

Amnon shrugged. "Why not?"

Eliza didn't think anyone could be coming looking for her. But just in case Yehuda Barak did get her letter and came to Kfar Hannah, well, she wanted him to know she still existed.

19

CAMP ALEPH

THE FACES OF THE PEOPLE ELIZA SAW IN FRONT OF HER WERE exactly like her face seven months ago: eager, desperate, confused. Most of all, the faces were thankful for release from the prison of those DP camps, where life had been put on hold and one was forever waiting for official notice to be able to begin to live again. How well she remembered! And how hard it was to start over again, even when one was free. It was like cranking up an old Victrola—learning how to laugh, to have hopes, to cherish dreams.

But her job was not to tell these people that those sensations would return in time. Her job was to teach them how to fight and how to live with the expectation that they might soon again face death. None of them objected. Each had volunteered to be here. Israel was a cause they could understand, a nation they considered worth fighting and dying for.

She spoke in Yiddish. There were immigrants from Poland, Czechoslovakia, France, Holland, Austria—all the nations of Europe. Most had only Yiddish as a common language, that and the suffering they had endured. All bore numbers on their arms.

The task was made more difficult, not by the different nationalities of the people she was dealing with, but by the different types of weapons they were using. These new soldiers held in their hands whatever the army had given them, and she had to teach them how to take apart, clean, put together, and use each of these weapons. She divided them according to weapon and taught them that way, dashing from one group to another, then letting them change rifles and learn how to use one another's in case they had to pick up a different weapon on the field.

A month, the month the truce gave her, was not enough time to train her pupils to use a variety of weapons competently. Eliza didn't even have that month. She had a week with each group that came through Camp Aleph. And in the beginning, she had no ammunition. She could teach them the various positions to fire from, but how could she teach them accuracy and how to correct for the vagaries of each weapon when they didn't have a chance to fire at anything?

She complained to David, who was in charge of Camp Aleph. He asked, "Would you rather have the bullets for target practice or for the enemy?"

It wasn't much of a choice.

The first time she heard mortar fire at Camp Aleph, she thought the Arabs had broken the truce and the camp was under attack. But she noticed that none of the regular soldiers were panicking, not running and ducking for cover. This could be either misplaced bravado or a complete lack of sense. Or—

She rushed to David's office. "David, have we been—" She stopped suddenly and stared.

"Resupplied," David finished for her. But he noticed she wasn't really paying attention to him. She was staring at the officer who had just brought in truckloads of weapons. He took a guess. "Do you know each other?"

They didn't answer. They walked toward each other, turned, and left together. David went to the door to call after them. "Eliza, it would be nice if your troops could have target practice with real bullets from now on." She paid no attention. "After lunch, of course," he added.

"You," she said.

"Eliza." Her name sounded so good on his tongue. "I didn't hear from you."

"You didn't? But I sent you a letter."

"You did?"

Yehuda didn't look older. He looked tired, but there was still a youthful strength about him. "What are you doing here?" he asked.

"Training the new immigrants. They're going to be thrown into battle as soon as the truce is over."

"You left Kfar Hannah."

She smiled. "Obviously. Though I guess I'll go back when they no longer need me here. I don't really have any place else to go."

"You could marry me."

"Don't be silly," she said quickly.

He turned and continued walking across the camp. She hurried after him. Had she offended him? No. He had been joking. She had to confess to herself that she really didn't understand Israeli men. "What have you been doing?" she asked.

"I've become a smuggler."

"Really?"

"Well, semi-smuggler. During the truce we're not supposed to bring in arms. But you must know by now what would happen if we didn't."

"We'd be fighting with pickaxes. Are a lot of arms getting through? I hope so."

"We're not supposed to talk about it."

"But you can tell me. After all, you did just ask me to marry you." She tried to keep her voice light, teasing.

"But you refused."

"Only because I knew you were joking."

"I wasn't."

She shook her head. "How could you possibly want to marry me? You don't know anything about me."

"You don't know anything about me either."

"But there's less to know about you, I'm sure."

"Thanks."

"Look—" She pulled her shoulders in tightly and glanced up at the sky. No, she wasn't going to say anything meaningful, because he wasn't being serious, even though he seemed solemn enough. War. He probably just wanted someone to write to, to fantasize about. "I'd like to see more of you," she said with a smile.

"I'd like to see more of you, too," he replied, his eyes sliding down her body. So that's what he really wanted. "Then you can tell me all your deep dark secrets." He brought his eyes upward again.

But she never got a chance to tell him anything. Yehuda couldn't even stay for lunch. Camp Aleph wasn't the only base he had to supply.

By the time the month-long truce ended, Israel had not only vastly increased its manpower, but also, thanks to several countries and many private sources, added greatly to its weaponry, including an air force, which it later used effectively in the Negev. So successful were the Israeli troops after the truce that the British became frightened that Israel would capture the entire Palestinian mandate. At Britain's urging, the United Nations imposed a new truce on the warring parties, to take effect on July 18, 1948. Count Folke Bernadotte was to draft a plan for a workable, livable, viable peace treaty for the former British mandate.

When Eliza read through Bernadotte's first proposal in the paper, she knew a viable plan for peace was not at hand. The Swedish diplomat intended to dismantle Israel as a state, deny Jewish rights of immigration in the future, make Ramle and Lydda, and thus the international airport at the latter, free zones, and hand Jerusalem to Transjordan. The only thing he was willing to give to the Jews was the Galilee; and though Eliza was sitting in the Galilee, the proposed treaty did not make her happy. Too many lives had been lost to allow it to be implemented.

Even Bernadotte saw that. He changed his plan to be fairer to Israel. He would allow Israel to remain a state. But Ramle and Lydda would have to go back to the Arabs, and Jerusalem would be put under UN control. The Arab refugees would again have the right to reclaim their property and return home.

On September 17 Count Bernadotte was assassinated, presumably by Jewish terrorists. "This is really politically devastating for Israel," David said to his officers at Camp Aleph. "However, this does give us the opportunity to arrest all the members of the Stern gang we can find, and at least get them out of the way."

Eliza just shook her head. Partisan politics, especially Israeli partisan politics, was something she was not ready for yet. She kept her eye on the paper, on the international reaction to this stupid act of political assassination. Now Israel would be forced to give up everything.

To counter political pressure, to get more land, so that they would have to bargain away less, Israel attacked the Egyptian forces in the Negev.

By December, a year and a month after Eliza had arrived in what was then Palestine and was now her country, Israel, the United Nations had given up calling for truces. Now it demanded that the parties in the Middle East negotiate a permanent armistice. Finally, all sides were ready to quit fighting, at least for the time being. Territorially, Israel had most of what she wanted. The old city of Jerusalem had been lost; Egypt still had the Gaza strip. Israeli troops had failed to take Jenin, in the north, but the Beit Sha'an valley was theirs, even though along the Hula valley the settlements were easier targets for Syrian guns on the Golan Heights. Still, a peace of sorts was welcome.

Eliza rejoiced when she was finally able to return to Kfar Hannah. "Let this be the end of my wars," she said to David at the farewell party the regular army threw for the volunteers.

"Don't count on it," he replied.

David's pessimism seemed unfounded to her. By March of 1949 Israel's application for membership in the United Nations was approved, and in May 1949, the Jewish Star of David was proudly raised at the United Nations in New York. Eliza saw pictures of it, and she wept. She remembered her mother cutting out and sewing neat little Stars of David on the family's coats. In 1941 the symbol had meant death. Now it meant life. If only Israel had existed before the war. If only nations had opened up their gates so that her people, her lover, her family could live.

A living memorial—Adam had wanted that from her. But her gift to him would have been the State of Israel.

20

THE GROCERY STORE

"WHAT ARE YOUR PLANS NOW?" DVORA ASKED HER.

Now? Eliza wondered.

"Of course, you're welcome to stay here. But now that the war is over, I imagine you want to be getting on with your own life."

How could she explain to Dvora that she hadn't any life to get on with? "How much time do I have?" Eliza asked.

"Time?"

"How long will you allow me to stay here? You see, I'd like to explore Israel. I haven't really seen much of it except Kfar Hannah, the army base, and Haifa."

"You can have all the time in the world," Dvora assured her. "We appreciate all you did for us during the call-up."

"You did for us" was the giveaway, Eliza decided. She, as opposed to those who actually belonged. Would she always be the outsider? She sighed. "Let me think."

"Naturally. I'm not pushing you, Eliza. I'm only considering your best interests. Kfar Hannah really is no place for a woman alone, especially a woman your age. You need to start over. There are lots of refugees pouring in from Europe now, settling in Tel Aviv, Jerusalem. Maybe you'll find somebody there."

Eliza smiled. "I never knew you were a matchmaker, Dvora."

"I'm not. I just know that living alone is no fun. I didn't get married until I was twenty-five."

"I can't understand why."

"Neither could I. Think about where you want to go. Think about what you can do."

Where could Eliza go? Well, she could go anywhere within the borders of the new state. What could she do? She had never done anything except fight. Oh, yes, she had studied history for one year. But as far as work went, what did she know how to do except feed and guard chickens, do laundry, and work in the kitchen?

The chickens. That was how she'd met Yehuda Barak. Then he had come back to Kfar Hannah for the independence celebration, and they had made love in the dust. He had arrived at the army camp and had asked her to marry him. Then he had disappeared.

Was he dead? It was possible that he had been killed and she had not heard of it. But she thought she would know.

Did he simply not want to see her again? Probably. It was, after all, a very strange relationship. But then she figured it was no stranger than a lot of others that had sprung up during wars. Except that this time it concerned her.

She could go to Tiberias. She had his address. She could just say she was sightseeing and had stumbled on Rehov Bialik. Maybe she would find him sitting at the kitchen table with a wife and a baby.

Forget it. She couldn't go to Tiberias. She wasn't that forward. Except that she was almost twenty-eight now, and the formalities, the ever-so-polite manners she had learned in her youth, no longer applied. They had stopped applying years ago in Europe, and certainly in Israel they didn't stand a chance.

Eliza smiled, remembering when she was a teenager. Oh, how Adam courted her, coming to her father's house for tea, talking to her parents, being nice to Lina and her husband, then perhaps having a few moments to speak with her. How sweet those times seemed now! How innocent! How full of life!

She wondered how people courted in Israel. She knew Tzippi was mooning over a boy she had met from Kibbutz Degania, but that was a teenager's way. What about adults? Or were adults already so tied up with obligations that they didn't have time for real romance?

Make your move, Eliza, she told herself. All you can do is fall flat on your face.

She asked Amnon to let her know when the next car was traveling anywhere near Tiberias. She hadn't long to wait. One was leaving on Friday morning to pick up supplies and drop a family off for Shabbat. There was room for her if she was willing to squeeze in.

It is impossible to say you're in love with a city with your first glimpse of it, especially because the sweep of the city is not visible in one take. But she could see that Tiberias had a lot to recommend it. It sat on the hill above the Kinneret, so that one could look down onto the Sea of Galilee and the nearby kibbutzim and their banana plantations. Not only was the Sea of Galilee below it, but within the city itself were curative springs that drew many people who believed the water could do anything from curing arthritis to banishing infertility. The city of Tiberias was an ancient one, and had served from the first century A.D., after the destruction of the Temple, as a center of Jewish learning. It held the graves of many great rabbis, including Rabbi Akiva, Rabbi Johanan ben Zakkai, and Maimonides. But it wasn't the graves that attracted Eliza to it; it was the city's beauty, its life.

It was hard to believe that so much of Tiberias had been in Arab hands before the war. There had been street fighting, as Yehuda had said, raids and reprisals back and forth among neighbors. Now the city looked peaceful, almost somnolent, ready for revival.

The car from Kfar Hannah dropped her off in the center of Tiberias, since she had said she simply wanted to see what the city looked like. From there, she had quite a hike to Rehov Bialik and the Mendelsohn grocery. It occupied the ground floor of what looked like a relatively new building of flats that had received only minor damage during the war. She should have realized that on a Friday the grocery would be crowded with men and women hurrying to complete their Sabbath shopping. Everything closed for Shabbat, not only to honor God, but so the people could have a day of rest and reflection after working the previous six days.

Through the window, she could see what she thought were both Mr. and Mrs. Mendelsohn dealing with their customers. Each business exchange was accompanied by at least a few moments of gossip. Eliza stood outside. People stared at her as they went in and out. She decided to go to a small café for a late lunch. When she returned, the flow of customers had slowed. She entered the grocery, walked up to the counter, and said, "Good day."

The woman smiled. "Are you looking for something that I can help you find?"

"Well, actually—" Oh, God, Eliza thought. What if she asked for Yehuda and he was dead? What a scene that would create!

"Yes?" the woman waited expectantly.

"Does Yehuda Barak live here?"

"Yehuda? My son?"

"Yes. He gave me this address once and—"

"Oh! Are you the woman from Kfar Hannah?"

Eliza was shocked. Yehuda had met her three times, and he had already told his mother about her? What had he said? "Yes," she admitted.

"Max, it's the woman from Kfar Hannah," Mrs. Mendelsohn

shouted out to her husband. That brought all activity to a crushing halt. Eliza was sure she was blushing. She tried to nod calmly at Max Mendelsohn. ''What are you doing here?'' Mrs. Mendelsohn continued. The audience of shoppers waited for an answer.

''I was just touring. I remembered that Yehuda lived here, and I was wondering—'' She let her sentence trail off, because she didn't know how to explain what she was wondering.

''Do you have a place for the Sabbath meal?'' Mrs. Mendelsohn asked.

''No.''

''Then come upstairs with me. You can't be alone for Shabbat. Come.'' The woman came out from behind her counter and led Eliza out of the shop. They went into the stairwell of the apartment house and up to the first landing, where Mrs. Mendelsohn unlocked the door to her apartment. ''Sit. Rest. Get what you want from the kitchen. Shower, if you like. We'll be up in a couple of hours. Maybe sleep. You look tired. In there is Yehuda's bedroom. No one is using it now.'' She returned downstairs, which left Eliza with the question: If no one was using Yehuda's bedroom, then where was Yehuda?

She took advantage of Mrs. Mendelsohn's kind offer. She slept. When she woke, the apartment was filled with the smell of chicken and potatoes. From beyond the door she could hear the sound of the shower running, as the Mendelsohns prepared for Shabbat. She sat up, took her brush from her bag, and brushed out her hair. Then she went into the living room. Mrs. Mendelsohn peeked out from the kitchen. ''There you are. Did you have a nice nap?''

''Yes, thank you. Is there anything I can do to help?''

''Just come into the kitchen and talk to me.'' Eliza obeyed. ''My name's Hattie, by the way. And unlike Yehuda, for whom everything has to be Israeli, we kept the name Mendelsohn, instead of changing it to Barak when he did.''

''Mine's Eliza Wolf.''

''Eliza—that's it. I had forgotten. I only knew you were from Kfar Hannah.''

''How did Yehuda come to mention me? I've only seen him a few times.''

''Ah, yes. Well, I nudge him, you know. Whom does he like; whom is he seeing? Ever since—well, I suppose Yehuda's told you all about that.''

''No,'' Eliza confessed.

''Ah, yes. He doesn't like to talk about it. I can see why he would avoid telling you.''

Eliza didn't know how to admit to Hattie Mendelsohn that she had barely talked with Yehuda at all. Their relationship had been mainly—well, she guessed, physical. And she certainly wasn't going to admit that to Yehuda's mother, of all people.

Max Mendelsohn came out of the shower and asked her if she would like to use it. "I showered before I came. Friday is shower day at Kfar Hannah, and I didn't want to miss mine," she said with a smile.

They had a comfortable meal together. Max and Hattie told her how they had come to Israel in 1933—just in time. "Max didn't trust the Germans," Hattie confessed, "though life was quite hard here when we came. I wanted to brain him. But now, of course, I'm grateful he was so determined."

"Yes," Eliza agreed. "We, my boyfriend and I, had been socialists before the war. We thought socialism would solve all problems, free everybody, make them happy. Adam's cousin Motti was a Zionist, so he came here. I remember how Adam used to argue with him all the time. Motti was right, of course."

"Socialism is still a good theory," Max said. "But no theory can hold up against tyranny. And worse."

"And this Adam?" Hattie wanted to know.

"He was killed during the war. We were partisans. He was killed fighting the Germans. We were betrayed. Later, we got revenge. But he was dead." They stared at her. She hadn't realized until that moment that she had been crying. She wiped her tears away. "I'm sorry," she said. Then it occurred to her that she hadn't mentioned Adam to anyone since her arrival in Israel.

"We understand," Hattie said. "When Yehuda lost Bracha, we thought he was going to go mad."

"How did it happen?" Eliza asked.

"He didn't tell you?" Max asked in turn.

"No, Max. You know how Yehuda is about Bracha and what happened to her."

"We didn't talk about the past," Eliza said. True enough. They didn't talk about much of anything.

"It's probably better," Hattie said. "At least in the beginning."

"Bracha and Yehuda were Gadna leaders. They took high-school students out for their paramilitary training. One day, right here in Tiberias, the city itself, they were attacked by a band of Arabs, and Bracha was killed."

"Immediately, thank God," Hattie said. "Only she and Yehuda had weapons. So Yehuda and a high-schooler who'd picked up Bracha's rifle had to hold off the Arabs until men from the nearby streets could grab their weapons and come running. It was horrible. Right here in the city. Yehuda never forgave himself. But what could he have done?''

"Nothing," Max answered to his wife's rhetorical question. "But you always think there is something. If they hadn't gone out that day, or if Bracha hadn't been standing where she was, or if they had realized there might be trouble." He shrugged. "Yehuda's never said much about it. At least not to me. More to his mother. But you could see after Bracha's death that he didn't have much desire for anything."

"That's why we were so glad when he met you."

Oh, boy, Eliza thought, have they been misled. "Mrs. Mendelsohn—"

"Hattie, please."

"Hattie, I think I'm here under false pretenses. Your son and I have met only three times. Although I think he's very nice, nothing of much significance has passed between us. I'm sorry." Well, maybe there was some significance to their meetings. He did make love to her. He did ask her to marry him. But she didn't really know him at all. "As a matter of fact, I haven't seen your son for quite some time."

"How could you? He's been out of the country."

"Out of the country?"

"Yes," Max said. "He's scavenging for weapons. Every once in a while someone comes to our door with a message, telling us Yehuda's in Czechoslovakia, France, Panama." He shrugged. "So we know he's safe. But what he's doing, we never ask and they never tell us."

"But the last message said he would be home soon," Hattie assured Eliza with a smile. "So we are hoping to see him any day now. Is your family with you at Kfar Hannah?" she said, changing the subject.

"I have no family. Not anymore."

"Ah."

"You also must have lost—"

"Yes. Though a few were lucky enough to make it to South America. We watch all the time for the names of those who might be related to us. But there are so very few."

"Yes," Eliza agreed.

"Would you like to see our scrapbook? All our pictures of Yehuda?"

"Don't bore her, Hattie."

"I'd love to!" Eliza said.

She and Hattie cleared the table and washed up while Max sat and read the Friday papers and listened to the radio. Then Eliza sat down on the couch while Hattie got out a large album of photos. Eliza smiled as she watched Yehuda turn from a baby to a young boy, from a string bean of a teenager to a very young man. She was shown a picture of his sister, Yael, two years older than he, who lived in Haifa, where her husband was an engineer for the navy. "And this is Bracha," Hattie pointed out. There was a whole series of pictures of the two of them together, holding hands, kissing, mugging for the camera. And then the pictures stopped.

"It's so late," Hattie said. "I hadn't even noticed. I'm waiting for grandchildren. Then this album will grow again." She smiled, but then noticed the shadow that crossed Eliza's face. "You can have children, can't you?"

"Hattie!" Max said.

"I only—"

"Yes," Eliza said. "I can have children."

"It was tactless of me," Hattie admitted.

"A legitimate concern," Eliza said. "It is late." She stood.

"Do you need more blankets? It can get cool up here, because of the lake."

"No. It gets cool in Kfar Hannah, too. I'm used to it."

"If you do need anything, let us know."

Eliza retreated to Yehuda's bedroom. He had been away so long. No wonder it no longer smelled of him. She undressed, took the nightshirt out of her bag, and let it fall over her head and body. She slipped under the covers and tried to think. Sadness. Maybe that's what Yehuda saw in her. The effect of loss upon the human soul. She closed her eyes. Pictures in an album. Her whole life was a picture album full of people who no longer existed. How could she live again? Instead, she slept.

She didn't know what woke her in the night. Other people might assume it was something from a dream, but she knew it was more than that. Her instincts were still sharp. Yes. There it was again. Someone was moving about in the living room. She lay back on her pillow and closed her eyes. Probably Max, looking for something to read or searching for a late-night snack. There were footsteps in the hallway now. And then at her door?

She sat up. The door opened. A shadow came in. The door closed. She couldn't believe it was Yehuda's father!

The light flicked on, and she was blinded. Before she could clear her eyes to see, someone was pressing his lips against hers, placing his hands against the warmth and heaviness of her breasts. She pushed him away. "Yehuda!"

He smiled. "What a pleasant welcome-home surprise. You in my bed."

"Yehuda!"

He lifted the nightshirt over her head and devoured her body with his eyes.

"Your parents are right next door!"

"So we'll have to keep quiet."

"You can't seriously be meaning to—"

But he was. And he very seriously went about it. "Don't moan so loud," he warned her. "And your giggles aren't very encouraging to me," he chided.

"If you persist in doing that I can't help but moan and giggle," she whispered back.

"I want you to be happy."

"I'll be happier if you'd lock the door."

"The door doesn't have a lock on it."

"Great."

"Just lie back and relax. If my parents come in, well—why are you so tense?"

"Take a wild guess and mention your parents again."

But it wasn't a wild guess he was taking. It was her body, every bit of it, loving her, caressing her, making her feel whole again. She wondered if there would ever be a time when she didn't make love surreptitiously. To make love openly had to be one of the real pleasures in life. She moved her hands down along the strength of Yehuda's back. She opened her legs to him and yielded herself up so willingly that she got lost in him, felt his heaviness, wanted him to smother her with his power. He placed his hand softly over her mouth when he felt she was coming. It took something away from the experience, because she had another fit of giggles. But she enjoyed it. He could tell by the wetness that gushed out of her.

She ran her hands along his body and held him to her, murmuring his name. He passed his fingers through her hair, kissing her neck, circling his tongue in her ear. "How long have you been here?" he asked.

"Just today," she answered. "Your parents are very nice."

"Nice, yes. But gossips. Did they gossip about me?"

"Yes. Your mother showed me all your pictures."

He took her hand and kissed it. "We'll talk tomorrow," he promised her. "Now I think I'd better clear out and go sleep on the couch."

He rose, but she caught his hand. "Yehuda, can you love me?"

"Yes. I think so."

"Maybe it's the answer then, for both of us."

21

PENSION BRACHA

ELIZA AWOKE THE NEXT MORNING TO THE SOUNDS OF CELEBRA-
tion. She had no idea what time it was except that it looked dark
out to her. Hattie had screamed in delight. Now she was cooing
with concern for her son, while Max went into the living room,
saying something man-to-man to Yehuda. Eliza couldn't catch the
words. Yehuda's voice in response sounded tired. She cocked an
ear and caught him saying something about going with them to visit
the relatives. His parents insistently rejected his offer, told him he
needed his rest; the relatives would always be there. She fell back
on her pillow, now only half-heartedly listening to outside sounds.
Words of parting, doors slamming—that's all she caught.

The door to the bedroom opened. "Alone at last," Yehuda said.

"I'm sleeping," she said without looking.

"No, you're not."

She looked. He was completely naked. She laughed. "Yehuda!
What if your parents forgot something?"

"Don't worry about it."

"I have to use the bathroom."

"Well, that's an excuse I'll accept."

She got up and passed him. He grabbed at her hand, but she
slipped away. She used the toilet, washed, cleaned her teeth, tried
to brush her hair. She heard the outer door open and Hattie call,
"Darling, I forgot to tell you. There's fresh cream just behind the
juice."

God, what would Hattie think of them now. Eliza stayed in the
bathroom until the door closed and it was quiet once more. Then
she came out and found Yehuda wrapped in a robe. "Don't worry,"
he said to her. "I know the sound of my mother's footsteps on the
stairs."

"Long years of practice?"

"You better believe it. Are you hungry?"

"Not yet."

"Do you want to?"

She looked at him and bit her lower lip. His robe had fallen open, and she could glimpse the length of his body. "Will your mother be back?"

"We can close the door."

"But last night you told me it doesn't have a lock on it."

"I'm willing to chance it."

"Maybe you don't have a reputation to lose."

He smiled and went toward her. She assumed that she wouldn't have a reputation, either, after a morning with Yehuda.

It was fun going to bed with him. Yehuda was kind and warm, considerate and comforting. Had he picked up a lot of experience in Europe? She felt shy and wanton at the same time. Although she wasn't a virgin, she felt virginal, as if this hadn't happened to her before. She wondered how she felt?

Hungry, it turned out. After making love to her, he leapt from the bed, showered, and dressed in a pair of khaki pants and a khaki work shirt, not too different from the uniform she had always seen him in. Then he went into the kitchen. From the bedroom, she could hear him moving about. When he came back, he was carrying a tray with pita bread, eggs, salad, and yogurt. "Sorry it took so long," he said. "I'm out of practice."

She slipped her nightshirt back on. "Service." She smiled. "I love it."

"Do you always look this good in the morning?" he asked her. She gave him a withering look, and he laughed. "If you want more eggs, let me know."

"Rationing?"

"Hey, I don't come home every day."

She bit into the pita, then asked, "If you can get eggs and bread and things from your parents' grocery, why try to steal from Kfar Hannah?"

"For my men, of course. Besides, you people had so many chickens. What did you do with all of them?"

"Get eggs, get more chickens. Good eggs, Yehuda. You have a talent for cooking them. I'll have to admit I've never really cooked much of anything, except squirrels."

"Sounds really tempting. More juice?"

He poured some grapefruit juice for her and a small glass for himself, too. They drank it in silence. She stared at him, but he seemed to be concentrating on eating. "I didn't hear from you for such a long time, I was afraid something might have happened,'' she said.

"I know," he told her, looking into her eyes. "I was afraid."

"Of what? The fighting?"

He laughed. "That, too. But no. I was afraid after I asked you to marry me."

"That I would accept?"

"Yes, I guess so," he admitted.

She felt something in her heart weaken. "Well, you needn't have panicked. We hardly know each other, after all. I won't marry you. Don't worry. I just wanted to make sure you were all right. Now I'll be going. You see, I don't know that many people in Israel yet, so I just like to check up on those I do know. Silly habit. I have places to go after breakfast anyway."

"Oh? Where are you going?"

"Just touring Tiberias. And then I think I'll go to Haifa. I have some friends in Haifa from Camp Aleph. And then—well, who knows? I've never been to Tel Aviv. Or Jerusalem. I don't know if it's possible to go to Jerusalem yet—"

"It is."

"So I'll go there. Time to get out and see something of Israel." She tried to sound cheerful, chipper, independent.

"Have you left Kfar Hannah?"

"Not really. Not yet anyway."

"So you're looking for a place to settle?"

"Yes. You might say that."

She thought that with her next bite of food she would vomit. She was trying hard not to cry. What did he want from her? It wasn't as if he considered her a whore, an easy woman. No. She would know if those were his thoughts. Maybe he was just—confused. Well, she also was confused, so that made two of them.

Why had she come here? What a mistake! What was she doing? Looking for someone to take care of her? No one had to take care of her. She knew how to manage that all by herself. Whom had she been kidding, in thinking she could find love again, have a normal life?

"Did I overcook the eggs?" he asked.

"No. They're fine. I like to savor them," she lied. How was she ever going to force this food down her throat?

"Would you like me to show you around Tiberias this morning?"

"No." She said it too quickly, too harshly. She smiled at him. No need for him to understand and maybe relish the fact that she had made a fool of herself by coming here. "I like to get the feel of a place alone."

"Silly."

"That's what I am. Silly."

"Let me show you the springs and the old synagogue. Can you ride a bike?"

"I haven't in years."

"We'll walk up the hills. Finish eating and let's get ready. As beautiful as Tiberias is, even this city gets hot in the middle of the day. Besides, my parents will expect us here for the midday meal."

Somehow she managed to finish her breakfast. Then, while he waited, she packed her things in her small duffle bag, and carried it to the door. "Leave it here," he ordered. "We'll have to come back anyway."

He led her downstairs, out back to a tin storage shed, which held the remnants of several old machines and two very rusty bicycles. "They don't ride as bad as they look," he said, trying to encourage her.

"I hope not," she replied.

It took Yehuda fifteen minutes to get the tires pumped up. He rolled the bikes one by one out of the shed and also brought along the pump and a patching kit for the tires. "Are you sure we wouldn't be safer walking?" she asked.

"Safer, yes. But would it be as much fun?"

She smiled at him and awkwardly mounted the bike, as if it were an animal. Really, this was ridiculous. It must have been about fifteen years since she had last ridden. She would fall and break her nose, have scabs all over her knees like a little girl. "The first part's all downhill," he yelled back to her, as he led her out of the alley.

Fine. Did she remember how to brake?

"It's fun once you get the hang of it, isn't it?" he called to her.

Sure. Except something was wrong with the seat; it kept jabbing against her in a most distressing fashion. Or was she simply sore from last night and this morning?

Up more streets, down others, until Yehuda finally stopped. "The springs," he announced. "In Roman times this used to be a spa. The water is supposed to have a lot of health-giving properties. They're going to excavate this whole area. I understand there was also a synagogue here. There're lots of Roman and Jewish ruins around. Megiddo, Hatzor. Tourists have always come to the Holy Land, and Tiberias has always been on their itinerary, especially in the summer. It's attractive because it's not hot, like the coastal plain. I love it here. Come on."

No rest for the wicked, she thought, as he biked onward while she trailed behind. They pedaled up a hill that evened out and brought a cool breeze. Yehuda stopped in the middle of it. He left his bike to one side and placed hers next to it. Then he took her hand and walked her across the street. They went through the garden gate of one of the hotels, so that she could have a clearer view. "It's beautiful," she said.

Below them lay the Kinneret. Yehuda showed her where the Jordan River exited from the Sea of Galilee. "It doesn't stop until it reaches the Dead Sea in the Negev. Look. They're still fishing, those crazy bastards," Yehuda said.

"Is it dangerous then?"

"If the Syrians and Jordanians want to make it so. You see, this will bring the Christian trade to Tiberias. The Sea of Galilee. The Jordan River, where John the Baptist did his work. Down there, that banana plantation is Ginnosar's. Have you ever been to that kibbutz?"

"No."

"Someday I'll take you. It's Yigal Allon's."

"Do you like kibbutz living?"

"No." He laughed. "I like to make my own decisions. Also, I have to admit, I'm not a farmer. And you?"

"I was born in Cracow."

He shrugged. "I was born in Munich. You can still like farming. Come. We can go back, but I want to show you something first." He took her hand and led her across the street to where they had left their bikes. There was an archway with a sign on top, but the letters were so obscure that she couldn't read them. He led her inside. The front garden was scraggly, the flagstones broken in spots.

He knocked on the door. An old woman answered. "So you're back," she said, after she had examined him closely.

"I promised I would be."

"You said after the war. The war's been over for months."

"I just got back. Honest. Last night."

"It's true," Eliza added, feeling she had to confirm it.

"Ay," the woman said. "So come in. I suppose you want to look around again. Even though it's Shabbat."

"Yes, I'd like that. Mrs. Krause, let me introduce a friend of mine from Kfar Hannah, Eliza Wolf." Eliza nodded at the woman, and the woman studied her as if she were an experimental specimen. "Come on," he said softly to Eliza. "We'll just look around then, Mrs. Krause."

"Don't take all day. I have important things to do."

"Yes, ma'am." Yehuda looked at Eliza as he pulled her up the stairs. The house had three stories. Yehuda took Eliza into every room. Each floor had two toilets with washstands and one bathroom. There were also washstands in the various rooms. The windows faced the windows of the houses on either side, except in the back and front rooms. The back windows looked out over the rear garden, which had orange and lemon trees, bougainvillea and a grown-over patio. "Ten rooms," Yehuda said to her.

"Umm."

"It needs work."

"I hadn't noticed."

He laughed, put his arm around her and gave her a squeeze. Why?

"You could put a very nice little garden restaurant out back," she suggested. "You know, for the guests, for tea. Or at night, during the summer, for a light supper."

He led her downstairs. They went through the parlor, the reception area, the breakfast room. Mrs. Krause just watched them move about. "Can we go see the private quarters, Mrs. Krause?" Yehuda asked.

"If you don't touch anything."

"We won't," he promised.

The private quarters Yehuda referred to lay behind the reception area. There was a small living room, two bedrooms, a bath and toilet; a back door led to a private section of the rear garden. "We could take the shutters down. That would let the sun in. I was thinking of also knocking out part of the wall, putting in a larger window. This feels too closed up for me."

"Umm," Eliza agreed.

"Do you like it?"

"It will take a lot of work to get it back in shape. What was the name of it, anyway? I couldn't read the sign."

"I think Mrs. Krause called it Happiness House. I want to call it Pension Bracha."

22

DECISIONS

YEHUDA THANKED MRS. KRAUSE FOR LETTING HIM SEE THE HOTEL again. "I have to have your decision almost right away," Mrs. Krause warned him. "I have other people waiting to buy."

"Tomorrow by five," he responded.

"All right. But after five, I'm going to have to open the bidding to all comers."

"Fine, Mrs. Krause. I promise I'll be here with my answer."

Eliza and Yehuda got on their bikes again. "Let's go down to the Kinneret," he called back to her.

Down was the key word. Eliza felt sure she was going to be killed. The road was very steep and twisting, and the brakes on the bike screeched in protest when she attempted to apply them. What was Yehuda doing? He was zooming down the road. At any moment he was going to fly over the hillside and get down to the lake the fastest way possible.

By the time the road had leveled out near Kibbutz Ginnosar, Eliza was a nervous wreck; her legs were shaking. Yehuda waved her on as if he were leading a patrol into enemy territory. She followed him up a dirt path through the banana plants. Finally, the bikes got mired in the mud, and she knew they had reached the Kinneret.

"God, I haven't done that in years!" he said, simply exhilarated by the speed, the danger. She looked menacingly at him. He laughed. "When I was a kid, that used to be my favorite ride of all. Let's go swimming."

"No suit."

"Swim in your underclothes."

"No thanks."

"Wading then?"

They went to the edge of the lake and splashed their feet in the water and let the waves ripple over their calves. "It's good to be back," Yehuda said softly. "All the other countries I went to were very interesting, but it's not like being home. Do you feel at home here yet, Eliza?"

107

"It's the only home I have," she answered.

"You shouldn't just accept Israel because of that. You should love the country. And there's so much to love about Israel. Each new turn in the road brings you face to face with the history of our people."

"I don't need a pep talk from you about Israel, Yehuda. I waited a long time to come here. I knew I had to come, to redeem something from what happened in Europe. I came for my family. For—others. I don't think you can understand that, not having been through the war."

"Ooh. We're angry."

"I just don't want any puerile lectures on what I should feel."

He looked over at her, while she stared straight ahead. "What's bothering you? The ride down to the lake?"

She shook her head. "No."

"Then what?"

"Nothing."

He put his hand on her back. She shrugged it off. "Was it something I said or did?"

"It's everything you say and do."

"That's honest, at least. But give me an example."

She sighed. "I don't understand you. We made love that night, the night of independence. Fine. We both needed something. I'm not arguing with that. So I don't see you again. Fine. That's all right, too, because it's war and things like that happen in war. You send a letter. I answer. I meet you at the base. You ask me to marry you. I come to Tiberias because Dvora, at Kfar Hannah, says it's time to start my life over elsewhere and I have no elsewhere to go to. You're in Tiberias. We make love again. You tell me you don't want to marry me. You take me to the pension and talk about how we could fix it up together. You're naming it after your dead sweetheart. I don't know, Yehuda. Maybe you're not normal; maybe I'm not normal."

He leaned back on his elbows, then fell all the way back, blocking the sun from his eyes with his arm. "How much do you know about Bracha?"

"Only what your mother told me. I saw the pictures in the album. She was very pretty."

"Bracha and I were engaged to be married when she was murdered. That was seven years ago. We had been in love ever since high school. She was standing right next to me when she was shot. The bullet blew her face away, killed her instantly. And all I've been able to wonder about these past seven years is why didn't that bullet hit me? Can you understand that?'' He grabbed Eliza's hand and pulled her down so that she was lying facing him. ''I go over and over it in my mind. Why was I standing where I was? Why wasn't I standing where she was? Why did they aim at her, not at me? Why were we on that street? Why hadn't we postponed the training? Why didn't we have intelligence telling us the Arabs would be active that day? Why did she die and I live? Her parents—I can still barely face them. I used to spend all my time over at their apartment. And now I feel like my very life is an insult to them. You see, I should have been able to protect her, save her. I didn't. I'm sorry. I can't expect you to understand.''

''Oh, honestly, Yehuda, you are so dense.''

''Thanks.''

''Do you think I can't understand guilt? Or love? Good God. And you think it's so hard for you. That's what makes you such a stupid boy. The issues for you, for all of Israel, are very simple. You know who your enemy is. You know what your enemy will do to you if you lose the war. We knew nothing. Who were we to believe? Were there death camps? Or were they work camps? Should we run and hide in the forest? Or should we stay with our families in the ghetto? Should we ask our neighbors for help? Or would our neighbors betray us, our children, to the Germans? Should we fall in love with someone, bear children, pretend there was hope? Or should we simply face death every day knowing there was no hope, no hope at all? Only insanity, bestiality.''

He took a piece of her hair and twirled it around his finger. ''Did you love someone during the war?'' he asked softly.

''Did I love someone during the war?'' she repeated bitterly. ''His name was Adam. He took me away from the ghetto of Cracow before the Germans could ship us out to a camp. He took me into the forest, where we joined the partisans. We slept together without benefit of marriage. Unbelievable for a girl like me. We had a child.''

She sat up abruptly. The sun made her dizzy, nauseous. Yehuda sat up next to her and grabbed hold of her shoulders. ''Eliza.''

''Yehuda,'' she mimicked harshly. He stared questioningly at her, puzzled, concerned. ''My lover's dead. My child's lost. And I'm here, starting a new life that's going nowhere.'' She grabbed her sandals and stood. She went back to the bikes. Yehuda followed. She said nothing to him as they climbed the long hill back into town.

His mother and father were waiting for him when they arrived at the apartment. ''Where were you?'' Hattie asked. ''It's almost dinner, and we have to open the store for a few hours. You know that, Yehuda," she scolded.

"Sorry, Mother. We were down at the lake and lost track of time," he replied.

"Well, dinner's almost completely dried out. But there's still some nice potatoes and carrots with a bit of meat."

"I'm sorry I can't stay to eat, Mrs. Mendelsohn," Eliza said. "I have to catch a bus." She put on the best smile she could.

"Oh, but you must stay and—"

Eliza walked past her and stuffed the last few items into her bag. Yehuda followed and stood watching her. She came face to face with him when she turned. "Good-bye. Good luck," she told him. She pushed past him. "Thank you for everything," she said to his parents. Then she quickly left before the speechless Mendelsohns could recover.

She hurried down the stairs. Heavy steps followed hers. It was Yehuda. "I said good-bye upstairs," she told him.

"You don't know where the bus station is."

"I can find it."

He walked along with her and guided her there. When they reached it, he bought her an orange drink, which she gratefully sipped. She had made up her mind to take the first bus that came along, no matter where it was going. The first bus that pulled in was from the north, and it was going south to Tel Aviv. Good. She needed a city to get lost in. She paid for her ticket without saying good-bye again to Yehuda, which turned out to be unnecessary in any case. He got on the bus after she did and took the seat next to her. "This is really stupid," she told him.

The bus pulled out of the station toward the south.

"What happened to your child?" he asked.

"Why should that matter to you?"

He put his arm around her. "Because *you* matter to me."

She started to cry, but quickly brushed the tears away. There was still no time to be human, not yet.

"What happened?" he whispered.

"Adam, my—"

"I know."

"He was killed. Our camp was destroyed. The Germans had somehow found out where we were; and when the men had gone, they came and killed the women and children. Mina and I were out hunting. I really am a very good shot, you know."

He squeezed her shoulder. "I'm sure you are."

"Anyway, I knew it wasn't safe for Mina, my daughter, anymore. I took a chance and left her with a village woman Adam and I had run across before the war. The woman threatened to put her out in the cold to freeze to death. But she didn't. I went back to check. After Poland was liberated, I was sick. Typhoid. I couldn't get back to the village right away. By the time I did, the woman had left, just disappeared. But I know from the villagers that the woman was alive after the war was over and that Mina, too, was alive and healthy. Supposedly, they went to Cracow. At least, that's what they told the people in the village. I went to Cracow. I stayed for about a year looking for them. Nothing."

"But your child's alive?"

"Yes. That's what I keep telling myself. She's alive. That's some sort of miracle, I guess. But I don't know what to do, how to find her, what name she's using even." Eliza shrugged.

He held her more tightly still. "I never knew you had a child."

"Why should you?"

"Can you still have children?"

"I don't know. I haven't tried. Besides, there's no way to replace one who's lost."

"No substitutes."

"No."

"And this man, this Adam?"

She smiled. "Oh, he was—" she looked up at Yehuda—"my first love."

"Bracha was my first love. I'm trying to make myself fit to love again."

"I think it's probably easier for me," Eliza admitted. "Even though there has been less time to recover. You see, we avenged his death and the death of the others. And, to be brutal, I got used to seeing those I loved die. I learned to hang onto memories, to what was precious in our time together. I don't even feel that guilty about surviving. Maybe if I had been in the camps, I would. I'm planning to live a very full life, I guess, for all those who can't. I don't know. I've lost everything, Yehuda. But I need to go on. I must. To choose otherwise would be wasteful."

Yehuda looked past her out the window. She smiled. "You better get off at the next stop, Yehuda. Your mother will be worried."

He looked down at her. "Do you really think I'd let you see Tel Aviv alone after I gave you such an excellent tour of Tiberias?"

"Another tour like that, and I may never be able to walk again."

"I want to marry you."

"Don't start that again."

"But in a way, it feels like a betrayal."

"Exactly. So get off at the next stop."

"But—"

"Yehuda! Don't do me any favors. I need someone who cares about me, who's willing to let me love him. I need someone who, when he reaches out at night, will be reaching out for me."

"I understand."

"Good. So good luck to you. Maybe one day we'll see each other again."

"Are you trying to get rid of me?"

She turned away from him before she said, "Your company's very pleasant, until you open your mouth."

He laughed. "It's buttoned shut," he promised her.

True, he didn't say a word the rest of the trip to Tel Aviv. But if he had, she might not have heard it anyway. She fell asleep from the jogging of the bus, rousing only briefly as it bumped to a stop and started again.

When it pulled in to the Central Bus Station in Tel Aviv, Yehuda woke her. "We're here," he said. Now what, she wondered.

They climbed off the bus and looked around. Unlike Tiberias, a pretty city set on a hill, surrounded by all that was beautiful, Tel Aviv was a modern big city, crowded and noisy, smelling of bus fumes and vegetables, chickens hanging in the open air to be sold. And outside the city, encroaching on it each morning, were the sand dunes upon which Tel Aviv was founded.

"Where do country bumpkins go when they come to Tel Aviv?" she asked Yehuda.

"Let's try the beach," he suggested.

Since Tel Aviv lay along the beach, it wasn't far to it from any place. Eliza watched the waves come in, then ran to meet them. Except for Haifa, which was really a port city, she hadn't had a chance to frolic in the sea. Now she did. Yehuda took off his shoes, but he simply sat in the sand, watching her. When she came back to him, her dress was wet; sand and salt clung to her legs. "I wish I had bought you a pail and shovel," he told her.

"Don't be so superior," she warned. They sat together silently on the beach and watched the sun lower itself into the Mediterranean. Eliza sighed at this completion of the day. She turned to Yehuda. "Shall we sleep out on the beach tonight? Or do you have a better idea?"

"Better than an idea, I have a friend."

His friend's name was Marco. He spoke both Portuguese and Spanish and had traveled to South America with Yehuda, on the same mission. Marco's wife, Paula, was from Italy. She and Eliza found a lot to talk about; they had been in several of the same DP camps, even though they had never met. What language Marco and Paula spoke together, Eliza didn't know. Certainly, it was a Romance language. The four of them spoke Hebrew, although Paula's was still very elementary. Eliza supposed she should be grateful she had been thrust so quickly into Israeli society at Kfar Hannah. At least she could make herself understood and could understand. Marco was telling them about the new job he had with the customs service. "I'm trying to decide whether I'll grow rich on bribes or if this is going to be the one customs service in the world to be totally honest," he confessed.

Yehuda laughed. "Next time we see you, you'll have a villa."

"Next time you see us we'll have a baby," he said proudly.

Eliza's face lit up as she congratulated Paula. "It was my dream in the camps," Paula told her, "to have a baby. To prove they could not destroy us."

Yehuda looked at Eliza and took her hand. "And you two?" Marco asked. "What are your plans?"

"We're planning to open a hotel up in Tiberias," Yehuda said. "Just a small pension really, ten rooms, but it will be a pleasant place. Right now it needs a lot of work. The previous owner really let it run down after her husband died. Tiberias has been short of tourists lately. But now that the war's over, I'm looking forward to a booming business. We hope to have it open in a month or so, to catch the summer trade. Tiberias is a little bit rainy and cold in the winter, but still pleasant, just right for a vacation. When we get enough money, we'll put heaters in the rooms. There's a lot that can be done."

"Do you have any experience working in a hotel?" Paula asked Eliza.

Eliza was confused. Should she correct Paula's impression that she was in on this with Yehuda?

"Eliza doesn't yet, but she will. Since she's made *aliya*, immigrated to Israel, she's been at Kfar Hannah. A real farm girl." Yehuda laughed. "That's how I met her. When I tried to steal one of her chickens. Then, during the war, she helped train the troops. Now she's going to have a real home; we're going to have a real home, together." He put his arm around her and kissed her cheek.

She was still trying to decide if this was for the benefit of Marco and Paula or if Yehuda had planned all of this without asking for her help.

Paula smiled. "So when's the wedding going to be?"

"Very soon, because I have to plunk down the money for the

pension tomorrow night, and I want to get to work on it right away.''

"No honeymoon then?" Paula asked.

"Working on the pension will be our honeymoon," he assured them.

They talked long into the night; Marco and Yehuda over old times, friends in common; she and Paula about Israel and how they found it. But internally, Eliza was debating with herself: Just how close to insanity was Yehuda?

Marco promised to wake them at six the next morning, so they could catch the bus back to Tiberias. That gave them, if Eliza figured it right, five hours to sleep. She took the couch; Yehuda took the pillows off the chairs and slept on them. They didn't say anything to each other, after Marco and Paula left them, except good night. What else was there to say that wouldn't take hours of lengthy discussion and a lot of screaming? She'd wait for the bus ride home. Home?

23

GOING HOME

"I DON'T BELIEVE YOU," SHE TOLD HIM, AS THE BUS FOR TIBERIAS pulled out of the Central Bus Station.

"Seeing Marco and Paula together convinced me that it was the right decision," Yehuda said solemnly.

"Whose decision was it?"

"Ours, of course. We'll tell my parents when we get back. I'll have to see Bracha's parents and tell them. That will be difficult. But you're right: Life isn't to be wasted."

"Yehuda, did you ever ask me what I thought?"

"I'm sure I must have."

"No, you didn't."

"Well, what do you think?"

"I think you're crazy."

"Do you have something against the hotel? It'll be hard work, sure, but fun. Interesting. Something that will unite us."

"I'm speaking about marriage."

"Another thing that will unite us."

"You didn't ask me."

"I did ask you!"

"You took it back."

"You're being childish, Eliza. I told you what my problem was. You accused me of being wishy-washy in my affections toward you. I'm no longer wishy-washy. I love you; I want to marry you. So what do you have against that?"

Her eyes rolled upward. "This is insane."

"Where shall we have the marriage? My place or yours?"

By nightfall, Eliza had returned to Kfar Hannah. Her legs were stiff from all the bike-riding yesterday, and her mind felt as if the wind were blowing through it. Yehuda had taken her to his parents' apartment and announced their impending marriage. Hattie and Max had been overwhelmed. Maybe that's what Eliza was feeling, too. Overwhelmed. And unsure. She'd have to admit to that. She would continue to be unsure until Yehuda saw Bracha's parents, talked to them, to see whether he could in his heart make another commitment. Until then, even though everyone in the settlement asked where she had been, she decided to remain silent.

Yehuda showed up on his bicycle the next day at 12:30, just in time for dinner. The way he walked up to her in the laundry and smiled at her led her to believe that everything was going to be all right. "Did you tell everyone?" he asked.

"No. No one. I was waiting."

She led him into the dining-room hallway, where they washed up before eating. Then they took a seat together at one of the long tables. "How did it go last night?" she asked.

"Mrs. Krause was glad to see me. And get the money. By the way, we owe my parents a small fortune. I hope you don't mind paying that off for the rest of our lives."

"And Bracha's parents?" She waited nervously.

He exhaled. "I told them I had met someone. Mr. Shemtov brought out the brandy, wished me mazel tov, and hoped to be invited to the wedding. I think—honestly—that they were happy for me."

Eliza put her hand on his shoulder. "I wish I could ease your pain."

"You have."

She smiled. "Did you tell Mr. Shemtov the name of your hotel?"

"No. He'll probably think it's silly, naming a hotel after his daughter."

"I don't think it's silly at all. I think it's beautiful."

"Then maybe I'll name our garden restaurant Gan Eliza, or Café Eliza." They laughed. "We have to get married fast. Mrs. Krause is vacating next week."

She shrugged. "There's nothing to stop us now."

Yehuda raised his eyebrows. "Then the answer's yes?"

She laughed. "Of course."

All of a sudden, he was hitting his knife against his water glass. Eliza thought she was going to die—another embarrassing moment with Yehuda Barak. "Listen, everybody," he called when the dining room had fallen still. "I have an announcement to make."

Dvora called out, "Aren't you the soldier who tried to steal our chickens?"

"Yes," he admitted. "And now I'm stealing something else. Eliza and I are going to be married."

So much for eating the rest of her meal. Eliza sweetly accepted congratulations while Yehuda got together with Dvora and Amnon to plan the wedding. He assured Eliza later that it was a much better idea to have the wedding on Kfar Hannah. With the rationing in the cities, even with his parents' grocery, a wedding feast in Tiberias would be rather skimpy. But on a farm, it could be a real celebration.

Figuring the angles—it was something she would have to learn to do if she were to keep up with Yehuda.

Dvora bought her a new dress from village funds for the occasion. It was blue and white, "For a bride of Israel," Dvora explained. It was the most beautiful dress Eliza had ever seen. Maybe everyone feels that way about the dress she is to be married in, she thought. When Eliza slipped it on for the ceremony, she felt more gorgeous than she could ever remember. She hoped Yehuda saw her that way, too. She wore her hair up and pinned back. She thought it more proper, more formal for the occasion. Then Yehuda could take it down pin by pin after they were married, when they were alone together, wherever he was planning to take her to be alone.

The ceremony was held as the sun was setting, when the men had come home from the fields and had had time to wash. The children had eaten and were looking forward to time with their families. Kfar Hannah was crowded with Yehuda's family and friends from Tiberias, and friends of both from army days. This wedding really would put a dent in Kfar Hannah's food supply. Four of Yehuda's friends held the *huppah* while the rabbi recited the marriage vows in Hebrew.

Eliza, in a moment of sheer panic, thought she was back in

Poland, in Cracow, and it was not Yehuda, but Adam, at her side, in a fine black suit, while she wore a silk-and-lace dress. She saw her family surrounding her, her dear mother, her father, Lina, Hershel, Lina's children, Adam's brother. She looked across at Yehuda, in his open-collared white shirt and his blue pants, and wondered if he was thinking of Bracha. He stared at her, seemed to see only her, smiled as the Hebrew words of the ancient ceremony flowed on. He placed a ring on her finger, symbolizing their never-ending love. Then someone placed a glass under his foot, and he smashed it, commemorating the destruction of the Temple in Jerusalem. "Mazel tov!" the crowd shouted. She smiled at him. He leaned over and kissed her. Their lips lingered.

Despite Yehuda's later urgings that she eat well because they might not have access to all this food again, Eliza found herself merely picking at it. She was too nervous. Not about sleeping with Yehuda; that didn't bother her. She looked forward to that. But what was it like to be somebody's wife? She had seen her mother and father together. But this wasn't Poland. This was Israel. She wondered if Yehuda expected her to be meek and obedient. But then, she had never seen an Israeli wife who was obedient thus far. What would life be like with Yehuda? How would they spend their days together? Would they grow to love each other more, or less? Would they have children? Would they prosper?

When it was time to go, Tzippi brought Eliza the single cloth bag that Eliza had carried with her from Europe. "Don't be a stranger now," Dvora told her. "Bring the children, when they come along."

"And you'll always have a place to stay in Tiberias," Eliza assured her.

"Why should I want to go to Tiberias?" Dvora asked.

Eliza smiled. She would leave Kfar Hannah much as she had come.

Yehuda's parents had paid for a separate taxi to take Yehuda and Eliza on their honeymoon. For some reason, Eliza was not surprised when they ended up at Pension Bracha. "Wait till you see what I've done." Yehuda told her.

He helped her climb the stairs to the topmost floor. They went into the front room, where he lit a candle. He took her to the window. "Look," he told her.

The moon shone on the waters of the Kinneret, turning the lake into a silver jewel. "It's beautiful," she murmured.

"And it's all ours," he said. "Until they build across from us."

"Or we rent this room."

"Whichever comes first," he agreed. "Did you like our wedding?"

"Yes. It was fun. And I liked your friends, too."

"Not half as much as I liked Dvora," he teased.

Eliza laughed. "She's not too bad once you get used to her."

"Well, you don't have to get used to her anymore. I didn't see you eat much."

"I was too nervous," she confessed.

"About now?"

"No. Just about the future."

"Didn't you once give me a lecture about living one day at a time?"

"That was before, when I had nothing to live for. Now—"

"Now there's us." He took her in his arms. He kissed her cheek, her neck, her other cheek. And then he began undoing the buttons of her dress. "The window," she warned.

He blew out the candle. "No one can see now," he assured her.

She stood and watched his strong hands undo the tiny buttons. She let him drop the dress from her shoulders, lower her slip, unhook her bra. Her breasts stood free in the night air. The nipples crinkled. "You're so beautiful," he assured her. He placed his hands on her breasts, and she could almost see his mouth water.

She smiled. He looked up at her and caught her. "You like turning me into a dog in heat, don't you?"

She said nothing. He stepped back from her and removed his pants, his underpants. He was standing straight up, ready for her. "Nu?"

She laughed and pushed him down on the bed. He grabbed her, and they tussled. Despite her vision of his removing her hairpins one by one, they came tumbling out by themselves, until they and her hair were all over the bed. Somehow her dress had come all the way off, too, and she was lying there naked in the bed, pressed against the buttons of his shirt. She hurriedly undid them so she could feel his skin underneath, so that her breasts could rest against his chest, so that nothing could separate the entire length of their bodies. "Hold me," she told him, but his hands flew along her back, onto her rump as he squeezed and kneaded her. "Eliza," he begged. She sat upon him and felt him go into her. She looked down at him as he reached to encircle her breasts. And then he thrust into her, deeper and deeper, while she squeezed against him and felt free to whimper and moan in delight at a world made whole again.

24

BRIT MILA

ELIZA STRETCHED AND YAWNED AS THE DAY'S WORK AT PENSION Bracha was about to begin. She smiled.

"Why are you smiling?" Yehuda asked, with that nervous energy he drew on at the start of each morning. "We have so much work to do."

"I'm happy working alongside you." She leaned forward and touched his cheek. "Do you realize we're an old married couple?"

"Where does time fly to?" he teased. Then he stood abruptly. "The rooms," he shouted, "the garden, the kitchen—all awaiting our magic touch."

"Yes, sure," she said, as she took another sip of coffee. She wanted to enjoy her last moment of relaxation before she caught up to the routine of the day. Didn't Yehuda know the meaning of the word "lazy"?

But she wouldn't complain. Yehuda had been a good husband to her. He loved her, knew when to hold her, knew when to let her cry in his arms without asking why. Together they had worked beyond the pain of the past. Together they had worked! How much labor it had taken to put Pension Bracha right again. Yehuda figured two months. In two months they had the sign up, and had put the lobby, the sitting room, the dining room, and the parlor in order. It had taken another month to spruce up the next floor and to make the garden attractive enough so that someone would want to stay with them. They were spending all their money, while absolutely nothing was coming in. It was horrible. Yehuda borrowed from his parents, from his friends, from relatives. She sensed disaster.

But three months after their marriage, Pension Bracha opened for business. As an added extravagance, they took out ads in the papers, touting its homelike atmosphere, though Eliza had her doubts that people wanted to go to a place like home for a vacation. Yehuda also wanted to put in the ad that they were across the street from the sea, but she had strongly objected. They were nowhere near the Kinneret. "You cross the street and you can see it," he argued. But she had insisted that everything be legitimate, including their ads.

Hardly anyone stayed with them that first month they were open. This was good in a way. It gave them a chance to finish the top two floors. Then their weekend trade began to pick up: families from the larger cities and the low-lying plains who wanted some cool evening air to breathe; older people who held hope for the medicinal properties of Tiberias's waters.

The first time they were booked solid was over Rosh Hashanah. Unfortunately, half their guests were people who had loaned them money and stayed for free. But there was a sprinkling of tourists and a few repeat families from earlier in the year. Pension Bracha served breakfast and supper, which was essentially the same meal: bread, fish, salad, eggs, cheese. But for Shabbat and for holidays Eliza had to go all out and cook a full meal for however many were staying with them. Then she had to clean up. When Yehuda mentioned to her that they really should consider opening Café Eliza in the garden, with a sedate coffee bar, she warned him that it would not be possible until they had the money to hire help. It was an idea whose time had not yet come.

The winter months were hard again. The north was colder than the rest of the country, so who was crazy enough to come up to Tiberias for a holiday then? One day Yehuda returned home with the news that there were some crazy people. "I've just been over to Gali Tours," he told her.

She didn't have any idea what he was talking about, but she encouraged him to go on. "And?"

"For a small kickback—"

"Yehuda!"

"Eliza, please, that's the way things are done. I didn't invent it. Anyway, for a small sum on the head of each tourist, Gali Tours is willing to divert some of its Christian pilgrims to Pension Bracha. That means during their Christmas season we will be booked solid. Here's what we have to do before then: Open a gift shop."

"Insane."

"Postcards, stamps, candy, mementos, like little bottles filled with water from the Sea of Galilee."

"Wouldn't it be just as simple for them to fill their own bottles while they're at the sea?"

"Ours will be authentic. Maybe also water from the Jordan, in case they want to baptize anyone back home," Yehuda added thoughtfully.

"Surely you can find pieces of the true cross?"

He looked at her brightly. "An idea, Eliza! Very good. I'm glad you're getting into the spirit of our gift shop."

Her look at him could only be interpreted as "annoyed." "Yehuda, how can we run a gift shop, make breakfast and supper, clean the rooms, and still manage to breathe at night?"

When the deal with Gali Tours was set, they hired help: Shimon Ben Elezar and his wife, Alice. Shimon, from Morocco, had lived in Israel a little over a year. He had been floating around, trying to find work, going from kibbutz to *moshav* until he met Alice, an English volunteer on Kibbutz HaEmek. With little thought for the future, they had married, and continued wandering. Yehuda had heard about them through a friend on another kibbutz. The friend called the pair eccentric but hard workers. It was Yehuda who had gone to speak to them. He told Eliza later, "Shimon speaks Hebrew—Biblical, but it can pass—French, and Arabic. Alice so far speaks only English."

"Your friend said they were eccentric."

"They're not that bad. They're willing to come and work for us for very low wages, pocket money really, as long as they have a room and something to eat. They're tired of wandering."

She sighed. What could she say? They needed help, and they needed someone who could speak other languages. And they couldn't afford to hire anyone who wanted a bundle in wages. "Fine. Try them," she conceded. "But if they don't work out, they go."

"Of course."

They worked out. They *were* eccentric, but by Christmas, Eliza realized they were also valuable. The Christian tourists were charmed by Alice's Anglo-English. Alice manned the gift shop in the mornings after breakfast and in the evenings. She could sell anything. She even managed to sell Yehuda's bottled water from the Sea of Galilee, much to Eliza's dismay and chagrin. She still thought there was something unethical about that. Once, Eliza caught Yehuda filling the bottles from the tap. She was very angry with him. But he pointed out that their drinking water did come from the Kinneret or the Jordan. She gave up.

While Alice was inside, Shimon was outside, working on the garden, planning Café Eliza. Or he was inside, aiding Yehuda with the upkeep, helping Eliza with the cleaning. The four of them worked hard together, but it paid off. Thank God there were times when few guests came. That made up for the hectic weekends, the religious holidays, the unending tours. Finally, they were beginning to pay back their debts.

It was during one of those quiet periods, as he went over the books, that Eliza approached Yehuda and insisted in a peremptory way that she wanted their own quarters fixed up. Finally! "Where is the window you promised me?" she asked. "And the furniture. It's Mrs. Krause's. I want something light and lovely."

"We're not that well off yet," he told her, barely looking up from the books.

"And I want that second bedroom cleaned out. You've put God knows what in it. It's unusable."

"Fortunately, we don't have to use it," he continued, almost totally ignoring her. He was used to her carping. It was her release. Sometimes she got so tired she didn't think she would make it through the day.

"We're going to have to use it soon," she warned. "And I know how you put things off."

He finally looked up at her. "Are you expecting someone to stay with us that I don't know about yet?"

"Yes."

"He's such a good friend that we can't put him up in one of the rooms?"

She sat down on the sofa. "No. We can't put him up in one of the rooms."

"Who is he?"

She shrugged. "I don't know. It might not even be a he."

"Eliza." He drew her name out, then went to sit down on the sofa next to her. He stared into her eyes, and she knew he was afraid to ask, to guess, afraid even to imagine.

"I'm pregnant."

"The doctor—"

"I don't need a doctor to tell me I'm three months gone. Morning sickness tells me that."

He placed his hands on her shoulders and then touched her face. They had never tried not to have a child. But for the first year, nothing happened. Yehuda hadn't said anything; she hadn't said anything. A silence on the subject of children grew up like a hedge between them. Except when they were at his parents' house. Hattie was a great one for hinting, asking when it would be economically feasible for them to have a child. And now—what would Hattie say?

Yehuda took Eliza in his arms and held her against his chest. She could hear the fierceness of his heartbeat. "I'm—happy. I hope you are too."

"Of course. I wanted to give you children," she told him.

"I don't want the child to be just for me."

"I'll admit to feeling strange," she said. "I can't help but think back, compare. I can't help but feel as if something has been torn away from me. I loved Mina. With all my heart."

The sharpness of the image, her little girl the day she left her in Kowitz, came back to Eliza with such force that she stopped breathing. "Eliza!" Yehuda pushed her away and shook her. She smiled, even as tears ran down her cheeks. "I'm all right."

"Yes. Sure."

"I'm ruining what should be the happiest moment in our lives. Your first child."

"Our first child, together."

She leaned back, away from him. "You *will* get that second bedroom cleaned up? You have a few months to do it in."

The child was born six months later, just as she had predicted. It was a son. For this birth, she was in a hospital. In a way, she preferred the forest, where the baby came and, a few hours later, she was almost back to normal, as if having a baby was the most natural event in the world. Here in the hospital, people treated her as if she were sick. She told Yehuda, when he was allowed to visit, that she wanted to get home as fast as possible. But he wasn't listening. He couldn't stop kissing her, worshiping her for giving him a son. He held her hand and kissed it. "We'll call him Adam," he offered.

"No. You're very sweet, Yehuda, but there is more than one person to honor. His name will be Amihai, my people live. We'll call him Ami for short. All right?"

Yehuda smiled. "All right."

The *brit* was held at the newly opened Café Eliza, with Shimon and Alice officiating as host and hostess. Relatives, friends, and guests showed up for the occasion. Ami behaved himself very well, considering the circumstances. Only during the endless celebration did he become cranky and need to be put down for a nap. "Next time a girl," Hattie told Eliza, as she rose to take Ami inside. The smile fell from Eliza's face as if she had been struck. Yehuda stepped in. "One child at a time, Mother, please. Poor Eliza is not a breeding machine."

That gave Eliza time to escape. She stayed in their quarters for a while with Ami, enjoying the serenity. The second bedroom was now beautiful, just right for a child. And even the living room looked better, now that Yehuda and Shimon had knocked out part of the wall to put in a window. During her pregnancy, Yehuda had hired Pnina to come in every day to help with the cleaning and cooking. Pnina was from Yemen, and she made the tastiest food on the face of the earth. Eliza hoped she would stay with them even now that the baby had come.

Eliza put her pinky down and let Ami grab it. She cooed at the child, and he gurgled back. "Nothing will happen to you," she promised him. "You will be safe for all time."

25

JOURNEYING BACKWARD

"LOOK AT HIM TODDLING ALONG!" HATTIE EXCLAIMED. "I DON'T think any child's ever walked this young, not even Yael's."

"Hattie, he is thirteen months old. Down the street a girl walked when she was eight months old."

"But Ami walks better, I'm sure."

Eliza laughed and placed her hand on her mother-in-law's shoulder. She had gotten used to the routine of seeing her in-laws at least every Shabbat. When Yael and her family came from Haifa, they all gathered at Hattie's apartment above the grocery. When Yael was busy, Hattie and Max came to the hotel.

"And now Alice is pregnant?" Hattie said.

"Yes. She and Shimon are very excited. Pretty soon we'll have to turn Café Eliza into a kindergarten, instead of a restaurant."

"Will they stay with you?"

"Yes. They're looking for an apartment to buy. But they've assured us they want to continue working here. We'll just have to pay them more. But we can afford it. Now that Ben Gurion's taken to staying in Tiberias, we've become an even more popular resort."

"But he stays downtown."

"So? We get the spillover."

"It's so much work."

"The grocery's not?"

"We wanted Yehuda to become a professor."

Eliza sighed. "Yehuda is very, very happy. He likes hard work; he likes meeting people." Then she smiled, and said, "Did Yehuda tell you? When we went to Tel Aviv the other day for that Tourism Ministry seminar, we met some old friends of mine from the forest, Branek and Sóphie Weiss. We ran into them on the street. There was Branek pushing a baby carriage, while Sophie dragged along a two-year-old. They were bickering, as usual. They always used to quarrel." Eliza remembered with a smile. "I'm glad to see some things never change. He's working with the defense industries, still playing with guns."

Eliza didn't mention that lately Branek had been in Czechoslovakia clandestinely, looking for spare parts. He had told her how organized things were in 1952 in Europe, as opposed to the war years and directly afterward. "Maybe now," Sophie had suggested over coffee, "perhaps, it would be possible to locate—"

"Mina," Yehuda had finished.

"Yehuda knows all about Adam and my child," Eliza told her two old friends.

"At least she's alive," Branek said. "If Mina had stayed with you—God, you were so sick with typhoid—"

"I thought you were going to give it to the whole camp," Sophie said. "Me especially. You know, I always hated nursing."

"But thank you for taking care of me," Eliza replied.

"Yes, indeed," Yehuda agreed.

"Poland is still a den of anti-Semites," Sophie said. "The stories Branek came back with! Did you know that Poles killed many of the Jews who tried to return to their towns after they were liberated from the camps?"

"After Auschwitz, would anything surprise you?" Eliza asked.

"Anyway," Branek said, "all I'm telling you is that it is possible now to make a more efficient, effective check for the girl. You don't even have to go to Poland. You can do it through the government here."

"I wouldn't trust the bureaucracy with that sort of task. There are so many people searching for so many lost ones, why would they care about my little girl? I'd just get a runaround for years, possibly for the rest of my life."

"How old would Mina be now?" Sophia asked. "Not so very little. Nine, ten?"

"Ten in two months."

"Ten. My God. So many years," Sophie said wistfully. "We're old already."

"And what's worse, we were never young," Branek added, passing his hand over his graying stubble.

Eliza placed her hand on his. "But we were always strong."

"Almost always," Sophie corrected her.

Yehuda, on the return bus ride to Tiberias, told her how much he had liked her friends. "Yes," she agreed. "They were wonderful. At the time, maybe, we had doubts. But now, thinking back on it, the way we hung together, trusted each other, well, it kept us alive. And even when we didn't live, our deaths were purposeful.''

Yehuda didn't bring up Mina or anything concerning Branek's suggestions about Poland, so Eliza didn't either. She knew, after what Branek had said, that she would have to go, somehow find the money and make that trip. She couldn't live with herself otherwise, especially now that Ami had reached the age Mina was when Eliza left her with Wanda Zbyszek.

"So you're leaving Ami with Yael for two weeks?" Hattie broke into Eliza's remembrances.

Confused, Eliza asked, "What?"

Hattie was puzzled. "Yehuda said the Tourism Ministry was sending both of you on a program overseas so that you could convince people to come to Tiberias. Quite an honor that the two of you were picked."

Eliza was alone in the room with Hattie and Ami. Yehuda was not around to save her. What could she do but play it by ear? "Yes," she agreed.

"Yael will take good care of Ami. I wish I could take him in, but with the store—"

"Of course. I understand. Besides, Yael's two children have always played so nicely with Ami."

Yehuda and Max finally came back into the living room from the hotel kitchen, where Yehuda had shown his father the sort of refrigeration unit he was thinking of installing. Eliza looked at her husband and wondered what he was up to. But no one brought up the supposed trip sponsored by the Tourism Ministry again. There was no way she was going to get to the bottom of this until his parents were gone.

When they were once again alone and she sat feeding Ami his evening meal, she said to her husband, "So, what are you up to?"

"I told you about the refrigeration unit," he said, feigning ignorance.

"I mean about leaving Ami with Yael for two weeks while we are supposedly on some jaunt for the Tourism Ministry."

He looked at her sharply. "How did you hear that?"

"From your mother."

"That damned Yael! I told her to keep her mouth shut."

"Discretion is not one of her qualities."

"Obviously." He fiddled around with some paper on his desk.

"Well, I'm waiting," she said to him.

"Please don't talk to me in that tone of voice. It always scares me," he said.

She smiled. "Yehuda, stop teasing me. Nothing I do scares you. I only wish it did."

He turned. "That's not true. When you mourn for Mina, that scares me. I'm afraid I can't make you happy."

"Don't be stupid. You and Ami are my life now."

"Not all of it."

"Don't accuse me of not loving you enough, Yehuda, because I love you with all my heart. And I love our child."

"I'm not accusing you of anything. I spoke to a friend of mine, one of the men I searched for weapons with. He's with the diplomatic corps now. I explained our problem. He arranged visas for us, and letters of introduction to people he knows in Warsaw and Cracow. We're leaving on Thursday."

"When were you planning to tell me?"

"Wednesday night. Only joking, Eliza. Tonight, after my parents left. I didn't want them to see you upset. We've never told anyone. I assumed that's the way you want it."

"I think it's best."

"Fine. We have two weeks. It's slow here now. Shimon and Alice and Pnina can handle things. Even if we can't find Mina, at least people will know we're still looking." He turned back to his papers.

"Yehuda."

"Yes."

"Thank you."

"You're my wife, Eliza. I'd do anything for you."

Eliza returned to Cracow almost by the same route she left, except that she wasn't on foot this time. And she wasn't alone.

She and Yehuda arrived in Cracow by train. "Do you remember any of this?" he kept asking her. It hadn't been so many years since she'd left, yet nothing looked familiar. Even all the months she had spent in the city after the war did not bring a sense of familiarity to her now.

They checked into a hotel. That was new for her, staying at a hotel in Cracow. The clerk looked unhappy to see them, and glanced suspiciously at their Israeli passports. The atmosphere was definitely frigid. That night, there was nothing to do but walk through the streets. "Was it ever a city of light and happiness?" Yehuda asked her.

She smiled. "Oh, yes," she said almost fervently. "When—when we were all alive."

"It's so damn dreary now. It looks like they haven't done a thing to clear the rubble from the war."

"It's too dark."

"I have a feeling it's always dark in Poland."

Morning came, and the city did not look less gray. Ready to go, Yehuda stood at the window and looked out while Eliza hurried to get ready. "Where to first, do you think?" he asked.

"Kowitz."

He looked at her.

"The town where Wanda lived, where I left Mina."

"How do we get there?"

Eliza thought, and almost laughed. "Do you know, I've gone there several times, but always on foot. There was that first time, with Adam, when we hiked. And then when I took Mina through the woods to Wanda's cottage. On the way back, to check on her, I had three refugees from Cracow in tow. Then, after the war, well, I walked again."

"Walking takes time," he told her.

"There's a bus to the South Market; I know that. Maybe there's even a bus to Kowitz by now." She shrugged.

Yehuda hired a car and driver. The clerk at the front desk told him no car would be available for at least a week, but Yehuda mentioned several of the names he had introductions to and asked if it would be faster to arrange a car through them. The clerk then saw to it that a car arrived within an hour.

Eliza anxiously peered out the windows as the driver headed down the road to Kowitz. "During the war when I was here," she told Yehuda, "there were German soldiers traveling back and forth along this road, hauling supplies to the city. There was a quota each village had to fill. See! There. That's where I left the road with my three refugees. One could hardly walk. His lungs. I didn't have my rifle. I had buried it in the woods. I had to worry about the three of them and about Mina. It was a horrible day. Then at night I went to the village, listened outside the door of Wanda's shack, heard her speaking to Mina, encouraging her to eat. You can't believe how happy I was then."

The village of Kowitz was the same as it had been when Eliza returned to look for her daughter after the war. "Wanda will be here now. I have a feeling," Eliza said. "And Mina will be with her, too. How much paperwork will be necessary to take Mina home?"

Yehuda said nothing. He helped his wife from the car, and they went into the general store. Eliza immediately recognized the man behind the counter as the man she had spoken to after the war. He was grayer, in both body and spirit, but otherwise the same. She walked up to him. "Hello," she said. "You won't remember me, but I came here right after the war looking for Wanda Zbyszek. She had gone off to Cracow then. I was wondering if she had returned and where I might find her?"

The man looked at her, then suspiciously past her to Yehuda and the hired car beyond his door. "Wanda Zbyszek," Eliza repeated.

The man studied her then, very closely. "I remember you."

Eliza smiled. "Yes," she affirmed.

"You look better than you did last time you were here. But I still can't help you. Wanda Zbyszek left the village right after the war. No one's ever heard from her again."

A woman came out from behind a curtain. "Who is she looking for?" she asked the man.

"Wanda Zbyszek," the man said without looking at her.

"That one! So irresponsible."

"How do you mean?" Eliza asked the woman.

"Leaving, and now no one's here to do the laundry."

"She had a child with her."

"Oh, yes, that child. Said it was her mother's. I never believed that for a minute. If Magda Zbyszek had delivered the child to Wanda, why didn't Magda stay, talk to us, her old friends."

"Maybe Magda was collaborating with the Germans?" the man suggested. "Maybe the child was a German child?"

"The child was dark, darker than any German I've ever seen," the woman protested.

"What was the child like? Was she happy with Wanda?" Eliza asked.

"Oh, she was a happy enough child. Very quiet. What was she, only about three when she left. Always followed Wanda around like she didn't want to lose her. What a pair those two made! Of course, you never know what goes on in a child's mind. There were a lot of men visiting Wanda's place, but I suppose you knew that." The woman almost snorted her disapproval.

"No one's ever heard from Wanda? What about a special friend in the village?"

"We were all her friends," the man said. His wife gave him a hard look. "In the village we're all friendly," the man corrected himself. "But, believe me, if someone had heard from Wanda, we would have been told."

"Why do you want to know about Wanda? What's your interest in her?" the woman wanted to know.

Eliza looked behind her to Yehuda. The woman waited. Eliza said nothing. She took a slip of paper and an envelope from her purse. On the paper she wrote her name, her address, the phone number of Pension Bracha. Beneath that she wrote, "Wanda, please get in touch with me about my child, Mina. Thank you. Eliza." She folded the letter and put it in the envelope, then put Wanda Zbyszek's name on the front. Taking another piece of paper, she wrote her name, address, and phone number on it and handed it to the man. "This is my address, my phone number in Israel."

"You're a Jew. I thought so," the woman said.

"If Wanda should show up or you should hear anything from her, about her, please get in touch with me immediately. There's money in it for you. Lots of money." She handed the envelope to the store owner. "If Wanda ever does show up, please give her this. Please." The man looked at her and took the envelope from her hand. "Thank you," she said to him.

She turned to leave. "You know something about the child, don't you?" the woman called after her.

"Good day to you," Eliza said with a slight smile.

They returned to the car. As the driver was about to start it, Eliza impulsively got out again. Yehuda followed her to the edge of Kowitz, which wasn't far. There, lying almost up against the forest was the small, windowless shack. "You could blow it down with a feather," he said.

"That's where Mina spent two years of her life." Eliza went up to the shack and knocked. No answer. She opened the door. There was no one inside. She had hoped against hope that maybe the man had been lying, the way villagers always lie to strangers. Maybe Wanda and Mina were here, right here, living the same sort of life they had lived during the war. But the shack was empty. By the light from the doorway, Eliza wandered inside, inspected the table, the chair where she had left Mina sitting. She rummaged around hoping for some sign of a previous life. But there was no sign. Wanda and Mina had completely vanished.

26

CONTACTS

ELIZA AND YEHUDA RETURNED TO CRACOW AND PAID THE DRIVER. Over lunch she translated for Yehuda exactly, almost word for word, what had been said in Kowitz. She could barely stomach the food she was served. "Eliza," he warned, "you must not become emotional."

"First, why not? Second, how can I help it?"

"I know you can't help it. Why not? Because it interferes with the search. The chances of finding Mina now, almost ten years after you left her, are minimal. Minimal. You have to face that. Now. Because if you don't, after two weeks, you won't have the strength to go on with your own life."

"Maybe I won't want the strength."

"Don't forget all that we have made for ourselves away from this land of death."

She ate. In the afternoon they began making the rounds of government officials to see if they could help locate Wanda Zbyszek. One official was very reassuring. He said, "If she is still in Poland, she can be found. Everyone has to be registered. There is no way, anymore, for anyone to get lost."

With that assurance, Eliza saw night fall with some small amount of comfort.

"What do you want to do for supper?" Yehuda asked her.

"There's someone I want to try to find first," she said.

"That's what we've been doing all day," he almost complained.

She smiled and took his arm. She felt his warmth. It was very cold.

This time they walked through Cracow. She pointed out, as well as she could recognize them, the places of her youth. So much had been destroyed. Her school, her synagogue, the place where she had lived. A whole way of life had been slashed from the bone.

They came to a dilapidated building on the outskirts of the ghetto. This was where she had left the man she was now looking for, but Eliza had no idea whether he would still be there. She opened the outer door of the apartment house and beckoned Yehuda inside. There was a small pocket of warmth between the outer door and the inner. Once inside the stairway, it became cold again. Eliza climbed the stairs. Yehuda followed her. At the third landing she stopped and rang the bell of Apartment 10. The door opened. A woman about Eliza's age, with blond hair, looked out. "Yes?" she said suspiciously.

Stupid of Eliza to think that no one changes addresses. "I'm looking for a man who used to live here," she said. "I wonder if you have any idea where he might be. His name is Hershel Samovic."

The woman looked surprised. "There is a Jan Samovic living here now."

"Jan Samovic?"

"Jan!" the woman called.

A man appeared from around a corner, older and fatter than Eliza remembered him. "Hershel?" she said with a smile.

He looked frightened, then offended. He came closer to stare at her. "Eliza?"

Her smile broadened. "Yes!"

He seemed not to know whether to invite her in or whether to come out on the landing and join her. Finally, he decided that in was better, though he almost closed the door on Yehuda. "Please call me Jan," he whispered to her as they entered the apartment.

Eliza was puzzled. Jan was the most popular of Polish names. She couldn't figure out Hershel's reason, but naturally she would go along. The woman looked as confused as Eliza felt. "Helen," Jan said, "this is my first wife's sister."

"Helen," Eliza repeated. "I'm so pleased to meet you." They shook hands. Then there was a commotion in the kitchen that drew Helen's attention away from the visitors. It was the familiar sound of children squabbling.

"Come in, please. Sit down," Jan said.

"We've come at an inopportune moment," Eliza said.

"There is no opportune moment with these kids," Jan said wearily. Then he looked at Yehuda.

"Hershel—sorry—Jan, this is my husband, Yehuda Barak." They shook hands. "Israeli?" Jan asked.

"Yes."

"So. You got there after all," he said to Eliza.

"Yes."

"And how is it?"

"Compared to Cracow, a paradise."

Jan shrugged. "We haven't recovered. That's for sure. But not for publication." He smiled. "So tell me about your life."

"There've been changes here, too."

"You first."

So Eliza told Jan about her family, the hotel, her friends. He nodded sadly. "It's good to start over in a new place. Here, there are so many reminders. Too many."

"You could have left, too."

"There was no reason to leave, no reason to stay. Maybe it was shock, maybe inertia. And now? Well now I'm settled again. I have a job with the government, working as an engineer at the state radio. I met Helen there. She writes for the station. We have the children."

"And you're happy?"

"Who can be happy after what happened? They don't want us here. Still. After all that has happened, there is no shame. Poland wishes the Germans had wiped us all out. Though not officially of course. I changed my name. You're probably wondering about that. Jan sounds so Polish, doesn't it? When people first meet me, they don't know. I keep my sleeve rolled down so they can't see the number. But maybe someday—"

"Someday," Eliza scoffed. "Yesterday we were three million strong in Poland. How many of us were left alive after the war? Not more than three hundred thousand. And of those, how many fled when they had the chance? We will never be anything in Poland again."

"So why are you here?"

"She's looking for her child," Yehuda said.

"Ah. Forget her, Eliza. Forget her the way I've had to forget my children. They are ashes, all of them."

Eliza stood up as Helen returned to the living room with one baby in her arms, another hanging onto her skirt. "What beautiful, beautiful children," Eliza said to her. "How fortunate you are."

Helen smiled her thanks.

"We have to be going, Jan," Eliza said to her brother-in-law.

"So soon? You can't stay for some soup and bread?" He laughed.

"Come to Israel. If you can," she said softly to him. She took Yehuda by the hand and led him out of the apartment.

"Get me back to sunny Tiberias quickly," he told her.

"At least he still remembers his Yiddish."

"Do you think Helen was Jewish?"

She gave him a look of irritation. They retreated to a café near the hotel for something to eat.

The next day, Yehuda planned their assault on the government offices while Eliza read the paper. "Are you ready?" he asked. She seemed to be taking her time.

"Wait," she told him.

"Yes."

"Tadeusz Dlugosz."

"Is that a curse or what?"

"It's a name. The name of a friend of mine in the resistance. He's—my God, Yehuda—he's a high party functionary now. He's assistant to—we have to see him!"

"Today?"

"Yes."

"If he's so high up, will he see us?"

"Yes. We have to go to Warsaw right away."

"Eliza, we haven't finished seeing people here yet."

"Tadeusz will help us. This I know for sure."

They checked out of the hotel and took the first train to Warsaw. She had been to the capital of Poland only twice, as a child. It looked as gray as Cracow, but at least something had been done to restore it to its former magnificence, especially around the government buildings.

When they reached Tadeusz's office, splendidly large, with a carpeted reception area, Eliza assured the woman at the desk that Tadeusz would see her immediately. The woman was equally insistent that he most definitely would not.

"Please send my name in to him," she urged.

The woman discreetly picked up the phone and turned so that Eliza could not see what she was saying. The phone went down; the door flew open. "Eliza Wolf!" came the booming voice of a Tadeusz grown heavier and healthier than she had ever seen him in his youth. Power must agree with him. He grabbed her in a bear hug and held her tight. Then he pushed her slightly away. "Beautiful. So much better than the last time, with you and your typhoid fever. Talk about death knells. And who is this? May I assume it's your husband?"

"Yehuda Barak. Yes. My husband."

"Barak?" Tadeusz repeated. "Jewish or Israeli?" he asked in French.

"Both," Yehuda admitted.

"Ah, then we shall have to have several sharp disagreements about your government's policy of oppression." He said this with a smile. Then he led them into his office.

Eliza looked around. "This is much different from the way we used to operate," she reminded him.

"Oh, yes. Cellars, attics. Now, after our liberation by the Russians, the right has finally triumphed."

"Meaning you?"

"Among other forward-thinking people."

"You look great, Tadeusz. And Luba, how is she?"

Tadeusz's face fell. "Luba. Sit down, Eliza, Yehuda." They sat in the plushest chairs Eliza had yet seen in Poland. "Luba has failed to support the revolution. I'm sorry to say that Luba is in serious trouble. Her husband—"

"You didn't marry her!" It came out an accusation.

"She made other choices. Her husband has been guilty of running an underground press. I'm afraid he's been caught and sentenced to quite a heavy term, although in one of our better prison camps."

"I can't believe it!"

"You see, Eliza, the problem with working so long underground is that some people never get used to working within the system again. That was Luba's problem. But, you didn't come here to Poland to talk about old times, as exciting, or should I say stimulating, as they were. There is another reason, surely."

"The child."

"Yes. Tell me what you have done, and I'll see what I can do."

Eliza gave Tadeusz all the details of Kowitz and Cracow. Tadeusz wrote everything down, circling some of the words as he went. "Let me ask you this," he said to Eliza, "you can't have any children?"

"I have a child. A son."

He smiled broadly. "Congratulations. Mazel tov."

"Thanks, Tadeusz."

"Then may I suggest—no, that would be unfair of me. Let me tell you honestly, Eliza, that I will put someone on this immediately. I will have him check through the records of birth, death, marriage, divorce, health, employment. You know what it's like here. You know the bureaucracy. The wheels will turn. Slowly. But there are hundreds of thousands of people who have simply vanished. No, not in the camps. We know about them. The Germans were meticulous record keepers. I'm talking about after the war, people migrating all across Europe. You say this Wanda Zbyszek left Kowitz for Cracow. But what's to say that once in Cracow she didn't simply go one step farther, then another, until who knows where she is? What I'm saying is, don't get your hopes up."

"Everyone's been saying that to me."

"My feeling is this: You know Mina's alive; your little girl is alive. Cherish that thought above all others. But, don't get me wrong, we will try to find her."

Everyone tried. But when the two weeks in Poland were up, no one had found Mina. No one had found a trace of Wanda Zbyszek. The two of them had simply disappeared.

Once more Eliza and Yehuda boarded the train that would take them into Austria and a semblance of freedom. "We've left our address and phone number everywhere. If anyone finds out anything, we'll hear," Yehuda said, trying to comfort her.

They slept through Czechoslovakia, and awakened at the border crossing to Austria. "I will be so glad to get home," Eliza said. "I couldn't breathe there. Did you get that feeling? It was like living in a cemetery."

He took her hand. "Thank God you feel that way."

Eliza thought back to the visit she and Yehuda had paid to Luba, despite Tadeusz's warnings that Luba was no longer ideologically sound. It was pitiful to see how far the state had crushed an old friend. "I'm still fighting, Eliza," Luba had said. "I will not lose my ideals." But she had lost everything else. Her husband was in prison, her children were charity cases. Eliza wondered if Luba couldn't ask Tadeusz for help. Luba smiled at Eliza's naïveté. "I am poison to him now. All the years, all the times we saved one another's lives, that means nothing anymore. If you lived here, you would learn quickly. Only one loyalty is allowed, and that is to the party." Eliza remembered pressing money on her friend before she and Yehuda left her. She felt chilled, and she could not get warm again until they boarded a train taking them away. "I hope Tadeusz is right," Eliza said somberly.

"Right in what? He said so much."

"Right in his supposition that Wanda traveled to Cracow and kept on going. I couldn't bear to think of Mina growing up in that prison camp of a nation. Now, you know what I'm going to do, Yehuda."

"What, my darling?"

"I'm going to think of her as growing up happy, free, in some marvelous land with all the food and clothing she'll ever want or need. And you know what we're going to do when we get home?"

"No."

"We're going to have another baby. No matter how hard you have to try."

"I shall try very hard and very often," he promised her sincerely.

NEW
WORLDS

27

"WHAT AMERICA MEANS TO ME"

MINA PRYCHEK STOOD ON THE STAGE IN THE JUNIOR HIGH SCHOOL auditorium and tried not to be nervous. It was hard. Fortunately, she stood behind the lectern, so she had a place to rest her hands. And she could let her weight sink from one foot to the other. The lectern light shone down on her notes. Also, light escaped into her eyes, cutting off all possibility of seeing who was in the audience. Though she knew for certain about one person. Her mother was there. Her mother had promised to come. Mina supposed that all her teachers throughout her years in the Trenton school system were in the audience, plus the entire student body. The students were probably happy just to get out of class. A newspaper reporter was also there. She hadn't known this when she entered the essay contest, "What America Means to Me." Otherwise, she wouldn't have bothered.

"America," she began in her girlish, young voice, "I pass the Statue of Liberty, sailing through your golden portal. You lift me up and set me on the high ground.

"America, a home. I have been chased across Europe by war, famine and disease. I come here to this land of plenty, and you welcome me with the wide-open arms of a mother. You take me in; you comfort me; you dress me anew.

"America, I do not fear now that I am upon your shores. I see laughing, happy faces. I see hands outstretched in welcome. I feel the warmth of a people who have opened their hearts and their land to the many who have come before me. I see a land of promise, of opportunity, of love, of safety, of hope, and, most important, of dreams.

"I dream, America, of times I cannot really remember. I dream of days and nights of silence, when to utter a sound meant certain death. I recall cold nights when the only lullaby was the sound of gunfire and the cries of people dying. I remember the fear of hunger, of cold, of what life itself would bring.

"I have no fears now. I am happy, secure, well nourished, ful-

139

filled, and my dreams are of the future, when I, too, shall have the opportunity to stand before the golden gate and say to others, as you have said to me, 'Welcome to America. You are safe here. Free to say what you will, do as you wish. Most of all, you are free to dream and make those dreams come true.' "

Maria Prychek, in the balcony, led the applause for her daughter. She knew the essay by heart, saw it being written, heard the lines being memorized and rehearsed over and over again. It had gone well. Her daughter had not stumbled.

Now the man from the American Legion was going up on the stage to present Mina with a plaque. Mina was so small next to him. Yet she took the plaque confidently from him, shook his hand, then shook the hand of the principal, before retiring from the stage. Maria could see from her daughter's sudden slouch as she descended the steps from the stage that she was glad it was over. Maria herself would be delighted to bask in the glory forever.

How true her daughter's words were! How good and perfect the thoughts! What a refuge America had been for them! And now they were about to become citizens, she and her daughter, just in time to vote in the 1956 election. There was one thing she was sure of. She was voting for Eisenhower. Who else could stop the Russians from jackbooting their way across the whole of Europe? Look what they had done to her own country, her Poland—squirming, poor, and starving—now completely under the Russian heel. How thankful she was that she had gotten out.

Citizenship! To be an American citizen meant that she would be safe forever. Both she and Mina would be secure, never have to fear again. There were times when she had lived with dread, even here in America. But that was in the beginning. Now, life was perfection.

The beginning—she smiled as she remembered those frantic days. How confused and confusing it had been! Yes, it had been scary. But more than fear, she had felt the thrill of the challenge. She, unlike so many others, had been given the chance to re-create herself. Wanda Zbyszek was dead. Maria Prychek was being reborn. Out of whole cloth she had created a new woman. And she was very happy with the results.

No one would ever know of her triumph. She could not brag about the results of her efforts. She could not even confide in her own daughter. The secret of her past was one that Maria would carry to her grave. Her present? She was proud to be Maria Prychek.

28

ARRIVAL

MARIA REMEMBERED WELL HER VOYAGE TO AMERICA. IT HAD BEEN just as Mina had written. They had gone out on deck one day when they heard sounds of excitement. "Land!" people were calling to one another in various languages, but no one could miss the meaning of the word. Maria had pushed her way to the railing, picked Mina up in her arms and told her the significance of what lay ahead of them. "Now it will be all right for you to shout and yell as much as you want, the same as any other child," she told her daughter.

Mina had simply smiled that sweet little smile of hers, as if she had no need to laugh and play loudly like other children. She put her arms around Maria's neck and hugged her tight. Maria returned the pressure. She was glad now she had kept Mina with her, happy she had someone who loved her, someone to face the world with her.

"The lady," Mina said as the ship passed by the Statue of Liberty.

"Yes," Maria said, "and that's New York up ahead. New York," she repeated magically. Even in Kowitz they had heard of New York. "America," the wind seemed to whistle. It was so cold on deck. The winter crossing had been most unpleasant. Their coats had not been adequate to protect them from the winter gales. But now she would not go below until they were told to get ready to disembark.

"Will we live there, Mama?" Mina asked, as the tall buildings began to loom closer.

"I don't know where we'll live, what we'll do," Maria confessed. "But we've already been through the worst, Mina. Now everything will be better."

Maria had, as usual, spoken too quickly. She had not counted on all the lines they would have to stand in once they had disembarked. How could she forget the DP camps so soon, the lines, the officials who didn't care?

She and Mina were lucky. They had but one suitcase between

them. There were some people who had truckloads of goods. Where did they get it all? Did they bring it from the camps? Or were these Americans returning home? No. These people were from camps, just like she and Mina were. They must have been holding on to everything they could, just in case. Maria had left everything behind. All she wanted to bring to America was herself, the child, and her clothes. And when she reached America, the clothes would be discarded, too. She would buy something bright and lively and new. If she ever got the money.

"You are coming in with how much money?" an official asked her.

"My relatives are waiting for us right outside the gate," Maria told the man. "They have money. They are taking us in. Look. Here" She fumbled through her handful of papers. "Here's their letter. Also one from the captain, confirming their offer. And I know how to work. I can work very hard."

The man looked at her, at her anxious face, at the papers thrust out before him. "I'm sure you can, ma'am. Next station."

Maria shoved the papers back into her purse, took her suitcase in one hand and Mina in the other and moved on. Mina looked up at her mother a little doubtfully. "Don't worry," Maria told her. "We're getting closer."

She had to believe that each station they passed through would bring them closer to freedom. She would not let the shouts of despair from others less fortunate bring her down. They had come this far; they would make it all the way. All the way. There was a beige fence; on the other side of it people were waiting. These people were Americans. Real Americans. Somewhere out there must be her relatives.

Maria came to the last guard separating her from her future. She held out all her papers to him. One by one he tore off the bits he needed. He used his stamp over and over again to signify the importance of what she was carrying. Then he lifted his face to her and said, "Welcome to the United States of America."

She could only nod and smile and thank God it was over. The past was dead. Now there was a new beginning.

Or there would be if she could find the Novoveskis. Where were they? What would they look like? Had they come? Was there some confusion about the dates? Would she need to use a telephone? And how did one go about doing that here?

Some people standing in the crowd of Americans held up signs with names on them. Maybe her name was on one of the signs. She stood and searched. She saw people looking hopefully back at her. But her name was not held up high. Her only recourse was to go up to people and ask if they were the Novoveskis. She did this only to those she thought looked Polish. Though who could tell what the Novoveskis looked like now? After all, they were Americans.

"Excuse me, whom did you say you were looking for?"

The English was quick, too quick for Maria. She stood there, trying to repeat his words in her head while she looked up at this strange man before her. "Maria Prychek?" he tried.

"Yes! Peter Novoveski?"

"Yes." He smiled. She smiled. "I thought I would never find you in this crowd," he confessed. "I should have brought a sign, but I didn't give it a thought before I left. Confusing, isn't it?"

She continued smiling. She caught almost nothing of what he said. He noticed. "Let me take your suitcase," he said slowly. "We will go to my car."

Maria wanted him to take her suitcase if he really was Peter Novoveski. But what if he were a thief? Maria! she chided herself. This is America. And this is your cousin. Relax. For once.

Then Peter noticed what she held in her other hand. He leaned down. "This must be Mina. Hi, Mina."

Mina held back, circling behind Maria's hips. Peter simply smiled and stood. "Come on. Let's get out of this madhouse. Let's go home."

Home? Maria let him take her suitcase and then hurried after him, as he strode through the arrivals terminal. They were soon out in a parking lot of what looked like a car factory. There were cars everywhere, all sizes, all shapes. "Whose are these?" she called to Peter.

He stopped and turned. "What are you asking?"

"The cars. Are they being shipped someplace?"

He laughed. "No. We—those of us inside waiting for people own these cars. This is a parking lot."

"You own a car yourself?"

"Of course. How would I get to work without one?"

Of course, Maria repeated in her mind. Of course. Then it must be as natural in America to own a car as to breathe. She smiled down at Mina and squeezed her hand.

They reached Peter's car. It was huge, a Chevrolet, black and white. He opened the trunk and tossed her suitcase inside. Then he opened the passenger door, and she and Mina slipped in. Riding in a car! Oh, they had ridden in jeeps in the DP camps, and in trucks, too. But a car, that was something special. She would always remember this first sight of America, a land full of cars.

"We're driving to my house now," Peter told her carefully. "It's a bit of a trip, all the way to Trenton. If you're hungry, or you need to use the bathroom or anything, let me know." They both looked down at Mina, but Mina, as usual, said nothing. "All the relatives are waiting to meet you," he said to Maria with a smile. "This is the most excitement they've had since V-J Day."

Maria smiled nervously back at him. All the relatives? God, how was she to continue the masquerade with all the relatives? She was so anxious now that she definitely knew she would have to use the bathroom before they reached Trenton.

They did. They stopped at a small restaurant. She and Mina went into the ladies' room. When they came out, Peter had a bag with him. "I don't want to lose time, and Doreen will be mad that I gave you anything to eat, because they've prepared a feast for you. But I wanted you to start off right in America, so I've bought you two hamburgers."

Maria took the bag from him. When they were back in the car and he had pulled onto the road, she and Mina opened the bag and took out the sandwiches. "Meat," she said to Mina. They both smiled and started eating. Meat with onions in a roll, good meat, grilled. With tomatoes. "Good!" she pronounced. Peter looked very happy.

Maria and Mina ate the hamburgers quickly. The last meal they had had was breakfast that morning. Now it was growing dark outside. It had been a long day, and sometimes Maria's eyes would close. But she tried not to let them. She wanted to see everything. There was so much to see. She tried to read all the signs, in English. She looked at the houses and wondered what life was like inside, how life was different in America.

"Trenton," Peter told her.

"Trenton," she repeated. "It's a city?"

"Sort of. In some places, I guess," he said.

As he drove through the streets, she saw many cars like his parked along the curb and in the driveways. So many cars. Everyone must be very rich.

"This is where we live." He pulled his car up in front of a blue house with a gray roof and shutters. "It's called a duplex. That means another family lives on the other side. Someday we'll move to a bigger house. But this was all we could find after the war."

After the war. Yes, that was the phrase she could well understand. Everything was different after a war.

She and Mina didn't even manage to get out of the car before people came pouring down the front steps of Peter's duplex. Maria was overwhelmed, first by all the people, then by the fact that some were speaking Polish. Mostly, though, she was overwhelmed by her fear that she would immediately be recognized as an impostor.

Mina had been taken from her and was now wildly calling for her. Maria saw Mina being carried up the steps and into the house, reaching frantically back to her. "Mina!" Maria yelled, chasing after her, oblivious to those who were making an effort to hug and kiss her.

"Hey! Let the kid go!" Peter called. Maria turned. He was back at the trunk, getting her suitcase. No one heard him. She herself was being hustled up the stairs, asked all sorts of questions. She was so confused, she didn't know what to say or do.

She found herself in a room full of sofas and people. Mina had reached there before her and was crying hysterically. Did Mina know the enemy when she saw them? They were giving her candy, trying to stop the tears. Maria called to her daughter, and Mina fled into her arms. Maria rocked her and held her tight to stop the convulsive shaking of her shoulders. "She doesn't know who you are," Maria explained to them.

"How thoughtless of us," one woman said. How true that was! Poor Mina. Maria now looked slowly at the faces staring at her. She went from one to the other, man, woman, boy, girl. She could recognize no one. "I'm sorry," she said. "You will have to tell me who you are. Maybe I have seen some of you at some time, but it has been so long."

"Indeed, you have seen me," one woman said quickly to her in Polish. "I was at your christening. That was just before I left for America. I knew your mother well. When we heard she had died, it was awful. We used to play together as children. You don't remember me, your Aunt Basia?"

Maria smiled. She shook her head slowly, sadly. "I have heard of you, of course. My mother—" But then she trailed off. She didn't want to say anything about Maria's mother that might be incorrect. And what could she really remember of the woman? She looked down at Mina and saw that she had calmed down but was still not brave enough to peek out at everyone assembled there. Maria only wished she had the same privilege. But instead she stood up to the barrage of questions she knew she had to face. She tried to answer as honestly as she could. The questions she answered best were those concerning conditions in Kowitz during the war. That she knew well. And yes, she could definitely answer about the people in Kowitz. She told several amusing stories about the mayor and his wife. But she shied away from answering questions about her husband, her child, her family. All through the conversation, all through the meal, she practiced her tactic of avoidance. And then she indicated by several indelicate yawns and drooping lids that she was really exhausted. This was not in any sense a misrepresentation. She *was* exhausted. She had a headache. It had not been an easy day. Mina was asleep, "like an angel," as they all said, on her lap. "You must be tired, too," the relatives said to her over and over again, though that gave them no impetus to leave.

Finally Peter cleared them out. This was after the women had helped Doreen with the dishes. Soon those left were all in Peter's immediate family: his wife, Doreen, whom Maria had barely had a chance to speak to at all, and his two children, Michelle and Bobby.

There were two bedrooms upstairs, Doreen explained, one for her and her husband and one for the children. Down here in the living room, the sofa folded out. Maria and Mina could sleep on that, if they didn't mind. Doreen had said that almost apologetically. "We can sleep anyplace, and we have," Maria assured her. She helped make the bed, then woke Mina to use the downstairs bathroom, which she herself was thankful for. Tomorrow, Doreen assured her, there would be time to take a shower, get cleaned up, go shopping.

Maria turned off the light in the living room. She lay on the sofa bed and listened to the sounds from upstairs. She looked across at Mina, already sleeping soundly next to her. Tomorrow. Tomorrow they would do this, do that, do everything. For Maria tomorrow had arrived today. For so many years she had waited and now it was here. She was alive and well and living in America.

29

OUT ON HER OWN

DOREEN NOVOVESKI WAS A SAINT. AT LEAST THAT WAS HOW MARIA Prychek came to consider her over the next weeks. Doreen served as her protector and her educator. Which role was more important,

Maria couldn't decide. She supposed she preferred to be educated; she had always protected herself.

There was so much to learn about the United States. Just walking into a department store made Maria think she had died and gone to heaven. How could one country have so much?

The shopping forays were the ones Maria loved best. She held on to Mina while Doreen carried Bobby, who had been born after Peter returned from the war. Michelle, their older child, was already in school. The two women looked at clothes, dishes, appliances. Maria couldn't believe the appliances. If she had had a washing machine in Kowitz, the money she could have made!

The grocery store was another American miracle. Maria wasn't thinking of the corner grocery store, which was very nice and friendly, like the one in Kowitz but with more goods. It was the new supermarket, with everything carefully wrapped and packaged, looking as if it had come off an assembly line, that impressed her. Despite the continued rationing, everyone ate well here. There was no starvation. All segments of this rich society sped toward the future. For Maria that was good. The past was something she had to forget, to escape from.

The relatives and their questioning also demanded some evasive action on Maria's part. The family came to Doreen's almost every night, bringing clothes for Maria and Mina. She didn't need so many clothes, especially since even with the greatest of alterations some of the dresses would never fit. The relatives really came to ask questions and more questions. Soon the questions centered on her husband and, more dangerously, on Mina. Maria continued to try to make it painfully clear to them that there were some subjects, some areas in her life that were too devastating to talk about. Perhaps this was a mistake; it seemed that these were the exact areas they wished to delve into. How could she protect herself from their probing? She could run away. But these were her sponsors. She needed these people. And maybe they needed her, as their charity.

Doreen, her protector, finally told her what the problem was. "You don't wear a wedding ring."

"I sold my ring in order to bribe my way across the border to get to Vienna."

"And they can't figure out why Mina has your last name, your maiden name instead of your married name."

"The papers—the war made everything so difficult."

"The girl is so unlike us. They think maybe she is illegitimate, that you were, maybe, raped—or something."

Maria turned dangerously on Doreen. "What do they know about the war?"

"Only what they read," Doreen admitted.

"Exactly. They can never understand what it was like. All the death. All the fear. Mina and I survived. We don't owe anybody an explanation for that."

"Please, Maria. Don't get mad at me. I'm just—"

"I know, Doreen. You've been very, very good to me. Without you, without your letter, I would have been stuck under the Russians, as I had been crushed under the Germans. I will never stop being grateful. And as far as the others go, I know they mean well. They have been generous. But I owe my life to you. Not to them. And I will never apologize for keeping Mina alive."

Doreen looked puzzled. She was on the verge of asking more questions when she changed her mind. She took Maria's hand, then hugged her. "I'm glad you're here. I'm glad Mina's here, too."

Doreen was sincere. But Maria realized Doreen wouldn't be glad to have them there forever. The truth of the matter was that the Novoveskis did not have a very big duplex. For the past eighteen days, they had been rearranging their living pattern in order to make room for the needs of Maria and Mina. Those eighteen days had given Maria confidence. She had been out with Doreen; she had been out walking by herself with Mina. She knew she could make herself understood. What was more fantastic was that Mina's English was becoming even better than hers, the result of playing with her cousin Michelle Novoveski. It was time, Maria believed, to look for her own place to live. More important, it was time to look for a way to support herself.

Once Over Easy stood on a corner in a shopping district that was a ten-minute bus ride from the Novoveskis' duplex. Maria had passed by it often when she took Mina to shop from one side of the street to the other, from Ben Franklin's to Woolworth's. In the window of Once Over Easy stood pickle jars. Sausages hung from the ceiling. Of more interest to Maria, in one corner was tucked a sign: HELP WANTED.

Despite Mina's vehement objections, Maria dressed one day in the best hand-me-down she had received and made clear her intention to head for the shopping district alone. "You stay home and help Aunt Doreen with Bobby."

"Will you bring me something then?" Mina asked. She was becoming so American.

"I can't bring you something every time I go out," Maria protested.

"Why not?"

"Maybe a lollipop," Maria conceded. "But not more than that."

Mina smiled, pleased with her half-victory.

Maria didn't know what to expect when she entered Once Over Easy. It was ten in the morning. There were perhaps five people at the restaurant counter. Two women were sitting at one of the tables having coffee, and a few more were crowded at the deli department in front. It was a small restaurant, but pleasant. She stood and tried to assess whom to approach. Finally she figured it might be the man reading the paper behind the counter. "Excuse me," she said, as she stood before him.

He looked up and looked her over. Her blond hair was clean and combed in a pageboy. Her face was delicately made up with Maybelline. Her dress was a blue-and-white-print shirtwaist that fell sweetly over her body, sedately emphasizing her breasts, the curve of her hips. He was definitely admiring. "May I help you?"

"The sign in the window. I'd like to apply for the job."

He smiled. "You're foreign."

Her hand went to her neck. "Yes. But I have my papers." She knew it was always important to have papers.

His smile became broader. "Where are you from?"

"Poland."

"Are you a Jew?"

"No."

"I didn't think so. We're Jewish here."

"Oh." She wondered what he was trying to say. That he didn't hire Poles? Not that she would blame him. But maybe it was only something about the food. "Does that mean you keep kosher?"

"No. My wife and I, we're Jews. Does that make any difference to you?"

Maria gave him a puzzled smile. She shrugged her shoulders and swept the blond hair back from her eyes. "I'm new in this country; I have a little girl I need to support. I saw your sign and came in."

He raised his eyebrows. "No husband?"

"Dead."

He nodded. "You'll have to speak to my wife." He nodded toward the woman behind the deli counter. "Stella."

The woman looked up. The man pointed toward the window, then toward Maria. Maria walked toward Stella, who finished waiting on a customer with a smile and an exchange of one last bit of gossip. Then Stella stepped aside and Maria approached. "You're looking for a job?" Stella asked.

"She's Polish," the man called.

Everybody was involved now. Maria was sure her entire life history, as much as she would let be known, would soon be broadcast around the deli. "That's okay," Stella tried to reassure her. "Don't mind Sam. We have plenty of Polish customers here. Do you speak Polish?"

"Yes."

"Do you speak English?"

"I believe well enough."

"There's not that much English to speak here. Just how they want their food, how much meat they want sliced. What you need to be is fast and cheerful. How are you on fast and cheerful?"

"I can do fine."

"She has a child, but no husband," Sam called from across the room.

Maria shifted from one foot to another, feeling very uncomfortable.

"Don't mind him," Stella insisted. It was hard not to mind a man who shouted your life history across an open room, but Maria tried. "If you have a child, you might not want this job. We need someone for the early shift, from 6:00 to 2:30. That covers breakfast and lunch and the mid-morning shoppers. You won't have a moment to sit down and rest, except for your half-hour break. But the food you eat here is free. The salary's minimum wage, plus tips. They're not the greatest tippers who come in here. We provide the white apron to wear over your clothes. You can wear anything as long as you look respectable. You'll have to get a net for your hair. We can't have hair in the customers' food. For some reason, that's one thing they really get upset about."

Maria had been nodding all the way through Stella's recital. Now she spoke. "Then is it possible I may have the job?"

"It's possible if you want it."

"May I start next Monday, so that I may get my daughter settled?"

"You want the job?"

"Yes. Very much."

"Then next Monday's fine. Sam," called, "take care of the paperwork."

Maria was in such a rush to hurry home and tell Doreen the news that she almost forgot Mina's lollipop. Almost, but thank God she stopped in Ben Franklin's in time.

Doreen was not as happy as Maria thought she would be about the job. "But how can you work and have a child at the same time?" she asked.

"I worked in Kowitz."

"That was different. That was a small town. Trenton's not a small town."

When Peter came home, Doren told him the news before Maria could break it to him herself. "You're going to work at Once Over Easy?" he questioned.

"Yes. Why not?"

"I know the place. The Markses run it."

"Sam and Stella," Maria added.

"They're Jews."

"Yes. They told me."

"Do they know you're from Poland?"

"Yes. I told them."

"And they still hired you?"

"Yes. They said they had many Polish customers, and they asked if I could speak Polish. They seemed happy."

Peter shook his head. "You know, relationships haven't been so great here between Poles and Jews, especially not since the Jews found out what happened in Poland during the war. They blame us for it."

"You?"

"Not us. But, you know, the Poles. They say we were always anti-Semitic."

"Yes. Well—that's true," Maria said.

"What!" Doreen objected. "You think it was our fault?"

"It was someone's fault. Someone should have stopped it. I saw the trains that went to Auschwitz."

"The Germans did as much harm to the Poles as they did to the Jews. When will these people realize that?" Peter asked.

Maria bent her head in submission. "I don't want to refight the war. I simply want to start a new life. For that I need a job; I need money."

"My concern is also for my own wife," Peter said. "Doreen has enough on her hands with Michelle and Bobby. For her to take care of Mina, too—"

Maria looked up in surprise. "Oh! Doreen, no! That's not what I expected you to think. I realize that taking me and Mina in has been a sacrifice for you two."

"Not at all," Doreen tried to protest.

"But of course it has. You've shared your lovely home with us, your food, your company, your love. I know we've been putting you out, what with everyone having to leave the living room so that we can sleep. And here we are, always in the middle of everything.

You have been good to us, but we have stayed long enough. That is clear."

"Then what are you planning to do?" Peter asked.

"I start work on Monday. I was hoping that before then, you would help me find a place to live. I need someplace near the bus line, so I can reach the deli easily. Maybe there's someone who has a room to rent? That would be all Mina and I would need."

Peter shook his head. "You're asking the impossible. They're building houses like crazy, but still, there is a definite housing shortage."

"But we can try. There must be someplace."

There was. They found it through the church. The priest knew of a widow whose husband had been a dentist. She had sold all his equipment, and his office space remained vacant. It was attached to her house, but the former office area had its own private entrance. There were two rooms and a bathroom, more than enough space for Maria and Mina. "The child won't make too much noise, will she?" Mrs. Nowicki, their new landlady asked.

"No," Maria assured her. "Mina hardly makes any noise at all."

The relatives came to their rescue once again, casting old pieces of furniture in their direction, helping with towels and bedding, curtains, until finally the small apartment could pass for somebody's home.

By Monday Maria was ready to start a new life. She explained carefully to Mina how she would have to stay home and care for herself until the afternoon, when they could once again be together. "And someday," she told her daughter, "I promise you, cross my heart, hope to die, you'll be able to make all the noise you wish."

30

ONCE OVER EASY

MONDAY MORNING MARIA WAS WAITING OUTSIDE THE DOOR OF Once Over Easy by 5:45. A freezing rain was driving into the side of the building, and she just barely protected herself by huddling in the doorway. Before they went to bed the night before, Maria had made Mina promise to sleep late, play only outside in their yard, not to go away with strangers, to eat two good meals, one for breakfast, one for lunch. Then she was to take a nap until Maria came home.

The Markses showed up at five minutes to six. By that time Maria could feel herself turning blue. "You don't have to be such a good employee," Sam told her. "Six is fine."

"The bus."

"Whatever."

Before she knew it, she was taking down the chairs and wiping off the tables and the booths. The Markses were in the back, setting up the kitchen. When a black man came through the front door, Maria was stymied. She had seen blacks on the streets of Trenton but had never been face to face with one. She grabbed the order book Stella had given her. "May I help you?" she asked.

He looked at her as if she were crazy. Then he laughed. "I'm Harry. The cook. You must be the new girl."

She smiled. "Maria."

"Maria, great. Just keep your writing clear and pick up your orders on time, and we'll do okay."

He disappeared in the back, and she was making herself familiar with the layout of the deli when a woman came in, this one in her forties with blond hair, suspiciously blond. "You're new," the woman said. "I hope you'll last at least a month. I'm tired of doing everything. What's your name?"

"Maria."

"Maria? Too delicate. In here they'll call you Marie. My name's Carol. Yeah. I'm divorced. Why else would I be working a cruddy job like this? What's your reason?"

"I need the money."

"Hey, I like the sound of that one. Well, don't let anyone push you around. If you have any problems, we'll help. Unless you look like you're going to be a complete imbecile."

"Thank you," Maria said doubtfully.

By 6:25, five minutes before the official opening time of Once Over Easy, customers had started to drift in, leaving puddles and wet seats where the rain dripped off their coats. From 6:25 until 2:30 in the afternoon, Maria didn't have a chance to think of anything except the job. Sam even had to remind her to eat. She never thought anyone would ever have to remind her to eat. But she was so concerned with doing everything right that all thoughts of bodily functions fled from her mind.

"You did good, kid," Sam said to her when 2:30 came. She

looked up at the clock above the fountain counter. "I know," he said to her, "where has time flown?"

She looked puzzled. "You mean work is over?"

"This is all we're paying you for."

A bit confused, she took off her apron, got her coat from the back, and walked toward the front of the deli. Two more waitresses, who had come in for the luncheon crowd, were still working. "I'll be back tomorrow," she said to no one in particular.

"We're hoping," Sam called.

"Hold it," Stella said. "We have some extra cake that's going to go stale. Maybe your daughter would like it?"

Maria looked at Stella and tears started to form in her eyes. "Thank you so much. You are so kind," she said.

Stella shrugged. "It's stale. What can I say?"

Maria held the package delicately in her lap as she traveled by bus back to her apartment. Her thoughts turned to worries. What had Mina been up to during the day? She was such a good, obedient child, but America, even in the short time they had been here, was already changing her.

When Maria opened the door of the apartment, Mina came rushing to her. "Mama," she said, giving her a hug. "I've missed you!"

"I've missed you, too, darling. Look! Look what Mrs. Marks has sent you. Cake."

They opened the cake box at the table. Then, on dissimilar plates, they cut two pieces. Maria tasted it. It wasn't stale at all. "What did you do all day?" Mina asked.

"Worked. Worked hard." She put her hand in her purse and took out the tips she had transferred from her apron. Together they counted the change. Twice. Mina looked up at her and smiled. "We're rich."

Maria laughed. "Not yet. But soon we will be. And this is on top of my salary. Soon we'll buy you all new clothes, and you will be the prettiest girl in Trenton." She yawned.

"You're tired," Mina said.

"Yes. And my feet hurt."

"You should sleep."

Maria took her daughter's advice. She lay down on the bed and covered herself with a blanket while Mina gently massaged her feet. "You are the best daughter in the world," Maria said to her as her eyes closed.

When she woke up, it was five o'clock. She was startled that she had slept so long. Mina was sitting silently in the chair, watching her. It was already dark outside. "I hate the winter," Maria said, staring out the window at nothing.

"There's a library four blocks down the street from us," Mina said.

"Four blocks! You were supposed to stay at home."

"There was nothing to do. If you come with me on Saturday, I can get a card and bring books home."

"If you read too much, you'll ruin your eyes." She turned on her side and stared at the girl. She wondered how much Mina resembled her real mother. Did Eliza Wolf, when she was alive, read all the time, even when she was this young? Did she stare with such knowing eyes at her mother, her father? Did Mina look like Eliza? Maria could barely remember. It seemed so many centuries ago that she was Wanda Zbyszek, town laundress, town whore. And it might have *been* centuries ago. She was now reincarnated, and no one would ever know her secret. Or Mina's. Mina would be safe with her in this new land. There would be no train rides to oblivion for her, as there had been for her mother. The past was dead, for both of them.

"Can we?"

"What, darling?"

"Get a library card. It doesn't cost money."

"Yes. If it doesn't cost money, why not?"

The first lump sum of money Maria got together went for new shoes for herself. She felt guilty, because Mina could have done with a pair of boots that fit her better than the hand-me-downs. But Maria had to stand all day; and she discovered through Carol, that she needed special shoes if she was going to be able to stand at all by the end of the week. Then after those shoes, she began to start saving money to buy Mina a few small things so that she could entertain herself during the day. And small things they had to be, for after Maria paid the rent and the utilities and the grocery bills, there was not as much left as she had hoped. Still they were doing very well for two people who landed in America with nothing but one suitcase a few months before.

By summer, Maria had enough money and enough know-how to enroll Mina in a summer playground program run by the school. It was only in the mornings, but it gave Mina a chance to get out and scream without having to worry about Mrs. Nowicki next door. And it also allowed her to meet the children with whom she would go to school, to kindergarten. Mina, except for the funny sizes of some of her clothing, was now almost totally American. She spoke English with no accent. If Maria had been wise, she would have learned from her daughter, and both would have spoken only English at home. But Polish was still the language they communicated in when they were alone.

The summer was so beautiful in America. Maria would come home from work and nap, a habit she could not break. Then she and Mina would go out and walk around the neighborhood, share dreams together, walk downtown and get ice cream, then maybe listen to a band concert, or, more often, a neighbor fighting, almost equally entertaining.

Maria was pleased with the rhythm of her life. The Markses were very good to her; she began to know and like the customers who came in regularly. They liked her, too. Her tips were steady and sometimes generous. Some of the men occasionally gave indications that the tips could be even more generous for other services she might like to render, but she always laughed them off, joked away their suggestions. The one thing she had in America was her good name, or, rather, Maria Prychek's good name. And she wasn't planning on losing it.

Maria had Saturdays and Sundays off. She understood from Carol that on the weekends the Markses had a series of high school kids come in, who liked to make that extra money for a prom dress or for make-up, for anything their allowances wouldn't cover.

Maria saved Saturdays for things she and Mina could do together. At first they stayed in Trenton. But later they became more adventurous, and took the bus to Philadelphia and to New York. They were becoming quite adept at being tourists, discovering what lay beyond their own neighborhood.

Maria set Sundays aside for church and family. She took Mina every Sunday to the eleven o'clock Mass. Sometimes she felt guilty, because she knew Mina wasn't Catholic. Yet how could she bring her up as a Jew? It wasn't possible. There would have been too many questions to answer. She would simply have to assume that if a person was good, it didn't matter what religion she was. Maria didn't believe in certain concepts of the church anymore, like hell and salvation. She had seen too much in this world to allow her to believe the other world could be any worse.

After Mass, Maria and Mina would travel to one relative or another for Sunday dinner. She enjoyed this time with the relatives, but was also glad that it came only once a week. Sometimes the family was oppressive, filled with suggestions about what she should be doing for herself, for Mina. She thought she had proved that she could take care of herself and Mina just fine. But it always seemed not to be fine enough.

It didn't matter. She could be amused by the relatives now that
they didn't control her life. She could take what advice she wanted
and simply smile through the rest of it.

So she was satisfied and comfortable with her life. There were
absences, yes; there was more that she wanted. But there was no
point in being greedy. She had so much more than she had ever
hoped for, growing up in Kowitz, even waiting all those months in
the DP camps in Austria. If life was to be fuller for her, that would
come in its own time. Meanwhile, she had Mina, the Markses, her
co-workers, and her family. She considered herself very fortunate.

31

A MATCH

"WHO ARE YOU STARING AT, MOMMY?" MINA ASKED FROM BE-
hind her hands.

Maria looked down at her seven-year-old daughter. "In church
we don't stare at anyone," she explained. "We think about God
and the Virgin Mary."

Mina looked suspiciously as if she didn't believe her. Self-
righteously, Maria drew her eyes back to the priest, whereas a few
minutes before she had been staring at a man she thought she recognized. It was hard to tell. She could see only the back and right
side of his head. Maybe when, if, he went up to receive Communion, she would know where she had seen him before.

A few weeks ago Maria had celebrated her twenty-ninth birthday.
Twenty-nine, and she felt like an old maid. She was an old maid,
at least in her own mind, since she, if no one else, knew she had
never been married, never had a child. Even by reckoning her real
age, and not Maria Prychek's age, she was twenty-six. By the time
she was thirty, she would be a dried-up old prune. That's what they
called an old maid in America.

Carol, her friend and fellow waitress from Once Over Easy, had
remarried. She was in her forties; she was never too specific about
which forty she had reached. She had become involved with one
of the customers, not Maria's type certainly but, as Carol said,
beggars can't be choosers. She had retired from her job and told

Maria that now she spent her days sitting near the radio, folding the laundry, and waiting for her husband to come home. He was in his fifties, so they wouldn't have children around. It was just the two of them and the pretty house that Carol had to look after. Was Maria destined to work forever as a waitress, fated to listen to the radio alone on Saturday night?

Well, not every Saturday night. Through church and through the relatives, she had met a few men. She hated it when the family fixed her up. Afterward, they always wanted to know how it went. When she said okay, they couldn't understand why she was being so choosy. They expected her to be overwhelmingly grateful. Even in Kowitz she would not have looked at some of these men the family found for her, probably off the street. But soon, she realized, these men would not look at her; she would be too old. She wanted someone to admire her. She wanted someone to touch her. She had not been touched since she left Kowitz, except for one time in a DP camp, with an American soldier, because she wanted to know how different American men were. He wasn't. She knew she had to act virginal when she got to the States, but she didn't expect to turn into one.

There. He was going up to the rail now. Oh, yes, she remembered him. He sat at her table maybe once or twice a week, never saying much. He wished her good morning when she greeted him, gave her his order, left a nice tip, was very pleasant. But he never gave a sign that he knew she was alive, that she was more than the bearer of sausage and eggs, orange juice to start.

She sighed. Mina looked up at her. "Did you confess this week?" Mina asked.

"To what?" Maria wondered dolefully.

"Are you going up or not?" Mina asked.

Maria smiled down at her. Soon Mina would have her first Communion. How pretty she would look in her white dress. Doreen said that when the time came, Mina could probably fit into the one Michelle had used. It would save money. Those dresses were so expensive, and the girls only wore them once. Peter and Doreen, what lucky people they were! They had finally moved to a big house, with four bedrooms, and Doreen was pregnant again. Everyone in America was a success.

When it was their row's turn, Maria put down her missal and moved down the aisle. Her thoughts were less on receiving the host than on how she looked passing the row where her customer sat.

Mina wanted to make a quick departure from the church when Mass was over, but Maria lingered, ostensibly straightening the bow on Mina's dress, until she saw the man coming up the aisle. He was alone. Exactly as she'd thought from observing him. No wife, no children. She managed to enter the aisle in time to put him a little bit off balance. "Sorry," she said. Then she stared at him, as if she recognized him, which of course she did. "Oh, hello," she said cheerfully.

He stared back. Obviously, she had made no impression on him at all. "Aren't you—don't you come into Once Over Easy for breakfast sometimes?" she asked innocently.

He smiled. "Oh, yes! You're—"

"I work there, yes. I see you there sometimes."

"I'm sorry. That's so early in the morning; I'm spending most of my time thinking about the day ahead."

"I can believe it."

They were blocking the aisle. People were going around the bottleneck they had created. He touched her arm and eased her toward the door of the church. Mina was left to trail behind them. "I didn't know you went to this church," Maria said to him.

"I don't usually," he confessed. "It's not the closest one to where I live, but sometimes I like a change."

"I know what you mean. But this is convenient for us, not too far to walk, so we come here."

"Us?"

"My daughter and I." She looked around for Mina, who was now waiting patiently for her on the stone wall, probably snagging her dress.

"Your husband's not religious?" the man guessed.

"I'm—a widow."

"Sorry."

"The war."

"Yes. I haven't introduced myself, have I?"

"I haven't either."

"But I remember. You're—Maria."

She was pleased. "Yes."

"The name tag," he explained. "And they ask for you a lot."

"It's busy in the mornings. Yes, I'm Maria Prychek." She held out her hand.

"Jerry Jankowski." He took her hand in his. His handshake was firm but not overbearing.

"You're Polish, too?"

He nodded. "My real name is Jerzy, but that's not the sort of name you go through school with."

"In Poland it is."

"From your accent you must be from there."

"Yes. I came here about two and a half years ago."

"And do you like it?"

"Oh, very much. It's heaven."

"Are you here alone, just you and your daughter?"

"Oh, no. We have relatives who sponsored us. They were very kind to us when we first came over, helping with clothes and such. But now we have our own apartment, a bus ride away from most of them. It's nice. I work at the deli while Mina is in school. She's in school all day now, which makes it easier than when I first started." Maria laughed. "I'm sorry. I'm just rattling on."

"No. Please continue. You have a pleasant voice. I like your accent."

All of a sudden, she couldn't think of anything to use her accent on. He noticed. "Would you like a ride home?" he asked.

"It would be out of your way?" she suggested.

"No. My car's out back in the lot."

"Mina," she called to her daughter. Mina hopped down from the wall and came over to them. "Mina, this is Mr. Jankowski. He's offered to give us a ride home."

"In a car?"

"Of course in a car."

"Wonderful!"

It was a wonderful car, a large black Packard, so roomy that Maria could hardly believe it. She got into the front seat with Jerry; Mina took over the back. "Is that a radio?" Mina asked, as Jerry started the engine.

"Yes," he told her.

"Can we listen to it?"

"Mina," Maria censured. But Jerry turned on the radio and swiftly drove through the streets of the neighborhood to Maria's apartment.

They stopped right in front of the driveway, and Maria could tell that Mrs. Nowicki was peeking through the curtains. Usually, she and Mina did not come straight home from Mass. They took a bus to one of the relatives. Usually. "Would you like to come in and have some tea or coffee?" Maria asked Jerry. "I think I can even whip up something for Sunday dinner."

"Do you go out to eat on Sundays?" he asked.

"Most of the time we go over to one of the relatives'," she admitted. "But they won't miss us for one Sunday. And you?"

"I go home to eat with my parents."

"Oh." She knew she sounded disappointed.

"But why don't we stop at a phone booth, call everybody and let them know we have something better to do? Not in those words, of course. Then let me take you out to dinner."

"Sounds great," she agreed.

They went to a diner, miles outside Trenton. It was a gorgeous drive through the countryside with the windows down. It was luxurious. The diner was chrome on the outside, but inside it was extremely pleasant, with wood paneling and tables with a view out over a lake. Mina ordered a hamburger and chocolate milk; Maria let Jerry order for her. His choice was fried chicken with mashed potatoes and canned peas, which weren't very good. But the chicken was. She even followed his lead and picked the chicken up and ate it that way. For desert they each had a hot fudge sundae. "I'll never eat again," Maria said.

"I will," Mina begged to differ.

Jerry laughed. "You don't eat out much, do you?"

"Hardly ever. We save our money for the movies."

He nodded. "Do you go often?"

"Saturday matinees. We can't miss Buck Rogers."

"And they have double features on Saturdays," Mina stressed.

He smiled at her. "What grade are you in now, Mina?"

"Second."

"Do you like school?"

"Yes. All my friends are there."

"What do you do, Jerry?" Maria asked.

"Salesman. I sell industrial light fixtures. It's not very glamorous, but it pays."

She looked at his hands. "And you're not married?" There probably was a more delicate way of putting it, but she had to know.

"I *was* married. Just before I shipped out, I married a girl I had known a couple of months. It was a foolish mistake. I was away two years in the Pacific. It was about a year and five months too long for her."

"I'm sorry."

"We had the marriage annulled. The priest was good about that. We were both very young."

"So now you can start over."

"It's a matter of regaining faith," he told her. "Meanwhile, I'm living with my parents because of the housing shortage. You were lucky to find that apartment. But living at home's not bad, because I'm saving my money. Someday, who knows."

"Who knows about life?" Maria agreed. "It's always full of

surprises. Some not so pleasant, some—well, like today. This has been a real treat for us. Thank you very much, Jerry.''

"My pleasure.''

She saw Jerry Jankowski only once the following week. He came in on Tuesday to ask if she could go out with him on Saturday night. "Will you be able to get a baby-sitter for Mina?'' he asked.

"Mrs. Nowicki, next door, keeps an eye out for her,'' Maria explained, as she delivered his Breakfast Platter No. 2.

"Eight o'clock?''

"Sounds good,'' she told him. "Do you remember where I live?''

"Of course.''

She was happy the rest of the week. Naturally, she had to deal with Mina's disappointment that she wasn't going to be a part of their evening, not going to get a chance to ride in the Packard and get a hamburger; she told Mina that maybe there would be other times. Wishful thinking. She first had to get through Saturday.

Maria's immediate impulse was to buy a new dress. But she realized how dumb that was. She didn't really have money to fling around on new dresses. Besides, Jerry hadn't seen any of her old dresses, except for the one she wore last Sunday. So Saturday around seven she slipped into a green dress with a V neck that looked particularly good with her blond hair. Then she applied her make-up, including green eye shadow, very carefully. By 7:45 she was ready, waiting, and nervous. She wondered where they would go. Maybe to a movie? Maybe to dinner? Wherever would be okay with her. It was good to be going out with someone instead of sitting home. "Now you behave,'' she reminded Mina.

"What else is there to do?'' Mina wanted to know.

"No playing with matches or things like that.''

"Mom, the fireman came to our school. I know all about fire prevention now. The Red Cross came, too. I even know how to put on bandages.''

"Such an educated young lady.''

"Do you like Jerry?''

"Mr. Jankowski to you, Mina. And I don't even know him.''

"I like his car. It has a radio.''

"I remember.''

The doorbell rang. Maria tried not to rush to it. She counted to ten, rose from the chair, and went to the door. "Jerry!'' she said with delight, almost surprise. "Please come in. I'll get my coat.''

As she got her coat, she could feel his eyes swinging up and down her body. This green dress was the best she had. He turned away from her. "Hi, kid, how're ya doing?'' he said to Mina.

"Fine—Mr. Jankowski."

"Call me Jerry."

"Jerry." Mina smiled.

Maria brought her coat over and let Jerry help her on with it; then, she again reminded Mina to behave. Outside, Jerry asked, "She'll be okay?"

"If you glance toward the second window on your left, you will see Mrs. Nowicki sneaking a look. She keeps a close eye on everything we do. Mina will just listen to the radio; then, she'll go to sleep."

He helped her into the car. It seemed even larger, roomier than she remembered. "Have you ever been to Dante's?" he asked her.

"No."

"It's over toward Philly, a nightclub with dancing. Do you like to dance?"

She laughed. "I've never danced in my life, except the polka."

"No polkas here. But you'll catch on."

She didn't bother to tell him she had never been to a nightclub, either. This Dante's was extremely dark; there were red lights on tables covered with black tablecloths. "What would you like to drink?" Jerry asked, while a waitress in extremely skimpy clothing stood there waiting. Maria shrugged and started to panic. Would beer be inelegant? "Two Scotch-and-sodas." Jerry ordered. "If you don't like it, you don't have to drink it," he told her.

It wasn't that she didn't like Scotch; it was simply a new taste for her. Her relatives never served Scotch, and certainly she'd never bought any. But she was almost getting used to it when the band came out to play and Jerry told her that it was time to dance.

He led her to the dance floor and took her in his arms. "Watch your feet," she told him.

"I can't," he replied. "I'm going to be watching you."

Dancing wasn't as hard as she thought it would be. They did what Jerry called the fox trot. She got dizzy on the waltz, so he sat her down. The tango they just watched. Then he got up and taught her how to jitterbug. She felt he was tossing her around like a mop, but she finally got the hang of it. "You're crazy," she told him when he finally led her back to their table.

"My only exercise," he informed her. Then he ordered two more Scotch-and-sodas. She had to drink hers. She was thirsty.

In between the sets they talked. They talked about his sales trips and how lonely he got when he traveled. They discussed her work and how lonely it was when she got home. "Even with Mina?" he asked.

"Mina's not a man," she retorted.

"I've noticed. But I am." What did he mean? What did he want? And how did that coincide with what she wanted?

Around 12:30 he asked her if she was all danced out. Since she felt like she had been through a gymnastics contest, she said maybe she could do with a rest. By that time she had consumed three and a half Scotch-and-sodas. She let him assist her to the car. "I've had too much to drink," she told him.

"Nah."

"Yes. I'm telling you. You shouldn't have ordered them for me."

"You shouldn't have drunk them."

"I know." She lay back in the seat and let him whisk her home.

"Did you have fun?" he asked her.

"Oh, yes, Jerry. It was great. You know so many interesting things to do. You must have a fantastic life."

"Sometimes," he agreed. He pulled up in front of her apartment. "Is Mrs. Nowicki still up?"

"I doubt it."

"I didn't want her watching if I kissed you good night."

"Are you going to?"

"I think I just might." He leaned over, and she turned her head to face him. She raised her eyes and watched him come toward her until their lips met. She liked his lips. They were soft and sensual. They parted, and his tongue sank into her mouth. She leaned closer to him, not wanting him to escape. Her arms encircled his neck while his went around her under her coat, against the skin of her dress. "I taste the Scotch," he told her.

"Does it taste good?"

"Oh, yeah."

His lips went from her cheek to her neck. His hand went to the front of her dress, pressing against her breast, finding her nipple, teasing it. "No," she told him.

"Yes."

"Oh," she moaned.

"They're lovely."

"Jerry."

His other hand moved down along her hip, to her hem, her stocking. "No," she insisted. "Not in the car on a public street!"

"Mina?"

"She's asleep."

They got out of the car. He helped her up the steps to her entrance. She leaned heavily against him as she got out her keys.

The apartment was dark. "Where's the bedroom?" he asked her.

"Mina's in it."

"Great."

"The couch?"

"We'll learn how to make do."

Maria pulled away from him, looked in the bedroom at her sleeping daughter, then closed the door.

"She won't come out?" Jerry asked.

"I hope not."

"Come."

She went to him and let him take her in his arms. Her coat fell from her; his hands crushed her dress in his efforts to reach through the material. "Unzip it," she told him. The dress dropped. She was in her slip. She removed his jacket while he limply stared at her. Then he lowered the straps of her slip and her bra until she stood before him half-naked. "Jesus, you're beautiful."

She brought his head to her, moved it down to her nipples, so he could take them in his mouth. "I love it; I love it," she told him.

He pulled her to the couch and almost ripped the rest of the clothes from her, until she was naked. "You *are* a blond," he said.

"Did you think I wasn't?"

"Who knows nowadays."

"Are you going to undress?"

"Everything but the socks," he teased.

"Ugh."

She helped him take off everything. He was so hard, so beautiful; all she wanted was for him to fuck her. The couch was narrow; they tangled with each other. Jerry sat up and brought her with him. He placed her on his lap and went inside her. She shuddered and moaned and raised her eyes, pleaded with him to do it, do it hard. He watched her as he slowly thrust deeper and deeper into her. He enjoyed the way she twisted and turned upon him, trying to absorb every move he made. "Oh, baby, you are so good," he told her. "You are such a pleasure."

She said nothing. She was too busy savoring the hardness of him, the maleness, too busy feeling his hands on her hips, his lips on her neck, his hands pulling her hair to him. "Now," he said, and she hurried her movements, because she knew soon it would be over and she wanted all of him.

She collapsed against his chest, and he held her tight. "You, yes, you are a very good dancer," he told her.

He told her how beautiful she was as he dressed. She dropped her slip back on, put on her coat, and walked him to the door. "I'll see you?" she asked.

He leaned over and kissed her. "You bet."

32

A B S E N C E S   M A K E
T H E   H E A R T . . .

JERRY JANKOWSKI WAS NOT IN CHURCH THAT SUNDAY. NOR, DEspite her anxious waiting, did he come to Once Over Easy during the week for breakfast, for lunch, for anything.

She was angry. Oh, not at Jerry. She was the dumb one. She was the one who had let him have his way with her on their very first date. What was he looking for, a virgin? Probably. And she had proved she was anything but that. So had he, for that matter. She should have been coy with him, shy, trembling, anything but what she was. Now, she thought, he knew she was a whore. So why bother with her anymore? He had had what he wanted.

That entire week she was impossible. She had to be sweet to the customers at the deli, but after hours she spent her time snapping at Mina for every little thing she did. Mina soon slunk off and stayed out of her way. The only time she came close was when Maria cried, and then she tried to comfort her. It was no good.

But finally Maria took hold of herself, sat back, and thought. Why did she like Jerry? What was it? The car? The fact that he took her places? The fact that she desired him? Maybe she would desire anyone? Who knew anymore? So forget him.

By the end of the week she had made up her mind. She would never see Jerry again. So she had made a mistake. She had made plenty of mistakes in her life. What was one more? She had survived before. She would survive now.

When Mina went with Maria to confession on Saturday, Maria's penance took longer than Mina could bear. "What did you do?" she asked her mother.

"I was stupid. Don't be stupid, Mina."

"I get the highest marks in class," she bragged.

"Don't be boastful either," Maria warned. "Let's go. Let's go home."

Sunday morning they went to the eleven o'clock Mass as usual. Mina was in her best Sunday dress, carrying her white missal. Maria was in a sweater and skirt, wearing low heels. They slipped into a row about halfway down, the way they usually did, and began praying. Before they could finish and slide back onto the seat, Jerry joined them. "Hi," he said.

Maria looked at him as if he were crazy. He must have been, because he kept smiling as if nothing at all was wrong. Instead of attacking him in church, she became aloof, cold, monastic. Still, she could not help but feel the pressure of his hip as they went from their knees and back onto their seats throughout the Mass. She walked down the aisle for Communion, which was more than he did.

After Mass, he stepped out into the aisle to let her and Mina pass. She hurried up the aisle, Mina pushing after her, leaving Jerry in their dust. But not for long. "Hey," he called, as they stood outside, facing a rather drizzly Sunday morning, "what's wrong?" She didn't answer, so he went up to her and grabbed her arm to stop her. "You act as if you're not glad to see me." He'd finally noticed.

"Now why wouldn't I be glad to see you?" she asked.

"I don't know."

"Just because you didn't call, didn't stop in the deli—"

"Didn't send flowers?"

"Didn't do anything except make a fool of me." She turned and started for home. "Come, Mina."

He didn't follow her. She was glad and sorry at the same time. Mina trudged along behind her as the drizzle turned to rain. They had not brought umbrellas, and their coats seemed to absorb the water rather than protect them from it. When they reached their apartment, Jerry's Packard was parked in front. "The least he could have done was give us a ride home," Mina noted indignantly.

Maria ignored the car. She went up the steps and unlocked the door. Jerry had timed it perfectly so that he would be there when the door opened. "May I come in and talk to you?" he asked.

"I don't see what we have to talk about."

"Maybe we'll hit on something."

Reluctantly, regretfully, she let him in. He looked at Mina. "Hi, kid."

"Hi, Jerry." Mina looked at the two of them. "If you don't mind, I think I'll go into the bedroom and read." She turned and walked out of the living room.

"Smart kid," Jerry commented.

"Yes."

He put his hands on Maria's shoulders and said, "So, how've you been?"

She shrugged him off. "Fine."

"Look, I'm sorry I didn't get in touch with you. Last week I was traveling. One of our salesmen got sick. I had to take his territory *and* mine. This weekend my father wanted me to help paint the shutters. What could I say to him? I live there for free, after all."

"I don't recall asking you for an explanation."

"But you seem to expect one."

"Fine. Now I've heard it."

"So do you want to go out for lunch?"

"I'm really not in the mood. This rain is depressing."

"What do you want to do? Look, we have the whole afternoon. Let's not waste it."

"You're assuming that I don't have any other plans."

"Do you?"

"I told you, I see my relatives each Sunday."

"Let me drive you there, then. It will be better than taking a bus. It's awfully wet out there."

"Fine. Mina!" she called. "We're going now."

Mina excitedly came into the living room. "We're going out to the diner again?"

"Your mother wants to go see her relatives," Jerry said.

"Oh."

"Maybe next week. Okay, kid?"

Maria hadn't really planned to see the relatives this week, but she was stuck now. And then, when she got to an aunt's house, she had to answer questions about the man in the Packard and why she hadn't invited him in. She should have stayed home and napped.

On Tuesday, Jerry came into the deli, but another waitress got his table. Maria was filling in behind the counter. He ate breakfast, but before he paid his check, he asked her if he could see her on Friday night. "We'll go to the movies."

"Fine," she agreed. Maybe she shouldn't have; maybe she was still angry at him; but she also knew it would be more fun to go out on Friday than to stay in and listen to the radio.

He took her to a war picture, in which all the heroes were brave and valiant and all the enemies were dark and mustached and died in the end. One of the women died, too, but she had been a spy. So even though she had fallen in love with one of the good guys and could have made him happy, she had to step in front of him in the last ten minutes of the movie and take the bullet that was meant for him. As they left the theater, most of the women were dabbing their eyes, but not Maria. "That was the stupidest movie I have ever seen!" she told Jerry. "Why do people glamorize what was so horrible?"

"Maybe it's the only way they can deal with it."

"Do you glamorize your time in the Pacific?"

"I try not to think about it."

"That's best."

"Pizza?"

"What?"

"Would you like to go get a pizza?"

"What is it?"

He smiled at her. "How long have you been in this country?"

He took her down to an old section of town, well away from where she and her relatives lived. They went into a small restaurant that had red-and-white-checked tablecloths and old wine bottles with candles stuck in them and drippings all over the sides. "We'll start with basic cheese," he informed her.

They had to wait forty minutes for the pizza to be delivered. During that time they had a beer and Jerry asked her how the war was for her. "Lousy," she replied. "Impossible to talk about."

"Because of your husband?"

"I barely saw my husband after we were married. We were to-gether just long enough for me to get pregnant. Then he was off with the Home Army. The next thing I knew, he was dead, and I was getting ready to have Mina."

"Must have been quite a shock."

"There were a lot of shocks in those days. Kowitz, where I lived, was a farming village. We had a quota we had to fill for the Ger-mans. If we didn't have our quota ready, we knew they would kill us. Or force us to march across Poland into Germany, where they would use us as slave labor. That's why, seeing films like that, it's as if America didn't know what it was to suffer during the war."

"We knew. Our men died, too, you know. But, you're right. We weren't occupied. Were the Germans really as bad as the movies make them out to be?"

"Some of them were just young men, like my husband. You could see that they wouldn't have hurt anybody unless they were under orders to do it. But others loved the power they had over us, to take what they wanted, to kill, to destroy."

"Umm. Do you think about those years a lot?"

"Never. Not consciously. I'm glad I'm safe now."

"You don't miss your village?"

"Oh, sometimes," She smiled. "When the seasons change, I think of the farm. I liked the land. Here, everything is so close. I dream sometimes of having a little vegetable garden, some flowers, of going into the forest to collect wood for the fire." She laughed. "Silly, isn't it?"

He shook his head. "No."

"What do you dream of?" she asked him.

"Making it big. Having lots of money. Being successful. Having a family to come home to."

"You have all of that."

"The beginnings, maybe."

The pizza came. It was round and cut like a pie. Jerry removed a piece for her. The slice was dripping with cheese and tomato. How was she to eat it without smearing it all over her? He picked up his slice and started biting from the point. She followed suit. It was hot, but good.

"Delicious," she pronounced.

"You need an education," he told her.

"What do you mean?"

"You've got to stop living in this Polish ghetto, where your life is your relatives and your church. There's a whole world out there, you know. It's called the suburbs." He laughed.

She thought him crazy. "What are you talking about?"

"Someday maybe I'll show you. Tonight, eat your pizza."

When he took her home, she was determined that he would not set foot inside her apartment. She would not be so easy the second time. She had to make that clear. He got out of the Packard and came around to the passenger side to help her out. Then he escorted her up her steps. She turned. "Thanks for the lovely evening, Jerry." She held out her hand. He smiled, took her hand, and kissed the palm of it. The warmth of that kiss shot like fire up her arm and across her chest.

"May I come in?" he asked.

"I think not."

"Why?"

"Because."

"You don't want me?"

"I want you," she admitted.

"Look, we're not children."

"I don't want to be used. I don't want to be someone casual for you."

"A nice Polish girl like you? How could you be? Let me in. Let's make each other happy."

She let him in. Cautiously, she moved to close the door to the bedroom. She could see Mina's eyes wide open. Maria made a shushing movement with her lips. She wondered whether Mina remembered the other times, before they came to America.

"Is she okay?" Jerry asked.

"She's fine." Maria turned to him. Her mouth opened as she stared at his body. He held out his hand. "Come on over here," he said.

She let him take her in his arms and run his hands down her back, over her ass, under her dress. His hands were in her pants before they were anywhere else; his fingers were probing inside her. She moved herself so that she could press down on him, all the time struggling with her dress, pulling it and her slip over her head. She undid her bra, held her breasts up to his mouth, still feeling the pressure of his hand inside her. She moaned and exploded.

"Oh, baby, you really do need me," Jerry told her.

It was true. She needed him. She needed sex. But he had his needs, too. She unzipped his pants and slipped down on her knees. She took him in her mouth, circling her tongue around him, sucking on him until he came. Then he fell back on the couch, while she looked at him triumphantly.

"Nice," he told her. "Come on. Let's do it for real."

33

GAINING GROUND

SHE BEGAN TO SEE MORE OF JERRY AND LESS OF HER RELATIVES. She still went to church, for Mina's sake, but she stopped taking Communion. She had gone to confession several times, but the priest had insisted she stop fornicating, as he called it. It was impossible to stop fornicating with Jerry. She liked it; he liked it. And Jerry was right; they both needed it.

Maria realized that she was not playing it right with Jerry, that someday she would regret the fact that he always knew he could come to her apartment after a date. But he was something she had not had before in America, a steady fella, and she was enjoying it.

He did things with her that no one else would even consider. He drove her into the city, took her to plays, musicals, the best restaurants. And he did other things, too, which she would never have had the nerve to do herself. He once rented a motel room for her. That was the first time he had ever complained about Mina, how her presence in the apartment got in the way of their love-making. Usually, he was very good about Mina. Sundays were always family days, when they would do something together—go to the zoo or go to a ball game or find some forlorn meadow and pick wildflowers. Jerry was generous toward Mina, and Maria appreciated that.

Their relationship was three months old when Maria took Jerry to meet her relatives for the first time. He was very polite, but she could tell he found them overbearing. Well, who wouldn't? They had so many questions to ask him, he barely had time to eat. But he was good-humored and agreed with her that maybe he should go with her to the relatives once a month. Once a month suited her fine.

They had been seeing each other for a year, had just been through a false alarm, with Maria one week overdue, when Jerry decided it was time for her to meet his parents. She had never asked Jerry why she hadn't met them before. He talked about them, told her how they had married late. He was their only child, and they had been distressed about the failure of his first marriage. She hadn't pushed him into the introduction. She had a feeling that if they hadn't approved, he would have dropped her. She was afraid that if he dropped her now, no one would pick her up.

Maria spent a lot of time getting ready to meet the Jankowskis. She wore a gray suit she had bought especially for the occasion. It was much more conservative than most of her clothing. She worked on Mina, too, trying to get her frizzy dark hair to do something reasonable. It had been cut a month ago and already it was all over the place. If Mina's hair had only been blond and straight! She bought Mina a new pair of shoes and dressed her in a pretty little outfit from Sears. She looked adorable. Who wouldn't love her?

Jerry's plan was to go to church together, after which they would drive to his parents'. Maria was very careful during Mass. She didn't want to snag her nylons, have them run. "I hope they like me," she said to Jerry when Mass was finally over and they were getting into the Packard.

"Don't pay too much attention to them," Jerry warned her.

What was that supposed to mean? She sat in the car, her stomach churning. She looked back at Mina, who made a face at her. Somehow she had the feeling that this was not going to be a happy occasion.

Stefan and Ann Jankowski lived a few blocks from some of Maria's relatives. Their house was extremely neat. Their yard was fenced, and they kept a German shepherd in it. The dog barked ferociously as soon as it saw Maria and Mina get out of Jerry's Packard. "Sit, Rommel, sit!" Jerry demanded.

The dog didn't obey. It paced sullenly back and forth as Jerry led Maria and Mina up to the front porch. He rang the doorbell, to give his parents fair warning; then he opened the door and let Maria and Mina step in before him. The Jankowskis were waiting in a living room that had the shades drawn, to protect the carpet from the sun, and there were covers over the furniture, so that nothing could ruin the upholstery. Everything in the living room was neat and exactly placed. "Be careful," Maria said quickly in Polish to Mina, as they entered and waited to be introduced.

Maria decided halfway through dinner that Stefan and Ann Jankowski didn't believe in waste—not of money, food, or words. They spent most of the meal staring at her and, especially, Mina. Maria tried to talk to them, attempted to elicit some response, but they were having none of it. They answered in monosyllables, and Jerry did not help much. He sat and ate and seemed simply to stare downward. The only time the Jankowskis ventured a comment was to criticize Mina for not thoroughly cleaning her plate. Children elsewhere were not as lucky as she. Mina stared at her plate and looked as though she might cry. Maria felt like replying that her daughter wasn't used to eating in a mortuary, but she kept quiet for Jerry's sake.

After dinner, poor Mina couldn't go out to play. Rommel was outside, on patrol. No one could have been happier than the Prycheks when Jerry announced at about five o'clock that it was time to go home.

This time he did not insist on entering the apartment. He merely escorted them to the door and told them he would talk to them later. Mina walked into the apartment and exploded. "I hated them!" she screamed.

Maria looked at her daughter. Usually Mina could stand anything. "Why?" she asked. "What was wrong with them?"

Mina glanced at her mother and saw she was only teasing. "Oh!" she exclaimed. Then she went to her mother. They tussled and fell laughing on the floor. But Mina became serious again. "What if Jerry asks you to marry him? What if you have to go live with his parents in that house? Where will I go?"

"You'll come with me wherever I go. You're my daughter, after all."

"I can't live there, Mom."

"Me either."

"How did Jerry get such parents?"

"We can't pick our parents, darling. And besides, after today, don't worry. I might not even see Jerry. His parents didn't seem too impressed with us."

"You tried. You were very nice. And you looked so pretty."

"Thank you, darling."

"Even the dog didn't like us."

"Well, it was a German shepherd."

They laughed together, made themselves grilled-cheese sandwiches, then listened to the radio until it was time for bed. Maria put all thoughts of Jerry from her mind. Maybe, she hoped, he was adopted.

She didn't see Jerry the following week. She guessed that his parents had had a lot to say about her and Mina, none of it good. On Friday she was surprised at work when Stella Marks told her she had had a message from Jerry yesterday, just after she'd left, saying he would be dropping by her place at nine o'clock Saturday morning. Maria had kept Stella and Sam informed about her relationship with Jerry. Stella had been dying for details of the meeting with the parents. When she heard, she sent home an entire chocolate cake to make it up to Mina. "Some people!" she had consoled Maria.

Saturday morning Maria and Mina were having an argument that started when they got up and continued until Jerry knocked on the door at nine. "Hi," he said to them. He kissed them both and asked how they were doing.

Maria looked at her daughter. "Mina's feeling a little under the weather. So she wants to know exactly where we're going this morning."

Jerry smiled. "We're not going to see my parents. Does that make you feel any better, kid?"

Mina smiled. "I can be ready to go any time now."

Jerry laughed.

"I guess we didn't make too good an impression on your parents," Maria said.

Jerry gazed at her. "Go to your bedroom and look at your comic books for a moment," he ordered Mina. Mina retreated. "It's a fact that you were married before, that you have a child," he said in a very low voice to Maria.

Maria might have admitted, had she been totally honest, to a flash of regret. But she steadfastly said, "I can't change that."

"I like Mina. I think she's a terrific kid. Let's go. Mina! You can come out now."

Neither Maria nor Mina had any idea where Jerry was taking them. Being with him was always an adventure. But this time it didn't seem they were to travel far from Trenton. They drove a little bit past the outskirts of the city into an almost hilly area, where they rode over recently paved streets. "This is called Mill Trace," he told them. They drove up and down the roads that circled and curved around until Maria was sure they were lost. On either side of the roads were houses, some finished, some nearly finished, some just skeletons. "They left most of the trees standing," Jerry said. "When I saw the trees, I thought of you. Do you remember how you told me you used to go into the forest to collect wood?"

"I remember," Mina said.

"You couldn't," Maria corrected. "You were so young."

"I remember!" Mina insisted.

Jerry seemed to know exactly where he was going. He circled back and came to a house at the bottom of the hill, right near the entrance. He parked and told them to get out of the car. They went up the steps of the house. "More relatives," Mina whispered. But Jerry entered the house without knocking. The whole house was filled with carpets and drapes and furniture, but no people. Mina romped around, while Jerry and Maria walked each step, inspecting everything.

"Look at how big the kitchen is," Maria said.

"Country kitchen," Jerry told her. "So you can eat in it. It's facing east to get the morning sun. I understand most of the houses are built that way. Do you like the floor? It's tile instead of linoleum. More variety."

"Look, Jerry, there's a bathroom off the kitchen. But no bath in it."

"That's for company, a half-bath," he explained. "Let's go upstairs."

Mina was already up there, dashing around from one bedroom to the next. "Four bedrooms," she told her mother.

"There's a bath in the master bedroom and one for the other three. It's pretty big; it has a double sink," Jerry reported.

Maria looked around her in wonder. "It's a palace," she told him. She stared out the window. "Look, Jerry, it has a patio with a barbecue set on it. America is so wonderful. It has everything.

No one in Poland—well, definitely no one in Kowitz—has a house this grand."

"Do you like it then?"

"Sure. Who wouldn't?"

"Would you like to live in it?"

"This house?"

"Not this house. This is the model. But one like it?"

"Of course, I would like to live in it. It would be paradise."

"Well, say the word then."

She looked at him. "What word?"

"Yes."

"Yes?"

"When I ask you to marry me, say yes."

"Yes!"

"I haven't asked yet."

"Oh, Jerry!"

"Will you marry me?"

"Yes! Of course! But Jerry," she hesitated suddenly.

"Umm?"

"Where will we live?"

"I thought you understood. We'll be buying one of these houses. We're going to be moving into this Mill Trace subdivision."

She was even more cautious. "And who's going to be living with us?"

"You, me, Mina. And I thought, with luck, I could knock you up immediately, and we can have a few babies here and there. Sound okay?"

She opened her arms to him. "Sounds great to me."

Mina caught them hugging and kissing. "What's going on?" she asked.

Maria broke away from her husband-to-be. "Jerry's asked me to marry him."

"Where are we going to live?"

"In one of these houses."

"With whom?"

"Just us."

"Sounds fine to me."

"Gee, I guess my parents really made an impression on you two."

"Yes, Jerry," Maria agreed. "They certainly did."

34

PRIMIPARA

MARIA SAT IN DR. BRAUNSTEIN'S OFFICE AND LOOKED AROUND her. She had to be the oldest woman in the waiting room. It made her feel uneasy, being different. She smiled. She supposed that's what living in Mill Trace did to one, made one want to conform. Her pen was poised over the forms she was filling out. How many pregnancies? How many miscarriages? Did she have headaches, allergies, this or that? What childhood diseases had she had? How could she answer all these questions? How could she remember?

She hurriedly filled out the form as best she could, gave it to the receptionist, and waited. She knew she was pregnant. She didn't need a doctor to tell her that. But that's the way they did things here in America, her next-door neighbor, Marci Teller, had told her. She had to see a doctor every month and then, when it was time, go to the hospital. Marci should know. She had two children and was working on a third. What a racket that baby of hers made some nights. Maria wondered if it was American to be noisy.

She tried to read a magazine. No good. She was too nervous. She had been to a doctor only twice in America: when she first arrived and when she had her blood test for the marriage license. Of course, she had taken Mina to a pediatrician. The schools demanded that.

She wondered what effect this baby would have on Mina. Jerry was already ecstatic. Ever since the night of their wedding, they had been trying, trying so hard she got pregnant the second month. Jerry's parents couldn't possibly disapprove of her now.

Who were Stefan and Ann Jankowski to look down on her, anyway? All through the planning of the wedding, they treated her like a charity case. Ann Jankowski spent her time saying things like "Of course, the parents of the bride usually pay for this" or "Your mother should really be taking care of this instead of me." Maria was perfectly willing to plan and pay for her own wedding, but the Jankowskis preferred belittling her, rather than allowing her that independence. She had to hold her tongue for Jerry's sake.

177

The wedding itself turned out to be fun. Doreen Novoveski served as her matron of honor; Mina was the flower girl, over the Jankowskis' objections that it wouldn't look proper. All of Maria's relatives came, Jerry's also, and her friends from work. The Markses catered the affair. Mrs. Jankowski made some slighting remarks about how the deli owners were overcharging them, as people of their ilk will. Maria had to put her straight on that one, because she knew the Markses were charging only at cost. If she hadn't wanted to wed Jerry so much, she would have had second and third thoughts about a marriage that came with such in-laws. But Jerry was the one she fixed her mind on. He looked so handsome on their wedding day, and he told her she looked beautiful. She couldn't wear the traditional white, of course, but she did wear a quite nice powder-blue dress and the string of pearls Jerry had bought her for a wedding gift, despite the fact that she told him they had to save all their money for the house.

The honeymoon had been a riot. After leaving Mina with the Novoveskis, they had traveled to the Poconos and stayed at a hotel with a heart-shaped bathtub right in the room. How delicious! They had spent their days out hiking and horseback riding, which she thought was only for Cossacks, and their nights in the tub. If only all life could be like that!

There was a return to reality in a week's time, moving into their new house. Jerry went straight back to work, and she was left helping Mina adjust to a new school. Not that that was all Maria did. She spent plenty of time arguing with the builders about the little finishing touches they were supposed to put on the house, which they somehow never seemed to have time for until she threatened legal action. Those were the days when she could have let loose with a few choice words to Jerry, especially because he assumed she did nothing around the house all day except straighten all the magazines on the coffee table. But she couldn't complain to him; she wouldn't. He had given her all of this—the respectability of marriage, this house full of beautiful, new furniture, and, most important, a future to look forward to with joy, especially now that she was pregnant.

"Mrs. Jankowski?"

The door had opened, and a woman in white holding a pink smock looked out at the waiting room. "That's me," Maria said.

"Would you come this way, please?"

Maria rose, with a lot less trouble than many of the women in the waiting room. The nurse directed her into a small room and told her to take off everything and put the sheet over her. "Doctor will be with you in a minute."

A minute isn't long to strip, Maria thought, as she hurriedly divested herself of her clothing. She should have realized this "minute" would not be literal. She lay under the cold sheet for at least ten before Dr. Braunstein and his nurse made their appearance.

"How are we feeling today?" the doctor asked her.

Perhaps it was Maria's lack of experience with doctors, rather than the English language, that confused her. How was she to interpret "we"? She said nothing.

"A little nervous," the doctor answered for her.

After a while, she knew she had reason to be nervous. She had had many men feel her breasts and the insides of her, but none of them had done it on a padded metal table with another woman looking on. "Just relax," Dr. Braunstein said to her. It was hard going. "About three months along," he reported to his nurse. He had the nurse bring the chart closer, took another look at it, and then carefully reexamined Maria. He stood, threw his gloves in the waste pail, and said, "Why don't you get dressed, come into my office, and we'll discuss our course of action over the term of your pregnancy?" He smiled at her, then left the room.

Maria let the sheet slide from her and sat up. She felt queasy and decided right then and there that she didn't like playing doctor, being examined. She wasn't just some body, she was a person. Marci Teller had told her everyone used Dr. Braunstein, so he had to know what he was doing. But still, Maria didn't feel right.

She got dressed more slowly than she had stripped. It was especially difficult putting her nylons back on without having them look baggy. Then she opened the door and went into the corridor. She had to wait for a nurse to escort her to Dr. Braunstein's office. Then it was a good fifteen minutes before Dr. Braunstein himself made his appearance. He sat down in his chair, looked across at her, and smiled. She supposed she could see why women liked him. His hair was gray; he looked fatherly, unthreatening, though, after studying his unlined face, she believed his hair was prematurely gray. "So," he said. "You're pregnant. Are you happy about it?"

"Very," she said.

"And your husband?"

"Oh, yes. We wanted a child immediately."

"Immediately?"

"Ever since we got married."

"Which was?"

"About five months ago."

"So this is your second marriage?"

"Yes."

"You had one child by your first, your record states."

"Yes."

He sighed. "Was your first child adopted?"

She was startled. "No, of course not." Who was this man to be asking her such questions?

"Mrs. Jankowski," Dr. Braunstein started softly, "umm-let's see. You were born in Poland. Was your first child born in Poland, too?"

"Yes."

"During the war?"

"Yes."

"Mrs. Jankowski?"

"Yes."

"Do you know what the term *primipara* means?"

"No."

"It's a medical term used for a woman who is about to give birth to her first child. I'm afraid I'll have to use it medically on your chart."

"My husband—"

"He won't have to know, of course. No one sees the chart except medical personnel, and their professional ethics will not allow them to divulge information such as this. I don't know what the circumstances were—"

"The circumstances were that if I didn't take the child in, she would have been killed. The circumstances were that after the war she had no mother, no father, no one to return to. The circumstances are that no one must ever know she is not my child. Even she doesn't know. If I had understood you could know I never had a child before, I would never have come to a doctor."

"You can't have a baby alone in a field."

"Women have done it before."

"Not in America. Certainly, that would cause much more suspicion than coming in for medical care." He smiled. "Look, Mrs. Jankowski, your secret is safe with me. As far as I am concerned, you are having your second child. But medically, for your safety, your chart must say *primipara*."

"Fine. Just, please, don't ever let anyone know the truth."

Dr. Braunstein became her firm ally after their first conversation. He didn't even meet Jerry until she was taken into the labor room. Poor Jerry was so worried about the pain she was suffering.

Dr. Braunstein told him not to, that it was "always easier the second time around."

Maria certainly hoped so, because she couldn't stand to go through the first time around again. She didn't know such pain was possible. By the time the baby was delivered, she was too exhausted to be glad it was a boy. "A perfect baby," the nurse pronounced it. Maria did remember Jerry kissing her in the hallway, while she was being wheeled to her room. Then she almost didn't see the baby until she was leaving the hospital five days later. They named the boy Terrance Michael; they called him Terry.

Eighteen months later, she was in the delivery room again. Yes, it was easier the second time around. This time they had a girl, Kristin Brigida. She was a blond beauty right from the start. "Just like her mother," Jerry assured the wife he now worshiped.

Maria was happy with her family. Jerry was a successful salesman. She was a homemaker with two beautiful young children, and Mina, of course. They were living in the suburbs of Trenton. Now she really fit into the American scheme of things. More and more she was becoming totally American. More and more, no one, no matter how hard he searched, would be able to find Wanda Zbyszek in Maria Prychek Jankowski.

35

THE ENTREPRENEUR

"MINA," MARCI TELLER WAS SAYING, "YOU ARE SUCH A GOOD girl to be doing all that baby-sitting for your mother."

"She doesn't only baby-sit. She also helps me with the food," Maria corrected her friend. "She's twelve years old, after all."

"Well, I know kids who are twelve years old who just sit around all day reading movie magazines."

"She does that, too, Marci," Maria assured her.

"Good. At least she's normal. I was beginning to wonder if Mina was too good to be true."

"No need to worry about that. I think my daughter will be a typical American teenager."

"Then you've got problems," Marci remarked. "Listen, thanks

for making all these sandwiches. I don't think I could stand giving a party if I had to cater it all, too. You're a lifesaver. And Betty says you're catering for her tomorrow night?''

"Don't worry. I won't get bored. She didn't want sandwiches; she's serving something hot.''

"Well, she has the money for it. This is just for Al's bowling crowd, not his boss or anything. You know, your rates are too reasonable. Even though I'm benefiting from them, you should look into pricing. You could have a real business going here. Well, see you later. I've got to go vacuum one last time and hope the kids will understand I mean business with my threats.''

Marci left with her trays of food. Mina studied her mother. "You could make it a business," she told her.

"I'm not a businesswoman, I'm a housewife. Jerry makes the money in this family. Remember that, Mina. It's up to the man to support you.''

"But you said we got the patio furniture from your money?''

"My money is extra, for treats and things. And nicer clothes for you, now that you're budding.''

"Mom, please.''

"Well, it's hard to escape noticing. Here you are having your period and everything, like a real lady.''

"Ladies don't have periods; women do.''

"And correcting me all the time. You got that from living in America. In the old country—''

"Mom!''

Maria looked at her daughter. "Okay, you're right. I'll shut up. Come to me.'' She held out her arms to her daughter, and Mina quickly came inside them to receive her hug. "Marci is right, you know. I couldn't do any of this without you. If you weren't around after school to take care of Terry and Kristin, I think I might go crazy.''

"Next year Terry will go to kindergarten," Mina consoled her.

"God, I remember the first year we came here. Do you remember? When we were living at Mrs. Nowicki's? You went to kindergarten then, after the summer. And here you are, already in seventh grade. Soon you'll be in high school, and then—''

"And then college.''

"College? Not marriage?''

"Well, marriage, too. But college first, so I can learn to be somebody.''

"You are somebody.''

"I mean somebody who knows things. Do you think Jerry will send me to college?"

"Sure. Why not? If we have the money." Mina looked doubtful. Maria held her daughter tight once again. It was hard for Mina; Maria realized that. Not that Jerry deliberately slighted or ignored her. It was just that he now had his own two children, who were blond and beautiful like their mother. Mina was so dark and different. It was easy to see her as an outsider, especially lately, with her mood swings and her wisecracks. Everyone said that was part of growing up, but it could be trying.

The grandparents didn't help. Maria shouldn't have expected Stefan and Ann Jankowski to be anything but rigidly disapproving. She tried to console Mina with the fact that they barely recognized Maria's existence also. Maria knew it hurt Mina when they lavished gifts on Terry and Kristin for Christmas and Easter, birthdays and the like, but never thought to get anything for Mina. It was cruel. But they were cruel people. She didn't know how Jerry could come from such petty—and what did they have to be so proud about? It wasn't as if Stefan Jankowski were God.

"You know what, Mina?"

"What?"

"You've just given me a purpose for this catering madness."

Mina smiled at her. "What?"

"I'll save it for you, for college."

"I thought you said Jerry would pay?"

"I bet he will. But why take chances? What if something happens to his job? It won't be long now until you'll be going to college, really only a few years. So I'll put my money away for you."

"But you wanted to buy a new washing machine and—"

"No. College is what you want. College is what you'll get. Of course, this means we'll have to go about things a little differently."

"How?"

"Maybe we'll make menus, a set of menus with a set price, so people can see what's available. Naturally, we'll still be flexible, give people what they want, within reason."

They heard fighting in the background. "Terry, leave Kristin alone!" Maria shouted automatically. "I don't think I'm going to have another child," she confided.

"Sounds good to me," Mina said. "We have only four bedrooms anyway. And I really don't want to share with Kristin. She's such a baby."

"Almost three isn't a baby, Mina. Six months is a baby. Go take care of them now. I have lots of planning to do."

Plan she did. It was a real campaign. She told Sam and Stella Marks what she was hoping to do, and they were a big help, putting her in touch with other catering services, so she could judge how much she should really be charging. They also introduced her to wholesalers, so that her profits would be higher; and they showed her how to shop for bargains in the local farmers' markets.

Maria's time for her new business was limited. She still intended to be the perfect mother, which meant on many occasions dragging both Terry and Kristin with her on her early-morning shopping trips. While she was stuck at home with them, she perfected her recipes, especially her continental cuisine. Despite her promise to Mina that the money would go into a college account for her, Maria found herself spending plenty for a new double oven with gas burners. It bothered her a little that Jerry didn't even inquire about the three ovens in the kitchen. But then, he was so busy with his own work, the last thing he wanted to think about was problems at home.

When Mina came home from school, Maria could really get to work. Mina either helped her in the kitchen or kept the children out of the way. The Jankowski house was really in full swing from Wednesdays to Sundays, as word got around Mill Trace and then from Mill Trace to various other developments that there was this marvelous little foreign woman who could do wonders catering your party.

Maria always made the effort to see that her work did not interfere with what Jerry wanted. It took him a while to understand that he had to tell her a week in advance what he was planning to do during the day on Saturday and Sunday. Fortunately, mostly what he wanted to do was take care of the grass, read the paper, watch the ball games and the fights on their new television set. On Sundays he liked to take the kids to his parents after church. Mina, now that she was older, felt she could bow out. And Jerry wasn't so insensitive that he didn't know his parents would prefer Mina's absence— Maria's, too, which suited Maria just fine. She almost always had a Sunday brunch or a Sunday cocktail party to cater.

What amazed her was that she was getting rich. Oh, not rich like Jerry. He had become manager of the sales office, so he was home a lot more than he used to be, which she liked. But each Monday she went to the bank to deposit her weekend checks. And each Monday afternoon, she showed the balance to Mina. "Soon you'll not only be able to go to college, you'll be able to open your own," she joked with her daughter.

Mina was happy, except that lately she could see that her mother was working overtime, mentally at least. "What is it?" she asked on one of those Mondays.

"You know, I'm always going to be limited in what I can make."

"Menus?"

"No, money. Working out of the house limits me. If I had my own shop—you know how it is. Some of the women ask if I can bring glasses and plates. Some ask if I have anyone to serve, that sort of thing. Well, I can't arrange that from the house."

"So you want to take the money—"

"No, no. It's just a thought. Someday. But not yet. What would Jerry say? He expects his needs and the children's needs to come first. Which is right. I owe it to Jerry after all he's given to me."

"But you give him a lot, too."

Maria looked at her daughter. "What do you mean?"

"He gets his meals, clean laundry, two children that look like both of you, a neat house to come home to."

Maria smiled. "I'm afraid men don't see things exactly that way, Mina. They think those comforts come automatically with marriage. No. Maybe someday I can expand my business. But not now. Someday when Jerry's in a very good mood, I'll talk to him about it."

36

UPROOTING

MINA PUT TERRY BACK INTO BED FOR THE THIRD TIME AND CLOSED his door tight, after telling him to stay put. Kristin, the angel, was sleeping through all this. Meanwhile, her mother and stepfather were downstairs screaming at each other. Never before had Mina heard such anger between the two of them.

Terry was afraid. Mina didn't blame him. She was afraid, too. What could have brought about such a disaster? She sank down on the stairs, prepared to listen. She tried to pick up each word, as her mother and Jerry circled the living room, dining room, kitchen, and back again.

"You can't do this to me!" her mother was screaming, and not for the first time.

"I'm not doing anything to you! Can't you understand that? It's a move, a step up for all of us. It's more money; it's a better job. The company's newer; it's growing; there's more opportunity."

"In Dayton, Ohio? There's nothing there, Jerry. Nothing."

"You've never been there."

"I'd like to keep it that way."

"I've already accepted the job, Maria."

"Without telling me. Without even consulting me, you've accepted a job in another part of the country, far away from everything we know? All our relatives, all our friends, this house. This house that I love, that I've put my life into."

"We'll get another house. Houses are so much cheaper in Dayton, believe me. We'll get a house so big you wouldn't believe it."

"They have tornadoes in the Midwest."

"Maria."

"Jerry, I'm not going. You want another job, you can get another job here."

"I'm calling the real estate agent tomorrow. Can you have this house in order by tomorrow evening?"

"Jerry, I'm begging you."

"It'll be hard until we sell the house, I'll admit that. But then we're home free. The company's paying for a trip out for both of us to buy a new house. You'll like that."

"Jerry, listen." She began rustling in her desk drawer. "Look. Look at my books. You don't realize how well my catering business has gone. I've been thinking we can open a shop, just you and me. You can do the advertising and the selling. I can make the food, hire more people, and serve it, also. It will mean investing in silver, china, and glassware, but it will be worth it. I'm turning away customers, Jerry. This is the perfect opportunity for you and me to do something on our own, together. We can make a go of it, and it will be much better than your working for someone else."

"Maria."

"Look at my books!"

"Maria, what you have here is a hobby, something to keep you busy while the kids are small. I understand; and even though it's bothered me sometimes, I haven't stood in your way. But for you to suggest we try to make a living from your catering, well, as my mother would say—"

"Don't bring up your mother. Don't you dare! Jerry, this is not just a hobby; it's a living. Why won't you even look at my figures, listen to me?"

"What do you know about business?"

"I know a lot. I've been running one for years now. I've had to put up with all sorts of people, and I've managed to please them. I can do it, Jerry, and with your help we can expand beyond belief. And it will be ours. You won't have to depend on someone else."

"Just on you, right?"

"What's wrong with that? You depend on me; I depend on you. That's what I understood marriage was all about. Not your suddenly deciding to do something without telling me."

"I'm sorry, Maria, if I didn't make my intentions clear. I told you, after Bob got that promotion that should have gone to me, I was looking elsewhere. Now, what marriage means to me is supporting you and providing for you and the kids. Haven't I always done that?"

"Of course, Jerry. You know I appreciate all you've given me, but—"

"And if you think for one minute I'm going to depend on your catering business to support my family, you are just insane."

"Insane?"

"Insane," he repeated.

Mina sitting on the stairs, heard a loud crash. She didn't know what her mother had thrown at Jerry, but she could bet it was expensive.

"Maria! For Christ's sake!"

They were wrestling downstairs. Mina could hear the bodies shoving each other back and forth. Should she go downstairs and stop them? Should she call the police?

"Maria! Will you quiet down? Think of the children. What if they hear you?"

"*You* think of the children. What will it do to them to move all over creation? What about their family, their friends?"

"The children are too young to care. Kristin's only in kindergarten, Terry's in second grade. They'll adjust in no time."

"And Mina? She's in high school."

"She's been dragged from one continent to another. Going to Dayton isn't going to kill her. Besides, it might even be better for Mina. You're always complaining about the way my parents treat her."

"They don't *treat* her. They pretend she doesn't exist. They pretend I don't exist."

"So you won't have to worry about making excuses every Sunday not to visit them anymore."

"And my relatives?"

"Maria, people in the Midwest are very friendly. You'll love it. Give it a chance."

"Do I have a choice?"

"No, baby, you don't."

"I do if I get a divorce."

"Get a divorce? Christ, what do you have, your period or something? If you get a divorce, how are you going to pay for this house? How are you going to support the kids?"

"There's such a thing as alimony and child support."

"Are you trying to say you don't love me?"

"That's unfair."

"That's unfair? You bring up divorce, and I'm being unfair when I mention love. I've been through a broken marriage before, remember? I know what it's like. It's not fun. Look, Maria, I love you. We have two beautiful children. People in America move all the time. There's nothing to it. I know that because of the war and everything you want security. I can understand that. But I'm your security. As long as we're together, everything is going to be all right. Come on. Let's kiss and make up. I'll even sweep up the vase Mother gave us for Christmas last year."

Maria laughed between her tears. "That felt good."

"Love me?"

Mina heard them smooching and figured the worst was over. Trying not to make the landing squeak, she got up and went back to bed. Moving to Ohio? What was she to make of that? She knew they made tires in Ohio, that Columbus was the capital—wasn't it?—that the state bordered Lake Erie. But what sort of people lived there?

Like her mother, she didn't want to move. They were citizens now, she and her mother. They had been through the ceremony, been congratulated by the judge himself, received an American flag and a copy of the Declaration of Independence and the Constitution. But sometimes the fact that they were citizens didn't matter to other people. One time, in school, when they asked where she had been born and she told them Kowitz, Poland, they started calling her a Communist. She had tried to explain that they had fled Poland right after the war, but none of her friends knew which war she was talking about. They all thought it was the Korean War. Then they started accusing her of being a Russian spy. Mina had told her mother about it, but her mother had laughed it off, telling Mina that sometimes she had the same problem with some of her customers. Some people were just plain ignorant, her mother said.

Her mother was a very tolerant person. Maybe it was from living through the war, having all those horrible experiences in the DP camps. Mina only vaguely remembered them. In the camps they were always trying to keep warm. That Mina remembered vividly. And the waiting.

Tolerance. Her mother, in a way, wasn't like the rest of the relatives. Mina could recall one day when she had come home from catechism class and had said something nasty about the Jews. Her mother had been really angry at her. "Why did you say that?" she had asked.

"Everyone says that," Mina had defended herself. "After all, the Jews killed Christ."

Maria shook her head. "Is that what they teach you in church here?"

"Yes. That's what the nuns say. They always tell us to be thankful we weren't born Jewish, because then we would be guilty of the greatest crime ever committed."

Her mother had stopped her baking and sat down with Mina, taking her hand. "There was once a time when I thought as the nuns do," she said. "That the Jews were responsible for killing Christ; that if the harvest was bad, a Jew had spat in the field; that you had to watch your babies, because Jews were on the lookout for babies to kill for Passover. But when I got older, I realized how stupid these folk tales were. Because people believed them, they led to much evil."

"What evil?"

Maria looked at her daughter. "You don't know?"

"No."

"Someday you'll know. You'll ask and I'll tell you."

"Why not tell me now?"

"Because you're too young to hear. When you want to know, that will be time enough. In the meantime, you should try pointing out to the nuns that the Romans killed Christ. But I think the true theological belief is that we all killed Christ, because he died for our sins, so we could be saved. And also remember, when you make these remarks about the Jews, that when we came to America, Sam and Stella Marks hired me, not caring that I was Polish Catholic. It was their food we had at our table. Also, Dr. Braunstein, who delivered your brother and sister, is Jewish and a very good man. There are not Jews and Catholics. There are simply good people and bad people."

"But Jerry and the rest of the family—"

"I don't care what they say. Their ignorance doesn't have to be yours. I don't ever want to hear you say anything bad about the

Jews again. Respect for other poeple—that's what America is all about.''

So the next time the nuns brought up the fact that the Jews killed Christ, Mina had objected and pointed out that it was actually the Romans. She had been sent to Father Schoen, who had listened to her interpretation of general guilt for Christ's death and had replied, ''As far as I'm concerned, it was the Jews.''

Mina repeated this to her mother, and Maria had simply laughed. ''Just remember what I told you,'' she warned.

So now Mina was in trouble with the kids at school for being Polish and the kids at religious education for being tolerant. Maybe it was time to move to Dayton. Jerry was right about one thing at least: they wouldn't have to see his parents anymore. Yes, she was willing to give Dayton a try.

The next morning, Mina wanted to tell her mother it would be all right, but Maria was not in the kitchen. Jerry was there and told Mina to make breakfast for the children. ''Where's Mom?'' she asked, as casually as she could. Her mind was racing overtime. What if Jerry had killed her during the night? Maybe they had continued their argument after she fell asleep and in a fit of passion—

''Your mom's all tired out. It's best to let her sleep this morning. Walk the kids as far as the crossing guard before you go to school, okay?''

''Fine, Jerry.'' She waited until after he had left the house for work, and Terry and Kristin were busy with their cereal. Then she sneaked upstairs to her parents' bedroom. She opened the door and could see her mother lying on her stomach, hair straggled like a mop on the pillow. She tiptoed inside and stood watching. The blanket rose and fell regularly. Her mother was obviously alive. Mina guessed it was safe to go to school.

When she got home, Maria was cleaning. Her eyes were red. She had been crying. But she said. ''We've been waiting for you, Mina. I've an announcement to make.'' Mina sat down with Terry and Kristin at the kitchen table. ''Your father and I have decided— well, your father has had a terrific job offer. But it means that we are going to have to move. We'll be going to Dayton, Ohio. Won't that be exciting?'' They simply stared at her. Maybe she had not put enough enthusiasm in her voice. ''Now,'' she continued, ''I've cleaned your rooms, Terry and Kristin, and I expect them to stay clean. We have to sell this house so we can buy a new one in Ohio. Okay? So every night before you go to sleep, you pick up your toys and your clothes. And, Mina, you're going to have to help keep the whole house clean. I'm still planning to run my business until the very last day here.''

The real estate agent came by that night. She assured them they would have no trouble selling a house in the Mill Trace subdivision, because the schools were so good and the grocery stores convenient. She suggested that they get rid of the extra oven in the kitchen, but Maria held firm; it would stay until they moved.

The house was sold within a month. The family who bought it had three boys. One of the boys, the oldest, had already decided what changes he would make in Mina's room. That was upsetting, but it wouldn't be her room anymore in June, when school ended and they moved out.

Time went faster than Mina would have wished. Her friends at school gave her a party, at which everyone signed an autograph book they had bought her. They had Cokes and pizza. It was Mina's favorite party. The rest of the farewells were with the relatives. They had to go to each relative's house once, even though they kept seeing the same people over and over again. It got really tiresome. How many times can you say good-bye?

When the moving van came, Mina knew the good-byes were final. Despite all the promises about how they would see each other frequently, Mina didn't believe it. Her relatives hardly ever left Trenton.

The neighbors were the last to bid them farewell. Together they all walked through the empty house, reminiscing about the good times, the new babies, the barbecues, the ball games, the car pools.

Jerry was waiting by the car. Terry and Kristin were already in the back with a bag of food and some coloring books. Mina would have to supervise them all the way to Dayton, however long that would take. She would have to keep them quiet, since Jerry couldn't stand to drive when they were fighting with each other.

The Jankowskis pulled away from the curb, waving wildly to those standing there, yelling promises to write, especially at Christmas. Then they were headed toward the interstate.

"I was happy here," Maria said sadly. "For the first time in my life, really happy."

37

WAR AGAIN

"NOT WITH YOUR FINGERS, RON. EAT WITH A FORK," ELIZA suggested to her three-year-old son. "Yuk! Look what you're doing. Is that any way to eat a potato?"

"Looks like fun to me," Yehuda said, supporting his son with a twinkle.

"And you," Eliza ordered, "can put away your accounts during the evening meal, at least."

"Yes, ma'am." He threw his account book on the couch. "Now. How was school today, Ami?"

"Sassi threw sand in my face."

Yehuda looked at five-year-old Ami. Then he turned to Ron. He had to admit that neither of the boys looked very much like him. They both had their mother's darker hair, her beautiful brown eyes, her translucent skin, not yet hardened by the desert air. He loved them so terribly that when he looked at them he ached. "He threw sand in your face," Yehuda repeated. "Did you toss some back?"

"Mommy said to tell the teacher."

"Oh, God, Eliza! What are we raising here? Next time Sassi throws sand in your face, you throw pebbles in his. He throws a rock; you throw a boulder. If that doesn't flatten him, then you can tell the teacher."

"Your father's just joking, Ami."

"Hell, girl, we've got to toughen him up for the paratroopers. We want none of this sissy European crap that you're teaching him. Our sons are the valiant."

"Have such escalating tactics worked against the fedayeen?" Eliza asked.

Yehuda shook his head and shivered. Then he dug into his potato pancake, fried with onions, just as he liked it. "Don't ask me what to do about the fedayeen. Fortunately, I'm not in the government."

"But you're still in the army," Eliza said almost tensely.

"Aren't we all?" His eyes slid over to the newspapers lying on a side table. Small wars were being waged along Israel's border with Jordan, where the Arab fedayeen had been most active. Terrorist attack was followed by military operation was followed by terrorist attack. "They'll have to do something about it soon," he said to his wife.

"What, Daddy?" Ami asked.

"The bad people."

"Like Sassi?"

"Even worse than Sassi, if that's possible." Yehuda teased.

It was October 25, 1956, and life in Israel was not easy. Many of the friends Eliza and Yehuda Barak had made in the late 1940s and early 1950s had already left Israel for greener pastures: South America, North America, Australia, South Africa, some even back to Europe. These friends wrote glowing letters of the lives they were leading, full of economic prosperity with no threat of violence, no bomb shelters to run to. But Yehuda was practically born to his commitment, and Eliza had made hers after the war, in Poland and in the DP camps of Europe. Israel was their homeland. They saw no reason to turn away from it.

And, although life wasn't easy for the Baraks, it wasn't as difficult as it had once been. Pension Bracha was a success. Yehuda said they owed it all to Ben Gurion. He had taken to vacationing in Tiberias. True, he vacationed in the center of town, not on the heights where Pension Bracha lay, but his time there gave others the incentive to try Tiberias. After all, if it was good enough for BG, it was good enough for everyone.

The Baraks continued to employ Shimon and Alice Ben Elezar. The Ben Elezars now had two children, who chased around with Ami and Ron. Pnina still worked for them, along with Orit, a cousin of hers. Best of all, they had hired Yamima, another Yemenite woman, to cook for their restaurant, which caused many of the locals, when they had money for a night out, to come to Café Eliza for some spicy food.

Their customers were not rich. Pension Bracha wasn't that sort of hotel. But they were getting many families who had enough money to take a vacation. They were booking the middle-class tourists from Europe, occasionally an American or two, though Americans generally went for the newer, more modern establishments. They were doing well enough for Yehuda to suggest that they buy the house next to them, to create an annex for Pension Bracha.

Eliza was totally against it. It would mean reinvesting all their capital, and then what would happen if there was an emergency? She made a cogent argument against the deal, and then Yehuda said, "I've already signed the contract." Sometimes she had to wonder exactly what kind of partnership he considered their marriage to be. Oh, how she raged against him. Oh, how sweetly he listened. But it did not change his mind, nor was he willing to investigate breaking the contract. He and Shimon were going to work on the addition over the winter months, in an effort to have it ready in time for Passover. They would have to hire a plumber though, because it was Yehuda's dream in this new purchase of his to put a bathroom in each of the rooms for rent. Also, the wall between the houses would be knocked down, to allow more space for Pension Bracha's private garden and an expansion of the patio, so more diners could be serviced at Café Eliza.

Eliza was nervous. Yehuda was wagering so much on the future. She didn't count on a future. She still couldn't believe that a future was a certainty. The past always haunted her whenever she tried to plan a future. When she envisioned her children growing up through the years, passing through all the trauma and joys that life would offer, she forced herself to cut off her thoughts immediately. She could not count on life being there. Out of nowhere, life could easily be snatched away by forces no one could foresee. She had lived long enough to see destruction over and over again.

But perhaps she should keep her mouth shut about Yehuda's plans. He had faith in a future. She shouldn't let her fears infect the rest of the family.

"Did you read the papers about Hungary this morning?" Yehuda asked her, drawing her back into his real world.

"Disgusting."

"It reminds me of how we would have had to fight the War of Independence if we hadn't been lucky enough to get supplied from Czechoslovakia, of all places. I don't think they'd give us the time of day now. Look what the Russians are doing to those poor Hungarians. Tanks against Molotov cocktails. That's the sort of battle the Russians love fighting." He shook his head. "Thank God for France."

"They have been generous with the arms supply," Eliza agreed.

"More than generous," Yehuda said. "Yael said she can see armaments from France being unloaded in Haifa's harbor daily now. And I've got it from a friend that France is flying in shipment after shipment of armaments near Tel Aviv."

"Well, we need every gun, every bullet."

"We need every plane," he corrected her. "Air power. That's what we don't have enough of. And we need the pilots, we need— uh."

"We need, we need. You talk about the army as if it's our hotel," she teased. "Thank God you're not in charge of that, too."

"Can we go out and play?" Ami asked.

"Yes. But don't bother any of the guests."

They watched their two sons race out the back door into the garden. "Pretty soon I'll be putting them to work in the garden," Yehuda said.

"I'm sure they'll love that."

"They spend hours there now. I'll give them a hoe, a rake. What could be healthier? Speaking of hours, do you think now's the time to—"

"I can't believe you. Right after dinner."

"Can you think of a better time? The kids are out of the house. You don't have to be quiet. I can hear you moaning when I—"

"You know, Yehuda, ever since you've made that deal to buy the house next door, your interest in sex has increased. Do you find financial deals so stimulating? Or are you trying to exhaust me so I won't say anything?"

"I'm trying to keep your mouth busy in productive pursuits."

Eliza was trying to be angry, but she laughed instead. "Leave the dishes on the table," Yehuda suggested.

She crumpled her napkin and rose. Yehuda was waiting for her. He took her by the hand, then put his arm around her, wrapping her closer. His other hand touched her neck. He kissed her. Someone knocked on their door. "Shit!" Yehuda said under his breath.

"Alice is at the desk this evening, isn't she?" Eliza asked. "There shouldn't be a problem."

"But there always is, isn't there?" Yehuda said, totally annoyed. Before composing himself, as he usually did, he flung open the door. A man in fatigues stood there. "Coyote," he said. Then he turned and walked quickly out of the hotel.

Eliza stared open-mouthed at her husband. "Turn on the radio," he told her. She twisted the knob to Gallei Zahal. "Men of Tibet, Sons of the Soil, Sweet Rivers—" The voice droned on.

"Get the kids in so I can say good-bye."

She stared at him as he walked into their bedroom alone. Then she hurried to the back door. "Ami, Ron, come in now." She heard their complaints from the bushes. "This instant!" she insisted.

The children reluctantly came in, dragging sand with them. Yehuda had changed into his fatigues. He had his beret and his insignia in his hand when he came out to face his sons. He knelt down and beckoned them into his arms. He held them tight, kissing first one and then the other. "You help look after things now, boys. I have to go away for a little while."

"To reserves, Daddy?" Ami asked.

"Yes. Something like that. So you be good. I don't want to come home and hear that your mother had to scream at you all the time." He gave each one more kiss and stood up. Eliza came forward into his arms. She held him tight and felt every bone in his body. "You owe me one," he told her.

"You be careful. I want you to collect."

"Don't worry. You know me."

"I know I want to see you again when this is over."

"Don't worry! You won't have a choice. Get to my parents; give them my love."

"Right."

He was about to pull away, but then he squeezed her tight. "I love you, Eliza."

"I love you, too."

He hurried out the door, was gone. Eliza stood by the table alone, with her two children watching her. I love you. What kind of phrase was "I love you?" I want you, I need you, I worship you, I hate you, I argue with you. You can make me happy, sad, desperate, ecstatic; you are my world. Any of those would have been more accurate. "I love you" was too simple, too overused. Did Yehuda know how much her life was intermingled with his? Did he know she had no life without him?

"Eliza?"

"Alice?" She looked at Shimon's red-headed wife, standing in the doorway. She tried to concentrate, to come back to earth.

"What's happening?" Alice asked.

Gallei Zahal droned on; each code word meant more men leaving families, heading toward mobilization points throughout Israel.

"Alice!"

She turned at the sound of her husband's voice. "Shimon! Who's with the children?"

He ignored her. He was already dressed, ready to go. "Did anyone hear Wolf Pack?"

Eliza shook her head. "I wasn't listening. Someone came and got Yehuda."

"I better go anyway. I probably missed it. Alice—"

"Go on, Alice. Go back to your children. I'll take care of the desk tonight," Eliza told her.

Shimon grabbed Alice by the hand and pulled her outside, where they could have a quiet moment alone before he had to leave. Eliza tried to think of herself as a woman of experience. After all, she had been fighting half her life. Alice might need her support. But Eliza felt weak and worried, as if she had never been through this before.

"Will Daddy be home tomorrow?" Ron asked, as Eliza headed toward the front desk.

She turned back to her younger son. "I don't know when Daddy will be home, Ron. There's going to be a war."

38

OPERATION KADESH

THE SINAI CAMPAIGN DID NOT BEGIN UNTIL FOUR DAYS AFTER THE troops were mobilized. All during those days, everyone in Israel assumed Zahal was going to attack Jordan. Eliza certainly was one of those making that assumption. After all, most of the fedayeen attacks had come from across the Jordanian border. Jordan assumed the Israeli army had her in its sights; and there were vague rumors in the newspapers that if Jordan was attacked, Britain would come to her rescue. An Iraqi division was already supposedly marching into Jordanian territory to help defend the country. Egypt and Syria both had military pacts with Jordan. If they came in, it would be war on three fronts again, just as in the War of Independence.

The foreign guests staying at Pension Bracha mostly decided to cut their visits short. Eliza couldn't say she was offended. She had enough on her mind, wondering what was happening to Yehuda. Where was he? Alice was worried about Shimon. Everyone working at the hotel had someone to worry about.

On the night of October 29, there were rumors that Israeli paratroopers had landed in the Sinai. Both Eliza and Alice were puzzled. The Sinai was a long way from the Jordanian border. On October 30, when they woke up, it was clearer that Jordan was not the target after all. It was to be the Sinai Peninsula, Gaza, and Egypt's Nasser.

Some called it the Hundred Hours' War. That's how long it took for the Israeli army to sweep through the Sinai Peninsula from Gaza almost to the Suez Canal, taking Sharm el-Sheikh. The Egyptian soldiers were surrounded, captured, and interned; they were beaten back; they were deserted by their officers and forced to flee singly into the wasteland of the Sinai, where they looked for Israelis to surrender to before the Bedouin got to them.

Five days after Operation Kadesh began, Shimon Ben Elezar came back to Pension Bracha, to a hero's welcome. He shrugged it off. "Sorry to disappoint you women, but I was stationed along the Jordanian border." It was a letdown for him, perhaps, but not to Alice, that he did not see action. Despite their military agreements with Egypt, neither Jordan nor Syria had answered when Nasser called.

"And Yehuda?" Eliza wanted to know. "What have you heard of him?"

"Nothing." Shimon shrugged his shoulders. "I'm infantry, Eliza. That's not Yehuda's specialty."

What was his specialty, Eliza wondered. After the War of Independence, he had been placed in an artillery unit—because of his math aptitude. Maybe he was still in the Sinai, but it was hell waiting for him. She knew he was alive and walking around, because if he hadn't been, she would have been notified. A hundred and eighty families had had their men taken from them by this war. She thanked God hers wasn't one of them.

With Shimon back, running the hotel became easier, though there were no more than a handful of guests. She still went to the market every day to meet the truck from Kfar Hannah. She had an agreement with them for their best produce. Dvora, her old boss, had arranged it. Eliza was glad, since it allowed her to keep in touch. Kfar Hannah had lost one man, a captain in the paratroops. But as much as his death tempered the victory, it did not stand in the way of the elation all those in the market felt. They couldn't believe what Israel had accomplished, what a mighty nation they had become. Finally the Jews were a people to be reckoned with.

Yehuda came home ten days after Operation Kadesh was completed. In those ten days Israel had returned to its usual state, from elation to the biting of nails. Diplomatically, all countries had turned against her. France and Britain—Britain especially—had lost their nerve and bungled what was supposed to be a three-way action to free the Suez Canal from Nasser's nationalization. In the United Nations, only France still stood at Israel's side. The United States was making all sorts of threats, as were the Russians. What had happened to Israel's splendid victory? She would have to withdraw. She would receive nothing from the foray into the Sinai.

The first thing Yehuda did when he got home, aside from kissing his sons, was collect what was owed him before he left. Eliza had him take a long hot bath first. "What *is* that smell?" she asked him, when the bath seemed to have done no good.

"Axle grease."

"Come on. I'm serious."

"I thought you'd be glad to see me no matter how I smelled."

"You know I am, but honestly."

"Honestly, it's axle grease, and motor oil and all that sort of stuff. You wouldn't believe what the Egyptians left in the desert."

"All their men?"

"Aside from that. Tons of ammunition. So far, we've counted five thousand tons and there's more to go. Fuel, artillery, about a hundred tanks, and God knows how many jeeps and troop carriers. Which we desperately need. Do you know that a good number of our soldiers couldn't get to the front because we didn't have the transport?"

"I read about it. So that's what you've been doing? Working in the desert to bring back equipment?"

"Yes. Ever since the army swept through there. The first few days, I was down in Tel Aviv, coordinating with the French. We've got to get more planes, Eliza. Without French air cover, we might have been lost."

"Do you have to go back?"

"Yes. Of course. Why? Has something happened here?"

"I miss you."

"I miss you, too, but my unit needs me. And anyway, I'm in no danger; so you don't have that to worry about. Hey, did I tell you I climbed Mt. Sinai? It's so beautiful down there, Eliza. I'm going to hate giving it up."

She looked along his naked body as he lay there content, satisfied, maybe even anxious to get away again. "So we're going to have to give it up?"

"Ben Gurion's working to get something out of it, to salvage some of our aims. But with the Americans and the Russians—"

"Both of whom seem to be forgetting the way Russia is rampaging through Hungary," she protested.

"It's easier to gang up on Israel than on the Soviet Union. Do you think I should wake the kids before I go?"

"If you want. You're going to stay the night, aren't you?"

"I had planned on it." He smiled. "Why? Did you have someone coming over?"

She hit him. "Don't even joke about that. You don't know how worried I was. I mean, you could have been anywhere."

"I was. I was in Tel Aviv."

After breakfast the next morning, Yehuda left. Four days later, he was home for good. Militarily, the Sinai campaign was over. Diplomatically, it dragged on for months, until March 1957, when Israeli troops withdrew from the Sinai and Gaza, and United Nations soldiers took their place in Sharm el-Sheikh and Gaza. What Israel had gained was a lot of confidence, and also freedom of navigation through the Straits of Tiran and diminished fedayeen activity from Gaza. What it had lost was the respect of many of the nonaligned nations, who now saw her as an imperialist power because of her link with Britain and France in the Suez escapade.

But what did politics matter, as long as there was peace, for a while?

39

CAPTURING THE DEVIL

THE ALARM RANG AT SIX IN THE MORNING. ELIZA WOKE QUICKLY and turned it off. Yehuda slept, still and happy at her side. She was already tense. The night's sleep had done her no good. She couldn't understand her husband. They had enough. Why did he want more? He was always taking chances with the money they had accumulated from their hard work. She was willing to be just wealthy enough to have food to eat and a place to sleep, and to give the children whatever they really needed. But Yehuda didn't seem satisfied with her modest desires. Maybe it wasn't the money. Maybe it was a game to him. She didn't know. All she knew was that she could not go on like this much longer, could not suffer this strain in silence. She wasn't some high-powered manager. She was a simple woman who wanted simple things. Like peace and security. And love. Yehuda was so busy in the marketplace. Did he have time to love her anymore?

Perhaps she got her answer when he turned over toward her and placed his hand on top of her warm breast. "What time?" he muttered.

"Time to get up."

He moaned.

"You can stay in bed if you want to. I'll get the children ready for school."

"I want to get the sprinklers on in the garden. And we have that group of English tourists that wants picnic lunches. I have to make sure Pnina packs the right things."

He was out of bed. Another day had begun. Pension Bracha had expanded to thirty rooms. Even when there weren't enough tourists to fill the rooms, there was Café Eliza, which opened for lunch and dinner. Because they hired only Yemenite cooks, Café Eliza had quite a reputation for "authentic" Israeli food among the UN people who, when they weren't out checking on truce violations, seemed to be making Tiberias their second home. The breakfast room operated at Pension Bracha from 6:30 to 10:00 for hotel guests only. The front of the Pension Bracha Annex, as Yehuda liked to call the house next door, bought four years ago, had been converted into a milk bar, with several tables and a counter to stand at. It opened at 6:00 and stayed open until 12:00 at night. Eliza was in charge of the entire operation. It was simply too much for her.

She had tried to tell this to Yehuda when he was planning to buy another hotel, closer to town, whose owners desperately wanted to retire. What bargaining went on there! Yehuda gave here a blow-by-blow account each night, while she sat nervously pondering what she would do if he actually bought the place. She felt somewhat sure he wouldn't, because the owners were asking a lot for good will. But in the end, they figured that good will wasn't as important as getting out with a few years left to enjoy their retirement. So Yehuda and Eliza Barak had another hotel! They kept the old name, Gan Hofesh—"In case there really is any good will left," Yehuda said. She saw herself running back and forth between the heights and midtowns; but Yehuda informed her he had spoken to Shimon and Alice, and they had agreed to take over management of the new hotel.

Half of Eliza was happy about this development. It was much better for Shimon and Alice and their growing family. But they had been with Pension Bracha from the beginning. She didn't need to give them any instructions; they knew the whole routine as well as she did. Further, they were her friends. Whom would she talk to now that Alice would not be there? Yehuda? He was always busy with his deals.

Eliza showered and dressed, then went to make sure that the breakfast room would open on time and that everything offered would be fresh. Today she hoped there would be no crisis, no cook quitting mid-shift because one of the guests sent back his omelet.

Everything looked fine. She made up a tray and carried it back to their living quarters, where Ami and Ron were getting up, getting washed, getting ready for school. It was May. They wore only T-shirts and shorts. Both were looking forward to the end of June, when school would be over and they could spend the summer on their bikes, traveling throughout their part of the Galilee.

Eliza got the children off while Yehuda sat reading the morning paper, and then she went over once again to check on the breakfast room. She discovered that a French couple wanted breakfast in their room. She had to go up and explain to them that room service wasn't possible at Pension Bracha, since breakfast was a buffet. She had learned it was best to do this sort of thing herself; tourists could be rude and incredibly cruel. She had lost plenty of part-time help from the actions of ill-mannered tourists, while she felt she was equal to their threats never to come back again. This couple took it rather well. Eliza saw that the woman had a number tattooed on her arm. Maybe that made it easier for her to adjust.

When the French couple came down, Eliza watched them. She didn't know if the man was a survivor, but she could almost bet on it. They took more food than they could eat. They stuffed the rolls into their pockets. Eliza thought of her mother and her sister, her sister's children. How had it been for them? Should she have been there with them? Had it been wrong to flee from the ghetto and fight with the partisans? Why had she survived?

"Eliza?"

She turned.

"Problems?" Yehuda asked her.

"May I make an appointment to speak to you sometime?" she asked, almost sarcastically. It was safer to come back to her present problems.

"Sometime? We can do it now."

"I don't know if you're ready for it now. Maybe I'm not either."

He looked at her and smiled. "Okay. Now you've got my curiosity going. You know I won't be able to do anything until you tell me what the problem is. Come on. Let's go back to our place."

Why did he take her in his arms and kiss her when they got back to their living quarters? Sometimes he did not play fair. "This isn't our problem," she told him.

"Umm. You taste of butter and jam."

She took a step back. "Yehuda, have you noticed something about the way we live now?"

"Uh-oh. I guess this is serious."

"Yes. It is to me." She sank down on the sofa. "Maybe you married the wrong woman."

He looked almost scared. "What in God's name do you mean by that?"

"I'm not the same sort of person you are."

"I know. You're a woman, I'm a man."

"Look, Yehuda, please listen. When we started all this"—she waved her hand around—"it was fun, it was exciting, mainly because we were doing it together."

"And we were young and innocent."

"We were neither young nor innocent, either of us. Let's remember that. Now, I don't know. You go off each morning, God knows where."

"To look at real estate. You do know that, because I tell you."

"And you leave me with this hotel, the restaurant, the snack bar. I'm in charge. Of everything. I don't want to be in charge. That's not what I want out of life. Maybe some days I'd like to be able to sleep past six. Maybe there are things I'd like to do with the children. But I'm tied to this hotel. It would have been fine if you had simply stuck with Pension Bracha, but all the time you're full of improvements, making everything bigger and better. All the money we've gained, you've reinvested. For what? So we can work harder?"

Yehuda was annoyed. "I've always told you about my plans."

"That's exactly it! You've told me. And when I've objected, you've put your arms around me and told me again that everything was going to be fine."

"And everything is fine. Do you realize how much we're worth now compared with when we got married and had to borrow from my parents? My parents, dear, who've run a grocery store ever since they arrived in Israel. Talk about hours. The only day they have free is Shabbat."

"Well at least they have that," she shot back.

"I didn't realize you were overworked."

"Don't put it like that, Yehuda. If we were overworked, it would be fine."

"You mean you think I'm not pulling my weight."

"Not in the day-to-day running of things, no." There, she had said it. Now she had to sit there and wait for his reaction. He sat down next to her on the couch. She could see that he was thinking hard, that he was torn between anger and an honest consideration of what she had said. He looked at her finally, and grimaced. "So what do you want?" he asked.

"I've given that a lot of thought."

"I bet."

"First, I want an apartment. I want a place where I can raise my family away from the hotel, where I can wake up in the morning and not feel pressured. Everyone has an apartment, Yehuda. Even your parents don't live behind the grocery store."

"They live above it."

"Don't quibble. Further, I want you to hire more people."

"We have enough people to do the work, Eliza. It's not as if I'm making you to get down on your hands and knees every day to scrub the floors."

"But I have to be here every hour to make sure others scrub the floors, change the sheets and towels, get the linen off to the laundry in time."

"In other words, you want me to hire supervisory personnel."

"Exactly."

"Do you know how much that costs? Let's say I hire someone to run the hotel, to run the café, to run the milk bar. Do you realize that will more than double our monthly payroll?"

"And why double the monthly payroll when you can get me to do it for you for free? All right, let's make a deal. I'll continue doing this work, but I want to get paid for it. I want exactly what you would pay the three people who would have to be hired otherwise. That way I can save money for the apartment without giving it to your perpetual speculation."

"I don't speculate. I gamble, and my gambles have always paid off."

"Fine. Then start gambling on how long I'm going to take all this pressure."

"You've said the wrong thing, Eliza. I know you. I know that pressure only makes you stronger."

She shook her head. "You're speaking of the past, Yehuda, when the only pressure was to survive. Well, I've survived. Now I want more."

He sat back and put his hand on top of his head. "You realize you'll be ruining our profit margin."

"*Your* profit margin, Yehuda. I never see the profits. I've worked hard now for ten years straight. I've given you two sons. Now I expect something in return besides love and affection."

He smiled. "And my deep appreciation." He held out his hand to her and she took it. "Okay," he said.

"What does that mean?"

"I'll consider what you've said."

"Yehuda!"

"Look, there's a plot of land—"

She threw her hands to her ears. "I don't want to hear it."

"Plot of land," he continued, "that maybe I can get for a cut rate. How would you like a villa? It would be one of several villas, of course, high on the hill, maybe a bit cooler than down here in the winter. You see, there's this fellow—"

"No, Yehuda."

"He's in construction. He doesn't have the money for the land. I think I can swing that. Then we can subdivide and build on it. Villas, I think. It would go better with the terrain. But of course apartments would make a bigger profit."

"Yehuda, can't you see what's happening to you? You're in love with money."

He disagreed. "Not especially. But deals are something I really thrive on."

"I've noticed."

"Give me a year?"

"A year from today?"

"On May 23, 1961, you'll have what you want."

"Or you'll be looking for another wife."

Yehuda grinned. "I don't believe that." Then he was gone, out the door, and had left her with everything—again. But a year? She could hold out for a year.

He was back in the afternoon, looking anxious and distressed. "How are you?" he asked, when he found her in the hotel kitchen, helping to set up for the evening meal.

She stared at him as if he were crazy. "I'm fine. What's the matter?" Before he said it, she knew what the matter was. Somehow one of his deals had gone sour; they had lost everything. "What's happened?" she asked, her voice dropping at least an octave.

"You haven't heard?" He looked incredulous.

"Heard what?"

He took her by the hand and led her out of the kitchen and into the garden behind their living quarters. They sat at a small table. He continued to hold her hand. "Ben Gurion announced it to the Knesset. They've captured Adolf Eichmann."

"Who? The Germans?"

"We've captured him. Us. The Israelis. Somehow we got him out of Argentina. He's here in Israel. He's going to stand trial."

"Trial? What trial for such a man? He should be dead. Like all those he killed! Like my mother, my father, my sister, my nephews!"

"Eliza, Eliza." He tried to quiet her.

"Oh, God!"

Her two children came out of the living room into the garden, drawn by the commotion she was making. Her two sons stared at her, and she stared back at them. She didn't recognize them, or Yehuda. It was as if the years after the war didn't exist. It was as if she and Adam Feuerstein were still in the forest, fighting with the partisans, taking in those who had managed to escape from the labor camps. The death camps, where they—she looked around her, and the world felt very cold. "Where is Mina? Where is my daughter?" she asked. Yehuda tried to take her in his arms and comfort her, but it was impossible.

40

AT HOME IN DAYTON

MINA WENT IN THE BACK DOOR AND THREW HER BOOKS ON THE table. Her regret was immediate when she saw she had startled her mother. "Sorry." Her mother looked up at her, then down. "What are you reading?"

"The newspaper," Maria answered.

"But *what* in the newspaper?" Usually her mother just flipped through for the ads.

"It's a story that—it's about Adolf Eichmann."

"Who's he?"

Maria gave a strange laugh, shook her head, and continued reading. It was incredible that Mina didn't know who Eichmann was. But Maria had done her best to bury the past, for many reasons—most of them selfish, she would admit. Now that the Israelis had captured Eichmann, kidnapping him from Argentina and taking him to stand trial in Israel, the past wouldn't stay buried. She raised her eyes to her daughter. But maybe the story of Eichmann's capture wouldn't touch Mina. The girl was now so American. She did not have a keen sense of history. She did, however, have a keen sense of hunger. Following her usual after-school routine, Mina poured herself a glass of milk, made herself a bowl of salad, with a side dish of potato chips. She sat down across the table from her mother. "Don't eat too much or you'll never fit into your prom dress," Maria warned. She studied her daughter. Did the girl have a tendency to fat? Maria didn't think so. She tried to remember Mina's mother. Eliza Wolf had been thin, very thin. But those were the war years. Everyone was thin. Now, no more. Maria touched her own stomach, pressing it in. She had to watch herself. She would start looking like a German hausfrau if she weren't careful.

"Are we going to hem my dress today?" Mina asked.

"We?" Maria replied.

Mina laughed. She had been upset at first when her mother had suggested it would be cheaper to make, rather than buy, her prom dress, but it was looking better each time she slipped it on. And her mother was right. It was more important to save money for college than to spend a fortune on a dress for one night. Especially since she was only going with Bobby Lake. Now if Jack Coombs had asked her, that would have been a different story. But Jack was going with Celia Fenster. It paid to be a cheerleader.

"Are you excited?" Maria asked her daughter.

"About the prom? Yeah. I guess so. I hope it's fun. If it is, Bobby might ask me out for graduation night."

"I still don't like the idea of your staying out all night."

"But everyone does. That's part of the fun."

"Boys can get drunk and drive their cars into trees."

"So can men. Anyway, Bobby's too sensible. He's going to Oberlin."

Maria, glancing at her daughter, decided it would be best to stop trying to read the paper. "Are you upset that you're going to Ohio State?"

"No! It should be fun."

"I know you had your heart set on one of those girls' schools back east, but they're *so* expensive, and Jerry—"

"Look, Mom, you don't have to explain. Ohio State is fine. I know Jerry's saving up for the kids. I appreciate what *you're* doing for me."

"Jerry doesn't mean to be cheap with you."

"Of course he does."

"He doesn't really, Mina. It's just that—"

"I'm not his child. God, don't think I could forget that."

"Adolescence is difficult. I've been reading about it. And perhaps you haven't been as understanding of Jerry's problems as you might be. You could have stayed off the phone more, been more respectful of Jerry's political opinions.''

''Been more appreciative of his bowling scores?''

Maria laughed.

''Do you love him, Mom?''

''Of course I love Jerry! How could you ask such a question? He's been very good to me. And keep your voice down. Who knows when the kids will come in from playing.''

''I don't know who I'm going to love and marry, but I think it will be different. I remember Jerry being fun when you first met him, but now, every year he seems to be more like his parents.''

''May they rest in peace.''

''Don't be so sanctimonious. The only one broken up by their death was Jerry. Oh, yeah, and Terry and Kristin, because now they won't get any more presents from them.''

''I hope, when you go away to college, you'll learn more tolerance for other people.''

''Like Jerry? The way he talks about Negroes and Jews—''

''Mina!'' Maria cut her short.

''And the way he's treated you. He wouldn't let you set up a catering business when we moved to Dayton because people would think his wife had to work. How silly!''

''So, now I have my deli business.''

''Making salads and pickles?''

''It's buying little extras for you.''

''I go to school smelling like corned beef.''

Maria laughed again. ''Look, Mina, just because you're not getting along with Jerry, don't judge him too harshly. He works hard for us, he provides well. He doesn't go out and get drunk. He doesn't chase after other women. He loves us, yes, even you, though you go out of your way to aggravate him. As far as college goes, well, he isn't used to girls going to college, so he really didn't think it was insulting when he offered to send you to a secretarial school.''

''Or to a nursing school.''

''He's thinking about your future. Women should have a career to fall back on, in case they don't get married. I think you should be a teacher myself. You've always been good with children. And everyone respects teachers.''

''I don't.''

''Well, that's because you're a student. Just wait a few years.'' She sighed. ''I'm looking forward to seeing you graduate. It will be so exciting, my own daughter graduating from high school. I never graduated from high school, you know.''

"You didn't?" Mina was shocked.

"No. They didn't have a real school in Kowitz. The boys used to go to the next village for formal education. Girls attended a church school run by the nuns, where we learned to read and write, add and subtract. But it didn't last long. Our main education was to be out in the fields or working in the home. Things are so different here. It's so much better in America." She looked up at the kitchen clock. "Let's get going on that dress. Soon it'll be time for dinner."

They worked for about an hour on the dress. Maria marked it and basted up the hem. Then she showed Mina how to take little stitches to secure the hem. "And don't pull too tightly on the thread, or the material will pucker," she explained. She left Mina upstairs to work on it and hurried to the kitchen to prepare dinner. They would have pork chops tonight, with applesauce and scalloped potatoes. Jerry had to have his potatoes, even though he needed to watch his weight now. She kept trying to serve him rice, and he kept refusing.

At 5:20 Jerry pulled into the driveway. He came into the kitchen and gave her a kiss. "Hard day?" she asked, as it seemed she had been asking forever. "Not too bad," he said. "Do you have the paper?"

"It's on the table."

"Maria, you've folded it to the inside again."

"Sorry."

"Where are the kids?"

"Terry's over at the Maddoxes', Kristin's playing with Cheryl, and Mina's upstairs hemming her prom dress. She looks so beautiful in it. Wait till you see her."

"Do you know the boy she's going with?"

"No. But he's bound to be nice. Everyone at her high school is."

"No high school boy is nice, Maria. I remember."

Maria smiled. "Mina can take care of herself."

"She has a mouth on her," Jerry agreed.

"Be nice. She has only a few more months here before she goes away to college."

"And during those few months she'll complain about everything I say or do and then still insist that I owe it to her to lend her the car. When I was growing up, I either walked or took the bus. And I didn't talk back to my parents."

"Jerry, do you honestly think Mina is any different from any other teenager in Dayton?"

"No. And that's what's wrong with this country. These kids have no respect for anything."

"Shh. Calm down. Let's leave Mina alone and let her be happy."

"As long as she follows the same policy for us."

"Go read the paper. Dinner will be ready on time."

He sighed and walked out of the kitchen. At 5:45 Mina came down to set the table and call in her brother and sister. At 6:00 everyone was seated waiting for Maria to place the food on the table. Jerry got the first pick of the pork chops; then they were passed to his ten-year-old son and eight-year-old daughter. Mina and Maria got what was left. "So, kids, how'd it go today?" Jerry asked.

"Can I have a baseball mitt by the end of school?" Terry asked.

"As usual, I see," Jerry said grimly.

Maria smiled. "Your father wants to know how things went in school," she corrected her son. "He doesn't want a shopping list."

"Oh, things went pretty well. We're seeing lots of filmstrips now, because we've had to turn in our textbooks so the teachers can do inventory."

"Don't you have nearly a month of school left?" Jerry asked.

"Yeah. But I don't care."

"We're getting ready for finals," Mina put in. "If Dexter Price doesn't pass English, he won't be able to get his athletic scholarship."

"Sounds right to me," Jerry said.

"Why? He's an athlete, not a scholar."

"Are you trying to tell me that athletic scholarship is an inherently contradictory term?"

"What did you do today, Kristin?" Maria cut in quickly.

"We played doctor."

"Oh, God," Jerry said.

"The pediatrician came and told us what it would be like to go to the hospital to get our tonsils out. I was the nurse who brought ice cream to the patient."

Jerry looked relieved. "Did you read the paper today?" he asked his wife.

"I glanced through it."

"Did you see what the Israelis have done?"

"Yes."

"It's a crime, you know, kidnapping someone like that. It's just going to open everything up again when everyone's ready to forget. Eichmann's an old man. He's living a useful life with his family." Jerry shook his head. "I don't know."

"Who is this Eichmann anyway?" Mina asked.

"And it's going to be bad for the Poles," Jerry added. "People are going to start asking questions all over again. Why didn't the Poles do this for the Jews? Why didn't the Poles do that? Hell, it was war. It was every man for himself. It's not like it was our fault. Don't you agree?"

Maria shrugged. "I don't really want to talk about the war again. Okay?"

"Sorry, darling. Well, do you want to hear what we're getting at work? A computer. Can you believe it? It's taking up the entire lower floor of the new office building. But the higher-ups say it will make the company much more efficient, so we've got to learn to work with it. I've got to go back to school. A two-week course sometime this summer. On the plus side, it's going to be at some lake resort, and wives are invited." He smiled at Maria. "Nothing like a paid vacation."

Mina half-heartedly listened as summer plans were discussed. She had her summer all set. She'd be working at a day camp from 9:00 to 3:00, then she would come home and help her mother with her work. At night she would get together with her friends and go swimming or to the movies or, best of all, shopping for clothes for college. It was going to be so exciting, she could hardly wait. All that independence. No one arguing with her all the time.

After dinner, she helped her mother clear up and stack the dishes in the dishwasher. Then it was time for homework. She paused at the entrance to the living room. Her stepfather was watching television. She picked up the paper he had left lying on the table and found the story her mother and father had been discussing. Israel, Argentina, war criminal, justice, Eichmann. She tossed the paper down. News was for adults who had nothing else to do with their lives. She hurried upstairs. Before she studied, she might have time to sneak in a call to Marsha, if she kept it to under an hour.

41

OHIO STATE

"ARE YOU SURE YOU'RE HOLDING THE MAP RIGHT?" JERRY ASKED Maria impatiently, almost nervously.

"Yes."

"Maybe this is downtown Columbus. It sure as hell doesn't look like a college campus to me."

"The sign back there said Ohio State," Mina said, putting in her two cents' worth from the back seat.

"Even Fordham was nothing like this." He stopped the car, ignoring the honking behind him. He called out to a group of students passing by. "Tri-Oaks Tower?"

"How embarrassing!" Mina said. She sunk deeper into the back seat.

"Take two lefts, a right, two lefts, a right," Jerry said to Maria.

"Well at least we're getting a chance to see the campus," Maria consoled him.

"I hope you brought several pairs of sneakers with you," he said to Mina.

"Sneakers aren't popular this year."

"Then sore feet must be. You're going to have a lot of walking to do."

Mina looked around her. It was big, sure. But she had known that. She would adjust. She would find her way around faster than anyone. She hoped. "There it is!" she leaned forward and shouted, unfortunately into Jerry's ear.

He jumped and ground his teeth. "Sit back," Maria urged her.

They pulled into the circular drive of Tri-Oaks Tower. There were students with arm bands directing them to inch forward. "This is a dorm?" Maria asked. "It looks like a city block. And where are the three oaks?"

"Probably the dorm's sitting on them," Jerry said.

Maria rolled down her window and paid attention while the girl student said, "You can unload everything here. Then pull around to parking lot A."

"Is parking lot A easy to find?" Jerry asked.

"It's half a block down this road to your right," the girl explained. "If A is full, try B. That's two blocks down."

"And if B's full, can I just drive home?"

The girl laughed. Jerry turned off the motor. He, Maria, and Mina quickly unloaded Mina's worldly goods—everything, that is, that she wanted at college, and that was plenty. "You two wait here," Jerry told them, "I'll be right back. I hope."

Maria and Mina stood anxiously on the sidewalk. Mina looked around, smiling broadly. "Do you think one of these girls could be my roommate?"

"I hope not," Maria said. "It would be better if you arrived at the room first. Then you can choose your bed and dresser and things."

Mina had written to her roommate, Lydia Friedan from Cleveland. Lydia was going to bring a blue rug from home, so Mina had gone out and bought a blue bedspread. Mina was bringing an iron, Lydia an alarm clock, Mina a radio, Lydia a record player. Both would bring their records. They had exchanged pictures, but sometimes you couldn't tell with pictures. Lydia had brown hair, like Mina's, but straight, not unruly. She looked a little bit heavier than Mina in the picture. She was Jewish. "You could have asked to room with a Catholic," Jerry chided her. But Mina had wanted everything to be different at college; she wanted to experience the new, the exotic.

"There's Jerry," Maria said. She waved her hand at Jerry, who was mopping his brow as he approached. "Parking lot B," he told them. "I hope to God they have elevators in this building. I don't think my heart can take much more of this."

Mina wasn't listening. She had grabbed a suitcase and a laundry bag and was forging on. Jerry had a suitcase in each hand. Maria would stay by the packing boxes until they returned.

The first thing they heard when they entered the lobby was a ding. "Thank God. An elevator," Jerry said. First they had to check in at one of the welcoming tables. "N to R," Jerry said.

Mina lined up. "Mina Prychek," she told the student aide when it was her turn.

"Top floor, 809," the girl told her. "Better get used to waiting for the elevator."

Mina held the precious key in her hand. She smiled at Jerry and led him on. It didn't take them long to get on the elevator; it was getting off that took forever. It stopped on every floor up to the eighth. Mina hurried out of the elevator and down the corridor. It was buzzing with parents getting their daughters' room set up. "Here it is!" Mina called to Jerry. She tried the door. It was locked. She fumbled with the key and pushed the door open. She looked inside. "Paradise!" she exclaimed.

Jerry looked over her shoulder. "You could have joined a convent and had a bigger room," he informed her.

She was not to be deflated. They carted her goods into the room, and then Mina turned to get ready to make the trek back to her mother. "Hold it," Jerry said. "You decide right now which bed you want and which desk and dresser. Otherwise, when we get downstairs, your mother is going to fret."

"Does it matter?"

"Not really. But it will make your mother happy."

Mina chose the bed, desk, and dresser to the right. She walked to the window and looked down. "You can see everything from here."

Jerry joined her. "This isn't a college. It's a city. Come on. Let's get the rest of your stuff."

Maria was waiting anxiously for them. "Well, what's it like?"

"Beautiful!" Maria answered.

"Small, confining, claustrophobic, and not worth the money," Jerry corrected her. They grabbed the rest of Mina's things, and all made the elevator trip. "This reminds me of a lousy hotel I once stayed at," Jerry said under his breath to Maria. She smiled at him. When they reached the eighth floor, Mina danced out of the elevator to her room. Hers! She proudly opened the door for her mother. Maria looked in. "Interesting," she said to her daughter.

"Isn't it going to be great!"

"It's a little like where we used to live in Kowitz."

"What?"

"Nothing. Let's get started making this look like home."

Jerry left them. He said he was going to go down and explore the campus. If he got lost, they should try the police station. Mina and Maria unpacked, hung up clothes, put books away, made the bed, hung up the towels and Mina's mirror. Then they had to drag the suitcases down to the storage room in the basement. Up once again they went. They explored the bathrooms and the shower room. "This is like a DP camp, only more modern," Maria said.

"Mother, why do you compare everything to the war?"

"Sorry. You'll have to admit, it will take some getting used to. You have your robe?"

"Yes, of course. And my shower cap. And my toothpaste and toothbrush. And my soap and towels."

Maria put her arm on her daughter's shoulder. They walked back to the room and found the door open. A voice was saying, "This room is about the size of your closet, maybe smaller."

Mina stood in the doorway and got her first glimpse of Lydia Friedan. "Hi," she said. "I'm Mina Prychek."

Mother and daughter looked up at her. Lydia came forward. "Mina! You look exactly like your picture."

"I hated that picture. It's the one they put in the yearbook."

"None of you kids liked your senior pictures," Mrs. Friedan commented. She looked past Mina toward Maria. "Hello there. I'm Naomi Friedan."

"Hello. I'm Maria Jankowski."

"Oh, I thought—"

"I am Mina's mother. I've remarried."

"Oh."

"Not divorced. Widowed."

"Oh," Naomi Friedan said again, with a smile. She looked around the room. "It's going to be a tight fit. Especially since I've found girls always fill up the space allotted to them."

Maria smiled.

"Well, they'll manage, I guess," Naomi concluded.

Her husband, Saul, came to the room at almost the same time Jerry returned from his wandering. After introductions and greetings, Jerry informed Maria and Mina that he had found a place for lunch, if they didn't mind grease. Mina promised she would see Lydia soon. The Jankowskis and the Friedans exchanged goodbyes; and then Mina and her family were out on the sidewalk again, watching with some hauteur the new arrivals struggling to retain grace under extreme pressure.

"It's a hamburger joint," Jerry turned back to say to them. Then he led them onward, walking at least five paces ahead.

"She's nice, don't you think?" Mina said to Maria.

"She certainly seems to be," Maria said. "But just remember, even if you discover she's not nice, you get along with her. You have a whole year to spend together."

"Don't worry. I can get along with anyone."

Maria looked meaningfully ahead of them.

"Anyone my own age," Mina corrected.

They ate fitfully, not because the food was as bad as Jerry expected, but because after they ate it would be time to say good-bye. Maria kept thinking of last-minute bits of advice to give her daughter, and Mina was concentrating on getting back to the room to get to know her roommate and the others on the corridor. Jerry kept worrying about how he was going to find his way off campus.

After they ate, they walked back to parking lot B. Fortunately, their car was not hemmed in, as several other cars looked to be. Jerry embraced Mina. "We're going to miss you, kid. I don't know whom I'm going to argue with. Maybe your mother."

"I'll try to come home often enough to keep you in fighting trim," she promised him.

Maria hugged her daughter. "You've never been away from me. I've protected you always."

Mina pulled back from her mother and smiled. "What a funny thing to say."

Maria touched Mina's cheek. "What should I say then?"

Mina threw her arms around her mother. "I'll miss you so much. You've been my best friend, even when you were impossible."

"Thanks."

"This girl is full of compliments today," Jerry pointed out. He opened the car door and reached across to pop open the passenger side. Maria got in.

Mina watched, almost with tears in her eyes, as her parents left the parking lot and made their way slowly into what seemed to be city traffic.

Then they were gone. Her parents were gone. For the first time in her life, she was alone. She turned around and looked back at Tri-Oak Towers. Boy, was she going to make the most of it!

42

ROOMMATES

MINA DESPERATELY HELD HER SLIDE RULE IN HER HAND AND TRIED to figure out her chemistry problems. She had entered Ohio State with the secret ambition to be a doctor. Now in her second semester of both chemistry and zoology she knew she had made a big mistake. There were some things she was good at, maybe. Science wasn't one of them. Well at least this farce had served to get her science and math distribution credits out of the way. Her foreign language requirement was taken care of when she demonstrated her fluency in Polish. So here she was, left with the liberal arts and no particular direction.

She envied Lydia. Lydia had entered college knowing exactly what she wanted to do; she wanted to be a journalist. So far she had gone at her courses with gusto and had not changed her mind. In that, she was a rarity on the floor. Everyone had come to college with a preconceived idea of why she was there and what she wanted. Most of those ideas had changed dramatically. Like that one poor girl who wanted to become a nurse. She discovered very quickly that she couldn't stand to be around sick people, so she changed to public health administration. She claimed it would still give her a chance to hang around doctors and meet one to marry, but she wouldn't have to get dirty in the hospital itself.

A lot of the girls talked about marriage, how they would maybe spend one or two years in college, but they didn't expect to graduate. They wanted to meet Someone and have him carry them away, preferably on horseback. Mina often thought that would be simpler than trying to decide on a major; but she had spent close to a year here already, and she hadn't met any real Prince Charmings. She had gone to mixers; she had been fixed up with many blind dates; but she knew she wasn't the eye catcher a lot of the girls at Ohio State were. She was rather ordinary.

Lydia also didn't date a lot. But she didn't have to. She had joined the newspaper in her first week and worked there in her spare time. They didn't date there. They went in groups to movies, dances, and social events. Sometimes Mina tagged along, but she always felt like the odd person out. They were all so clever and verbal. She was the simple observer.

Not that Lydia didn't try to make her feel a part of everything. Mina had been so lucky to get Lydia Friedan as her roommate. What some of the girls had to put up with, well, she never could have done it. Lydia and she were considerate of each other. They had an unwritten schedule, by which each could have the room to herself for a while a few days a week; the other braved the elements to study in the library. It made life more bearable to have a short time alone.

Lydia, like Mina, spent all her extra money on food. The dorm food was indescribable. They often had to fortify themselves with hamburgers from the snack bar or pizza, free delivery guaranteed. By Christmas vacation they had each put on at least five pounds. They didn't know for sure how much they had gained, because they had stopped weighing themselves in November.

It wasn't only food and good times that they had in common.

They shared more than that. Their backgrounds mainly. Mina called herself a lapsed Catholic; Lydia, a Reform Jew. Only at Lydia's insistence did Mina rise one Sunday and take her roommate to Mass. That was one of the reasons Mina had looked forward to leaving Dayton, so she wouldn't have to go to church to make sure Terry and Kristin kept quiet. It wasn't necessary to be pious in Dayton, Ohio, Mina had tried to explain to her parents. There didn't seem to be much choice. "Very impressive," Lydia said when the Mass was over and they were out once again in the clear sun, on the windswept street. "But what does it all mean?"

Between the church and the dorm, Mina tried to give Lydia a short course on the Catholic religion. It was hard to explain the Virgin Mary to someone who didn't believe, or the intercession of the saints. Lydia looked at her as if she had pitied her simplicity. That made Mina defensive of what she herself didn't take seriously. Though she did imagine she would involve herself in religion when she had children. That always seemed to be the way.

During the High Holidays, Lydia reciprocated by taking Mina along to the services. Mina wasn't prejudiced. She was sure of it. But she felt very strange surrounded by all those Jews. She got the giggles in the middle of the Rosh Hashanah service when she thought of what Jerry would say if he could see her now. She embarrassed Lydia so much that her roommate tried to pretend she didn't know her.

On Yom Kippur, for the *Kol Nidre*, Lydia made Mina promise that if she felt the giggles coming on, she would pretend it was a coughing fit and leave. "Some people take this very seriously," she warned Mina.

Mina behaved herself that night. She read the words of the service for the Day of Atonement. They actually made sense. In a way, the Jews had it much better. They only had to feel guilty one day a year, not every day, like the Catholics. She wondered what Father Rolfe would say if she brought up that point to him next time she was home. Silly, she knew the answer. Catholics were saved by their faith; Jews were damned by theirs. Priests always had very pat answers for everything. That's why it was so hard to believe anymore. The older she grew, the less appeal simplicity had.

When she traveled to Cleveland with Lydia for one of their three-day weekends, she met the entire Friedan clan. Lydia's grandmother lived with them, and Lydia's older brother, a wine importer, was just back from a European tour, though he assured his family he would be making fewer trips overseas now that California was overtaking the European producers.

"You've traveled in Europe, I understand," Mrs. Friedan said to Mina.

"Me? No," Mina disagreed.

Mrs. Friedan looked at Lydia. "Didn't you tell me you were born in Poland?" Lydia said.

"Oh! Yes. I'm sorry, Mrs. Friedan. I thought you meant traveling in Europe when I could remember. Yes, I was born in Poland. But we got out of there when I was two or three, after the Germans had left but before the Russians took complete control. Then I was in a DP camp someplace in Austria, then, I think, in Italy. It's all hazy. I don't really remember much of it at all. By the time I was four, I was in the United States."

"With just your mother?"

"Yes. My father was killed in the war. He was a member of the Polish army and—well, I really don't know what happened to him, except he was killed. I never really think about that time. All my real remembered life has been in the United States."

"Does your mother ever talk about the war?" Lydia's brother, Alan, asked.

"No. She won't. Not even with my stepfather."

"Then I guess she doesn't discuss this upcoming trial with you," Mr. Friedan said.

"Which trial?"

"The Eichmann trial. Over in Israel. I would have thought she'd be interested, since a lot of the crimes took place in Poland. In Auschwitz, for instance."

"Auschwitz?" Mina looked around the table and saw that her ignorance was very annoying to the Friedans. "I'm sorry. I don't know Auschwitz. We came from a small farming village near Cracow."

"Auschwitz is also near Cracow," Grandmother Friedan informed Mina. "Most of my relatives from Germany—"

"Mom!" Lydia appealed to Mrs. Friedan. "Mina is my age. She certainly wasn't responsible. I don't think we should dump all this on her at dinner."

"Certainly not at dinner," Alan agreed. "Let's wait until after dinner." He smiled at Mina, and Mina smiled back.

"I honestly don't know as much as I should about the war," Mina admitted. "It's not been a popular subject in our house, though both my parents have mentioned the Eichmann trial. And next year I'm going to start on European history, so I'm sure I'll learn a lot more." She shrugged her shoulders. "I'm sorry."

She was glad that when Lydia visited her house, in Dayton, there were no political discussions. Everything went very smoothly. Jerry even put a car at their disposal for the weekend, so they could get to the movies and go shopping. Terry and Kristin were on their best behavior. Her mother proved herself a wonderful cook over and over again. Lydia really had a great time; Mina could sense that.

The next time Mina came home for a weekend, Jerry even asked how Lydia was doing. "You know, we've never had a Jew stay at the house before," he said to her.

They were both surprised to hear Maria burst out laughing over her needlepoint. "That woman's getting old," Jerry confided. "I thought Lydia was a very nice girl. Very well mannered."

"She had fun here," Mina said. "We've decided to room together next year, too."

"That's nice. Neither of you wanted to join a sorority?"

"No. Lydia doesn't approve on principle; and when I rushed, I just didn't feel that I fit in anywhere. So we're going to stay in the dorm, at least for next year."

When she got back to school from that weekend at home, Lydia was out. On Mina's desk was a folder with a note on top in Lydia's handwriting. "Over at the paper. In case you want to know more about Auschwitz. Open at your own risk! Don't lose anything; I'm writing a series. L."

Open at her own risk? Mina shook her head. Maybe Lydia should have been in the theater instead of journalism. She made everything so dramatic she could never be a newswriter. She'd have to stick to features.

Mina slid the note to one side and opened the folder.

Half an hour later she was in the bathroom, vomiting her guts up.

43

QUESTIONS THAT
CAN'T BE ANSWERED

DURING THE MONTHS OF THE EICHMANN TRIAL, MINA PRYCHEK bought the *New York Times* every day. Every day she heard of the innocents slaughtered. Almost every day Poland was mentioned, even if it was only Auschwitz, that small part of Poland that no one could ever now forget.

The trial started at the end of April, when she had what everyone considered more important things to think about—term papers and hourlies. It ended in the middle of August, when she had worked a full summer, not only for her mother but also for the day camp. What should have been a happy time for her was like ashes. Her life was ashes.

She could not understand. That was the problem. She read everything that was written about Adolf Eichmann's trial in the newspaper, the weekly magazines, and yet she could not believe that something like this had actually occurred in her lifetime. And she was there, occupying the same corner of the earth, the same small patch as those who had gone up in smoke at Auschwitz; as those who had been worked to death at other camps; at those who had been shot up against a wall, over an open pit, burned, mutilated, eviscerated.

Jerry tried not to let the subject be mentioned in the house. "They talk as if the Jews were the only ones to suffer during the war," he complained. "We all suffered. Even the Germans suffered. The Poles suffered most of all. That's what no one seems to understand. And look at the Jews. They're back on their feet again. Hell, they own half of this country."

"Don't you realize that's exactly the sort of attitude that allowed the Germans to destroy a people?" Mina asked him. "They played on prejudices such as yours; the Germans counted on those prejudices to allow them, even encourage them, to do their work."

"Hey, I fought in the war, kiddo. I was keeping my head down on a destroyer while the Jews were sitting on their fat asses in the Pentagon, taking their pickings of the women we left behind."

"Which Jews?"

"What?"

"Give me their names."

"What, are you crazy?"

"You've made a prejudicial statement. I'm asking you to support it with facts."

"Don't be ridiculous. Everybody knows—"

"I don't know. I've only met one Jewish man who was in the war. That's Lydia's father. He was a private with the invasion forces on D day. He fought his way through France and Germany. He saw the survivors of the camps. He said many of them lived only long enough to realize they had been liberated."

"It's all an exaggeration, you know. Just to raise money. Six million Jews? Think of it yourself. It's impossible."

But Mina had saved the account of the trial. She flipped back through the papers and found the one where there was testimony in mathematical detail of exactly how many could be killed at one camp in one day. Add that to all the camps, she told her stepfather. He waved her off. She showed him pictures, stacks of what could almost be recognized as human bodies. He told her not to be disgusting. "What's disgusting is that this happened, and nobody did anything about it," she argued. "Why didn't anybody stop it?"

"No one knew," he rebutted.

"No one could believe," her mother told her. Her mother had remained silent throughout most of the conversations Mina had had with Jerry; silent and moody the entire summer vacation. Maria kept house, made salads, pickled her vegetables for later sale, tended to her garden—and avoided her daughter.

"What happened?" Mina finally asked her. "Why didn't the people rise up?"

"You're talking simple solutions. Everyone wanted to live," Maria replied. "We were terrorized."

"I don't remember being terrorized."

"What do you remember, Mina?"

Mina thought back through the curtains of time. She shook her head. "I just remember our house being dark and cold. Except at night, when I could crawl into bed with you. I remember when the Russians came. You told me they were the Russians, and I was to hide under the bed. You told me not to come out. But they found me. They didn't hurt us, did they?"

"No."

"I remember helping you with the laundry, gathering wood. Most of all, I guess, I remember keeping silent."

"Do you remember why?"

Mina squeezed her eyes and thought hard. "No. Just that it was the most important thing, never to make a sound. What I find unbearable, Mom, is that all of this was going on and I never knew. Did you know?"

Maria shook her head. "No. That is the God's honest truth. Not until afterward did I hear about Auschwitz. I knew they were killing Jews. Yes, I knew that. They were killing Poles, too. Some who had relatives in the cities were given to understand that the Germans rounded people up, sent them off to labor camps, from which they never returned. Or, if a German was killed by the resistance or the partisans, the Germans would retaliate by simply grabbing fifty or a hundred people in the street, lining them up, and mowing them down.

"The resistance put one of its men in the village next to us. The Germans came to that town, asked if there were any strangers, anybody who had not lived there before the war. The people said nothing. The Germans took every fifth person from the rows of villagers—man, woman, child, it didn't matter—and killed them.

"When the resistance tried to put someone in our town, the Germans came, and the villagers gave him up. Kowitz was very loyal to its overlord. We were not heroes, Mina. Maybe it was dishonorable to survive."

"Could nothing stop them?"

"Something did stop the Germans. The Americans, the Russians, the British, even the French. But by then—"

"What did the priests say? Couldn't they have interceded?"

"The Jews were apart from us, Mina. You see, they were always foreign. So the priests said, 'Let the Germans have them; don't make a fuss; what are the Jews to us.' "

"And the Poles the Germans killed?"

"The priests were very much enamored of authority. The Germans had it; the priests respected it. War makes few people noble."

"I would like to think I'd have acted differently."

"Wouldn't we all?"

"I would like to think I'd have fought, as my father did. I can forgive you, Mom, because you're a woman, and women at that time didn't know they could be valiant. But the others?"

"None of us knew the extent of it. Radios were forbidden. We had none in the village. We were very law-abiding. I'll tell you how we found out what we did know. Several of the men and women would hold back a quantity of vegetables from the quota the Germans imposed—especially potatoes. These they took into

Cracow to sell. Food in Cracow was not only rationed, but also very scarce. People who had money were willing to pay on the black market. That's how we learned about German retaliation, about the disappearance of both Poles and Jews. But how many, no one knew. Until after the war, when we heard about Auschwitz, the other camps. And then no one could believe it.

"You don't remember the train station, do you?"

"No."

"I remember it. It's still vivid in my mind. One of the directional signs still said Oswiecim. That's the Polish for Auschwitz. I thought then of—all who had gone there and in what condition. But we boarded the train for Czechoslovakia and freedom. Freedom, Mina. Don't forget that. We're free now, and all that nightmare of war is in the past."

"Is it?"

"Yes. Of course."

"How can it be when people like Jerry still believe as they do? What was the point if the world learned nothing?"

"Do you think killing and dying can make people give up hating? Just try to keep love and tolerance perfect within yourself, and it will spread of its own accord."

"My mother, the original Pollyanna. What do you think should happen to Eichmann?"

"Oh, they should kill him," Maria said quickly. "Such evil should be wiped off the face of the earth. Though there is no expiation. Not for any of us."

44

ANOTHER FAITH

THE STATE OF ISRAEL EXECUTED ADOLF EICHMANN ON MAY 31, 1962, almost twenty years after Mina Prychek had been born. By then, both Mina and Lydia were completing their second year at Ohio State. Lydia breezed flawlessly along, never faltering in her desire to make journalism her career. Her classes became part of her life, not something separate from it, as most of Mina's were. What Lydia learned, she could apply. Mina's course work was a bit more speculative. During her sophomore year, she had delved heavily into history and philosophy. Philosophy made no sense to her. All these men in her book of readings, men only, devised a way of looking at and reacting to life that sounded good on paper, but who could apply it to actual living? She thought she would find an answer in philosophy, but all she found were more questions. Her professors were very proud of her. Questions satisfied them. She was the one who wanted to settle for answers.

History gave her answers. She had spent so many of her years being ignorant of even her own history that now she was determined to know everything. She started out with Biblical history, or prehistory, since a lot of the information was based on archaeology instead of the written word. The following year she would move on to European history in depth. She had decided to specialize in Eastern European Studies, which meant learning French, to complement her Polish and because French was the language used by so many Eastern Europeans.

Lydia was upset with her. "What can you do with Eastern European Studies?"

"Please. You sound like my parents."

"What do you want to do, get out of college and work in a grocery store?"

"I'm learning for learning's sake."

"How wonderfully naïve of you."

"Lydia, don't be so cynical. I can always get a job doing something, even if it's only going back home and helping Mom pack pickles."

"Are you sure you'll be able to go back home when they get a whiff of what else you're up to?"

"How indelicately you put things. The study of religion is always mind-broadening, Lydia. As a journalist, you—"

"Studying is one thing, converting is another," Lydia pointed out. "Even my mother thinks you're crazy. And she's Jewish. Very Jewish."

"And you're not?"

"No. I can take it or leave it, preferably leave it. You don't understand, Mina, that religion isn't just belief; it's family. Do you know what family is? It's fights, arguments, guilt. Goddamn, is it guilt." Lydia was sitting in the chair opposite Mina's, facing her squarely, staring directly into her eyes. "What are you going to say to your parents?"

"Well—I don't think I'll be inviting them to the conversion ceremony."

"I can honestly see your stepfather raising a pogrom against the synagogue."

Mina burst out laughing. "I know. Wouldn't that be something?"

Lydia shook her head. "Are you sure you're doing this for all the right reasons? Or are you really just trying to get back at your parents for something?"

"I think the reasons are right." Mina tipped her chair back and placed her feet on Lydia's bed. Lydia looked annoyed, but she didn't say anything. "I need a faith, Lydia. I can't be godless, like certain other people, who happen to be roommates. Maybe being Catholic does that to someone. You have to have someone to fall back on."

"But why the god of Abraham, Issac, and Jacob?"

"See, there you're wrong. The Jewish religion is not concerned with God; it's concerned with ethics. There's no substitute for doing what is right. There's no way to squirm out of it by confession or being born again. It demands that situations be faced, choices be made."

"If you think Jews are more moral than anyone else, you're wrong," Lydia said. "I could tell you stories just about members of my family. My own brother, for instance. I think he pads his expense account."

"Your brother's cute."

"Do you want to come up this summer when he's home, and I'll fix you up?" Lydia suggested.

"He's too old for me, Lydia. And remember last time, when he asked my opinion of the wine and I said it wasn't sweet enough?"

"Yeah. That did rather turn him off, didn't it? 'Fruity' yes, but 'sweet' is a word he abhors. Anyway, I think he's got someone in France. At least he spends enough time there."

"That's where the wine is."

"There's also wine in upstate New York. I don't see him trotting up there too often."

"Will you come to my conversion ceremony?"

Lydia squinted. "Will there by much mumbo-jumbo?"

"The rabbi's Reform, Lydia."

"Oh. You mean he'll be dressed as a Protestant minister? Okay, I guess I can face that. But what I can't face is your parents. They'll think it's my doing."

"Don't worry. First of all, I don't think they'll come. Second, they're already a bit pissed with you because I told them it was your idea to get an apartment next year."

"How very Catholic of you. I thought we were facing situations squarely now that we were becoming Jewish?"

Mina laughed. "Jerry's afraid we'll have parties."

"Hell, yes!"

"That we'll become wanton hussies."

"Sounds good. How many are in your class, by the way?"

"My conversion class?"

"Yes."

"Three. Two want to marry Jews. I'm the odd one."

"How true."

"I'm not doing it for love."

"Just another one of your enriching experiences. Only two others, huh?" Lydia considered it. "I guess that means I won't be able to get lost in the crowd."

Lydia was wrong. She actually was able to get lost in the crowd. The conversion ceremony was held at Temple Sinai, the Reform temple, on Friday night, and there were plenty of congregants, including the families of the married couples-to-be. Lydia's mother came down to Columbus for the ceremony, at Lydia's invitation, not Mina's. "For protection," Lydia whispered to Mina. But she need not have worried. Jerry Jankowski was not in attendance.

Mina had tried to break the news of her impending conversion to her parents as smoothly and compassionately as possible. She'd waited until they had watched Jerry's favorite show, "Leave It to Beaver," which Terry and Kristin loved, also. Then she had asked her parents if she could speak to them in the kitchen for a moment. She knew that Jerry was torn between watching more television and his duty as a parent. From the solemn look on her face, he guessed he'd better hightail it out to the kitchen.

They sat at the kitchen table, Jerry, Mina, and Maria. "You're either pregnant or you're flunking out," Jerry said threateningly.

She gave one of her disgusted sighs, then piously drew herself erect. "I've made a commitment that I think will displease you," she announced.

Maria's face lit up. "You're getting married."

"Mom, no! For God's sake, I hardly ever date."

"You'll meet someone. Don't worry. It's only a matter of time," Maria consoled her.

"Maria!" Jerry said. "Let's get on with this. What's the problem?"

"I've given this a lot of thought."

"We understand. Hurry up, my television time is running."

"Fine. Then I'll just come right out with it. I'm converting to

Judaism." She did not even see his hand as it snaked out and flashed across her face. But she did feel it. Her hands flew to her face. She was shocked. No one had ever hit her before, except for her mother's few spanks on the rear. She could not stop the tears that came to her eyes and fell down her cheeks.

"Never," Jerry said. "You will never become a Jew."

"Jerry, leave us," Maria said.

"You become a Jew, and you will never set foot in this house again," Jerry warned her.

"Don't say or do anything you will regret," Maria told him. "Now, please leave."

"No. This is my house, my kitchen. Everything is mine. Don't try to tell me when to come, when to go. This kid of yours—"

"Don't say another word!" Maria snarled at him. She stood up, pulled Mina up by her arm and dragged her from the room. They raced up the stairs into Mina's bedroom and locked the door. Mina opened her mouth to speak. "Shh!" Maria said to her. Silently, they sat on the bed and listened, but no footsteps followed.

"Just like old times," Mina joked. But her heart wasn't in it. She burst into tears.

Maria held Mina in her arms and rocked her, saying words to her in Polish that Mina hadn't heard for a long time. "Why did you tell him? Why didn't you just do it?" Maria finally asked. "You knew what this would do to him. He can accept a lapsed Catholic. He can't accept you as a Jew."

"I can't live my life by his prejudices."

"But you could have managed to keep it from him until you were out of the house for good, couldn't you?" She shook Mina slightly. "Couldn't you have?"

"Yes. I suppose so," Mina admitted.

"And now what am I to do? How will I make this right?"

"Maybe this is the one thing you won't be able to put right," Mina said. Embracing one another, they sat silently on the bed together. Then Mina pulled away. "Why haven't you said anything? You've made no objections. It doesn't bother you?"

Maria shrugged. "Well, you're twenty years old. You're not a baby. When I was your age—well, never mind that. I assume you know what you're doing. Am I right?"

"Yes."

"Because conversion is not something you can just do and forget about."

"I understand. Believe me."

Maria placed her hand on her daughter's cheek. "What was it

that attracted you to Judaism? I assume you've been to their services. Was it the music? The prayers?"

Mina shook her head. "Nothing like that. It's the ethical aspect." Her mother laughed. "Oh, I know you don't have any respect for the Jews. I've heard you and Jerry agree about how they always try to get things for the best price."

"But then, don't we all?" Maria said. "No, that's not why I was laughing. I was thinking."

"Of what?"

How could Maria tell Mina? And yet might this not be the perfect moment? No. No! If she told her, Mina would never keep her mouth shut, and then Jerry would be asking questions. Maria Prychek took in a Jew? Would he mention it to the relatives back in Trenton? Would they somehow find out she was not Maria Prychek? Could her citizenship be taken away? Could she be sent back to Poland? No. She would say nothing. The past must always be buried. For her safety and for the safety of her child, Eliza Wolf's child. She smiled, "I was just thinking what an interesting family we will make. My husband the anti-Semite, my daughter the Jew."

"And my mother?"

"Your mother will always be your mother."

Her mother helped her pick out the dress for the conversion ceremony. It was a simple white cotton summer dress, the kind that needed to be ironed, which put Mina off at first. But it was the only dress that looked not only becoming but also respectable. "Your confirmation dress was white," Maria reminded her.

"I remember. I hated it. It made me all itchy."

"You were such a pretty little girl. Ever since the first time I saw you."

"Everyone always made fun of my kinky hair. They still do. Combs were not made to undo my tangles."

"I'm glad you're going away this summer. It will give Jerry time to relent."

"The Silent Hulk."

"Be respectful. Isn't that one of the Jewish commandments: Honor thy father and thy mother?"

"One of the Ten Commandments, Mom. They're for all of us. I wish God had included a respect-thy-children one."

"Well, there must have been a reason he didn't."

Maria sat in the row with Lydia and Naomi Friedan. She seemed a bit uncomfortable; she looked around as if she had never been surrounded by Jews before, which was undoubtedly true. It was a miracle that she was even here. But Jerry had finally relented, saying gracelessly, "Well, she's your kid. Do what you want with her." Thank God Mina had taken that counseling job on Lake Erie. It would keep her away the entire summer.

She stood before the rabbi now in her white dress and listened carefully while she and the others were asked the questions leading to their conversion.

Did she enter Judaism of her own free will? As much as anyone had free will, she wanted to answer, but she supposed a simple yes would suffice.

Did she renounce her former faith? She remembered this part. She had had to renounce her former nationality and allegiances when she became an American citizen. For one fleeting moment she thought of her immortal soul, but then she thought of the Catholic church and the Holocaust. Renounce she did.

Would she pledge her loyalty to Judaism? Yes.

Did she cast her lot with the people of Israel? The rabbi had earlier explained that this wasn't a political questions. It didn't mean she had to become a Zionist. The people of Israel were Jews. Yes. She did cast her fate with them. Her stepfather cast her fate with them, too.

Would she lead a Jewish life? As Jewish as Lydia's, she promised herself.

Would she rear her children in the Jewish faith? She answered yes. She hoped to. But at this point in her life, she knew neither whom she was going to marry or if she would have children.

Would she have her male children circumcised? She remembered the evidence given at the trial, how Jewish boys were turned over to the Germans simply because they were circumcised. But there was no fear of that in America. Everyone was circumcised here. It was hygienic.

Her pledges were made. She and the other two repeated the Shema' Israel in Hebrew and in English. She was a Jew.

She returned to the pew and sat next to her mother. They held hands tightly until the service was finished. Then they filtered out to another part of the temple for Oneg Shabbat. "Be strong," her mother said to her. Then Maria happily noted that the cake she had baked was the first to be finished.

45

NOVEMBER 1963

THE APARTMENT LOOKED A MESS. MINA STOOD IN THE "CONVEN-ience" kitchen, the kind where one could barely turn around before hitting the eating counter, and tried to straighten things up. Lydia sat in the living room–dining room–all-purpose room, shredding open her envelopes, letting little pieces of paper fall around her, as if she had terminal dandruff.

Mina sighed loudly. Why did Lydia find neatness so offensive? Mina had been trying to find out ever since they moved into the apartment. Lydia had never given Mina a glimmer of being such a pig when they were in that small dorm room. But as soon as they hit a larger space, Lydia found it too much of an effort to take care of the basic necessities, like hanging up her clothes. Even when she'd had her boyfriend over, she saw no reason to clean up.

At first the roommates fought over certain hygienic or aesthetic standards. But Mina was not a warrior. Nor was she a maid. She simply decided that she would keep up her standards and pointedly tell those who came over which part of the apartment was hers and which was Lydia's. It worked, mainly because Lydia had no shame.

"I'm picking them up," Lydia said. She got down on all fours and gathered the little pieces to her. Mina's territory was in front of the chair. Lydia's was the entire sofa.

"What's news?" Mina asked her.

"You know when they say no news is good news?"

"Yes."

"They're right."

"I can't believe you actually resorted to a cliché to make your point."

Lydia collapsed on the couch. "Nobody wants me."

"Surely somebody."

"Not so far. I've written to all the papers I can think of, and no one will give me a chance. I'm not even asking for a decent living wage."

"Don't worry. They wouldn't have given you one anyway."

"Do you know what this means? I'll probably have to work for some house organ, some newsletter, disgrace my name as a journalist by doing public relations. Mina, am I such a bad writer?"

Mina came from the kitchen and sat down on her clean, neat chair with its newly starched slipcover. "You're not creepy enough."

"A compliment from you?"

"Look at the portfolio you put together. All the articles are beautifully written, but most of them are features. You've never actually showed up at the house of a rape victim ten minutes after, or followed around the mother of an accident victim, asked her how it felt to lose her son-slash-daughter. I honestly think you're just too polite to be a reporter, too civil. Too decent."

"But I've planned my whole life around it, ever since I started reading 'Brenda Starr' on Sundays."

"Have you noticed that life isn't always like the comics?"

"Yes, but I was hoping."

"Maybe when you do your internship, something will develop."

"Mina, I'm doing my internship in Akron. Grime city."

"At least, if you get a puncture there'll be a spare available."

"What will you do when I'm gone?"

"Clean up?"

"Ha ha. No, really, Mina? I'm worried about you. I wish you'd stop demonstrating and all that. You're meeting weird types."

"I stopped demonstrating for civil rights last year. This year I'm doing something about it."

"Tutoring kids?"

Mina squirmed defensively. "Look, if I had all the time in the world, I would go south and join in. But I don't. I still plan to finish college. And the demonstrations on college campuses are getting us nowhere. They're making no impact. However, I do consider it important to prepare Negro children for their rightful place in our society; and if I can do that by tutoring three times a week, I'm willing. At least I feel I'm accomplishing something."

"Maybe you should get your teacher's certificate, like your mother wants."

Mina shrugged. "I don't want to be a teacher."

"What *do* you want to be? God, Mina, this is our senior year!"

"But it's only November. The world is young. I'm thinking about the Peace Corps."

"Dear, I love you, but what could you contribute? They're looking for home economics majors."

"I have languages."

"Do they speak Polish in Africa? What about social work?"

"I'm not that patronizing."

"It's a skill you can develop." Lydia saw that Mina was getting annoyed. "I worry about you, dear. Who's going to protect you from yourself when I'm away for six weeks? You have to admit, you do tend to get involved quickly. Hastily? Precipitously?"

"I'll behave," Mina promised. "You just see that you don't meet some tire worker and elope."

"Not likely. You know I can't stand a man who doesn't have enough money to get a manicure."

Mina, unlike Lydia, did not really spend much time thinking about her future. True, last year she had become incensed by the offenses against humanity in the South. She could not understand such barbaric treatment of one American citizen by another. But demonstrating had proved an empty experience for her. It was exciting, sure, but she soon realized that demonstrating in Columbus, Ohio, was not going to make a difference to those poor people in Birmingham.

She kept silent about her political activities when she went home to visit. Jerry, true to his word, had never really forgiven her for becoming a Jew. How would he feel if he knew she had become a "nigger-lover," too? She couldn't put her mother in the precarious position of defending her on such a major issue a second time.

Things hadn't felt right at home the last time Mina had visited, in October. Terry and Kristin were fine. Terry was in junior high, now, into sports, which made Jerry proud. Kristin was eleven and spent her time with Mina discussing her girlfriends and how awful some of them were. No, it wasn't the kids. It was something between her mother and stepfather. Mina was self-centered enough to suppose at first that it had to do with her. If such was the case, she went well out of her way to be extra nice to Jerry, discussing his favorite subject, John F. Kennedy's presidency, which Jerry considered a personal badge of honor. It was as if Kennedy had legitimized Catholics in America, whereas Mina saw the vital president as legitimizing youth and new ideas. Whatever their reasons for approval of the man, both could agree that John Kennedy was the best thing that had happened to the country in a long, long time, maybe ever since the end of the war.

Maria did not join in the love-fest. Had she become a closet Republican, Mina wondered. Her mother was on edge her entire visit. But she refused to talk about it when Mina got her alone. She just said something vague about how things work out in the end, whatever that was supposed to mean. Mina worried about her mother. What was happening that she couldn't share?

Maria didn't know how to stop it. What does a woman do to end her husband's love affair? She could throw a temper tantrum, insist that he stop seeing the "other woman." His response could be simple refusal. Then what would be her position? She would have already been defeated.

She wondered when Jerry had started the affair. She had no inkling, no sudden burst of knowledge. Maybe she still wouldn't have known if he hadn't come home smelling of another woman's perfume. He didn't desire her less; he didn't sleep with her less. But once she knew, she had to refuse Jerry. She couldn't bear to think of him making love to her, then slinking off to make love to another woman.

She wondered often if their fights over Mina had driven Jerry away? But why? She never accused him. She simply defended her daughter's right to choose the way she wanted to live her life. Mina, after all, was not a child. True, they still supported her, but that did not mean they could control her mind, her faith, her beliefs. Jerry wanted control.

Jerry had controlled her, his wife, for too long, Maria thought. And now she was caught. If Jerry left her—and who knows what he was planning with his mistress, his lover, whatever he called the woman—Maria would not be in good shape. She supposed she would get the house, custody of the children, child support. But what about maintaining her standard of living? Divorce wasn't so uncommon in America anymore. Maria knew women who were divorced. They kept up appearances, but they were living on the edge of poverty.

Maria was angry. She was angry not so much at Jerry as at herself. She remembered her catering business in Trenton, how well she had done financially. Here in Dayton, her pickles and salads brought in very little. She was now almost totally dependent on Jerry—not just emotionally, but financially, and that was worse. Emotionally, she would die inside if Jerry left her. She was already crippled by his betrayal. But what would she do financially? Would she be put in a position where she would have to beg Jerry for money? For herself, for their children? Would she be so humiliated?

She had been a fool. To give up her financial independence had been a mistake! Love does not conquer all. Marriage does not provide unending security. She knew that life was not made up of certainties, and yet she had allowed herself to believe that now her life was being lived on a sound basis. The certainties: Jerry loved her; he would always love her, always want her, always worship her and the two children she had given him. Dumb, Maria. Other women could give him children, too. Other women who were younger, prettier, less demanding, more admiring, more worshiping than she was.

What could she do to save herself? Should she wait for the ax to fall?

Maria had read a lot since coming to Dayton. She didn't have as much to do, with the children getting older and her workload less, so she read. Books, magazines, newspapers. There was talk about the need for women to develop a concept of themselves as independent people. Women were not simply extensions of the men they married. She had to laugh at that one. As of now, she was an appendage of Jerry; and if he chose to cut her off, she would wither very quickly. She cursed herself for falling into this trap.

There was an article in *Ladies' Home Journal* about surviving an affair. Maria read it. It suggested being loving, understanding, kind, compassionate. In other words, the woman again sacrifices everything, including her self-respect, her true emotions. She left the magazine open to that article and placed it on Jerry's side of the bed on a night that he said he had to work late. She made sure the bed light was shining on it. Then she turned her back and tried to sleep.

She heard Jerry come in. He was whistling. It must have been a good fuck. He entered their bedroom in his stocking feet. Good old Jerry, living by the clichés. She heard him go to his side of the bed and sit down. His hands fingered the magazine she had left for him. Was he simply tossing it aside? Or did the title catch his guilty eye? She didn't know. She didn't dare turn around.

She lay silently and made her breath go in and out regularly. She heard Jerry taking a shower, almost felt him slip on his pajamas. He got in bed and turned out his reading light. "How long have you known?" he asked, his voice tired and dead.

"Months," she answered, her back still turned.

"I'm sorry."

She said nothing.

He pressed his body against her. She felt revolted. "I'm sorry, Maria," he whispered intensely.

"Why?" she had to ask.

"She was—so available," he answered.

Maria closed her eyes in disgust.

"I won't see her again," he promised.

"Do you work with her?" He didn't answer. Okay, so he worked with her. And when he saw her again in the morning, he would forget his promises of the night before to his wife. "Well, Jerry, if you work with her, you have a real problem, don't you?"

"I can take care of it, if you can forgive me."

She turned to face him. He looked guilty, expectant, waiting for a scolding. Were all men just little boys, after all? Did they all grab for what they could get? "I can forgive you, Jerry, if you can decide what you want. I mean, really decide. If you want her, then you don't want me. You don't want the children. You don't want our life together. Think about it. Good night." She turned away from him again and waited. His hand gently traced her spine from her neck down to her rear. Then he fell silent next to her. "I love you, Maria," he whispered.

The next day was silly. That's the only way Maria could describe it. At eleven o'clock the doorbell rang. She opened the door to find a delivery man, who handed her a set of keys and a bouquet of flowers. The flowers, she knew, must be from her apologetic husband, but the keys? She looked out into the driveway. There sat a spanking new Thunderbird, red, flashy, dare she say sexy? The delivery man's? "Enjoy the car," he said to her.

She stood stupidly on the doorstep, watching him drive away with a companion in an old heap. She walked down to her Thunderbird, gazed happily at it, then fumbled with the card accompanying the flowers. "Paul at Tarsus" was all it said. No, wait, on the back was added, "Don't drive it until I can confirm the insurance." She laughed. Dear Jerry. Thank God he hadn't changed too much.

Maria went into the house to call Jerry's office. She knew she probably wouldn't be able to reach him. He was always in conference, but she had to try. "Margot?" she said, when his phone was answered.

"No, sorry. This is a temp."

"Oh. Is Margot sick?"

"Oh, ah, I believe she's been transferred. Would you like me to try to find her new extension for you?"

"No. No, that's all right." Maria slowly put down the phone. So it was Margot. How very common of Jerry! His own fucking secretary! The bastard! She put down the flowers before she tossed them at something. She tried to calm herself. After all, what was there to get mad about? She knew he was sleeping with someone. So why not Margot? Except that the bitch was married herself! God! Damn!

Maria controlled herself. She had no choice. She had to make everything seem normal for Terry and Kristin. She had to be sweetly enthusiastic about the present their father had given her, a new car. They were excited. They wanted to take a ride. She told them to go inside and do their homework.

When Jerry came home, he wanted everyone in the family to go for a ride. "I think it would be better if you and I took the car out first," she strongly suggested. "To work out any bugs."

"Whatever you say." He was being so damned agreeable.

She got him into the car and drove him out on the highway. "It was Margot!" she screamed at him.

"I know it was Margot. Watch the road."

"Margot! How could you?"

"How did you find out?"

"I called your office. You had a temp."

"Yeah. From the office pool. I told you I'd handle the situation. It was a lateral move. Margot didn't lose anything in the deal. And I gained back my wife. Didn't I?"

"Margot! You bastard."

"Pull over."

"What?"

"Up there. Into the park."

She did as he told her and stopped the car. "You should not drive when you are emotionally upset," he told her.

"I'm not driving."

"Look, Maria, I have had a very trying day."

"Oh, God!"

"You wanted me to end it. I've ended it. I sent her packing. It was not something that was easy to do to someone who had meant a lot to me over the past year."

"Year!"

"Almost. Our anniversary—"

"Oh, Christ!"

Jerry leaned back in the plush new car. "I can't win, can I? She hates me. And you hate me. I should have continued the affair."

"You still can, Jerry. We can simply get a divorce."

"Oh, fuck that, Maria."

"Everyone's doing it."

"I'm not doing it. And neither are you. People survive affairs, Maria. If their love is strong enough."

"Oh, don't talk to me about love. Not when you've just mentioned your anniversary with that tramp."

"Don't make me defend her, Maria. What do you want me to do? Take out a whip and beat myself with it?"

"Sounds good."

"Castrate myself?"

"Sounds even better."

He laughed and put his hand on her hair. "I love you. Can you honestly say you don't love me?"

"Right now?"

"Can't love me?"

She looked at him, at his lips, his cheeks, his eyes, his receding hairline, the wrinkles around his mouth. She leaned forward and let her lips gently touch his. "You hurt me, Jerry."

"I know. I'm hurting, too, Maria. I feel confused and battered. But I don't want to lose you."

"I don't want to lose you, either."

He pulled her to him over the gearshift. Their hug was awkward. "Whatever happened to cars with a single front seat, where two people could cuddle up in comfort?" he asked. "Let's go rent a motel room," he suggested.

"The kids."

"The kids can get along without us for a few hours."

"It would be too much like—"

"I want to be alone with you, Maria. Romantically alone, like we haven't been in a long time. Just you and me. No phone ringing, no television, no children squabbling. Just you and me with no clothes on, enjoying ourselves. Okay?"

She started the motor. "Where to?" she asked.

"You pick."

She laughed. "Don't want to go where you've already been?"

"Just stay away from the Starlight on Second."

"God. Motel Tacky?"

"Tryst."

She shook her head. "Jerry, you're impossible."

The first time they made love, there was more sadness than joy. The second time, uneasy laughter. The third time, a definite renaissance. "You'll have a heart attack," she warned him.

"You didn't think I had it in me, did you?" he replied proudly.

She lay in his arms and silently had to agree with him. She didn't think he had it in him, not three erections in one night. But then, there was never time for three goes at home. There was always too much interference. Now she knew that would have to stop. Whether they rented a motel room or somehow got rid of the kids, they had to set aside more time for each other, time to nurture their love. She smiled and sighed when she thought of it. They spent more time working on the lawn or cleaning the house than they did on their marriage. It had never occurred to either of them that a marriage needs work, too. The tie that binds had always been on automatic. But no more. She would make sure neither she nor Jerry ever took their marriage for granted again. The good things in life had to last.

Two weeks after her confrontation with Jerry and their promises to each other of love's renewal, John F. Kennedy was assassinated. It was ironic how she marked that terrible event on her mental calendar. An event that shattered so many illusions, so many hopes and dreams for the America she loved, served to heal the remaining wounds between Jerry and herself. They clung together for comfort and support. They knew they would survive. They had seen war and death and villainy, and they knew that life went on.

For the children, though, life would never be the same. The death of Kennedy was the beginning of betrayal, the loss of promise, the end of dreams.

46

FIRST SIGHT

MINA WAS CAUGHT IN THAT WINTER OF DEPRESSION. SOMEONE IN Dallas had assassinated the president of the United States.

Life drained out of the country; it became a land of despair.

People marched grimly on, aware now that madness was crisscrossing the land. Picking up the torch remained a dream while the country disintegrated. Civic responsibility was transformed into civil strife.

The assassination happened at an appropriate season of the year, just as winter was deadening the land. The leaves crumbled; the skies grayed; the wind blew away the last of dreams. Mina, along with other students, got ready to go home for the Christmas holidays. She dreaded going home, expecting the tenseness that had been so evident during her last visit. But a surprise was waiting for her. The holidays were more intimate, more joyful than they had been in a long time. There was a new tenderness, a new respect between her parents, a deeper sort of love.

Over New Year's Mina had the house to herself. Jerry had driven Maria and the children over the mountains of Pennsylvania to Trenton to visit the relatives. Mina sat in solitude New Year's Eve, watching the Times Square ball drop on television. But she wasn't really lonely. She thought of next New Year's, when she would be out of college, on her own, and she wondered, half-scared, half-expectant, what life was going to be like for her.

Mina returned to Ohio State for her last semester with a renewed commitment to find something to do after college. Her toughest course was going to be Diplomatic Documents of Central Europe 1913-1947. She also had a course in French reading, one on Scandinavian history, and another on how to become a historian. The last was a recruitment course for the graduate program, but she knew she was through with studying. Learning was fun, but so was doing.

She had to admit that doing was less fun than it had been last semester. Lydia was missing. She was in Akron and had written to say that she was suffering from air pollution. Aside from that, she was writing obits and making the coffee run. So Mina's apartment was finally neat, but lonely.

She began to put in more hours at the Community Center. The students she tutored were older, tougher. While she was teaching them how to read and compute, they were telling her about their exploits in petty crime. They always ended their tales with, "But don't worry. We won't rob *you*." Sometimes, when she left the center, she wasn't quite sure of their sincerity.

Her favorite pupil was a boy named Chester. He was fifteen, waiting until he was sixteen to drop out of school. She amused him, she was sure, by all her pep talks on the American way: Get an education, get ahead. She found his cavalier attitude toward life and responsibility somewhat charming, when she should have found it frightening in someone so young.

One day she came to the center for her session with Chester, among others, to find he was not present. This was not unusual, but she felt it her duty to try to find out where he might be. "Has Chester gone AWOL?" she casually asked his friends.

"Police picked him up last night, B and E."

"B and E?" she questioned.

Stupid of her—breaking and entering. "Well, isn't he out on bail?"

They laughed at her.

"Parental recognizance?"

"Ain't got but a mother, and where she's at no one knows."

Mina was not the type to go herself and bail Chester out. For some reason, jails and police and the like were not her thing. She wanted to stay as far away from them as possible, despite all those elementary school lectures about policemen being your friends. Somehow, not trusting anyone in a uniform was more of a certainty for her.

But she couldn't let Chester rot, or even be sent away to reform school. He knew enough about crime already. She trotted up to the Community Center's legal affairs department. She had never been up there before, because, as much as she distrusted cops, she distrusted lawyers more. And from sensing the atmosphere in this office, she realized she was right. The kids downstairs still had their defiance. The people in the legal affairs office were burned out. Desperation, no. Just dull bleakness, from living with the knowledge that they were about to be screwed again.

"May I help you?"

Mina glanced at one of the few white faces in the room. He had on a shirt and a tie, but compensated for that formality by having his shirtsleeves rolled up, even though it was the middle of winter. His hair was wavy and brown, his face pleasant, his eyes tired. She walked over to him. "Yes," she said.

He waited. Then he smiled. "How may I help you?"

She sat down across the metal desk from him. "Maybe I should wait my turn."

"You're here now," he pointed out.

"I have a student. His name is Chester Jackson. He's been arrested for breaking and entering. I believe he's still in jail. I don't think anyone's around to bail him out."

"You'd like to know how to do it?"

"No. I—"

"You're not big on police stations?"

"Right. I have an aversion to uniforms and confinement."

He flipped over to a new sheet on his legal pad and wrote down the information she gave him. "I'll try to take care of it on my way home," he told her.

"Could you let me know what happens?"

"Name and phone number?"

"Mina Prychek, 237-2373."

With relief she left the legal affairs office and returned to her tutoring. She gave Chester a few fleeting thoughts that evening while she was doing a passable translation of French into Polish for her documents class. When the phone rang, she was deep into the meaning of a Polish word she was almost ready to call her mother about. Startled, she picked the phone up and rather breathlessly said hello.

"Did I catch you at something?"

"Translation." She tried to place the voice and couldn't. Was it one of Lydia's friends? The previous semester, she'd had more boyfriends than Mina had ever managed.

"I've checked on that character of yours."

"Excuse me?"

"Is this Mina Prychek?"

"Yes, this is she."

"Maybe I should start again. Hello, I'm Ted Eisenberg."

"Who?"

There was silence at the other end of the line. Ted Eisenberg. Ted Eisenberg. Was he in one of her classes? Which one? "Ted Eisenberg, legal affairs, Community Center," he tried again.

"Oh! Oh, yes! Sorry. I don't think I knew your name."

"Well, it's Ted."

"Hi, Ted."

"I'm calling you about this Chester Jackson you were concerned about."

"Yes."

"Did you know that he has a record of—"

"Yes. Well, either he's been pretty graphic in describing his real exploits or he has a great imagination."

"I don't think he's been lying to you. And I don't think I did him too much of a favor by going down there."

"Why?"

"The police had him registered under the name Oliver Twist."

"Oh?"

"Does that mean anything to you?"

"We were working on the book. It was part of his English class assignment in high school."

"Well, at least he got something from his tutoring."

"Surely the police—"

"They had no idea that Oliver Twist wasn't his real name."

"Hmm. Is Chester—"

"Can't find anyone who wants him. Anyway, I'm afraid there's too much evidence against him. He'll get what legal representation the public defender's office can provide, but chances are he's going to go to a juvenile home."

"Can't you help, somehow?"

"I'm not a lawyer, Mina. Just a law student. Sorry."

"Well, thanks for trying."

She let the phone sink back into its cradle. A feeling of depression hit her. What good would Oliver Twist do Chester now?

47

CAREFUL
DELIBERATIONS

ON HER SECOND TRIP TO THE COMMUNITY CENTER THAT WEEK, she and her students commiserated over Chester's incarceration. They all agreed with her that he was a cheerful crook and that life at the center wouldn't be quite the same without him. They even told her they would now consider leaving their clothes and books in the gym lockers again.

While Mina was helping one of the girls learn how to read well enough to fill out at job application, she looked up to find Ted Eisenberg watching her. "Hi," she said with a smile.

"So this is where you work."

"Volunteer."

"Ah, yes. What would this center do without Ohio State volunteers?"

It was a question she didn't have time to answer right then. "Thanks again for the effort," she told him, anxious to get back to the job application.

"What time do you finish? Maybe I can give you a lift home."

She studied him. Did she really want a ride home from him? On the other hand, did she want to walk those blocks in the cold and then wait for the bus? "Five, five-thirty?" she said.

"Fine. Just come up and get me."

He turned and walked away. Cute buns, Mina thought, then censored herself. Soon she would start sounding like Lydia!

"That your man?" her student asked.

"Certainly not."

"Why not?"

"Because I don't know him. Now, let's get to the concept of being bonded."

She had two more students to go, one in English, another who had trouble pronouncing the "Declaration of Independence," much less understanding it. Sometimes she thought tutoring was just as meaningful as spitting against the wind. At ten after five, she was ready to close up shop.

She went up and sat in the legal affairs office until 5:30, while Ted Eisenberg was helping a woman who had two small children and had been served an eviction notice for nonpayment of rent. Mina heard him explain to her the legal action she could take to forestall the eviction for a week. In the meantime, she had to get herself to a city social worker to see if there was any way she could get the funds to pay her rent. When the woman got up and turned around, Mina saw that she was younger than Mina herself. How could the woman have saddled herself with such horrendous problems at such a young age?

Ted straightened his desk, turned off the light, and stood up. She rose and joined him. "How depressing," she said to him.

He shrugged. "It's an endless cycle of depression. You're lucky. You see the young ones. They still have some spirit left."

They walked silently to his car, parked along the street. She could see why no one bothered it. It looked like it barely ran. Ted opened the door for her, and she slid in, glad to be out of the cold winter wind. She shivered slightly and rubbed her hands together. "Don't worry," Ted said, as he joined her. "The heater will be going in a moment."

The car started. She was surprised. Ted carefully pulled away from the curb and out of the neighborhood. Only when he got on the highway did he speed up. "Do you want to go out to dinner?" he asked her, as if it were a sudden inspiration.

She considered it. "I have so much work."

"But you do have to eat. Chinese? That won't take long."

She smiled. "Okay." She had never had Chinese food until she and Lydia moved into the apartment and Lydia began bringing it home. It was a taste Mina was still developing. When they got to the China Palace, she let Ted order for her. "You don't keep kosher, do you?" he asked.

Mina was shocked. What made him think she was Jewish? "No," she answered.

He ordered hot-and-sour soup for two, one shrimp dish, one pork dish. "We'll share," he told the waiter. "Now," he said, as he poured tea, "tell me all about yourself."

She laughed. "Nothing to tell."

"Just a student with a social conscience?"

"Not much of that anymore," Mina admitted. "Changing the world is hard work. Demonstrating is more fun."

"More visible. Highly intoxicating. What are you studying?"

"History. I'm a senior."

"What are you going to do with it?"

"Don't ask. You'll make me homesick for my roommate. That's one of her favorite questions to me."

"Why would the question make you homesick? Has she left college?"

"No. Just a journalism internship in Akron. She'll be back in March, but the apartment is lonesome without her."

"You live in an apartment alone? You're lucky. Right now I'm rooming with three other second-year law students, and it's an awful bore."

"Don't you like the law?"

"It's a living." He smiled. "And someone's got to do it."

"What would you really like to do?"

"I don't know. Fly to the moon. Discover Atlantis. Move the Dodgers back to Brooklyn."

"Hush now," she told him. "Lawyers can't be dreamers."

"Do you have a boyfriend?" he asked.

"No one special." She gave him a safe answer.

"Why not? Ohio State's a big place."

"Too big to find anyone."

Their soup came. She was glad. She chided herself for not being more inventive. She should have talked about Biff, Mr. Fraternity; or Floyd, the Jock; or Trevor, Mr. Sensitive Sociologist. Except that none of them existed. She took a gulp of the soup. He should have warned her. She had never had hot-and-sour soup before, only wonton. She started coughing, making an absolute fool of herself.

"Are you all right?" he asked anxiously.

She took out a tissue and wiped the tears away. "Good soup," she managed to croak. But she was able to finish it without embarrassing herself further.

She listened while Ted told her about his undergraduate years at Kenyon College, where he had majored in English. "I wanted to be a writer, but I couldn't sit still long enough. My mother said I could become either a doctor or a lawyer, or join the family business."

"What does your family do?"

"Commercial printing. My older brother's already involved. We never got along as children. I can't imagine being stuck in the same business with him all my life. And the sight of blood makes me faint. So—"

"So you set your foot along the path of righteousness."

"What?"

She laughed. "You're going to become a public defender," she guessed.

"God, no. What gave you that idea?"

"Your work at the Community Center."

"Oh. That's just to salve my social conscience. No. I'm going into some sort of money-making law."

"Become a company lawyer?" She almost sneered.

"Heavens no. After reading Sloan Wilson? No. I'm thinking of a small family practice. Wills and such. Real estate. Maybe a few divorces here and there for excitement."

"In other words, misery pays."

"I never said I was an idealist. I guess you are."

"No." She shrugged. "I'm not anything really. I'm sort of enjoying myself while I can."

"That sounds promising. I like a girl who knows how to enjoy herself."

"I didn't mean it in any particular way."

When he took her home that night and asked to see her again, she agreed. "This Saturday?" he suggested.

"Why not?"

Mina discovered there were certain advantages to not having a roommate constantly in attendance. Saturday nights with Ted led to weeknight study dates, first at the library, either his law library or her documents library. Library dates led to apartment studies, where each piled up books and got in a good two or three hours of work before one of them would break, first for food and then—well, it was hard having someone of the opposite sex so close, so available.

It had always been their intention to save the fun for Saturdays. Those were the nights when they kissed after the movies, after pizza, when they huddled together against the cold, had snowball fights in the late-evening hours. But it was hard not to yearn for the kissing when they were alone together in her apartment, when there was no one there and their bodies were so close and tempting.

She started it first, she guessed. She looked at him one night when he was standing at the refrigerator. He turned and saw her eyes. He closed the refrigerator and went to her. Why that night was different from all the others, she didn't know. He had often kissed her, fondled her breasts through her sweater, let his hand run down over her rear, while she had meekly kept her hands on his back, his hair, his chest. But tonight he eased her sweater up over her head, and she didn't stop him. She simply looked at his lips as he stared at her breasts, as he ran his hands over her bra, then moved them behind to unhook it. His head fell down on her and she embraced it, held him to her while his mouth found her nipples.

She moaned. He backed away, took off his shirt, unbuckled his pants. She was scared. He went to her again. "I'm not going to hurt you," he told her. And she believed him. He unzipped her jeans and pulled them off. Her underpants went along with them. She half-lay, half-sat naked on the couch. He removed his pants and stood there in his underwear. She closed her eyes tight, and he laughed at her. He lifted her up until they were standing together body to body, and she could feel him hard against her. Would she be disgusted? Would she love it? What would happen to her?

He placed her hand inside his underpants. She didn't know what to do. "Just hold it," he told her.

He renewed his assault on her body, finally sinking down and kissing the hair between her legs, jabbing out his tongue and licking her. She sank down on the couch, her legs lifted to his shoulders as he continued. She closed her eyes and was lost in the pleasure. His hands came for her breasts, and she felt something happen that she could not describe. Her body shook, and she knew she was going to die, but instead she floated. Ted urgently said her name. "You're wet enough now, Mina. It won't hurt."

He lifted her up and sat down where she had been. He placed her on his lap. "Just work me into you," he told her. She felt his cock pressing into her where his tongue and fingers had been before. Then she felt pain and wanted to pull back, but Ted held her and pushed forward until there was no barrier between them. He held her hips and moved in and out of her until he came and lay back with a smile.

"Are you okay?" he asked her.

"Hold me."

She pressed her sweaty body against his sweaty body. "I'm ashamed," she told him.

"Yeah," he said seriously. "I understand."

"I've never—"

"I know. Believe me."

"Do you—"

"I love you."

"I can take care of myself."

"Yeah. Sure. We didn't use anything."

"What?" she asked.

"Birth control."

"Oh, God."

Next time they did. And the time after that. And all the days following when he came over and they could not concentrate on their studying, not until they had tumbled onto her bed and devoured each other once, sometimes twice. They agreed that this was not good for their grade-point averages, but they could not stop.

She got her period. They celebrated with a bottle of wine. Ted taught her how to give him a blow job. "What do I get out of it?" she wanted to know.

"The pleasure of seeing me happy," he answered her mockingly.

She was happy when he was happy. He seemed happy when she was happy. But all the time in the back of her mind, she heard the eternal message: Nice girls don't. What did Ted think of her? What was going to happen to them? She was afraid.

48

THE PRODIGAL'S RETURN

TED PICKED UP THE PHONE WHEN IT RANG. IT WAS A NATURAL reaction maybe, but it could have been her mother. Mina glowered at him. "Hello?" he said.

"Who's this?" someone at the other end shouted.

"Whom did you wish to speak to?"

"What have you done with Mina?"

Ted handed the phone to Mina. "Hello?"

"Mina! Obviously, I cannot count on your good sense to guide you through without me. Who's in our apartment?"

"Lydia!"

"Yes. Remember me? Your roommate? Or have you made other arrangements?"

"Don't be silly." She paused. "When are you coming home?"

"This Sunday. If there are any condoms under the bed, remove them. Not for my sake, you understand, but Mother has decided to come to Akron to pick me up and then drive me to Columbus. What would I do without her?"

After Mina got off the phone, she explained the situation to Ted. "The end of paradise," he joked.

Mina was ecstatic to see Lydia again. She bustled in and brought the place to life. Her mother was distressed by Lydia's added layer of verbal vulgarity. "She thinks she's in *Front Page*," Naomi Friedan confided to Mina.

"It's the real world, Mother," Lydia retorted.

They went out together and had a nice, safe dinner at one of the saner, more conservative restaurants before Mrs. Friedan headed back to Cleveland. Mina and Lydia waved a wan farewell, then hurried into their apartment to exchange six weeks of gossip. "You first!" Lydia insisted.

"No. You."

"All right. They've offered me a job."

"I thought you hated Akron."

"Hey. You have to start someplace. I'll be doing obits and rewrites for a mere pittance. But at least I'll have something on my résumé. And I like the people. They're fun. Except they drink too much. And smoke too much. And—well, okay, so they have their faults. But I'm relieved to know what I'll be doing come June. I thought no one was ever going to hire me. I'll give you the nuts and bolts later. Out with it! Who is he?"

"Ted Eisenberg."

"Jewish?"

"I never asked."

"Ted Eisenberg. Jewish. Daddy will be pleased."

"Come on, Lydia. He's just a friend."

"How much of a friend?"

Mina sighed.

"That much?"

"It's happened."

"My God! You? Little Mina Prychek. The one with the Elmer's Glue between her legs."

"It's not funny, Lydia. It's—"

"So, did you like it?"

"Yes," Mina admitted.

"I told you you would. You have to trust me on these things."

"Lydia, do you feel any—shame?"

"Well—" Lydia considered it. "I did the first time. But then, he was a real bozo. I told you I caught him picking his nose. But the second time? No, I rather liked Richard. A bit Nordic perhaps, but there was something about him that was rather cuddly."

"He was a good ten pounds overweight."

"That must have been it then. When am I going to get a chance to meet this Ted Eisenberg?"

"What bothers me is, what does it all mean?"

"Honey, it's just a fuck. It's not the end of the world."

Mina frowned. "Your mother was right. Look, Lydia, I'm not the kind of girl who can sleep around and enjoy it."

Lydia took offense. "I don't consider two men sleeping around. Sleeping around, hell, that's at least three. Besides, I'm not planning to get married. So what should I do? Hold off until I'm thirty? Let's be sensible."

"You see, what if this is just a one-semester thing?"

"I'll talk to Ted. I'll set him straight."

"No thanks."

"No, honestly."

"Really, Lydia, you've done enough for me already by making the apartment available these past six weeks. Without that, I would have still been walking the straight and narrow."

"That's right. Blame it on your oldest, dearest friend. So when am I going to meet this hunk?"

"He's not a hunk. He's a law student."

"Oh, Jesus, Mina. Your conversion wasn't just a whim. You're going all the way with this Jewish thing."

"Stop it! You'll meet Ted soon, and you better like him."

But Lydia didn't get a chance to meet Ted until the following Saturday, because she had not only her classes to resume, but also her work at the paper. She never got home before eleven at night, a point well noted by Mina and Ted, who managed to compress their sex/study dates into this new time.

For the all-important first meeting, they decided on Saturday brunch. Ted had a western omelet and a bagel; Mina, pancakes; Lydia, a greasy hamburger and a Coke. Although both Ted and Lydia were from Cleveland, they lived in different suburbs. They spent the brunch trying to find out if they knew anyone in common. They hit on one person, from the B'nai B'rith youth group, whom they both detested. That out of the way, they talked about Lydia's experiences in Akron and Ted's summer and after-school work as a commercial printer. Mina sat silent, observing her two friends and listening to their animated conversation. "Well," Lydia said at the end of the brunch, after Ted picked up the check, "I approve."

"Gee, thanks. I was desperately waiting," Mina finally said.

"You know, Mina is such a strange, intense child that I thought, God, she's going to pick some creep. But so far, Ted, you seem perfectly normal. I think you'll be good for her. Of course, far be it from me to push this relationship, but let me remind you that in

April we have to tell our landlord if we want the apartment for next year. I certainly won't want it. I'll be in Akron. However, as a cozy little love nest for a young married couple, it wouldn't be so bad, would it?"

While Ted laughed, Mina sat there blushing, wishing she could kill Lydia. Afterward, when they were alone in the apartment, she protested. Lydia couldn't understand what had made her so angry. "Men need a little push now and then," she insisted.

"Ted and I have never said anything about marriage!" Mina shouted.

"Well. Now the subject will be harder to avoid. Believe me, someday you'll thank me. And yes, I will be your maid of honor."

Before she jumped Lydia and pulled out her hair, Mina turned around and slammed out of the apartment. Everything was ruined. Ted would think she had put Lydia up to this, that she had somehow indicated to Lydia that she planned to marry Ted. Now he would probably believe she was pressuring him, making demands. Ted would—oh, who the hell cared what he thought? She kicked through the snow, went into the first theater she could find, and sat through a French film shot entirely in shadows. During the middle of it, she got up to get some popcorn. She guessed that that was when she missed the "symbolism" everyone was talking about when the lights finally went up.

49

A FAMILY AFFAIR

TED KICKED A STONE AHEAD OF HIM ON THE SIDEWALK AND HURried on. Mina half ran after him. She didn't understand him today. Yesterday, he had been fine. He had crammed for an exam a week ago, got back the results, and was third in the class. Of course, she never had any doubts about how bright he was. Yesterday he had bought her a bouquet of daffodils to prove conclusively that spring had finally reached Columbus, Ohio. Today he wouldn't even let her walk by his side. "Ted!" she called.

He stopped and waited for her. "I'm not in training for anything, am I?" she questioned.

The way he looked at her made her think she was in training for something; she just didn't know what. "My parents called last night."

"That's nice," she told him.

"Really?"

He started walking again, this time more slowly. She could finally catch her breath and still keep up with him. As she walked, she tried to figure out what Ted was implying about the phone call from his parents. She knew she was always overjoyed to receive a call from her mother. There was so much they had to share. She assumed Ted felt the same way about his family.

"Passover's Friday night this year. Did you know that?"

She confessed she didn't. She hadn't really been to a seder yet, which she supposed did not make her a good convert; but it always fell during the week sometime, when both she and Lydia had something serious to do, like study.

Ted stopped, turned and faced her. "My family knows I've been seeing someone. They want me to bring her up for the seder."

"Well?" she responded in her most noncommittal fashion.

Ted turned and walked on. "You don't know my family," he called to her, as he picked up speed again.

"You don't know mine either," she yelled forward.

She had of course explained her family to Ted. He found her situation vastly amusing. He even teased her, telling her that Jerry sounded like a person he'd love to meet. "Jerry has his good points," Mina defended. "He also has his prejudices. But then, don't we all?"

Ted had spoken to her mother several times on the phone, just to say "Hi, how are you doing?" It was always an embarrassing conversation for him, but it paid off. Her mother assured Mina that Ted had a very nice voice; he sounded so polite over the telephone; when was she going to meet him? And then her mother would try to extract from Mina exactly what sort of relationship she had with Ted. Mina always replied with something like, "Oh, you know, just a friend." She didn't think her mother would ever forgive her if she knew Mina had lost her virginity.

"Trial by fire," Ted mused.

"What?"

"Nothing. So, what are we going to do?"

"That's up to you, isn't it? They're your family."

"My grandmother will be there. My brother, his wife, their two-year-old, my sister, her husband, my father. My mother."

"You don't think they'll like me?"

"I'm afraid."

"Well, if you think I'm acceptable to sleep with but not to take home to your family, you should tell me now."

He put his arms around her, hugged her, kissed her. "Jerk," he said. "Here I'm trying to protect you from a fate worse than death, meeting my family, and you give me a line like that. My family is—"

"Meshuga?" she tried.

"No. That would be charming. Um, how can I put it? Have you ever seen crows picking at the carcass of a dead animal? That's my family."

She laughed.

"And the seder brings out the worst in them. Any argument they've had for the past ten years, they bring up again. My brother had this beautiful girlfriend he brought to the seder. She made it past the hard-boiled eggs but fainted into the matzo-ball soup. Mother convinced him she was too frail to bear children. So then he found Mrs. Hale and Bitchy, and she fit right in. How can I expose you to that?"

"I can take care of myself."

"You think so? You who are too shy even to bring up marriage? You had to have your roommate do it for you."

She lowered her eyes. "That's a misinterpretation on your part. I didn't *have* Lydia bring it up. There's just no stopping her when she starts talking. In any case, counselor, you're the one who's supposed to bring up the subject of marriage."

"I love a woman who knows her place," he teased. "Look, do you want to talk about marriage?" He watched her blush. Then he pulled her off the sidewalk and lifted her onto a stone wall. "It's money," he told her. "I've been trying to figure out how we can manage on what I get from my parents. I'm not going to ask them to support me when I'm married."

"You mean they won't pay for your last year in law school?"

"Oh, yeah. They'll pay for that, and they'll pay for my room and board. I won't ask them to pay for *our* room and board."

"But I'll be graduating this year, and I can work."

"I won't have my wife working for me."

"Or is that just an excuse?"

"For what?"

"For not wanting to get married. Not wanting to marry me."

He lifted her down from the wall so that her body was close to his. "Do you think you're the first girl I ever slept with?"

She smiled. "No."

"Do you think I spend every extra minute of my time with you just on the off chance that I can fuck you?"

"Umm. Maybe." She grinned up at him.

"I want to marry you, Mina, when I can support you."

"Is that a proposal?"

"Not yet. Maybe you better meet my family before we talk marriage. I'm going to give you a chance to back out." He took her hand and pulled her back onto the sidewalk. "Don't bring anything along that makes you look pretty. Don't pack anything you wouldn't want my mother to see, because, chances are, she'll go snooping in your suitcase. Do bring something for indigestion."

Lydia was thrilled that Mina was going to Cleveland for the seder. First, it meant that she could get a ride with them to Cleveland, now that her own mother also had insisted that she show up for the seder, since it was on Friday. Second, "This means he really is serious about you."

"He talks about meeting his family as if it were a war game."

"Darling, if you're going to be Jewish, you're going to have to understand about the Jewish family. The unfortunate part of it is that you'll have to meet everybody. The fortunate part is that half of them won't be speaking to the other half. Don't try to be diplomatic. Just let it all hang loose. And—I have had one of my brilliant ideas!"

She ran to the phone and called Ted. When she put the phone down, she turned triumphantly to Mina. "Don't I always protect you? The second night of the seder you'll spend at our house. I think Ted was crying with gratitude when I hung up."

Despite Lydia's vast store of bawdy stories from her internship in Akron, Ted became more and more morose as they inched toward Cleveland in his car, which should have been junked years ago. He was so worried that Mina almost believed she should start panicking. "What if I stay with Lydia?" she suggested halfway to Cleveland.

"I should have thought about that sooner," Ted replied. "But Mom has already prepared Arthur's room for you."

"Does the room have a window with bars?" Lydia guessed.

"It's not the bars I'm worried about; it's the hidden camera."

"You're joking," Mina said.

"I hope so."

They dropped off Lydia with promises to be on time for the next night's seder. Then they drove the ten miles through traffic to Ted's house. Mina was impressed. The house, old and brick, was on a street with little traffic, set back from the sidewalk and surrounded by a well-landscaped lawn. "Beautiful," she told him.

"Umm."

"Ted, smile and be happy. We're together."

"I hope you feel that way by Sunday evening."

As soon as they pulled into the driveway, the back door opened, and a woman in an apron came out. She waited smiling, anxious, as Ted turned off the motor and opened the door. She didn't look like such an ogre. Mina sat in the car and watched while Ted and his mother embraced. She really felt like an outsider. Then she opened the door and went around the car. Ted broke from the embrace and held out his hand to her. "Mother, this is Mina Prychek."

"Mina," the woman said with a smile. "Welcome."

"Thank you, Mrs. Eisenberg."

"Please call me Adele. Come on in, please. You've had a long ride. Ted, get the bags."

Mina let herself be escorted into the kitchen, which seemed occupied by food, food, and more food. "You've been very busy."

"I know," Adele commented. "A mother's work, right? Let me take you to your room so you can freshen up. I've been so anxious to meet you. Ted's been protecting you like a hidden treasure. Everyone in the family is wondering what you're like."

Mina smiled and followed Adele up the stairs. Ted came quickly behind them with the bags. He dropped his off in front of his room, then followed his mother and Mina a few steps down the hall to Arthur's room. "Here we are. You're right across from the bathroom here," Adele explained. "I'm sorry the room doesn't look more feminine."

"It's fine," Mina said. "Very nice."

"Well, you take your time and settle in. Ted, why don't you come downstairs and talk to your old mother."

"In a minute, Mom. Just let me see that Mina has everything she needs."

They watched while Adele disappeared downstairs. "Now was that so bad?" Mina asked him.

"Not yet."

"She seems very, very nice."

He stared at her and nodded. "I didn't say my family wasn't nice. Did I?"

"Then what exactly did you say?"

"Do you have towels and everything?"

They looked around and found that there was an extra set in the bathroom. "If someone uses them, here's where you can find more." Ted led her to the linen closet.

"I'm fine, Ted. Go down and see your mother."

"Take my advice. Shower now, while there's still hot water." He turned and left her.

Mina smiled and hugged herself. She walked across the landing and heard Ted downstairs with Adele. She should take his advice and shower, she supposed, but instead she walked into his room. It was full of high school pennants and college pennants, pictures of Ted on the baseball team, photos of what she took to be his senior prom, his radio, a dolphin from Sea World, a penknife, his bar mitzvah photo. She smiled as she lovingly looked around. She wished that Ted were here so she could hold him, both his past and his present.

Instead she walked out of the room and took a shower. She put on a wine-red dress that Lydia had assured her made her look totally nondescript. Her heels were conservative and black. Her hair was, as usual, brown and frizzy. Why had she been cursed with such hair, when her mother's was so gorgeously blond? Not a single gray hair on her mother. Oh, well. She supposed if she could ever see a picture of her father, she would understand.

As she was going downstairs, Ted was coming up. "I left you some hot water," she told him.

"You look beautiful."

His eyes told her she did. "I'm supposed to look nondescript."

"Impossible. I'll be down in half an hour."

Mina went into the kitchen and offered to help. "Not necessary," Adele said. "Sit down in the living room and read."

"I'm really used to working, Mrs. Eisenberg."

"Adele."

"Adele. Please let me do something. I can't just sit around and watch you work."

"Well—if you'd like, you can set the table."

"Fine. Great."

"There'll be ten of us." Adele walked Mina into the dining room and showed her where the silver and the dishes were kept. Mina happily set about her task, anxious to show her competency. She was arranging the wine glasses when Ted's father arrived home and introduced himself.

Her only disappointment about Ted's father was that he was bald. She wondered if Ted also would lose his hair in the distant future. Ted came down, looking extremely handsome in his suit and tie. "Joe, take a picture," Adele called from the kitchen. Joe lined them up against the sofa in the living room and snapped twice. Mina smiled through her flash-cube blindness.

Then Joe disappeared with Adele while others began ringing the doorbell. Mina tried to keep them all straight. There was Arthur, Ted's older brother. He was married to Laurie. They had a two-year-old son, Josh. Then there was Claire, Ted's sister, and her husband, Stan. There was Grandma Rosen, whom Claire and Stan had picked up from the Jewish Home on their way over. The one thing Mina immediately liked about Ted's family was that she didn't have to say anything. Everyone else did the talking, all at once.

It was almost time for the seder when Adele looked at the table, tsked, and started rearranging the silverware and the plates. Mina felt an inward plunge of the knife. Quietly, she said to Ted, "I guess I didn't set the table the way your mother likes it."

"Darling, you'll never do anything the way my mother likes it. Get used to that fact. Ask Laurie or even Claire. They can give you day-by-day evidence."

At the table Mina was placed between Ted and Arthur. During the reading of the seder, Ted occasionally put his hand on the back of her neck, gently ruffling the underside of her hair. Mina wanted to tell him to stop. His mother was watching them like a hawk. Or was it like a lioness with her cub? By the time they got to the soup, everyone was ready to talk about something other than the ten plagues. "So how're the law studies coming along?" Arthur asked his brother.

"Just fine, Art."

"You know," Arthur confided in Mina, "Ted was too good to come into the family business, so now Mom and Dad are putting out, sending him to law school."

Mina nodded.

"You suffer for your children. That's what life's all about," Adele remarked. "Right, Laurie? Well Laurie wouldn't know. She's put Josh in day care already."

"Nursery school. You know what my nerves are like. I can't stand that screaming all day."

"Josh is a normal, healthy child. He's exuberant. He loves life," Joe proclaimed. "Would you take that away from him?"

"All I want to take away from him are his vocal cords," Laurie retorted.

Mina smiled down at Josh, who had left his chair and was circulating around the table. He placed his greasy hands on her dress. She touched his golden-brown hair. "Do you like children, Mina?" Adele asked.

"Oh, yes," Mina said.

"Why?" Claire asked.

"I suppose it's because I have two half-siblings who are much younger than I. It was fun helping my mother with them, watching them grow up."

"Your mother's a divorcee?" Joe wondered.

"Widowed."

"Prychek's a Czech name," Grandma Rosen said.

"But Mina's Jewish, Grandma," Claire said. "Anyone can see that."

"I can't stand the Czech people. They smell."

Ted rubbed his hand across his forehead. "Thank you, Grandma, for your input. Stan, how's the business going?"

"Slow season, April. But soon people will start coming in for Mother's Day."

"Stan owns a card shop," Ted explained. "Claire helps out there."

"She had a miscarriage last year," Adele explained. "But now they're trying again."

"Oh," Mina said. She stepped on Ted's foot under the table, and his hand went to his mouth to cover his laughter.

"Something's caught in Ted's throat!" Adele shouted.

"Nothing, Mom," he assured her.

"Ted's the youngest," Arthur explained to Mina. "Nothing's too good for him. No one expected anything from him except that he live like a prince."

"Did you have ambitions to be a lawyer?" Mina asked.

"That's not the point, is it?" Arthur replied. "You know, each child should get a piece of the pie, a piece. Claire here got a big wedding, I got four years of college and a chance to join Dad in the business. Ted had to go to Kenyon because everyone at the high school said he was so special. Then he had to go to law school because he was too special to get his hands dirty."

Mina bit her lower lip. Then she said quietly, "Don't criticize Ted in front of me."

"Ooh!" Grandma Rosen exclaimed. "A fighter. We haven't had a fighter in the family since Aunt Marla died."

"Just ignore him," Ted said under his breath.

"That's what you specialize in, isn't it?" Claire said to her younger brother. "Ignoring us."

"I'm here, aren't I?"

"Mom had to beg you to come. She told me. She was crying. Crying. Your own mother."

"I'm saying nothing. Just to have you all with me is what makes me happy," Adele put in.

"What would make me happy is if you'd all shut up," Joe added for good measure.

"Prychek? That's a Czech name, isn't it?" Grandma Rosen repeated.

"It could be," Mina agreed. "But in this case it isn't. It's Polish. I'm Polish, was born there, born a Catholic. I converted two years ago."

Afterward, when she thought about it, Mina was pleased with herself. She felt that she had added not only drama to that particular night, different from all other nights, but also another chapter to the Eisenberg saga of dramas. It certainly drew the daggers away from poor Ted's throat. Her favorite moment was when Adele, before she would eat with it, wiped the silver Mina had set out.

Ted was wrong about one thing. She didn't have indigestion after the meal. She didn't really eat anything except the soup and a hard-boiled egg. She was grilled so heavily after her pronouncement of unfavorable paternity, she didn't have a chance. "Well, that was the seder," Ted said to her when they went out later for a walk, despite the fact that the temperature had dropped and it was misting slightly.

"You understated the situation," she chided him.

He put his arm on her shoulder. "I wouldn't blame you if you demanded to be taken to a motel room."

"Do scenes make you horny?"

"I meant, if you didn't want to stay at my house."

"Oh, I'll stay. Unless I'm kicked out. But I will be locking my door tonight. Not that I don't trust your mother, but I'm averse to suffocation by pillow."

"So, now you know why I didn't ask you to marry me. I couldn't do that to you."

She laughed at him and brushed his cheek with her hand. "The Bible says that when a man marries, he leaves his own family and cleaves to his wife, whatever the hell 'cleaves' means."

"We'd still have to see them every now and then."

"Your grandmother's right. I am a fighter."

"Then if I asked you, would you say yes?"

"Ask and find out."

He stopped. The mist fell on them, making their hair shine under the streetlight like diamonds. "Mina Prychek, will you become my wife?"

"Yes."

They kissed, and it was like the first kiss ever. "We'll be happy together," she promised him.

"I've learned at my mother's knee: Nothing is ever perfect."

"I love you. That's perfect enough for me."

"I want to sleep with you."

"Don't you always?" She smiled. "You know, now that it's official, you have to come home and visit my family."

"Don't get mad, get even?"

"Let's go tell your parents."

"And aggravate my mother's heart condition?"

It wasn't until they reached the Friedans' house the next evening that they could really celebrate. Adele and Joe Eisenberg had reacted glumly to the news. On the other hand, Naomi and Saul Friedan broke out the champagne. Mina didn't really think it was for her and Ted alone. Alan, Lydia's older brother, had shown up this Passover with a Frenchwoman he had met on one of his wine-buying tours overseas. "Zimone," Lydia dramatically called her, though of course her name was Simone. Mina enjoyed speaking French to her, even when she discovered it was more formal than Simone was used to.

Lydia and Mina used the excuse of cleaning up after the seder to escape from the rest of the family. It was in the kitchen that Mina related the intimate details, word by word, expression by expression, of Ted's proposal. Also, she gave a blow-by-blow account of the seder. It took Lydia to make her see the funny side of every comment, every action taken, including the greasy prints on her wine-red dress.

Ted came in and caught them at it. "Okay. You've had enough fun at my family's expense," he warned.

"I think not," Lydia protested. "This is good for at least two more hours of yocks."

"All right, I'll make a deal with you," he told her.

"Always the lawyer," she chided.

"You can go on talking about my family as long as you listen to my version of my first meeting with the Jankowskis."

Lydia laughed so hard that her mother came in to see what had happened. "Family matters," Mina explained seriously.

50

DAYTON
RAPPROCHEMENT

MARIA STOOD BEFORE THE FULL-LENGTH MIRROR IN HER BEDROOM
and combed her hair. In the mirror, she could see Jerry lying naked
on the bed, watching her. He had come home earlier from work
today, not because Mina was arriving with her boyfriend for dinner,
but because he had played golf with several business associates and
didn't see the need to go back to the office. Now he had showered,
splashed himself with some sort of cologne, and was watching her.

"Come 'ere," he ordered her.

She turned and faced him, smiling. She was glad he was still
taken with her body. She was not a young woman anymore. Past
forty, she struggled against the thickening of her waist; her breasts
hung pendulously instead of standing erect. Her hair was still blond,
cut shorter now, but the wrinkles around her eyes and her mouth
were clearly visible.

"Come 'ere and show me what I like," Jerry said smokily to
her.

She walked over to the bed, spread her legs, and watched while
Jerry's mouth sought her out. She gazed over her husband's body
as his tongue slid down and inside her. Jerry didn't look so bad
himself. He made less of an effort than she did to stay in shape, but
he still didn't have much of a belly, and his cock was still hard for
her. What more could she ask for?

She carefully eased herself down on the bed so his mouth did not
lose contact with her. She took him in her mouth. Her hands pressed
from his rear to his thighs to his balls, squeezing them, caressing
them. She began to moan softly with Jerry still in her mouth. Jerry
liked to hear her moan. And she had good reason to. His fingers
were now where his tongue had been, his tongue higher, flicking
back and forth against her. "Jerry," she called to him.

His face was turned toward hers now, his hands pushing her
shoulder down flat against the bedcover. She raised her hips to him;
he slid into her; she wrapped herself around him, pleading with
him to make it last forever. He made it last long enough. She smiled

261

while he kissed her lips, her neck, her breasts. "You're still my favorite lay," he told her.

"You're a bastard, Jerry," she whispered.

"I love you," he said into her neck, so she almost didn't hear.

She put her arms around him and held him tight. He could tease her now about the other woman. Did that mean it was in the past? She hoped so. They never discussed Margot, not after that one day, before he had sent the flowers and the car. All she had said to him, all she had begged of him, was, "Please don't do this to me again."

He didn't. At least she didn't catch him at it if he did. He was more attentive to her, more loving. And she made a point of being more inventive sexually. She had been a whore before; the least she could do was be a whore to please her husband. She wanted to keep him satisfied, or maybe she simply wanted to keep him worn out.

Jerry's affair, though, was a lesson taught and learned. She could forgive him, but she would not forget the fears that had formed in her mind. Her main fear was of being left with nothing after giving everything. And that was also her main lesson. Some day Jerry, Catholic or no, might pick up and leave her. And then where would she be? She had had her warning. She was not foolish enough to disregard it.

"We're going to have to shower again," Jerry told her.

"I don't mind."

"Together?"

"Okay. But this time you stand in the back, because you're taller than I am and you always take all the water."

"Complaints, complaints." He got up and pulled her up after him. They went into the shower and quickly washed, toweled dry. "What time is Mina supposed to get here?" he asked.

"She said they'd be leaving around four, so they'll be here in time for dinner certainly." She took a new bra out of her drawer. "You'll remember to be nice," she warned him.

"Aren't I always? I'll pretend he's a client."

"He is, actually."

"Ted Eisenberg? I don't remember his name on any of our lists."

"I think he's in the market for a bride."

"Come on! Mina getting married?"

"I think that's why they're coming here, to tell us."

"Poor guy. Someone should warn him."

"Warn him what? There's nothing wrong with Mina."

"Not if you appreciate a woman who has an opinion on everything."

"Come on, Jerry."

"You have to admit she's not like our other kids."

"She's not our kid at all." Jerry looked at her. "She's my kid," Maria added quickly. "But you'll do very well as the father of the bride."

"I'm too young for that. They'll think I'm her brother."

Maria looked him over, evaluating. "No, dear, I don't think they will."

He laughed. Maria was glad they could laugh again when discussing Mina. For so long after her conversion, Mina had not been the subject of much humor. Maria thought Jerry would never get over not only Mina's rejection of Catholicism, but also her acceptance of Judaism. Did he care so much for Mina's sake? Or was it more for the sake of what his relatives and his friends would think?

But Jerry had come around. Maria had made sure of that. Slowly, surely, she had reintegrated Mina into Jerry's life. He had to see— she insisted that he see—Mina's decisions were hers alone to make. If they were wrong, she alone would suffer from them.

Maria was happy that Mina was now a Jew. Once again a Jew. It seemed right, as if somehow the spirit of her mother still lived through the child. It made Maria feel less guilty to be alive and surrounded by such bounty while Eliza Wolf and her world had been atomized.

She sighed. Unhappy thoughts did not belong on what she knew was going to be a happy day, the day her daughter was bringing home the man she would marry.

Maria was in the kitchen with Kristin when an unfamiliar car pulled into their driveway. "What a heap!" Kristin commented. But Maria didn't hear her. She had whipped off her apron and was out the door before the car could even come to a halt.

She waited expectantly while Mina opened the car door and hurried to her. They hugged. "You better like him," Mina whispered. Maria hugged her in assurance.

Ted Eisenberg got out of the car apprehensively. He was pleasant enough looking, Maria decided. His face was open and young. No hardships yet. She walked toward him and extended her hand. "Hello. You must be Ted Eisenberg. I'm Maria Jankowski."

Ted took her hand. His grip was pleasant, nothing distinctive by which to be either repulsed or attracted. "Mrs. Jankowski. I'm pleased to meet you."

Terry and Kristin had come out to join them. Mina hugged each of them, though Terry backed off somewhat. Thirteen-year-old boys don't like to be seen hugging anyone, especially sisters. Ted introduced himself to them. "Help with the bags," Mina ordered Terry.

"You're in my room," Terry informed Ted. "Do you like science fiction?"

His answer was lost to Maria and Mina. They watched Terry, talking constantly, escort Ted upstairs.

"Well, what do you think?" Mina asked expectantly.

"What's to think?" Maria replied. "I saw him for only a moment."

"Can't you tell he's wonderful?"

. Jerry chose that moment to join them in the hallway. Mina gave him a quick kiss. "Okay, how much is he worth?" Jerry whispered.

"Oh, Jerry!"

Jerry smiled. "So is this the one?"

"I think so." Mina positively beamed.

"Can I give you away now?"

"Ha, ha."

Ted was coming downstairs. Jerry waited. Ted saw him and stopped, his eyes flicking to Mina. Then he came steadily down the stairs. Jerry moved forward and shook his hand. "Hi. I'm Jerry Jankowski. Welcome to Dayton."

Maria smiled. Jerry actually was going to treat him like a client. "Come on into the living room. Let me fix you something to drink."

Poor Ted. In the next hour Jerry grilled him about how he had met Mina, what he was studying, how he was doing with his studying, what he was planning to do afterward, what his family was like, even about his values. Mina sat there only for moral support, since Jerry wouldn't let her get in a word, for either affirmation or defense. When her mother called, Mina set down her cocktail and was glad to help in the kitchen. "Jerry's scaring him away," Mina said.

Maria shook her head. "Ted doesn't look like the type to scare easily. Besides, it's Jerry's responsibility to find out all he can about Ted. I know you think he doesn't have any drawbacks—"

"Oh, yes, he does."

"He does?"

"His family."

Maria laughed. "Do you remember when we first met Jerry's parents?"

"How can I forget? Gloomsday."

"Thank God they're both dead," Maria said, crossing herself quickly. "Years ago, when Jerry told me we might have to move his mother out here to live with us, I thought I would die. Thank God she did first. That was the best thing about moving to Dayton, leaving his family behind.''

The buzzer on the stove rang. ''Should I go in and tell the men to get their asses to the table?'' Mina asked.

''Well, not exactly in that fashion.''

''Leave it to me.''

Maria served roast beef with parsley potatoes, salad, and beans. Jerry had brought home a couple of bottles of a very nice Burgundy. Even Terry and Kristin were allowed to have a glass, though the wine was wasted on them. They couldn't finish it. The meal went along pleasantly, with everyone talking in turn, everyone polite. Mina smiled happily at Ted. She hoped he noted the difference between her family and his. No tears, no scenes. Just a clean, decent American Friday-night dinner.

Jerry, naturally, was going to ruin Saturday by taking Ted out golfing, but that would at least give her and her mother time to dissect the relationship.

They moved into the living room for coffee. Terry and Kristin were dismissed to the family room for television.

Ted looked around when they were all settled and said, ''As you might have guessed, Mina and I actually came here to ask your— well—blessing on our marriage.''

''You're married!'' Jerry said.

''I meant impending marriage.''

Maria looked at her daughter. Mina was beaming.

''When are you planning to get married?'' Jerry asked.

''Sometime this summer,'' Mina answered.

Jerry looked at Maria, then asked, ''Can you make it in July?''

''Are you and Mom going away in August?''

''Sort of. There was something we weren't telling you until it was firm, but with you wanting to get married, it's only fair that you know.''

''Okay.''

''I'm moving up. I'm joining another company. It's in Chicago.''

''No!''

''Sorry, kid, but yes.''

''You can't move!'' Mina said to her mother.

''It's only Chicago,'' Jerry butted in. ''It's not like it's the end of the world. Ohio and Illinois are almost contiguous.''

''But leaving? Where will I call home?''

''With your husband,'' Jerry pointed out.

She gave him a dirty look. ''This is so typical of you.''

"It's really a much better job," Maria interrupted. "More money. Jerry will be happy."

"So you're going to sell this house?"

Jerry nodded. "You're going to have to come home and sort out what you want, take it with you."

Mina was clearly annoyed. But she tried to control herself in front of Ted. "I mean, how will it be coming home if I've never lived there? What about all my high school friends? And how can I sort out all that junk?" she said almost under her breath.

"We're moving in August. So that's why it would be better to have the wedding in July. Will it be here?" Jerry asked. "Will it be a religious ceremony?"

"If you consider Reform religious," Ted said.

"We don't belong to any temple," Jerry said. He smiled.

"He knows, Jerry," Mina cut in. "We thought of having it at the Hillel in Columbus."

"Columbus?" Maria didn't like that idea.

"Or at Temple Sinai in Columbus, where I was converted."

"No," Maria said.

"No?"

"No. This is your home."

"For a few more months, anyway."

"You can speak to the Reform rabbi here. You can marry here in Dayton. That's the way it should be done. If you want a small wedding, that's fine; but it should be here. I'm not going to see you married in some strange place I don't even know."

"But, Mom."

"That's fine, Mrs. Jankowski," Ted said. "I'll call the rabbi after the Sabbath. We'll speak to him on Sunday."

"But, Ted."

"No, your mother's right, Mina. It should be here."

"As it is, there's not much time," Maria said. "The invitations have to be engraved. The hall has to be rented for the reception. Your gown. What will we do about your gown?"

"Why don't you women discuss that tomorrow while Ted and I golf," Jerry suggested. "This sort of panic makes them very happy," he confided to Ted.

Maria and Mina weren't exactly panicked the next day. They were simply lying dreamily on Maria's bed, talking. They had decided, if possible, that the wedding be held in the same hall as the reception. That way they wouldn't have to worry about the synagogue being occupied. Later that day Maria would call restaurants and hotels, and they'd try to settle on a price and a place. They would have a small wedding, make every effort to limit it to a hundred people, fifty from each side. "We have to invite more than a hundred, but most of the relatives in New Jersey won't come," Maria estimated. "However, your father's friends here at work will. They'll consider it a duty. I'll bet you get a lot of nice presents from them."

"Ted and I are keeping the apartment Lydia and I have shared for the last two years."

"That rattrap?"

"Mother. It's not all that bad."

"Maybe not for newlyweds."

"We've lived in worse."

"Now *there* is the distinct truth," Maria agreed.

"So tell me, what did you think of Ted?"

"He's very nice."

"No, honestly."

"He's very nice," Maria repeated. "What can I tell you about him? He makes a good impression. He's very sincere. He acts like he's in love with you. He likes to avoid arguments. Which is good if he's going to have to live with you."

"How do you know he likes to avoid arguments?"

"The way he immediately agreed to have the wedding here. That was nice of him."

"He is nice."

"That's what I said before."

"We're going to be the happiest couple alive."

"Umm."

"Don't you believe me, Mom?"

"Do you know what I read the other day?"

"A new recipe?"

"What a fresh mouth you have. No, a book. I picked it up in the library while I was waiting for Terry to get books for his term paper. It was by a Friedan, a Betty Friedan. I picked it up because I thought she might be some relation of Lydia's. The book is called *The Feminine Mystique*. You should read it."

"Why?"

"It's a book about men and women."

"I know all there is to know about that."

"What do you know?"

"That Ted and I are going to get married. That our life together is going to be perfect." She smiled.

"Nobody's life is perfect," Maria said seriously.

"Mine will be."

"Don't depend on anyone but yourself, Mina. In the end, that's all you're going to have."

"I thought—well—I sensed that at one time you and Jerry were having problems. But lately it looks as if things are better between the two of you."

"They are. Never been better. But I relearned a lesson I had learned before. Never take anything for granted. Not love, not security, not even life. I was a fool not to take up catering again when I moved to Dayton. I don't take in a fourth of what I was earning in Trenton, not with the salads and pickles I make here. Chicago has one of the biggest Polish populations in the country. Did you know that? When I get there, I'm going to restart my business."

"Does Jerry know?"

"He will."

"What will he say?"

"He'll accept it or he won't. Whatever. But I'm going to make sure I will never have to fear being left to fend for myself again. Do you realize I'm over forty, Mina?"

"You don't look it."

"But soon I will. Rely on yourself, Mina. There's too much uncertainty to do otherwise."

Mina shook her head. "It's the war," she told her mother. "That's why you're so insecure, maybe. But I barely remember the war. I remember Mrs. Nowicki's apartment, yes. And I remember how good it was when Jerry married you and we seemed to have everything all at once. That's the way it's going to be with Ted and me, Mom. We're going to have everything."

Maria leaned over to her daughter and kissed her cheek. "I pray to God you will."

51

CHICAGO, 1967

MINA WATCHED WITH PLEASURE AS TERRY TROMPED THROUGH THE kitchen of the Wilmette house in his spiked shoes and baseball uniform. "I bet you have girls swarming around you," she teased her half-brother.

"Sometimes," Terry admitted with a shrug.

Mina sighed. Why did Terry get all of their mother's good looks? He had blond curly hair, a light complexion. He was tall and cute. And he had a girlfriend who was driving their mother crazy by calling all the time. Or at least that's what Maria had written her.

"Do you think you'll be in line for an athletic scholarship?" Mina asked Terry.

"Are you kidding?" Kristin cut in. "Whenever he has the chance to get his hands on the ball, he drops it."

"Hey, shut up!" Terry yelled.

"I'm sure not every time, or he wouldn't be on the team," Mina corrected her half-sister. Maria had also confessed in a letter that Kristin was more impossible than Mina had been. Hard to believe, but Kristin refused to do things around the house, like pick up her own room. Instead, she spent money at the shopping malls. Their bill from Sibley's and Carson's grew each month. Yet Kristin claimed she had nothing to wear.

"So how's Chicago?" she asked the two of them.

"It's better than Dayton," Terry told her. "There's much more to do."

"But it's colder," Kristin said. "And the high school's full of cliques."

"I got to worry about college applications and SATs now," Terry said.

"Not until the summer surely?"

"Yeah, well it seems awfully close. Though I'm looking forward to being a senior. We'll have the run of the whole school."

"Ha!" Kristin rebutted.

"Where do you think you'll go to college?" Mina asked.

"Probably the University of Illinois. It's far enough downstate to be away from the parents, but I can still get up here on the weekend if I need to."

"How's Mom been?"

"Busy," Kristin stated. "She's spending all her time with her business. I can't even come home and expect to find a meal on the table. Too bad we're not one of her customers."

"She brings home stuff she has left over," Terry defended his mother. "We always have plenty to eat. And she's always home for dinner. At least when Dad is."

"Why don't you two get together and make dinner for your parents?"

"Why should we?" Kristin asked. "That's not our job."

"Well, let's see what you have in the refrigerator for tonight."

Mina found some ground meat. By the time she took it out, both kids had disappeared. She shook her head. They obviously thought she was going to ask them to help. Instead, she went about cooking by herself. As she did so, she thought of Ted, of what he must be doing. Probably eating out.

Jerry was the first to arrive home. He opened the door and yelled, "I'm home," but his children were upstairs listening to their music. They didn't hear him. Mina came out of the kitchen. "Mina! Is that your rental car out there?"

She nodded. "Hi. How are you, Jerry?"

He came forward and kissed her cheek. "Trouble at home?"

"The kids look fine."

"I meant with Ted."

"Afraid you'll have me on your hands again, Jerry? Sorry. Everything's going great with Ted."

"Then why the surprise visit? You could have called. I'm sure your mother would have made other arrangements so she could have been here."

"Frankly, I didn't know how things would work out. I've been up in Wisconsin, taking a familiarization tour sponsored by several resorts up there. I have to be back in Cleveland by tomorrow night. So if the tour had lasted longer, I wouldn't have been able to make this stop. But I thought you could put me up for one night."

"We can put you up indefinitely," he assured her. "What are you doing in the kitchen?"

"Making dinner."

"I hope you're showing Kristin how."

"She doesn't seem to want to learn."

He shook his head. "That girl. Listen, I'm going up to change. Then let's have a drink and talk."

While Jerry was upstairs, Maria returned home. The first thing she did was walk into the kitchen. Her mouth dropped open in surprise when she saw Mina at the stove. Then she screamed with delight. "Mina! And I thought maybe Kristin had actually—"

"No." She came forward and gave her mother a big hug. Oh, it was so good to be back in those arms. "How are you? I hate to say it, but you look tired."

"I am tired. I was called upon to give an estimate for two weddings today. Weddings are the worst, Mina, believe me. These mothers can drive you crazy."

"In other words, your business is going well."

"It's going too well. I've had to hire an accountant. Pretty soon, instead of having only general help, I'm going to have to have an assistant. I have an idea of who it will be, but I want to see that she works out as well as I think she will. But, please, let's not talk about my business. What's happening with you? Why are you here?''

Mina gave her the same explanation she'd given Jerry. By that time Jerry had joined them. ''What are you making?'' he asked.

''Chili.''

''Well, I guess we'll hold the wine. Chili calls for beer. I hope you made it nice and hot.''

''Threw in a whole can of powder.''

Their meal together went well. Everyone talked at once, of course, and Mina became confused and started to get a headache. She was used to being at the table with Ted alone, used to hearing him meander on about his day, his frustrations, his semitriumphs.

''How's Ted's family?'' Jerry asked, as if guessing her thoughts.

''We manage not to see them as much as possible.''

Jerry laughed. ''I still remember his grandmother at the wedding.''

''Wasn't she a bigot,'' Maria added. ''I don't know how she got her face in so many of the photographs. How do you put up with them?''

''We don't really. I thought it was going to be awful when we moved to Cleveland. I was really upset with Ted for wanting to establish his practice there. But it's worked out okay. We join them for dinner about once a month. Sometimes I even manage to miss that by being away.''

''Yeah. What's it like to travel every place?'' Terry asked. ''It must be great to be a travel agent.''

''I like to travel,'' Mina admitted. ''So it's nice in that respect. But it can get awfully tiring to be wined and dined everywhere.''

''Tell me about it,'' Jerry said. ''You look like you put on a few pounds, so it must be agreeing with you. Or are you pregnant?''

''Now you sound like Ted's mother,'' she told him.

''Forgive me.''

''How long can you stay?'' Maria asked.

''I have to be back tomorrow evening.''

''So let me cancel my day's appointments, and we can go around together.''

''Well—'' Mina said. ''I was really hoping to have lunch with my favorite stepfather.''

''Uh-oh. She wants something,'' Jerry guessed.

''Can you make it?''

''It will mean canceling lunch with the mayor of Chicago, but for you, anything.''

Mina did spend the morning with her mother, visiting her mother's office in a suburban shopping center and examining the brochures and price lists. "You must be rich," she commented.

"Now I'm in the black. Just now," Maria said. "For the first two years I was heavily in debt, just setting up the business, getting started, getting my name known. Now I'm in demand and I'm going to make the most of it. That's why I need the assistant. I wish you and Ted were living here. We would work perfectly together."

"Yeah. I could bring in the Jewish business."

Maria didn't think it was a joke. "Yes. Between the Jews and the Poles, we would have Chicago all wrapped up."

"But you'd need an Italian assistant, too."

"True."

"Mother, I was joking."

Mina left Maria seriously contemplating Chicago's ethnic diversity when she set off for downtown to meet her stepfather. She had to admit that Jerry had done well for himself. The office building was new and bright. His company was located on the eighth and ninth floors. Jerry was on the ninth. He had a receptionist and a secretary. They had obviously been alerted to expect her, because they were extremely pleasant to her.

Jerry greeted her warmly, then took her to a local seafood restaurant. "Have to watch the weight," he admitted. "I'm getting old."

"You still look good," she told him.

They ordered. Then Jerry looked at her. "So now. What does little Mina want? I assume this is a business lunch."

"Yes."

"How right I was! Let me guess. Ted's not making it financially, and you need a loan."

"Wrong!"

"Oh?" He sat back. "Well, this is a pleasant surprise."

"Ted's doing okay. He's happy with the law firm he's joined. Someday he hopes to move out on his own, set up his own practice. But right now he's getting the sort of cases he wants. Mainly real estate and wills. Though lately he's been taking on more divorce work."

"You got to watch out for that. They say those women get desperate."

"I'm not worried."

"Not yet anyway."

"Jerry, I didn't come to speak about my married life."

"Okay. I'm listening."

"One of the partners in Ketura Travel wants to sell out. I want to buy in. I can't seem to get a loan."

"Naturally. You're a woman."

"Thank you. I'm fully cognizant of that. I want to know—well, I was wondering if you—"

"If I would lend you the money?"

"Yes."

"How much?"

"Ketura Travel is a small firm now, but I really believe travel is going to become a big industry. People are starting to have more leisure time. They're going to want to spend it away from home."

"Don't try to sell me on travel," he told her. "Sell me on yourself."

"But you know how competent I am."

"No, Mina, I don't know. Travel agents, what do they make? Eight or ten grand a year? Peanuts. And you want me to sink money into that business? Listen, let me tell you that when your mother was starting her business here, I didn't give her a penny. I didn't approve of her owning a business. I wanted her home with the kids. I wanted her to be there with dinner ready when I got home. Doesn't Ted want the same thing from you?"

"But you obviously didn't stand in her way," Mina evaded.

"No. Because your mother said she was going to do it whether I liked it or not. So what was my choice, throw her over? But I don't like it. I didn't like it in Trenton, in Dayton, and I don't like it here."

"Aren't you proud that she's making so much money?"

"She's not making that much yet. Proud? Look, when I married your mother, it was to take care of her, give her the security she so desperately wanted. I wanted to give her a home. Now she's giving me the message that she doesn't need me anymore."

"Oh, Jerry. Of course she needs you, but she needs something for herself, too."

"She has something for herself. The house and the kids. And you still haven't answered my question. What does Ted say?"

"Ted's used to my working."

"I thought when you two married, the idea was for you to work only that first year, while he was finishing law school."

"Yeah."

"So why did you start working again when you moved to Cleveland?"

"Because I like to work. And anyway, what was I going to do, sit home and watch television?"

"Why didn't you try getting pregnant?"

"Because I don't want a child now. There are other things I want to accomplish first."

"Then why did you get married?"

"Because I loved Ted. God, you're dense."

Jerry laughed. "You don't insult people when you're asking them for money, kiddo."

"Look, Jerry, buying into a business doesn't mean I won't have time for children. I'll have more time, because I'll be the boss. I can make my own hours. And this opportunity might not come again." She sighed. "I've never asked you for anything. Not anything, Jerry."

Jerry sadly shook his head. "Mina, even if I wanted to give you the loan, which I don't, I don't have that much liquid capital. Do you realize how much that house cost?"

"Mom told me."

"With the mortgage, the insurance, utilities, the car payments, I can't give you a lump sum. Especially not with Terry getting ready for college soon. Yours isn't the only future I've got to think of. What about Ted's parents?"

"I wouldn't think of asking. I want to keep my involvement with them at a minimum."

"You know why you can't get money from the bank, don't you? You're not only a woman, you're also a young woman. You're expected to have children and to drop out of the labor force."

"I don't intend to do that."

"Do you intend to have children at all?"

"Sometime."

"Is Ted willing to co-sign your loan? Is he willing to borrow the money under his name?"

"He's tried, Jerry. We don't have enough collateral."

Jerry ordered coffee and thought. He looked her over and grimaced. "Okay. I'll do this for you. Do you have any of the financial information with you?"

She patted her briefcase. "I have it all."

"I'll put you in touch with the loan officer who handled your mother's application. Your mother's paid back her loan. You can use the same collateral she did. I'll co-sign." He pointed his finger at her. "But if you default—"

"I won't, Jerry. I promise you."

"You better not."

52

JUNKET

TED SAT ON THE BED AND WATCHED HER PACK. "YOU KNOW, MINA, I really don't want you going over there at this time."

"The trip's all set, darling. I can't back out now."

"You *can* back out. All you have to do is phone, say it doesn't look safe, and that you'll come when the situation cools down."

Mina sat down on the bed, facing him. The first thing he did was put his hand on her thigh. She gave him a discouraging look. "Ted, I have worked my ass off, sending form letter after form letter to all the lists I could buy cheaply. I've joined Hadassah. I've joined the League of Women Voters. I've joined the Chamber of Commerce. If I had less of a conscience, I'd even join the Junior League. The reason I have done all this is not because I'm a joiner, but because I want people to get to know me, to think of me as a friend, to realize when they are planning a trip, Ketura Travel will be there to help them with those plans. That's why I give free lectures to high school groups, to college groups, to adult enrichment classes. Here I'm getting a chance to open up a whole new realm of expertise for Ketura. If you think I'm not going to go over to Israel now, you're crazy."

"Have you been reading the papers?"

"Of course."

"Then you might have read that Gama Abdel Nasser has closed the Straits of Tiran. Or have you watched television? Seen the mobs in Cairo crying out for Jewish blood?"

"Fortunately, Ted, I will not be in Cairo."

"I'm thinking of forbidding you to go."

"Look, Ted, you take care of your law practice; I'll take care of the world."

"May I quote you?"

She went to her dresser drawer and tried to find nylons without any runs. Somehow she never seemed to be adequately supplied. "It's only two weeks," she told him with her back turned. "You can live alone for two weeks, can't you?"

275

"What I'm worried about is living alone forever."

She turned and smiled. "You only wish."

He stood and walked over to her. He took her in his arms. "Are you going to bother me while I'm packing?" she inquired.

"You're damned right I am." His lips pressed against hers, and the nylons fell to the floor. She felt his hand slide up under her skirt. She tried to put her heart and soul into what Ted was doing to her, but she was afraid tonight would be almost totally one-sided. There were too many things to worry about, like what the weather was going to be like. Should she wear shorts? How many dresses should she take?

Ted broke away. "Am I bothering you, by any chance? Or are you just ignoring me?"

She looked guilty. "My mind is racing."

"Better take care of me or someone else will."

"If I must," she teased. She undid his belt buckle, and unzipped his pants. Then she knelt before him and took him in her mouth. He loved it, she knew. Sometimes, she supposed, it wasn't really her mouth, her tongue that got to him. It was the fact that she was kneeling, willing, submissive.

When he was about to come, he pushed her back onto the rug, lifted her skirt and tugged down her pants. "Miss me," he ordered her. She spread her legs and accepted him, holding tight onto what she knew so well. She felt the pleasure come then. It radiated around her hips like a belt made from the sun. The sun. How hot was Israel in the latter days of May?

After checking in at the El Al counter in New York, Mina discovered that over half of the travel agents who had planned to go on this junket had canceled. Not that this meant the plane wouldn't be full. The travel agents' places had been taken by young men, all flying home to their military units in Israel. For the first time, she wondered if she should be disturbed by the news reports coming from the Middle East.

Mina had never studied the Middle East in college. It had never been an area of interest for her, not like Eastern and Central Europe, which were so much a part of her own history. What she knew of Israel and its Arab neighbors she had learned from the Cleveland papers and from the United Jewish Appeal.

Her trip to Israel was motivated by the fact that there were so many Jews in Cleveland, as well as Christian groups, who expressed interest in seeing the Promised Land, the Holy Land. Either she or her partner in Ketura Travel had to be more alert to this market or they would lose customers. So when the chance came, when the Israeli Tourism Ministry last January had offered this comprehensive view of the country, including hotels, restaurants, and tours throughout the land, she couldn't pass it up. She had never expected, in May 1967, to stumble into a country at war.

She sat next to a young man named Moshe. Since she was in the aisle seat, he spent most of his time calling past her to friends across the aisle. They spoke Hebrew, so she didn't know what they were saying. Finally, when a meal was served, Moshe settled back, and she had a chance to smile at him, ask him if he was going home to visit his parents.

Moshe shrugged. "If there's time. First, though, I must report to my unit. And you? Are you going home to rejoin your family?"

"Oh, no. I'm a travel agent. Your government invited a few of us to come over, so that we can encourage our clients to visit Israel."

"If there's an Israel left to visit," he added grimly.

Oh, God.

By the time she had disembarked at Lod Airport, she had received the names and addresses of five of the young men on board and invitations to visit their homes, see how real Israelis live. She hoped, as she wished them well, that she would not have to see how real Israelis died.

An official of the Tourism Ministry was there to meet her and her group after they got through customs. They boarded a modern bus and were driven into Tel Aviv, to one of the larger hotels along the beach. Before the official let them off the bus, he explained that the service they would receive would be a little rougher than ordinary. "I'm sorry to say," he told them, "that many of our hotel workers have been called up to their units."

"Is there any danger of war?" One of the agents called to him.

The official looked as though he wanted to lie, but he didn't. "Yes," he admitted. "But we have plans to evacuate you as soon as we have any knowledge that it's beginning."

An agent two rows behind Mina said to his companion, "Don't you believe it. The first thing the Arabs will do is bomb the airport. If there's a war, we'll never get out of here."

It was looking more and more as though Ted had been right all along. But now that Mina was here, she was going to make the most of it.

Her tour of Israel began on May 26. For four days they made their base in Jerusalem and traveled south. Again, the tourism officials apologized for not allowing them access to certain areas.

"Military matters have intervened," it was announced, superfluously. All the agents, as a matter of habit, had picked up their morning copy of the *Jerusalem Post*. All noticed more absences from the hotel staff. Many had decided that touring Israel might be more congenial at another time, in a different climate, and had left the country.

Mina had called Ted once, to assure him that everything was fine. He didn't believe her. But there was something about the spirit of the country, its officials, who tried to make believe everything was normal when it obviously wasn't, that appealed to her. She decided that to leave now would be desertion; so she stayed, and she pretended she didn't see worry on the faces of all she met. The Arabs surrounded Israel. Their threat to exterminate the country seemed more real every day. She wondered if she would know how to fight, if and when the time came?

53

CHAOS

THE TOURIST CENTER FOR THE NORTH OF ISRAEL WAS SET UP IN A hotel in Tiberias. The hotel had six stories, and from the balconies on the eastern side one could look down over the Sea of Galilee. In the banquet room, hotel owners and tour operators had set up booths so that the few travel agents left could peruse, inspect, and make decisions about what they wanted to see and what they didn't.

Mina was impressed by the breadth of services offered at one of the booths, Barak Tours, with a list of Pensions Barak, which dotted the north. "Are you interested in seeing any of our hotels, taking our tours?" someone asked her.

She looked up to see a man in his forties. His hair was graying, as was his mustache; he looked fit and pleasant. "I'm interested that you're offering a comprehensive package," she told him. "What sort of tourists do you attract?"

"All kinds."

"No, I mean what sort of economic level, religion, that sort of thing."

"We have enough tour guides so that we can offer tours for Jews or Gentiles. Most of our customers so far have been Europeans, but we are hoping for more American trade. Where do you come from?"

"Cleveland, Ohio."

"Ah, that's—"

"In the middle of the country. I'm Mina Eisenberg."

He smiled. "Yehuda Barak. Could I convince you to visit my hotels with me, maybe get an idea of what I can offer, what services Barak Enterprises provides?"

"A personal tour? That would be great."

"I'll try to get a few more to join us."

"Slim pickings," she told him.

"Yes," he agreed grimly. "The timing of this tourism extravaganza was unfortunate."

By lunchtime, Yehuda Barak had managed to corral two more travel agents. He took them across the street to his first hotel, Pension Bracha. They inspected the rooms, the lobby, the kitchen. "No television," one of the men commented.

"Not yet."

"What do people do in the evening then?"

"There's radio, if you want to sit and listen. Also Tiberias has several cafés and clubs." Poor Yehuda could probably sense that the man was not thrilled with his answer, Mina thought.

For lunch they were taken to Café Eliza. It opened onto a beautiful patio garden. They were eating when a woman walked over, and Yehuda stood. "This is my wife, Eliza Barak. Eliza, these are a few of the travel agents who have braved this terrible time to take a look at what we can offer."

She smiled at them all. "Thank you for coming. Please feel free to ask any questions or to see anything you'd like." She nodded and was gone.

After lunch Yehuda took them to several more of his hotels, which were scattered in the Tiberias area.

"Are your other hotels throughout the Galilee like these?" Mina asked.

"Yes."

By the time they were back at their more modern hotel, it was nearly six o'clock. When they thanked him for his hospitality, he offered to buy them drinks. Mina accepted. The other two were worn out.

Mina had a beer at the bar. The beer was pretty horrible, and she could well understand why Yehuda ordered a Tempo, which was something like a lime soda. "Well, what did you think of the hotels?" he asked her.

He asked it with such pride that she regretted having to give him her honest assessment. "They're very charming."

"But—"

"But," she agreed. "They're not modern. They're not chrome and glass. Americans, I'm sorry to say, don't go for charm. What they want in a hotel room in Israel is exactly what they would want in one in Chicago or San Francisco."

"So you think I should give up hopes of the American market?"

"I wouldn't say that."

"What I want is the sort of trade I get from the Europeans. They stay at my hotels; they take my tours. It's all arranged by the agent. Naturally, the commission is generous."

"I don't think you can expect that. At least not from me. My business depends on repeat customers and on customer satisfaction. I have to say that they are not going to be satisfied with showers that don't have even a curtain over the door, where they have to use a mop or whatever that thing is, to keep the water from running along the hotel-room floor."

"Just on the side. It's common in Israel."

She smiled. "But it's uncommon in America. However, I certainly will keep your hotels in mind for the few Americans who would like to experience the real Israel."

"Okay. I like your honesty. What about my tours?"

"What about them?"

"Will you take some of them?"

"When will I have time?"

"Tomorrow. You'll still be here tomorrow?"

"But the Tourism Ministry—"

"Forget them. My tours will be better. You'll see more, understand more. Come over for breakfast tomorrow morning. You can see how much better our breakfast is than what you are getting here. Then I'll take you to see the real Galilee. I know every stone of this land. It's in my blood."

She agreed, mainly out of guilt, because she knew she could steer few customers to his hotels. Early the next morning she went to the breakfast room at Pension Bracha, where she was met not by Yehuda, but by his wife. "Mina Eisenberg?" the woman asked.

"Right," Mina said. She noted that the woman was pleasant-looking, also in her forties, maybe a little bit plump, but what one would call pleasingly so.

"I'm sorry to tell you that my husband has been called away."

"To his unit?"

Eliza Barak nodded. "Yes. I didn't want to say that, because I didn't want to frighten you."

"Oh, I've been seeing men disappear ever since I got here. It doesn't frighten me, but it must be awful for you."

"It's the waiting," Eliza confessed. "The not knowing. But that's not your problem. Our son will take you around. If you're still willing to go."

"Oh, I don't want to be any trouble. I can just go back next door and go on the regular tour."

"No. If you don't mind, Yehuda especially wanted you to go on our tour, because he wants you to know we have something to offer to your Americans."

Mina felt somewhat pressured. "Fine," she agreed. "But won't it interfere with your son's day?"

"His class was to report to the post office today to handle the mail. I'm afraid the regular postal carriers have all been—"

"Called up?"

"Yes. But Ami can substitute first-aid service for postal operations. And he can do it at night. Besides, he's anxious to drive his father's car."

"That's understandable."

"Please, help yourself to the buffet. Ami will be with you in a few minutes."

Mina noted that the breakfast buffet had about everything one would want to eat for all three meals. She wished her stomach could accept more than a simple roll and coffee.

"You're not eating anything."

She looked up to see a medium-tall youth with pale skin, freckles, and brownish-red hair. Ami, if that's who this was, definitely looked more like his father than his mother. "I'm used to very small breakfasts," she apologized.

He shrugged and sat down. "It's okay. But you should be like most tourists and grab yourself a picnic lunch while you're at it. I'm Ami, by the way."

She smiled. She liked the easy way he had about him. She decided that today would be an adventure.

Ami took her on three of the tours listed in the Barak Tours folder. He was able to accomplish so much in one day because the tours overlapped. One was for Christians, one for Jews, and the most interesting one was for amateur archaeologists. "You can dig anyplace in Israel and find a potsherd. Most of them date back to at least the time of Joshua," he explained.

"But you can't take them home with you?" Mina guessed.

Ami gave her a typical Israeli shrug. "Theoretically, no. If you find something in its entirety, the authorities must be notified. But all those little pieces—no one cares. I think that all our ancestors did was make and break pots. It gives the tourists a real thrill. And it's better than chiseling names on walls."

"Were you born in Israel?"

"Oh, yes."

"So then you're a Sabra?"

"Yes. And my brother, Ron. Naturally, since he's two years younger than I am. And you? Are you a Sabra American?"

Mina laughed. "No. I am an American. But I was born in Poland."

"Really? Hey, so was my mother."

Mina quickly recalled the pleasant woman at the buffet. "And she came here before the war?"

"No. She wasn't that lucky. She came after."

"Oh. I'm sorry."

"Don't be. She wasn't in the camps or anything. She was a partisan. A fighter. Her family, though, they all perished. She's the only one alive, though I think she said we have an uncle somewhere left in Poland. She doesn't talk about it much."

"Yes, I know. I was just four, I think, when we got out of Europe and traveled to America. I don't really remember much of anything. Just that I was glad to be out of there."

"Yeah. That I can believe."

"Are you worried about your father?"

"Of course."

"That was a stupid question."

"I mean, it would be different if I were in the army. Then I could do something about what's happening. Now we're being treated like little children, rolling bandages, delivering the mail. We've had our Gadna training. I know how to put a rifle together after taking it apart."

"How old are you?"

"Sixteen."

"Sixteen is too young to fight."

"Not when what you're fighting for is your country."

For the last part of the trip, Ami took her up on a hillside. They drank water from the same canteen and ate some of the food he had packed for lunch. It was peaceful where they sat, with the wind gently sailing through their hair and cooling their bodies. "Look over there," he told her. "To the north. Up on the tel."

She knew by now that that was a hill. She looked north to the high ground. "That's Syria," he informed her. "Can you see the sort of twinkling in the sun? Dotted around the land basin?"

She strained to see. "Yes."

"Those are our kibbutzim. When the Syrians spit, it lands on our farms, our villages. Each kibbutz has bomb shelters, all over, but especially next to the children's houses. The children sleep in the bomb shelters at night now. No one knows what's going to happen. If our men have to fight Syria, many will be slaughtered taking the high land. The Syrian fortifications are deep, well dug in.

"There," he told her. "Look to the east. That's Jordan. From your hotel you have a better view, but here you can see clearly enough. Ever since our state was founded, Jordan has been sending infiltrators across our common border to kill us. Farmers in the fields carry rifles in case they are shot at. Our women have been raped and murdered by these infiltrators. My father's first girl-friend—well that's who Pension Bracha is named after."

"You must hate the Arabs."

He lifted his shoulders. "Hate? No. I don't know any Arabs. My father knows some. I only wish they would leave us alone, let us live in peace. But that seems impossible for them. Hatred of Israel is the only thing that unites the Arab countries. If we didn't exist, they would be at each other's throat."

"What do you think is going to happen?"

"Oh, there will be a war. Any day now. We have almost complete mobilization. Israel can't exist with all its men mobilized. You've seen what it's done to everyday life."

"And you're not worried about being up on this hill alone?"

"No. If they come, when they come, it will be against the state, not against you and me on this hill." He looked at her. "But you're nervous?"

"Well, you shouldn't have talked about infiltrators, Ami."

"Don't worry. I know hand-to-hand combat."

"And I know how to scream, but who's going to hear us?"

He smiled, stood up, and pulled her up. "Okay. Back to Tiberias. If you've seen enough?"

"Yes. It's really beautiful. It's a shame that—"

"That so many people are willing to shed blood to own it?"

"Something like that. Actually, I was going to say that it's a shame we can't all live in peace, but I thought that might sound too simple-minded."

"Not that simple-minded, just too simple."

They got into the car, and Ami drove south toward Tiberias. "So, what did you think of my tour?"

"You were great. Do you act as a tour guide?"

"Sometimes, especially when we have teenagers from Germany."

"Oh, my."

"Yes. It's not easy. I try to look upon them as though they are like other people. But then I remember what happened. I had a sister who didn't make it. Half-sister really. My mother told us about her during the Eichmann trial. Maybe that's why you and I get along together. You have her name."

"Mina?"

"Yes."

"Well, believe me, Ami, if I were your sister, we wouldn't be getting along together. I know from my own family. Siblings like to fight."

He smiled. "Maybe. So what about the tour?"

"It's good. I'm going to give it my seal of approval, especially the archaeological one."

"My father will be pleased."

They drove companionably back toward Tiberias, talking about school and studying and traveling. "Good luck to you," she told him when she got out at her hotel. "I'll definitely be in touch with your father."

"I hope so," Ami said. After he drove off, she couldn't decide whether he meant he hoped she got in touch or hoped his father was around to be gotten in touch with.

When she entered the hotel, the official from the Tourism Ministry was waiting for her. "Where have you been, Mrs. Eisenberg?"

She was taken aback by his formality. Usually it had been Mina. "I've been out with a representative of Barak Tours," she said.

"I wish you had let me know."

"I did tell the desk."

"We have been looking all over Tiberias for you."

"Why? Has something happened? To my husband?" Her voice had continued to rise.

"No, nothing like that," he assured her. "The rest of the group went back to Tel Aviv before lunch. They are now on a plane flying out of Israel."

"You mean it's no longer safe to be here?"

"For your comfort, it might be better to reschedule the rest of the trip."

"You mean war is about to begin?"

"Mrs. Eisenberg—Mina—I don't know what's happening. I simply received orders to escort the group back to Tel Aviv for departure."

"And I've screwed up those orders."

"Slightly."

"Well, I guess we better get back to Tel Aviv now, then."

"I don't know if you'll be able to get a plane out, but, yes, Tel Aviv will be the safest place for you."

"Unless they bomb it."

"Please, Mina, pack your bags and let's go."

The official was anxious not only because he had failed to get her to Tel Aviv in time, but also because he had orders to report to his unit as soon as he delivered her. He wanted to be able to stop and kiss his wife and children good-bye first. Mina honestly believed during their trip south that they might be the first two casualties of the war. The way he was driving was criminal. But they made it back to her sea-front hotel, where she was dropped off and told to check with the front desk for further arrangements.

The front desk was a madhouse. There were people screaming for attention. She became enraged. Who were these tourists to be so hysterical about ensuring their own safety when those who were going to have to do the fighting and dying were going about life with such dignity? It took her a while to realize that these weren't tourists trying to get out. This was the world press trying to get in. Thank God she had a room.

She pushed through the throng to ask for her room key from a harried clerk. As she turned around, key in hand, she bumped into someone. She had no intention of excusing herself; the crowd was too raucous for common civility. "Mina?" she heard.

She looked up. There, with her brown hair pushed under a military cap and dressed in a dashing set of khaki fatigues, stood her favorite newsperson of all time. "Lydia Friedan? What the hell are you doing here?"

54

LIVES TO SHARE

ON THE NIGHT OF JUNE 3, MINA SAT IN HER HOTEL ROOM AND waited for Lydia to return. She was hungry, anxious, and a little angry at her friend. Where was she? How long did it take to get registered as a journalist? Then she remembered the crowd downstairs. Maybe she'd wait all night to eat.

She thought of calling Ted, but what would be the sense in that? He would want her to come home. Naturally, she was planning to fly home now, but it had been a long time since she and Lydia had had a chance to sit down and talk. They had seen each other over the holidays, but always in the company of Lydia's family or Ted. In neither case could they have an old-fashioned giggle and exchange real information.

That was one thing Mina missed when she got married, the closeness with her women friends. Now she had to center her social life around the couple concept: Mina and Ted this; Mina and Ted that. It was not so difficult to do in Cleveland, since no one from the old circle at Ohio State had moved there. But still, she missed Lydia and the openness with which they communicated.

The door smashed open. The whirlwind entered. "Finally!" Mina said.

Lydia closed the door and slumped against it. "Where is American efficiency? That's all I'm asking."

"All? I've never known you to stop at one question before."

Lydia tossed something on the bed toward Mina. Mina picked it up. "A press pass for me? How sweet of you."

"Please. No sarcasm, Mina. I told them you had the runs, and therefore couldn't stand around waiting for them to get organized."

"How do travel agents get press passes?"

"By having loyal friends like Lydia Friedan."

"The last I heard I was supposed to fly out of here."

"How the hell can you fly out of here at a time like this? There is simply too much going on. Come on, let's go down to the bar and put out feelers."

"What will we be feeling?"

"Mina, Mina, will you never grow up?"

They went to the bar, which was almost as crowded as the hotel lobby had been. Lydia had her own technique for procuring drinks. She went behind the bar and poured them herself. The bartender didn't seem to mind at all. "I know you still take milk," Lydia said to Mina, "but tonight we can go with something a little stronger."

Mina took a sip of a liquid that struck her as being a poor imitation of Scotch. "Now tell me all," Mina insisted. "What are you doing here? Last time I heard, you were safely in St. Louis, writing about the deterioration of that great American city."

"Well, I'm not here to cover the war, not the front-line stuff. My editor doesn't trust me to do that. So he sent some macho bozo instead. I'm doing the human-interest bit."

"How did you arrange that?"

"By lying and claiming I had more than twenty relatives I could contact who could put me on to others. But it won't be hard to find people. Everyone wants to talk about the war."

"Yes," Mina said, remembering Ami on the hill.

"And what are you doing here?"

"Press." Mina flashed her press card.

"Before that."

"I came with a group of travel agents. Today I was out getting a private tour. When I got back to the hotel in Tiberias, I found that all the other agents had been bused south and then flown out of the country."

"What does Ted say about all this?"

"I'm afraid to call him. He'll only want me to come home immediately."

"You should call him anyway, Mina. Otherwise he'll start panicking. Especially if he hears that all the other agents have flown home, and you've turned up missing."

"I can't turn up missing."

"Whatever."

"I'll call him later. Now, tell me, what's going on with you?"

Lydia launched into her saga of life in St. Louis. She had been there a year, having spent the first two years after college in Akron. But she saw that the *St. Louis Post-Dispatch* had possibilities. She didn't especially care for the city itself, but the paper had national and international reporters, and that's what she hoped to be.

"No regrets, then, about this dedication to your career?"

"None," Lydia informed her. "Any regrets about getting married?"

"No." Mina smiled. "I'm still in love. Ted was the right choice for me."

"Maybe. Though I still have hopes for you. I see you're not tied down with children, and you're working."

"Don't read anything into it. We're just getting started. We need to make money."

"Mom wrote that you bought into Ketura Travel. Is that making money?"

"It's an investment. I pay back the loan every month to a Chicago bank. I have to. Otherwise, Jerry would kill me. He co-signed the loan."

"Good old Jerry. How is he?"

"He's fine. They're all doing well. Mom's working hard. Her business is well established. See, it's possible, Lydia. My mother has always worked in one fashion or another, and yet she managed to have three children."

"Maybe someday I'll find someone. For my mother's sake, I hope so. Though now that Alan and Simone are married, some of the pressure is off. Oh God, there's Handsome Harry. Let me check in with him, so that if he calls our editor, the paper will know I'm on the job."

Lydia disappeared into the crowd of men. She moved easily in their company. The woman had no sense of fear. She was back in less than thirty minutes. Then she and Mina spent hours at the bar, talking until they figured it was safe to call Ted. It was three in the morning in Tel Aviv, and the lines might not be busy.

Ted was at home, assessing the latest reports from the Middle East. That immediately boded ill for the conversation. "Mina, where the hell are you?" he shouted into the phone.

"I'm in Tel Aviv. I'm at the hotel. I'm safe. Lydia's here."

"Lydia's there, and you're telling me you're safe! You know how crazy she gets."

"She's here as a reporter, Ted. I'll hardly see her."

"Damn right, because you're going to get your ass on a plane and fly right home."

"Probably from there you think that's the right thing to do. But it's very calm here. Believe me." Well, she wasn't exactly lying. Earlier she and Lydia had taken a stroll. There were few cars on the streets, and those that were out had their headlights painted blue.

"The calm before the storm," said Ted, given to clichés in a crisis.

"Ted, this is a once-in-a-lifetime experience."

"To live through a war? You did that in Europe. Remember?"

"The consensus is that whatever happens won't take long."

"Don't you love me enough to come back to me?"

"That's unfair," she told him. "Be content knowing I'm safe and satisfied. I can take care of myself."

"Maybe too well."

"Keep the home fires burning, darling," she retaliated, with a cliché of her own. Then she hung up.

"Trouble?" Lydia asked.

"Sometimes Ted doesn't understand me," Mina admitted.

When Mina awoke the next morning, Lydia was nowhere to be seen. She had left a note saying she would be back at some unspecified time. Mina showered and dressed and went downstairs. They were still baking bread, at least. She had a solid meal, then approached the woman behind the front desk. "Will you be checking out today?" the woman asked.

"No. I'm staying. I just want to know if there is any place I can go to offer help. I understand you're using volunteers."

The woman smiled at her, as tears welled up in her eyes. "Thank you," she said. Then she cleared her throat. "The Iriya, you can't miss it. No. 27 bus will take you there. Ask the driver."

She understood from the people in line that No. 27 usually came every five to ten minutes. Most of the buses in the city were missing. They were being used to transport the soldiers to the fronts—all three fronts. By the time a bus arrived, Mina had made several new friends and gotten a lot of advice.

At the Iriya she had to confess that she was a simple tourist. They were hesitant about using her; but she told them she was staying anyway, and they might as well assign her something. She didn't care what. "Do you speak any languages besides English?" One of the women in charge asked.

"French and Polish."

"Any Yiddish?"

"Just French and Polish."

Mina was assigned to a *gan*, which was like a child-care center in the United States. She was placed with the younger children, those who couldn't talk yet. Their mothers were all busy trying to keep the economy going while their fathers were waiting for the Arabs to attack. After a day there, Mina simply wanted to know why, when one baby started crying, they all followed suit. There was one phrase in Hebrew she learned to coo rather quickly. "*Ha kol biseder*"—all will be well. No one seemed to believe it, though.

When she returned to the hotel that night, she found Lydia waiting in the lobby. "Thank God you're here," Lydia said. "I thought I'd have to send Ted a telegram edged in black. What do you smell like?"

"Baby burp." Mina explained what she had been doing all day.

"Oh, Jesus," Lydia said. "Is this a story or isn't it? A great addition to my piece. Thanks, Mina. Keep it up."

"What's happening?"

"As far as I can figure out, the Israelis have nearly given up hope that anyone's going to come to their aid and help keep open the Straits of Tiran."

"I thought Lyndon Johnson—"

"They thought so, too. But there seems to be a certain hesitation on America's part, despite the guarantees we gave Israel after the Sinai campaign. Anyway, now it's just a matter of time."

When they woke up the next morning, they discovered the time was now. Lydia's phone rang. She grabbed it. "Can you tell me any details?" she begged. She listened, then almost slammed the phone down. "Don't ask, because Harry the Great doesn't know."

They got dressed and sped their separate ways. Mina reported for work at the *gan* once again. The children were sending up a constant wail. Maybe they knew.

The radio was on perpetually. "Please, please tell me," Mina had to beg over and over again. As the hours passed, the faces of the women grew less grim. By evening, there were uncertain smiles. A good sign? If only she knew.

For three days Mina did not see Lydia at all. They left each other notes, so they knew each was alive. But that was all. Between June 5 and June 8 Israel had managed to destroy the Arab air force and take all of the Sinai, including Sharm el-Sheikh, therefore reopening the *casus belli*, the Straits of Tiran. Israel had pushed Jordan beyond the Jordan River to the east and recaptured Jerusalem. Rumor at the *gan* had it that Israeli troops who had fought in the Sinai were being transported quickly to the north to wrest the highlands from Syria. Mina thought of Ami, how he had told her that all the Syrians had to do was spit, and it would land on a kibbutz. What would they throw down at the soldiers of Israel?

Despite the battle up north, the streets of Israel were filled with joy. After being under the sentence of death for so long, there had been a reprieve, brought about by their own hands. The Arabs, who had boasted of the coming destruction of the State of Israel, who had declared that the Jews would be pushed back into the sea, had been vanquished in the most inglorious fashion. Mina could not help but walk around with a smile on her face, even if she *was* only an observer.

The night of June 8 she returned to her hotel and opened the door of her room. "Aah!" her roommate shrieked. Startled, Mina couldn't figure out what was wrong. Had she waked Lydia out of a nightmare? Her friend sat up, half-naked. A fraction of a second later, Mina noticed another head, peeking out from the covers. "Mina, what a surprise!" Lydia said, regaining some social graces. "Mina, this is Tuvia. He's with the press office. Tuvia, Mina."

Mina nodded. Is this what Lydia called "developing a source?" "Should I leave and come back?"

"Why don't you just leave, dear. I'll meet you down at the bar in just a teensy while," Lydia suggested.

Mina nodded, sighed, and went out like a martyr. But how could she complain? She recalled all the nights Lydia had studied late at the library to give her time alone with Ted.

Lydia's teensy while turned into an hour. Either Tuvia was having a problem or they were enjoying an exorbitant moment of postcoital bliss. When Lydia finally showed up, she had Tuvia in tow. Mina could see why Lydia had attached herself to him. There was a slight thickening about his middle, but he was a good-looking guy. "Excuse me a minute while I call my wife," he said.

Mina stared hard at Lydia as he walked away. "Glad to note he's ever the dutiful husband," she hissed.

"Darling, there are no scruples when one is on a story. By the way, Ted called. A second interruption by the Eisenberg family. I told him I had just seen you, that you were serving mankind in a child-care center. You'll be glad to know he said he wished he were here."

"Great. If I had been in my room, where I rightfully belong—"

"I draw the line at a *ménage à trois*."

"I'm surprised."

Tuvia came back. "She's fine. The kid's cutting a new tooth, and she's worried about it."

It seemed rather incongruous to discuss tooth-cutting when so many men had recently been killed or wounded. Tuvia looked distracted for a minute. "So"—he finally glanced up at Mina—"Lydia says you're a journalist, too."

"I cannot tell a lie, Mr.—uh—"

"It's Colonel Tuvia," Lydia explained. "No last names."

Safer for the wife, Mina thought.

"Just call me Tuvia," he granted with a smile.

"I'm really a travel agent. Lydia got me the press pass."

"A travel agent? Good. Yes. Even better than a reporter."

"I've always thought so."

"So. Lydia wants me to take her around to see what we've won. You will come, too? Soon these lands will be open to tourists."

"And you'll be one of the first to see it," Lydia exclaimed. "What a story that will make back in Cleveland. Ketura Travel's expert on the Middle East."

But it wasn't the agency Mina was thinking of. It was the urge to share in the victory. "I'd love to see everything," she told him.

They left the next day. By that time Israel had taken the Golan Heights. The kibbutzim above the Sea of Galilee would no longer be spat upon. At the *gan*, Mina explained her plans. Some of the women were jealous, though they happily let her know that several of their men were on the way home. The babies were also smiling, as if some of the joy older Israelis were feeling had been transmitted to them.

Tuvia had an Uzi with him. This gave Mina pause, but he assured her it was only in case they ran into stragglers. She was glad to see he also had a radio. Their first stop was Jerusalem. On foot they made their way to the western wall of Solomon's Temple. The area in front of it was crowded with soldiers and weeping women. Tuvia told them to write a wish on a piece of paper and stick it into a crevice. "Will our wish come true?" Lydia wanted to know.

Tuvia shrugged.

Mina wrote on a piece of paper, "No more war." She was sure that thousands would do likewise in the next few weeks.

They toured the old quarter of Jerusalem. Arab merchants were open for business, ready to bargain. Tuvia took them, with the aid from some Armenian shopkeepers, to the twelve stations of the cross and to the Church of the Holy Sepulchre, built over the spot where Jesus was said to have been buried. "The Arabs act as if nothing has happened," Lydia commented.

"Oh, they know something has happened," Tuvia told her. "But Jerusalem has been overrun by so many different armies in its time. Armies come and go. The *shuk* is eternal. Besides, they are still in shock. The time will come when the shock will lessen. The fear will begin, and then the anger."

From Jerusalem they went to Bethlehem. Before driving to Manger Square, they stopped at the tomb of Rachel. Weeping women were leaning against the stone. It was unbelievably depressing. "Why?" Mina asked.

"For lost sons," Tuvia told her.

From Bethlehem they went to Hebron, to the Tomb of the Patriarchs, where once so many Jews had been massacred.

By nightfall they had reached Beersheba. Lydia and Tuvia shared quarters. But Mina was glad to be alone. It gave her time to think and to realize how little she knew the Bible. The Sunday School stories of her youth came back to her, but they were blurred by time. It made her wish the Gideons had reached Israel.

The next morning they headed into the Sinai. "We can't go all the way to the canal," Tuvia told them. "But we'll make it to Sharm el-Sheikh."

They passed through Eilat and headed south. "Over there," Tuvia said. "Mount Sinai. Someday, Mina, that will be open to tourists. There is a monastery there, Santa Catarina. A steep climb. Your healthier clients will love it."

As they moved farther into the Sinai, the signs of battle became more evident. Some of the dead had not yet been taken away. "Theirs," Tuvia said grimly. "Don't worry. We'll pretty it up for the tourists."

They stopped at Dahab, taken over by the Israeli army, with whom they shared rations. Lunch was longer than it might have been due to Lydia's quest for human interest. There was joy on the surface, until the men started talking about those they had lost.

Tuvia hurried them on, to Sharm el-Sheikh, where more of the army waited. He encouraged them to go swim, see the fish and the coral. "We have no bathing suits," Mina protested.

"The men won't mind."

She looked at those tired men in fatigues and was sure they wouldn't. It was so hot that she went into the water in her sundress. All she had to do was lie flat on the water and peer downward with open eyes. It was an underwater paradise.

But the time for pleasure was limited. They sped back up the coast to Eilat for the night. Lydia sent off her story during dinner, then she and Tuvia again disappeared.

The next day they zoomed north, cutting across the West Bank until they hit the kibbutzim below the Golan. After checking, Tuvia informed them they could not go up on the heights. "They're still cleaning out the bodies."

Mina agreed. "Yes, let's give it a miss."

"I don't know," Lydia said.

"We're *not* going," he told her. "We'll drive through Tiberias on the way back to Tel Aviv."

"Can we stop?" Mina asked.

"In Tiberias?"

"There's a family I know. I want to see if the husband is safe."

Tuvia was happy to stop at Café Eliza. It was time for dinner, in any case. While they ate, Mina looked around for one of the Barak family. She saw no one. "Excuse me," she asked one of the waiters, male and looking tired, probably just home from the service. "Do you know if—how Yehuda Barak is?"

"Yehuda? Sure. He's back at his place. He came home this morning with me."

Mina smiled.

"Do you want me to call him?"

"I don't want to disturb him."

"Why don't you give us his address?" Tuvia suggested.

After dinner Tuvia drove to the outskirts of Tiberias, where a series of villas had been built. "Nice," he said. "The tax collector must not be on to him yet."

"He's a very nice man and he works very hard," Mina corrected him.

"Don't we all, but some of us live on a government salary. Just remember, Mina, we have to get back to Tel Aviv tonight. My wife's expecting me." He said it right in front of Lydia, without guilt. Mina couldn't understand it.

They went to the Barak house and knocked. Ami opened the door. "Mina!" he exclaimed happily. They heard a dish drop. "Aiy, Mother! She's been on edge ever since my father left. And now that he's back, it's going to take her a few days to get over her relief. Come on in."

"Just for a minute," Mina said. "We have to get back to Tel Aviv."

By this time Yehuda had come to the door. He embraced her like an old friend. "I didn't think you would still be here."

"I couldn't leave," she told him. "I was worried about you, so we stopped at Café Eliza."

"Yes. Come on in. Let's have coffee."

They settled in the living room. Eliza brought out coffee and cake, fruit and nuts. "Please, this is too much," Mina told her.

"It's standard hospitality for Israel," Tuvia explained.

"So tell us your story. It might be in the papers in the States," Lydia tempted Yehuda.

He laughed. "Only put in my story if you're going to mention my hotels and my tours. Other than that, my story was everyone's story. We fought; we won. We paid a price for it."

"I hate understatement. Give me something vivid."

"Oh, Lydia, I'm sure you can supply your own purple prose,"

Mina censored. "Ami, I thought of our trip to that hill all the time the war was on. You must be pleased now."

"Yes."

"It's a war Ami and Ron won't have to fight," Yehuda added.

Mina looked from one of Yehuda's sons to the other. Ami was light; Ron was dark. Ron definitely looked only fourteen, and had dark eager eyes and a shy smile. She nodded to him, and he almost blushed. She hoped to God this would be the last war. Eliza, sitting there, so calm, so collected. How did such women stand it? Knowing that their husbands, their sons, must learn to fight, must be prepared to die to save the state. She thought of Ted. If anything happened to him, she would not be able to go on. People said you could, but she knew she couldn't. For the first time since she got to Israel, she wanted to go home, to be with her husband, to share his life.

"Where were you?" Lydia persisted in asking Yehuda.

"The West Bank. Not Jerusalem, though. I was with the mopping-up forces that pushed through Jenin toward Nablus and then over to the Damiya Bridge on the Jordan River. Then I was trucked to the Golan, but I wasn't needed. We had already paid the price there."

"That's where Israel lost most of her men, wasn't it?" Lydia inquired.

"I don't know the figures. I know it was hand-to-hand combat. Something you don't see much in war anymore." He shook his head. His wife put her hand on his shoulder.

Tuvia looked at Mina and Lydia. "We've really got to go," he told them.

There was a quick exchange of business cards between Mina and Yehuda and a promise from her to steer tourists his way. Then they were off to the south. The next day, while Lydia stayed to find some more human-interest stories, Mina boarded a bus for Lod Airport and flew home.

55

YOM KIPPUR, 1973

MINA KEPT HER EYES CLOSED IN THE HOPE THAT SHE MIGHT BE able to get back to sleep. Not that she hadn't heard Ted getting up. It was unbelievable how much noise that man could make, into the bathroom and out again, opening the closet to get his clothes, then into the bathroom again, squeaking the drawer open. Mr. Considerate. She stretched and turned over. At that point he gently closed the door. She tried to cut off the noise coming from the other side of the door. Ted was getting Sam dressed to go to the synagogue with him, and Rachel had to go "potty" so she could eat breakfast with them. That should take about half an hour. Then maybe, just maybe, Rachel would let her sleep. Or, more likely, the door would open and Rachel would want to know what was on the day's agenda.

Yom Kippur, the Day of Atonement. Mina, trying to get back to sleep, justified this to herself by the fact that she had little to atone for. She had produced a male heir for Ted. For herself, she had produced the sweetest little girl in the world, although everyone warned her to beware of Rachel once she entered her teens. Even her mother warned her of that, which Mina found particularly incredible.

Mina's family, as well as her business, was thriving. Ever since her return from Israel in 1967, she had had as much business as she could handle. She had taken Lydia's advice and gotten in touch with the press. She had told about her experiences during the war, and had been in the papers, on television, and on radio talk shows. It was free advertising. She had had the newspaper stories laminated, and they were now hanging on the wall in her office. Since then, she had managed to travel to Israel each year, and had become *the* expert in Cleveland on trips to that holy land. Ted had even gone with her twice.

What a difference these last six years had made in their lives. She and Ted were no longer young. That was the first thing she had to face. They were definitely cut off from the culture that had developed a few years after they'd left college. They didn't take drugs;

they didn't demonstrate. They were solidly middle class. That didn't mean they had voted for Nixon. Neither she nor Ted was a member of the Silent Majority, which the government seemed to be relying on so heavily. But they couldn't understand why taking drugs and dropping out needed to be part of the effort to bring the soldiers home from Vietnam. Nor did they share the belief that Watergate was simply par for the American course. Could they turn away from the values they grew up with: honesty, diligence, hard work, patriotism? They were over thirty; they were part of the system.

She smiled into her pillow. Maybe they did do things somewhat differently from others their age. For instance, in deciding when to have a child. She remembered getting off the plane in Cleveland after her first trip to Israel. Ted was standing there, unsmiling, angry. She reached up to kiss him, and he vaguely brushed her cheek with his lips. "Your mother wants you to call her as soon as we reach home. Needless to say, she is hysterical."

Ted had overstated the case. Her mother wasn't hysterical. She was worried. It was Jerry who was going crazy. "What kind of idiot are you?" he yelled at her. Mina would like to think the concern was for her, but she could bet that half of it was for the loan he had co-signed.

After that heated conversation with her parents, Ted ordered, "Get undressed; shower."

He was so angry that she didn't think of arguing with him. When she got out of the shower, he was waiting for her naked. Somehow she didn't think Ted was exactly horny. He had her spread her legs; then he methodically pushed his way into her. When he had finished, she asked, "What was the meaning of that? Male domination?"

"Forget the feminist crap, girl. I'm getting you pregnant."

As tired as she was, she laughed. As a former Catholic, she knew the rhythm method well. Ted's timing was off. Before he tried it again, she would convince him to return to their former methods of protection.

Nine months later, they had Sam. The *brit* was one of those family affairs she would gladly forget. She was quite thankful when, two years later, they had a girl. No *brit* then—just naming her in the temple. In between Sam and Rachel, they bought a house, much like the one her mother and Jerry had first bought in Trenton; except that this one was older, in an established, professional neighborhood. Even if Cleveland lacked charm, the house didn't. They also hired full-time help, an immigrant from Mexico, who was doing her best to make sure the children were bilingual.

Ted had his own office now. Real estate law needed someone who was charming and serene, especially at closings—when so many last-minute problems, not to mention hysterics, came up. Ted was good at the part. He also specialized in tax law, so he had many rich clients who were using real estate as an investment, a hedge against the future. Ted was making investments of his own, too, which she wasn't too pleased about. But he always said, "If my clients can trust me, so can you." She pointed out that if his client's income was kaput, she wouldn't have to suffer.

Not that she saw suffering in their future. Life was good, rich, thick with enjoyment.

The door opened. "Mommy," her little Rachel's voice called.

Life was filled with all good things except enough sleep.

By the time Ted came home, she and Rachel had listened to records, done their exercises, taken a long walk around the block, and made some soup and sandwiches for their menfolk. When Ted walked in the door, he looked pale and despairing. Every year he tried to fast; every year he came down with the most horrendous headache. "Eat something," she ordered.

"Did you hear the news?"

"What news?" She looked behind him for Sam, to make sure nothing had happened to her son, the Prince.

"Israel's been invaded."

"What!"

"I heard it at the temple."

"Invaded on Yom Kippur? No one would do that."

Except maybe Syria and Egypt.

It was awful; it was tragic, but Israel would recover, Mina thought, after she had absorbed the first shock. She had been there. She had seen what happened in 1967. This war, too, would be swift, terrible, final.

The war started October 6. For the next ten days there was no sign of victory. There was simply death piled upon death. There was no hope; there was no joy. On October 18, finally, good news. Israeli troops were on the West Bank of the Suez Canal. They were pushing into Egypt proper. Egypt's Third Army was cut off. In the north, where Mina had been only last year, whose kibbutzim she had visited, there was also a turnaround. Territory that had been overrun in the first days of war by the Syrians had been retaken. The Israelis also pushed forward, to within twenty-two miles of Damascus, their artillery able to pound the suburbs, if they so chose. And then, on October 24, Mount Hermon, where she had sledded, where others skied, Israel's Switzerland, was retaken.

The newspapers wrote about a great victory over incredible odds, as if this were a basketball team coming back after being twenty points down in the last quarter. But this was war, and war meant death. War meant destruction. Mina felt sick at heart, tired, defeated.

Ted made sure he was home each night of the war to watch the news. At first, the children didn't know what was happening. They tried to talk to their father and mother when the news was on. But they were shushed. Soon they learned there was to be no conversation until the news was over.

"Lydia looks good in fatigues," Ted said once.

Mina almost laughed. Though they hadn't seen Lydia in person since last December, they now saw her on television at least once a week. Her move to television had been something of a fluke. She was in Vietnam when one of her colleagues began interviewing her about the press's influence on the course of the war. Some television executive in New York saw her and liked her face. She got her shot as network correspondent. She claimed it was better than the army for seeing the world. Now she was in Israel again, reporting from the northern front.

Sometimes Mina felt jealous, envying Lydia her freedom. Lydia had not married, did not have children. She had no regrets. She had told Mina at Christmas that she preferred to be Auntie Lydia. And she was, not only to Mina's children, but also to Alan's and Simone's little girl. She was Lady Bountiful, arriving with spectacular gifts from all over the world. Lydia's mother was disappointed, but were mothers ever satisfied?

The last word on that night's news went to Henry Kissinger, Secretary of State. "Now it's all over except for the negotiations," Ted said.

Mina went into the kitchen. "And the cancellations," she added.

"Trouble?" he asked.

"Not compared to the grieving widows, orphans, and parents," she answered. "But trouble enough. Let's just say Israel's not going to be a hot spot in the travel market this holiday season."

"But you've diversified."

"Oh, yes. If they won't go there, they'll go somewhere. People who love to travel, travel no matter what. Don't worry. The business will still be there. Wash your hands, kids!" she called.

During dinner, both she and Ted focused on what the children had to say. There was not much that was terribly fascinating, but what there was was cute; the kids were definitely cute. After dinner, Ted helped her clean up, more to be with her than from feeling any need to lessen her work load. "What would you do if I quit?" she asked him.

"The travel business?"

"Yes."

He shrugged. "Fine with me. You've paid off the loan. Your business is in good shape. You could probably sell your interest for quite a profit. But you'd have to decide if you'd be happy staying home."

"I don't know. This war had made me wonder what's important and what isn't."

"And have you made a list?"

"No. Not yet. It seems to me that we go along and go along, and everything is happy, and then all of the sudden there's no more happiness left."

"Give yourself time to mourn."

"Mourn what? That's what I asking myself. Because, what have I lost?" She looked at him, waiting for an answer.

"Maybe we have lost the concept of our invincibility. Isn't that what a strong Israel means to us? That we are safe?"

Or secure. Maybe that was it. Like her mother, Mina needed to be secure. Was that why she had married and had children, whereas Lydia opted for independence? But then, what did Israel's near defeat have to do with her own security? Perhaps someday she would figure it out.

56

NOVEMBER 1973

ELIZA SAT BY HER SON'S BED AND SILENTLY CURSED. SHE CURSED her husband; she cursed God; she cursed the State of Israel. She cursed her son Ron for lying in this hospital, dying.

The nurse told her to pray for a miracle; the doctor told her not to expect a miracle. Ron lay there like a slab of meat, unmoving, uncaring, almost ceasing to be.

Ismailia. What a fiasco in a war of fiascos! Crossing over to the west bank of the Suez Canal had been enough. What had been the purpose of trying to take Ismailia house by house, enduring sniper fire that had cut down so many soldiers? And all for nothing. The fight for Ismailia had been abandoned, but only after Ron had been shot by the enemy and dragged away by his buddies.

They came by to see him, those who lived in Beersheba, the city to which he had been medevaced. They always asked Eliza what they could do for her. But what was there to do? She waited. The doctor said it would make no difference if she wanted him transported north, so that she could be closer to home. She had a feeling that he simply wanted Ron to be disconnected from the tubes and machines so that he would die. Maybe they needed the bed for some other body. She bitterly accused the doctor, and he backed off.

No one had to do anything for Ron. She was there, talking to him, singing songs, washing him, combing his hair, pretending that each day he was getting better. The only way she knew that she was lying to herself was when Yehuda came down each weekend and she saw in his face how much their son was deteriorating.

"Let's take him home," Yehuda begged her.

"No!"

"Eliza," he said very carefully, "there's nothing there. He's brain dead. The doctor—"

"His heart."

"Can go on pumping indefinitely, but he will never live again."

"No!"

She cried. It was worse when Yehuda came. During the week she could pretend. She could talk to Ron about the years since his birth, how his teachers had all loved him, said he was going to be something special. How he had taken up the trombone in high school and driven the neighbors nuts. And all his girlfriends. Ron was so handsome, so sweet. Everybody loved him. Even in the army, he was superior. She and Yehuda had been so proud when he received his paratrooper wings. He was the pride of the neighborhood. Ron had wanted to go to Europe after he served in the Army, maybe America, too, see lots of different places before he settled down to study. She would take him there. He might have to go in a wheelchair, but together they would manage. She would point out to him all the places she and Yehuda had seen only last year. London, Paris, the Riviera. Ron would like the Riviera. All those girls going topless on the beaches. What a wild one her boy is!

"Mom."

Ron! But no. The voice had come from behind her. She turned. Ami was standing there, staring down at her. Tears poured from her eyes. She had not seen her firstborn since the war, even though she knew he had been wounded. Now all she could feel, as she stood there, was guilt. "Ami. I thought Ron needed me more."

"Of course he did," Ami agreed. He was on crutches. He had lost a leg on the Golan. But he'd been told he was very lucky. He had lost it below the knee, so his rehabilitation would be relatively easy. When he saw the condition of the other wounded soldiers while waiting his turn for physical therapy, he knew the doctors were telling him the truth.

During his weeks in the hospital, his father had kept him informed of his mother's vigil. His father had let him know that there was no hope for his brother, and he had shared his father's tears. He had even begun to accept the inevitable death of his brother. It was easier for him, when so many of his friends had died retaking the Golan.

What a war this had been! He had been demobilized a few months before it began. It seemed that he and the others had just had their getting-out party, and then this, this war beyond belief, beyond words, almost beyond tears.

Now, in Beersheba, he looked for some place to sit. Feeling weak, drained, dead inside, as he saw Ron lying there, so beautiful, so perfect, he swallowed hard to hold back the tears.

His mother was fussing over him. She stood up and helped him into the chair. He held onto his crutches and reached over to take his brother's hand. It felt warm and dry to the touch. He wanted to shake it, tickle it, squeeze it, anything to wake Ron up, to hear his teasing and mocking and joking. His mother brought another chair and sat down next to him. "He looks better today, don't you think?" Eliza asked.

Ami held onto the hand, but turned to his mother. "Mom." He shook his head. "You know that it's over."

"Your father put you up to this!"

"No! I spoke to the doctor myself. I spoke to the doctor here. Dad took the EKG to Jerusalem, to Hadassah, to a specialist. Mom, we've got to let Ron go."

"No!"

"Mom, listen to me. Ron has already left us. It's just his body here."

"His body is enough."

"What are you doing, Mom? This is like having him stuffed and kept around the house."

She slapped him hard across the face. He took her hand and brought it to his lips. Then lowered his head and cried. When he recovered enough to speak, he said, "Whatever you are trying to keep alive can be kept alive without this travesty."

She held Ami to her and wept.

In the afternoon Yehuda found the doctor. All tubes were taken out, all machinery disconnected. Together, as a family, they sat at Ron's side and watched his chest rise and fall, weaker and weaker, until with a shudder it stopped, like an engine stalling.

His commanding officer came to Ron's funeral, along with as many soldiers from his unit as could walk. He was buried on a hill overlooking the Kinneret, where the breeze gently swayed through the grass, where all around them they could see the land the Lord had given them.

During the *shiv'a*, Eliza sat and listened to the empty words of comfort. "Do you know what I wish?" she said to Yehuda when the seven days were over. "I wish I had perished in the Holocaust."

THE
SEARCH

57

CHICAGO, 1976

MINA SAT IN THE SECOND ROW OF ST. ANTHONY'S CHURCH, directly behind her mother. Next to Mina sat six-year-old Rachel. Then came eight-year-old Sam and Ted. Mina had given her children strict orders. "Don't squirm!" Ted told them, "Pretend you're asleep." So far the children had been good, but the ceremony hadn't started yet.

Jerry, sitting next to Maria, looked around and up the aisle. His eyes dropped to Mina. He said, "I hope the bride hasn't had second thoughts about your dumb-ass brother."

Mina smiled. The organ music had been playing interminably. Poor Terry. It was impossible to think of him getting married. She still saw him as the preadolescent he was when she left for college. She would have to admit that she barely knew him. For instance, who would ever have thought Terry would turn out to be a veterinarian? She had never actually seen him pull the wings off butterflies, but she had also never seen him sleep with a rabbit in his bed, or whatever vets are supposed to do when they're young. When she had asked him about his vocational choice, he had said, "Hey, a man's gotta avoid the draft any way he can."

Thank God he managed to do that. What a waste his death would have been! Not that Terry's draft avoidance had stopped Jerry from spouting on about "our patriotic duty," but even Jerry must have been glad not to see his son slaughtered on some foreign battlefield for a cause no one understood.

Understanding had been hard to come by in the family over the last five years or so. Terry had studied his pants off so his grades would be high enough for him to stay out of the war. Kristin had decided to go to Kent State. She had been there, protesting, the day of the massacre, when four of her fellow students had been gunned down. And who could count the injured from this civil war, not only physically injured, but spiritually, morally? Kristin had been lost to her parents for several years. There was no way to explain her position to her father. Jerry wasn't the sort of man to listen to others. He wasn't the sort to believe that wisdom could come from children. And Kristin didn't dispense her gems in the sweetest fashion. The result was a series of shouting matches whenever they were together, which wasn't often. Certainly not after Jerry discovered that Kristin had been spending some of her allowance to buy marijuana. Mina was glad she was in Cleveland, and those two were in Chicago. Even her mother was disgusted with Kristin after she asked for the money to pay for an abortion.

Mina and Ted saw more of Kristin those years than her parents did. She often came for a weekend from Kent State. But she knew the rules at Mina's house: no drugs, not screwing around, no really gross language. She abided by them. At those times she seemed a very normal college student.

Today, two years after her graduation, she was serving as maid of honor for her brother's wife-to-be. She had spent a year bumming around Europe and had come home to inform her father that she would appreciate financial support while she got an MBA. She wanted to go into international marketing. Jerry was so grateful that she had finally seen the light at the end of the tunnel—a career in business—that he would have given her up to half his kingdom. So Kristin had exchanged her Indian shirts for man-tailored ones and was about to go after the buck. Mina guessed it ran in the family.

The announcing chords of the organ sounded. The guests stood as the wedding processional began. Terry and his best man, a fellow veterinary student, entered from the side door. Mina saw her mother turn to stare at her son. Then Maria looked up the aisle and waited. Her face was sad but happy as the bride made her way slowly down the aisle on the arm of her father.

Mina almost giggled as Ellen Regan, the bride, passed by. She was remembering what Jerry had told her before the rehearsal dinner he gave in the couple's honor last night. "You'll recognize her. She looks like an Irish setter." Well, she might have last night, with her red hair flapping about her ears. But today she looked absolutely gorgeous. Mina glanced back at Ted, remembering her own wedding. He placed his hand on Sam's head and smiled. Had it really been twelve years ago?

Mina was proud of her half-brother. He hadn't fumbled, not even when placing the ring on Ellen's finger, not even the kiss. He got her squarely on the mouth. They must have been practicing. During the recessional, they looked idiotically happy, no doubt glad to have the ceremony over with.

People started to file out. The Jankowskis and the Regans assured each other that their children were the happiest couple in the world and would remain so. And, they agreed, the ceremony was wonderful. Mina grabbed her mother by the elbow and said, "Listen, Mom, you enjoy the reception. I'll take care of everything."

"But there's—"

"Don't say another word. If I see you give one order, I'll do something drastic."

With that, Mina grabbed Rachel's hand and dashed up the aisle, turning to make sure Ted was tagging along with Sam. It was really too much. Her mother was providing free catering for a reception for 250 people. That took a lot of arranging and preparation. On top of that, Jerry was giving the happy couple a honeymoon in Hawaii. Terry would really have a wedding to remember.

Mina was one of the first to arrive at the reception hall. She found her mother's chief assistant and told her that, whatever problem might come up, she was the one to handle it, not her mother. Maria Jankowski was not to be bothered on this day of all days.

Fortunately, there were no problems—if the fact that several people switched place seatings was discounted. But then, after the dinner no one really sat down. The band the Regans had hired was quite good. She and Ted were prepared to dance the night away. "Do you remember the dancing the night of our wedding?" she asked him.

"Which dance do you mean?" Ted replied with a wicked grin. "The one where my father danced with you or the one when my father danced with your mother while your father danced with my mother?"

She laughed. "Did you ever see four more unhappy people? And your grandmother, sitting in the corner and looking as if one of my family was going to come and cart her off."

"Hilarious," Ted said sarcastically.

She disagreed. "It was funny. And now poor Jerry has to deal with the Irish."

"I don't know what America's coming to," Ted agreed.

Someone cut in. It was her stepfather. "What are you two giggling about?" he asked her.

"You."

"Not again."

"We were just saying how terribly American your family has become."

"Well, you know what they say about the Irish."

"Yes, I do, Jerry, and please don't repeat it here."

"I actually broke in to take you to one of the tables."

So that's why he was dancing her around in such an errant manner. They landed in front of a table filled with people she didn't recognize. Or did she? "Oh, my God!" she said. "I haven't seen you in ages."

"Only one since you moved away from Trenton," Doreen Novoveski said.

Mina couldn't believe it. Here were Peter and Doreen Novoveski, who had written that letter to her mother all those years ago, inviting her to America. And now they sat at the wedding of Maria's son. They looked older, heavier, but happy. They had not managed to get to Mina's wedding; but then, none of the relatives from Trenton had. A matter of principle? Or disappointment? But that was in the past, and, anyway, Mina had had enough problems with the relatives who had come.

"How are Bobby and Michelle?" Mina asked, surprising herself that she remembered their children's names.

"Both married. Bobby has three children now; Michelle, four. It's crowded at Christmastime," Peter said.

"And Thanksgiving," Doreen added.

Someone came up and slipped an arm around Mina's waist. It was her mother, "So you see how well Mina's turned out, from that skinny little girl you brought over here?" she said to the Novoveskis. They smiled back at her, making no comment. But what could they say? "I'm so glad you could come," Maria added. "It's such a pleasure to see so many of you here."

"Oh, we go a lot of places together now that Tony, Peter's brother, bought that van. It makes traveling fun and inexpensive. I hope you received that present from Aunt Basia."

"Yes, we did," Maria confirmed. "It was so nice of her to crochet that afghan for Terry. She must be in her seventies now."

"Seventy-two," Doreen confirmed. "She did so want to come to this wedding, but her travel plans were all set."

"She's traveling?"

"Didn't you write her, Doreen?" Peter asked his wife.

"Well, I thought we'd be seeing Maria soon enough. We could tell her then."

"Tell me what?" Maria asked with a smile.

"Aunt Basia's in Poland now," Doreen announced. "She said she had to see it one last time, though she's strong as a horse. She's visiting all the places of her youth, including Kowitz. When she comes back, she should have plenty of news for you. I'll write it all down and send it to you."

Mina felt her mother's hand tighten on her waist, her body shift closer to her.

"That's wonderful," Maria said. "Please excuse us now. Mina and I have to go check on the refreshments."

"You haven't lost your touch there," Peter assured her.

Maria leaned heavily on her daughter as they pushed their way toward the kitchen. "Mom, there's nothing to check in there. I've taken care of it." She studied her mother. "Are you all right?"

"Yes. Of course. There's not much left, is there?"

"Because everyone's eaten like pigs, Mom. And they've all had plenty to drink. Come on. Let's rejoin the party."

"No. You go. I'll stay here for a while. The noise," she added lamely.

Mina was undecided. The bustle out in the hall could get on anyone's nerves. Yet her mother was used to it. On the other hand, her son had gotten married today, and that had taken months of preparation. "Do you want me to get you anything?"

"No. I'll be out in a couple of minutes."

Mina made her way back to the reception, where she spent some time circling among Ellen's relatives, assuring them that she was delighted to meet them. But she kept an eye on the kitchen door. If her mother was not out of there soon, she was going back. She checked on her own family. Her children were dancing with other children; Ted was dancing with Ellen. She smiled fondly at them, then made her way back toward the kitchen. Almost there, she met Jerry. "Have you seen your mother?" he asked her.

"She's in here," Mina said, as she pushed her way through the doors.

Maria was exactly where Mina had left her, but she looked paler. "Mom, are you all right?" Mina asked.

"What's the matter?" Jerry asked his wife.

Maria looked up angrily at the two of them. "Would you stop making a fuss."

"I told you not to overdo it," Jerry chided.

"I didn't overdo it."

"You're not a young woman anymore."

"Oh, bullshit, Jerry. I'm exactly your age."

"This language she picked up from your sister, Kristin," Jerry said to Mina.

"Mom, maybe you should go home," Mina suggested.

"I'm not ruining my son's wedding, thank you very much." She stood up and rocked back on her heels. "I'll be fine. Let's go." With grim determination, she led them back out into the hall. Ellen had already disappeared to change into her going-away dress. It wouldn't be long now before people would start to depart.

Kristin caught the bouquet. That must have been planned. A limousine was waiting to take the newly married couple to the airport. "Don't try to get through security with those bags," someone yelled from the crowd. Mina briefly wondered what had been done to the suitcases. She waved as the limousine pulled briskly away and turned to make sure Ted had a tight grip on the children.

The party broke up with much regret. All vowed it was the best wedding ever—and it would be until the next one. The relatives from New Jersey wanted Jerry and Maria to come out with them for drinks, but Jerry begged off. "Maria put this whole thing together, and she is very tired. I'm taking her home and putting her to bed."

"Still doing that, eh?" Peter said.

Maria smiled wanly. "I could use some rest," she admitted.

Mina stayed until the only people left in the hall were the catering staff. She made sure they would be well supervised, before she and Ted and the two sleepy children made their way back to the hotel. They put the children in one bed; then, they slipped into the second. "Do you think, if we're very quiet, they won't wake up?" Ted asked.

"Have you ever fucked anyone who's asleep?" she asked tiredly.

"Isn't that the way we usually do it?"

"You bastard."

He nuzzled into her neck. "Only joking. Hey, what was wrong with your mother? She seemed to lose her oomph halfway through."

"I think it all got to her. She's been working like crazy on this. God only knows how she's going to overextend herself for Kristin."

"Kristin strikes me as the type who will have a very sensible wedding in a judge's chambers."

"Don't be too sure. Weddings are for the memories."

"Let's remember ours. Or a little past it."

"You're insatiable."

"That's because you're so incredible."

"I'll take that as a compliment."

58

THE LETTER

A MONTH HAD PASSED SINCE TERRY'S WEDDING, AND THERE WERE days when Maria didn't even think of Aunt Basia's trip to Poland. Obviously, nothing had been discovered. She would have heard. Or if something had been discovered, surely people would believe that Aunt Basia was old and confused, rather than believe what she said she had found out about Maria Prychek.

How long was Aunt Basia's trip supposed to last? Maria should have asked Doreen. But she had not worried about survival for the longest time. She had not had to. She had survived and been happy in her new land. A husband, three beautiful children, a house in which she could fit all of Kowitz, a business that thrived, grandchildren. No one could take all that away from her.

What was the worst that could happen? Say Aunt Basia discovered that she wasn't actually Maria Prychek: What difference would it make thirty years later? She had been a good citizen. She had done everything an American was supposed to do. Would anyone fault her now for taking that chance when it had come along all those years ago? Would Jerry?

Jerry loved her. Of course Jerry loved her. They had grown used to each other, they had lived together so many years. Sure, their marriage wasn't perfect. She knew that sometimes Jerry had other women. When he traveled, she knew he took advantage of his isolation. But there had never been another affair like the one in Dayton. There had been no single woman to whom he had become attached.

It was true that at times her work annoyed him. He wanted her available to do his bidding, pick up his dry cleaning, make his meals, appear at his side for business dinners. She made it a point to tailor her schedule to his needs.

She had been a good wife. Jerry couldn't deny that. She had been a helpmate. She had contributed substantially to their finances. She had even promised Jerry that when he was ready to retire, she would sell her business, so they could travel around the world together. That's what he wanted.

Together they had seen their children grow and prosper. Certainly, there had been problems, but who has children without problems? And Jerry was happy with the children now. He couldn't blame her for any trouble they might have caused, though he faulted her for being too gentle with them. But that's what mothers were for.

No. Everything would be okay. And if it wasn't okay, if Aunt Basia brought back the news that the woman Jerry had been living with all these years was not Maria Prychek, Jerry wouldn't care. He loved *her*. Love made everything else unimportant.

Jerry was sitting behind his desk studying charts of national sales figures when his secretary entered with the mail. "Anything interesting?" he looked up to ask.

"Two more applications for VISA cards, three magazine subscription requests, ten copies of memos from this office to the New York office."

"Glad to see everyone's covering his rear, as usual."

"But you did get something personal."

He looked quizzical.

"I didn't open it, since it was marked personal."

"That's not like you, Mrs. Quaid."

She laughed and went out.

Jerry riffled through all the letters Mrs. Quaid had opened and stamped with the date until he found the "personal" envelope. It was postmarked Trenton and had no return address. He was surprised. Usually the only time they heard from Trenton was at Christmas. Perhaps it was someone complaining about the wedding or not getting a thank-you note.

He opened it. It was a short letter, handwritten, with no signature, no date. "We thought you should know," it began. He leaned forward and read:

"We thought you should know about this. It took us a long time to decide to write this to you. At first we were going to go to the authorities. But then we decided that since she is your wife, we will leave it up to you.

"Your wife is not who she says she is. She is not Maria Prychek. Maria Prychek died during the war. Maria Prychek had no children.

"Your wife is an impostor. What are you going to do about this?"

Believing the letter to be absolute nonsense, Jerry nevertheless reread it several times. What did this mean that Maria was not Maria? What garbage was this? Some new émigré had come over to Trenton and begun telling stories? He felt like calling those gossips now and telling them where to get off.

His mind circled around all the relatives in Trenton, especially those who had come to the wedding. Was something said then that he hadn't heard?

Or was something said that he *had* heard? Aunt Basia going to Kowitz. That was it. Had she gone to Kowitz and dug out some dirt she now wanted to spread around?

But this wasn't Aunt Basia's writing. Aunt Basia was an old woman. The hand that wrote this was firm and strong.

Maria. Of course Maria was who she said she was. How else had she found out about the Novoveskis' offer to bring her over here? Their letter had been sent to Maria Prychek. How well he knew that story!

How well *did* he know it? After the war, Europe had been filled with refugees. Many people assumed new identities or lied about their past. Look at all the Nazis and collaborators who now lived in the Chicago area. Look at all the Nazis—

Christ! What was wrong with him?

He had to know. He picked up the phone and dialed Maria's office. It took her a while to get to the phone, but she sounded incredibly cheerful. "Jerry, hi. What's happening with the father of the groom?"

"Maria, can you meet me at home? Now?"

"Now? It's the middle of the afternoon."

"Maria, please."

"Are you all right?"

"No."

"Okay. I'll leave in five minutes. I'll see you soon. Take care of yourself. Do you think it's—you're not having a heart attack, are you?"

"Maybe."

"Jerry! Then get to the hospital."

"I'll see you in about half an hour."

She was waiting in front of the house when he pulled into the drive. She ran over to his car, helped him open the door. "How are you? What's wrong?" she asked. Her face was tense with worry. "Let's go to the hospital immediately."

He took her arm, grabbed it firmly, and marched her inside the house. She stood there in her coat, amazed by his manner. The foyer seemed like an echo chamber. He handed her the letter.

As she read the letter, her face turned white. When she finished, she dropped it to the floor, went into the living room, and collapsed on the sofa. Jerry went after her. "Who the hell are you?" he asked.

Terrified, she looked up at him. "I'm your wife."

"Who the hell are you?" he repeated.

"Jerry, you know who I am. We've lived together for—"

"You are not Maria Prychek, are you?"

"Does it matter what my real name is? Does it change what we are to each other?"

"What did you do during the war?"

"What do you mean what did I do? You know what I did. I tried to survive."

"You managed very well, didn't you?"

"I managed to live, yes. Was that a crime?"

"I don't know. I guess it all depends on how you managed it."

"Whom have you been speaking to? What do you know? Jerry? Jerry!"

Jerry was walking away from her, out the door. She ran after him, grabbing his coat. He shrugged her off and pulled away.

"Jerry, please," she begged. "Talk to me."

"I can't," he told her. He opened the door to his car, got in, and started the motor. She held onto the door handle. "Let go," he mouthed through the window.

She wouldn't. He started rolling slowly down the driveway. Her hands lost their grip as she watched him leave her.

59

GOING HOME

MINA WAS HANDLING THE LAST-MINUTE, AFTER-WORK TRADE AND was about to close up when the phone rang. She automatically picked it up and said, "Ketura Travel."

"Mina Prychek, please."

She was surprised. No one had used her maiden name in ages.

She tried to put a face to the voice, but couldn't. An old school chum? "This is Mina Prychek Eisenberg. How may I help you?"

"Mina, this is Jerry."

"Jerry! I didn't recognize your voice."

"Come home. Tonight!"

"Jerry? Is this Jerry Jankowski?"

"Of course, it's Jerry Jankowski. Get your ass to Chicago tonight."

Now that sounded like Jerry. "What's wrong, Jerry? Is Mom okay?"

"I expect to see you in a few hours."

He hung up. She couldn't believe it. Her stepfather made this outrageous request, then hung up! Well, what should she do? Something must be wrong. Jerry could be demanding, but not stupidly so.

Yet how could she suddenly disrupt her life? She'd call her mother, find out what was going on. She first tried the catering office. Maria had left in the middle of the afternoon. No, she had not come back. Home? No answer. Something had happened to her mother.

Mina checked the airline schedules and booked herself on an 8:10 flight to Chicago. She drove home as quickly as she could through the rush-hour traffic. Her housekeeper was anxious to go home and was not pleased when Mina asked her to come early the next day, because she wouldn't be there and Ted had to get to the office.

When Ted got home, she was upstairs in the bedroom packing an overnight bag. "What's this?" he asked, leaning against the door frame. "And I thought our marriage was a happy one."

"Ha, ha," she said without turning. "Jerry called me. He gave me explicit orders to, quote, 'get my ass,' unquote, to Chicago."

Ted went up to her. "Is something wrong?"

"Obviously. But I don't have any idea what it is. I think it has something to do with my mother. I tried to reach her and couldn't."

"Your mother?"

"Yes. And now I'm worried. Jerry wouldn't say over the phone what it was. Probably wanted me to be a nervous wreck for a few hours. By the way, Mrs. Mendez is coming early tomorrow, so my leaving shouldn't interfere with your work too much."

"Fine. Don't worry about that."

She turned to face him, surprised. When did he start looking, not old exactly, but more mature? "Can you handle the kids?"

"More to the point, how will they handle me?" He smiled. She held open her arms, and they hugged. The phone rang, but they didn't break for air.

"Mommy!" Sam called.

Mina picked up the extension in their bedroom. "Hello?"

There was silence at the other end. Or, not really silence. Mina heard a lot of traffic. Then a voice said, "Mina?"

"Mom!"

"Mina."

And then Mina heard the worst sound, the sound of her mother sobbing. "Mom, where are you?"

"Mina, come home," her mother begged.

"I'm coming home, Mom. I should be at the house by ten. Where are you now? What's happening?"

"By ten?"

Her mother's voice was so high-pitched, she sounded like Rachel. "Yes, Mom, by ten."

"I'll go home at ten then," her mother said. "Please don't be angry with me."

"I'm not angry. Why should I be angry? Mom, what is all this?"

"Do you still love me?"

"Of course I love you. You're my mother."

"Good-bye, Mina."

"Mom!"

Mina looked at the phone, dead in her hand. Ted took it from her and listened. Then he put it down. "What was that all about?" he asked her.

"God only knows, but I am suddenly very sick to my stomach."

"Let me drive you to the airport."

"No. I'll need the car when I come home. And the kids need to eat." She grabbed her bag.

Ted followed her down the stairs. "You call me the moment you find out what this is all about. The moment," he insisted.

Mina hugged her children good-bye and warned them to listen to their father, for a change. Then she was out the door and on her way to the airport.

Maria stood slumped in the phone booth, unable to move. Someone rapped on the plastic door, an old man with a folded newspaper. A businessman in a hurry. Maria pulled herself upright and opened the door. The man said something to her, some grumbled complaint, but Maria did not hear it.

She walked. She had been walking since Jerry left her, all through rush hour, into the night. Now the blackness matched her despair.

What was she to do? Resurrect the woman she had buried over thirty years ago? To what purpose? But she had to. Now she had no choice. Jerry wanted the truth. What she couldn't understand was why he couldn't love her without the truth. What difference would a name make to him? Yes, she would tell him. It's true. I'm not Maria Prychek. I'm Wanda Zbyszek.

Wanda Zbyszek. She had not even thought about that name for years. How could she suddenly become that person again? That person, the town whore. What if Jerry found out about that? What if he demanded they go to Kowitz so that she could prove to him that this time she was telling the truth? Oh, yes, they would remember Wanda. She had lived in the little hut at the edge of the village. The men found their way to her whenever they had needs a more decent woman would not fulfill.

How could that particular truth help either her or Jerry now?

Why had Jerry turned on her so quickly? If he loved her, he would stick by her. But instead he thought she was some sort of criminal and that was the reason she had taken a new name. Didn't he understand what it was like then, with the Germans leaving and the Russians closing in? She had seen her chance and she had taken it. Was that so un-American of her?

Mina would come. Mina would solve everything. Mina would talk to Jerry, calm him down. Jerry respected Mina. They yelled at each other, but they could still communicate. Mina was calm, rational. She would make everything better.

But what if Mina started asking questions? What if she asked if she was really Maria's child? She was, yes—in everything that mattered. She had come to her when she was a baby, and Maria had raised her, loved her, cared for her, protected her against the truth.

What if protecting her against the truth wasn't what Mina wanted? What if she also demanded the truth? How angry would Mina be that Maria had kept her heritage from her? How many times had there been when Maria could easily have told Mina the truth, if the truth had not been a threat to her own safety? During the Eichmann trial, when Mina had asked so many questions, how easy it would have been to say, yes, this is an evil man. This is the man who is responsible for the death of your parents. Then she could have told Mina what she knew of her father and her mother. So little, but maybe it would have been something for Mina to hold on to.

When Mina converted to Judaism, Maria could have stepped forward and told her there was no need. "You are already a Jew," she could have said to Mina. "Your mother died because she was

Jewish; your father, too. Your aunts, your uncles, your cousins, your grandparents, all dead, all ashes someplace in Poland.''

But Maria had said nothing because she was safe. She was secure, an American citizen married to a respectable American man. She had two beautiful children of her own. And how would they feel when they knew?

Knew what? Of what was Maria guilty?

The world bore down on her. She was alone. Isolated. Unforgiven. Again, maybe forever, the outcast, living in a dark hovel, sought out for sin but not for love.

Was there any reason to survive any longer? If she could not be Maria Prychek, whom could she be? If she weren't Jerry's wife, Mina's mother, who was she?

She was nothing. A shadow. A shade. She had counted on love to sustain her. She had counted on commitment to save her. But both had failed. She was alone. No longer either Maria Prychek or Wanda Zbyszek; she was a nonperson.

The traffic rushed by her. She could feel the cars at her back, whispering to her, whistling by her skirt, tempting her. It would be so simple. And there really wasn't any other answer, was there?

She glanced quickly backward. The traffic light changed from red to green. The cars surged forward, all hoping for that quick trip home, where it was warm and safe, where spouses and children waited, where love suffused all with a golden light. She turned and walked a few faltering steps forward. Each step drew her closer to the curb.

And then, with a quickening pace, she stepped out into the rush of traffic. Accompanied by the blare of horns and the screeching of tires, she fell beneath the cars and knew no more.

Mina felt her stomach tightening and her hands sweating as she drive a rental car toward her parents' home. She usually enjoyed the drive from the airport. She took back roads, where the houses were tall and imposing and reflected the riches inside. But today there was no pleasure. Just fear of what she would find when she reached home.

It was 9:40 when she arrived. Jerry must have been watching at the door for her, because he rushed right out and almost pulled her from the car. She whipped her arm away from his grip. ''What is this all about?'' she asked him almost angrily.

''Come inside. Have you seen your mother?''

''Obviously, I have not seen Mom, Jerry. I just drove in from the airport. But she called me before I left Cleveland. She will be here at ten, since that's when I told her I would arrive. I gather she doesn't want to be alone in the same house with you. What the hell is going on?"

She was taken aback when Jerry suddenly burst into tears, right there on the sidewalk. She put her arm on his shoulder. "I can't find her anywhere," he admitted. "I've called her office. She didn't go back there. I've driven around the streets. I didn't spot her. I've gone into restaurants, bars. She's nowhere."

"Come one. Let's get inside." She gently pushed him forward and got him into the living room. "Let me fix you a drink," she offered.

"I don't want a drink."

"Dinner?"

"I can't eat. I'm worried. I'm so worried."

She sat down opposite him. "All right. What are you worried about?"

"Your mother."

"Obviously. You had a fight. A bad one. Did you hit her?"

"Have I ever hit your mother?"

"No. But I've never been called by both of you and been ordered to show up here either, so I have no idea what's happened."

"It was a letter. I got a letter from Trenton. I reacted—badly. I— I thought I was justified. When I knew what the letter writer said was true, I didn't give her a chance to explain. I walked out. But I didn't mean to walk out on her. I love her. You know I love your mother."

"Where's the letter?" Mina asked.

Jerry nodded toward the lamp table. Mina stood up, took it in her hand, and read it. "It's not true."

"It *is* true," Jerry said. "Maria—whoever—didn't deny it."

"What did she say?"

"I don't—God, I don't even remember. I kept thinking about that Nazi housewife in New York."

"Oh, God, Jerry!"

"All right! I overreacted. But what would you do if you found out something like this?"

"Well, now I have found out 'something like this.' According to this letter, I'm not even Mina Prychek. So who *is* my mother? And who am I? I want to know. But I sure as hell don't think my mother is a Nazi. Or a collaborator of any sort. I don't think Mom's ever done a cruel thing in her life."

"What are we going to do?" Jerry moaned.

"We'll wait for Mom to return. And then we are going to sit

down like reasonable human beings and talk this through. And, Jerry, if you once raise your voice, I'm going to knock your teeth down your fucking throat.''

He looked up at her and almost grinned. "I brought you up well.''

She smiled at him. "Damn right you did,'' she said lovingly.

They waited. Mina didn't start to worry until eleven o'clock, because she figured her mother wanted to be sure Mina was here before she returned. At eleven, there was no Maria. "She should be home by now,'' Mina commented.

"Maybe she's not coming home. Maybe she won't come home,'' Jerry said. "I can see why she would be angry with me. Those damn busybodies in Trenton.''

Mina watched the minutes tick by. At 11:23 the phone rang. "That's her,'' Mina said.

"You take it,'' Jerry said. "I don't want to scare her off.''

Mina picked up the phone. "Mom?'' Jerry watched. She seemed deflated. "No, Ted, she's not home yet. I'll call you later, okay? Yes, I love you. No, I'm not angry. Good-bye. Ted,'' she said needlessly to Jerry.

"Damn!'' Jerry replied.

The doorbell rang at twelve o'clock, just as Jerry was considering alerting the police. "She doesn't have to ring the doorbell, for Christ's sake,'' Jerry said. He got up and rushed into the foyer. When he threw open the door, Mina was behind him.

It was the police, two officers who looked young enough to be Jerry's sons. "Mr. Jankowski?'' one of them said.

"Yes?''

"Mr. Jankowski, I'm afraid there's been an accident. Your wife is—''

"She'd dead, isn't she?''

"Yes, sir. I'm afraid so.''

The officers stepped back and let the family scream.

60

L O S S

"I MURDERED HER."

"Oh, Jerry," Mina had said.

"People die without love."

Mina remembered that conversation as she sat with her husband and children during the funeral for her mother. Overnight, Jerry had become an old man, guilt-ridden, despairing.

They had conspired to keep what had happened between the two of them. Neither Kristin nor Terry was to know about the letter from Trenton and the panic that followed.

It was a simple accident, they were told. Their mother had been thinking about something; she had stepped off the curb, been hit by one car, run over by another. Both drivers had stopped. Neither had seen the figure of the woman in the dark. There was no alcohol in Maria's body. It had been simply a fluke, the sort of mindless thing that happens sometimes.

The body, when they had identified it, had not even looked like Maria's. It was a blond rag doll. It had reminded Mina of a cat she had once seen die. The cat had been run over by a car, but no one knew it. The injuries were all internal.

Lydia sat on Mina's left. From time to time she held Mina's hand; occasionally she put her arm around her. Ted, on Mina's right, knew what had happened, knew the entire story. He tried to keep the children from bothering Mina.

The funeral was well attended, if that was any comfort. People from Jerry's office and Maria's co-workers from the catering business had come, to show their respect. Neighbors, too. But no one came from Trenton. They had not been notified. They were not wanted.

It was beautiful the day Maria was buried. The sun was shining. The mums were out in full force. It was a beautiful day to be alive. Mina held on to that as the earth thudded down onto the casket, burying her life line. To live without a mother to turn to was not to live at all.

323

Afterward, the closest of the mourners went back to the house. Maria's catering service provided a muted buffet, which they served discreetly. Mina went around, saying all the right things, nodding with understanding when words failed those who came to console. She hugged Kristin several times. Her half-sister looked as if she was not going to make it. Terry was stronger. He and Ellen were sharing their grief. Jerry merely sat and died a little more.

Lydia stayed until the very end. With her nose for news, she wanted to know how it had happened. When it was quiet, when they were alone, Mina told her. What annoyed her about her friend that day was that Lydia saw the story of her mother as a story for the feature page. Her former roommate didn't say anything, but Mina could see it in her eyes. "So your mother committed suicide?" Lydia said softly.

"It was an accident. Her back was to the traffic. She didn't see it. She was probably trying to cross the street—jaywalking, yes—and she got hit."

"Right." Lydia was not going to argue the point. "Needless to say, this is going to make it very difficult for you to find out the truth, but it can still be done."

"I know the truth, Lydia. She was my mother."

"Maybe."

"What do you mean 'maybe?' "

"Psychologically, yes, she was your mother. But it always struck me, and my mother, too, how different you were from your mother. Your hair, for instance. Hers was so blond and wispy; whereas yours? Many's the day I wondered how you got a comb through it. Both Terry and Kristin are fair and blond like your mother."

"Different fathers."

"Jerry's dark."

"What are you trying to do, Lydia?"

"I'm saying it would be interesting to know the true story behind all of this. You know how to reach me if you need help."

"I won't need help, Lydia. I know all I need to know about my mother. She was a good woman."

"Yes," Lydia agreed. "She was."

There was no pattern to the next few weeks. Mina spent her time flying back and forth between Cleveland and Chicago. When she wasn't in Chicago, she called every night to make sure Jerry was okay. He had sick leave stocked up at work. Now he took it. He found he couldn't sleep. The doctor prescribed sleeping pills, so he felt constantly drugged. Ted went to Chicago for the reading of the will. Maria had left everything to her husband.

Jerry announced to the family that he would be selling Maria's catering firm. Whatever profit he made, he would divide equally among the three children. He would also be selling the house. He couldn't live in it anymore. He gave Maria's car to Kristin. Whatever else of Maria's they wanted, they could divide among themselves.

Mina and Kristin spent an entire weekend cleaning out their mother's things. Some of the clothes they would keep for themselves; others would be given away. Pictures, papers—those would be boxed for Jerry to take with him to put God knows where. Jerry couldn't bear to watch them. Sometimes they had to rush downstairs to ask what he wanted done with such and such. "Jerry," Mina asked once, "can I take some of the pictures, the early ones? I'll return them later, when you want them."

"Take what you want," he said, waving her off.

Pictures, papers, valentines they had made for their mother in school, Mother's Day cards, report cards, Terry's detention slips, letters sent from college—what had their mother not kept? At the bottom of Maria's box of papers, Mina found a folder holding identity cards. Two of them were in Polish; others were from occupation authorities. All were in the names of Maria and Mina Prychek. Papers—her mother had always been so careful about papers. Papers had meant the difference between life and death at one time in her life. That was obvious. Mina slipped the identity cards and papers into the bag of photos she was taking. She would study them when there was time, and then decide what to do.

The weeks passed. Mina returned to her family, her business, her life. When Jerry went back to work, she stopped calling him so often, only once or twice a week. She wrote him letters. Sometimes she hated Jerry; sometimes she pitied him. Most of the time she loved him, because, despite what had happened, he had done his best for her, for her mother, when she needed him. Except—except that one last time, when it mattered the most, when none of them had been there for Maria. And then Mina would hate Jerry again.

61

FIRST STEPS

TED TOOK MINA IN HIS ARMS AND KISSED HER. SHE LAY FULL-length against him, comforted by his strength. "Did I tell you how glad I am to have the house to ourselves again?" he said.

"It wasn't as bad as all that."

"Yes, it was."

She shook her head against his cheek. But maybe he was right. It had certainly not been a happy holiday season. All the preceding years they had spent Christmas with her family in Chicago. Now her family didn't exist anymore. Mothers made families. Her mother was dead. She wondered if her mother and Jerry had lain like this, giving thanks when she and Ted with their two undeniably noisy children had departed for home. She didn't think so. Maria doted on the grandchildren.

Mina turned away from Ted and flopped over on her back. "Don't think," he warned her.

Impossible. How could she possibly not think of what her life was like now and what it had been like only a short four months ago? It was so strange, so terribly strange. She would be sitting at her desk, working, and suddenly recall she had forgotten to phone her mother on Sunday. Or Sam would get a part in a play, or Rachel would have a recorder recital, and she would think she'd have to take pictures, invite her mother to come to hear them, or call her mother to brag about them.

She supposed she had been selfish over the years. She had friends plenty of them, but her real confidants were Ted, her mother, and, when she saw her, Lydia. They had been enough.

After Maria died, Ted's mother had tried to make inroads. If Mina had been a kinder person, she might have opened her heart a little more. But she kept in her heart her first assessment of Ted's family: They were crazy, too volatile to be trusted. She could not forgive Ted's father for telling her that death was a natural part of life, when this particular death had been so unnatural.

"Jerry looked awful," she said to the ceiling.

"Well, what did you expect?" Ted asked. "Guilt does that to a person."

"Have any of your clients looked that bad?"

"Stealing money isn't the same thing as destroying someone."

"If only there were some way to take it all back."

"Oh, Mina."

"He's talking about taking early retirement."

"How old is he?"

"Fifty-six."

"Did you notice how he never once mentioned your mother the entire time he was here?"

"Yes, he did," Mina corrected him. "When he handed out the checks from the sale of her business."

"Oh, no. I listened very carefully. He never said her business, Mina; he said 'the business.' "

"Whatever. He got a good price for it."

"Yeah. I mean, I never got a look at the books, but it seems fair. What he really got a good price for was the house."

"He's going to need it when he retires. Kristin looked good."

"She's young. She has her studies, a whole new life to look forward to." Ted offered his assessment.

"I wish Terry had come."

"It's only natural that he would go to Ellen's family for the holidays."

"You're right, of course. Ted?"

"Hmm?"

"You know I can't let this rest."

"Don't start, Mina. It's been a trying ten days, and I don't want to go over this with you again."

"You handled a case like this once."

"Never."

"Yes, you did. I remember your practicing your opening argument here in front of the mirror. That adoptee looking for her natural parents. You were very noble about her right to know."

"Well, she found her natural parents, dear. Her mother wouldn't even open the door to her, and her father was in a state prison. And that's in this country. You were born in 1942—we think—in the middle of a war zone, and you expect to go back and find out who your mother was, who you are?"

"Thanks for being so supportive."

"Mina, Maria was a very wonderful mother to you. Jerry was a better-than-average stepfather. We have a good, solid marriage."

"Have you ever cheated on me?"

"Not yet."

"Not yet?" She slapped him on his naked thigh.

"Well, the statistics are against us. But that's not what I'm saying. I'm talking about what we have. Aside from our marriage, we have two beautiful children, perfect children. Look forward, Mina. There's nothing in the past but death and maybe some ugly truth you'd be happier not knowing."

She was silent for a minute, avoiding an immediate confrontation. Finally, she said, "I'll be taking a trip next Wednesday and Thursday. I hope to be home late Thursday night. Mrs. Mendez can sleep over if you need her to."

"Where are you going?"

"I'm flying to Newark, so I'll be in the New York–New Jersey area."

"In other words, you're going to Trenton."

"Support me on this, Ted. I'm going to need it."

"You're my wife, Mina. For better or worse, in wisdom and stupidity."

"Thanks. I guess that's your one hundred percent?"

She could feel him smile in the dark. She turned and put her arms around him once more. Would he ever know how much she needed him?

Wednesday morning, before she left her office for the airport, she called Jerry. He was on another line, so she was put on hold. For five minutes, she waited impatiently. When he finally answered, she told him she was going to Trenton. "Don't deal with those bastards," he said harshly.

"I'm not dealing with them, Jerry. I've just got to find out."

"If you do—"

"I'll tell you whatever I learn."

No one had ever informed the Trenton relatives of Maria's death. No one had answered their Christmas cards. They didn't deserve anything, except to be cut dead.

When Mina arrived in Trenton, where she had not been since the last time they visited Jerry's parents, she was amazed to see how dingy a city it was. She could remember her initial impression, when they had been driven there after landing in New York. It was their first real view of America, and both she and her mother had been so impressed. Now, she wouldn't live in Trenton on a bet.

She had brought a map of Trenton with her, though she had expected not to have to use it. From all her traveling, she had developed a good memory of the places she had seen before. But nothing in Trenton seemed familiar.

She stopped at a corner parking place and took out her map, turning it from one side to the other until she'd oriented herself. Then she drove toward the street where the deli Once Over Easy had stood. There was nothing on the street now but boarded-up storefronts, a public-assistance office, a small grocery store, and a drugstore. She remembered none of them.

She decided to try the drugstore first. The druggist and the clerks were all blacks, none of them older than Mina. They didn't have the slightest idea of what she was talking about. There hadn't been any deli here in years. If she felt like eating, there was a barbecue place two blocks over. She thanked them and went to the grocery store. This was run by a Korean couple. They didn't understand her; she didn't understand them. She shook her head in defeat and backed out of the store.

The public-assistance office also looked as if it would be a wash-out. She glanced around and mainly saw blacks and Hispanics. The people manning the desks looked as if they did not live in this section of Trenton. She waded hopelessly through a sea of young children. In one corner was a group of old women, chatting with each other. They were all white. Mina figured they were her best bet.

She went over to them and drew up a chair. "Excuse me," she said. They stopped talking and looked at her suspiciously, as if she were about to ask for a handout. "I used to live around here," she told them, as if they would be interested. "I'm trying to find a deli that was located on this street. Once Over Easy?"

"That hasn't been here for over ten years," one of the women said.

"Have the Markses retired?"

"Are you kidding? Stella and Sam? They have their kids and the grandchildren working in the store. But it's a long way from here. Over on the east side, in the Caldor's Shopping Center."

"How do I find it from here?" Mina asked, her voice livelier. She got three different sets of directions and a lot of disagreement over which would be the shortest and the easiest route, but she thought she had the general idea.

Thank God Caldor's believed in large signs. She located the shopping center without once getting lost and found there was a Waldbaum's next to it. The center itself was filled with little stores, some discount clothing, a drugstore, a card shop, a Radio Shack, and Once Over Easy, looking sparkling clean. Seeing it made her realize she was hungry. She went inside, and the old familiar smell hit her head-on. It sent the years reeling away so fast she felt faint.

She found a table and sat down quickly. The waitress immediately brought her a glass of water and a menu. Mina remembered how hard her mother had worked in this deli, how tired her mother's legs and feet had been, how she would massage them for her when Maria came home to that tiny apartment at Mrs. Nowicki's. "Are you all right?" the waitress asked.

She looked up at the woman. The waitress must have been leaning heavily toward forty. Her hair was bleached; she had on too much make-up. But there were smile lines about her eyes. "Could I have a tuna on rye with a side order of potato salad and a cherry Coke?" Mina asked. The old familiar order came back to her.

"No cherry Coke. Coke?"

"No cherry Coke?"

"Sorry."

"Coke's okay. Is Stella Marks here, by the way, or Sam?"

"They're both in the back."

"Could I speak to Stella, please?"

"Are you selling something?"

Mina smiled. "No."

The waitress disappeared. Mina kept watch. In another minute a small, white-haired woman appeared through the open door behind the counter. That couldn't be Stella Marks. Mina remembered Stella as big, imposing. But the woman was walking briskly toward her table. Mina stood. Mrs. Marks slowed her approach, looking puzzled. "Mrs. Marks?" Mina said.

"Yes."

"You don't remember me, I'm sure. I'm Mina Prychek. My mother—"

"God in heaven!" Stella said. "God in heaven! Sam!" she called.

Her husband, who also seemed to have shrunk over the years, came from the back. "Nu?" he yelled at her.

"Look who's here!"

He looked. He shrugged.

"It's little Mina. Mina Prychek."

Sam slapped his forehead and came toward them. Before long Mina had two luncheon companions. She told them how she had searched the old neighborhood for their store.

"It became impossible," Sam said. "Everyone had left. Egg salad, chicken salad, blinzes, herring—they didn't go over good with the new clientele. So we moved out. It hurt me, but we moved."

"And you," Stella said. "Tell us about your mother."

Mina said softly, "Mother's dead."

"No!" they both said.

"She died in a traffic accident early last fall."

Stella looked at Sam and shook her head. "Your mother was such a worker, that one. We were sorry to lose her."

"You'll be glad to know she stayed in the field," Mina told them.

"She had that catering business when she was here," Sam remembered.

"When we lived in Dayton, she made pickles and salads for various delicatessens; but when she moved to Chicago, she really hit her stride. She had a catering business that made her rich. Her own office and everything."

"Ambition. That's what new immigrants have that some of our own people don't," Stella said. "Sometimes I look at my grandchildren and wonder what's going to become of them. They live between New York and Philly, and they haven't even been to a museum. What kind of life is that?"

"Did she stay married to that guy—what was his name?" Sam asked.

"Jerry. Jerry Jankowski. Oh, yes. They had two children. Terry is married now. He's a vet."

"Vietnam, eh?" Stella said sadly.

"No. Veterinarian. His way of missing the war."

"Good for him."

"And Kristin is getting her MBA."

"They don't go into business nowadays," Sam said. "They study it. Learning by doing has no merit anymore."

"And you?" Stella asked.

"I married a lawyer. I have my own travel agency. We have two children."

Stella patted her hand. "I knew you would do well. You still like the tuna fish, I see."

Mina laughed.

"The bread's not as good as it used to be. The crust isn't as chewy. But what can you do? Only the regulars notice, and there're not many of them left," Sam reported.

Stella shrewdly assessed Mina. "You're not really here to discuss old times, are you?"

"No."

Stella nodded. "Not many people arrive in Trenton to discuss old times. Trenton *is* old times. So what can we do for you?"

"It's about my mother." Mina sat for a minute trying to decide how to start her inquiry without betraying the secret of her mother's final moments. "I guess I really never asked many questions of my mother when she was alive; and now that she's dead, I don't have a chance. You see, I was only four when we came over here. My mother was always reticent about the past. But I know how much she respected both of you, and I was hoping that maybe she'd confided in you.''

Stella shrugged. ''I wish I could help you, Mina, but your mother was very reticent with us, also. Not that we pushed it.''

''We were happy when she got married,'' Sam cut in.

''Yes,'' Stella agreed. ''Very happy. There was nothing we could do for her in that department. But here was this lovely young woman, working her tush off, with you, this young child, and there seemed to be no men in her life. Not that that was so out of the ordinary at the time. A lot of women were without men after the war. But she was a refugee and had been through those DP camps in Europe and everything, and we felt sorry for her. Sam's a great matchmaker. But she was Polish, Catholic, and we're not.''

''There was always a point with your mother beyond which we couldn't go,'' Sam added. ''The war, you know, brought out a lot of bad feelings between Catholics and Jews, Poles and Jews. I don't say it to offend you, but Jews were hunted down like animals in Poland. As much as we cared for your mother, that always came between us.''

''I understand,'' Mina said. ''During the Eichmann trial, my mother and I had long conversations about what happened in Poland during the war.''

''And what did she say?'' Stella wanted to know.

''That they never knew what was really going on; and when they heard rumors, they couldn't believe them.''

''Neither could we,'' Stella said. ''Sad times.'' She looked up and smiled. ''But now there are happier times.''

''Yes,'' Mina agreed.

''I know how it is to lose a mother,'' Stella said. ''There's so much that you have to say and no one to say it to. So you start talking to yourself and people think you're crazy, but it helps.''

''Especially when they thought you were crazy to begin with,'' Sam added.

Mina laughed. She picked up her pocketbook to pay the bill, but they insisted the treat was on them. Instead, she left a big tip for the waitress.

As they walked her to the door, they introduced her to the boy behind the counter, their grandson. Then, at the door, Sam said, ''You know, we don't even know your married name. It's not Mina Prychek anymore, is it?''

"Eisenberg," Mina said.

"That's a Jewish name."

"Uh-huh. He's Jewish."

"And the children?" Stella asked, concerned.

Mina laughed. "I converted in college. Then I met Ted. So there was no problem."

"What did your mother have to say?"

"She raised no objections at all. She just told me to make sure of what I was doing. I was very, very sure."

62

THE RELATIVES

MARIA HAD RAISED NO OBJECTIONS AT ALL. MINA THOUGHT OF her own words, as she drove across Trenton to a Holiday Inn close to where her relatives lived. Why had her mother made no objections? Jerry certainly had. He had been furious, insulted and insulting. But her mother had been accepting. Mina thought at the time that it was because Maria respected her daughter's choice, knew the seriousness of it, and understood its origins in the Eichmann trial. But maybe Mina had been mistaken. Could it be that her mother hadn't objected because she was Jewish herself? After all, when Maria lived in Poland, it wasn't safe to be Jewish. In Poland it was an offense punishable by death. What could be more practical than to become an instant Catholic? Then somehow her mother had found out about the letter the Novoveskis had sent Maria Prychek, adopted this Polish Catholic's identity as her own, and made her way with her daughter to the New World.

Except—except that Maria was Catholic. Mina was sure of it. When Maria talked of her youth, not her war days, but before, she spoke of superstitions and beliefs that were totally Catholic. Priests and demons and the Virgin Mary were involved in all of Maria's tales of good and evil, all of her morality lessons for little girls and little boys.

Besides, Mina remembered Kowitz. She remembered that dark hovel where they lived. She could vaguely recollect the people, though she was apparently only three when they left. She definitely recalled the time the Russians came and she had to hide under the bed. But they found her, and she had thrown herself on her mother for protection. The rest of that scene was a blur. It was just her mother holding her, and then everything was all right again.

Aunt Basia was wrong. Her mother was Maria Prychek. She did come from the village of Kowitz.

Mina was glad to get to the motel. She hadn't realized how exhausting her day had been, the travel, the talk, the thoughts. She lay down on one of the beds and closed her eyes for a few minutes. But then she opened them, because she had her duties as a mother to perform. It was 4:30, time to call home and see what the kids had been up to.

Sam answered the phone. He told her that he had gotten a hundred on his spelling test and was about to begin a science experiment. He needed the results for school the next day. "Why don't you wait for Daddy to get home before you try anything?" she calmly suggested.

"It's only with baking soda. Mrs. Mendez says she'll help. She's good in science. You know how Dad is."

"Well, okay. Are you sure it's not going to explode or anything?"

"It's supposed to be edible."

"Don't try it!" she ordered. Weren't nine-year-olds too young for science? "Put Rachel on the phone now, honey."

Rachel's little voice almost squeaked hello.

"Hi, honey, how are you?"

"I can't go back to school."

"Why not, sweet'ums?"

"Because the principal won't let me in unless you or Daddy comes with me. At lunch I squirted milk at Deborah through my straw, and she complained to the teacher. But *she* did it to me last week, and I didn't complain."

Life is unfair, Mina wanted to tell her daughter. "You know, that wasn't a very nice thing to do."

"Freddie threw up in the classroom. That wasn't very nice either, but he doesn't need to see the principal to get back in."

"Well, Daddy can handle it."

"No. I want to wait until you come back."

"Daddy will handle it, Rachel," Mina insisted. "You're not going to miss a day of school. Put Mrs. Mendez on. Now."

Mina had a short chat with Mrs. Mendez about dinner and Rachel's emotional state. Where had she gone wrong with her daughter? Already. She sighed. She decided to take a short nap. She couldn't go see the relatives yet, and she would need stamina for that visit. Besides, she knew she could count on Ted not to let her oversleep.

She checked her watch when the phone rang. If it was 6:30, it must be Ted. She picked up the phone. "Hello, darling."

"What am I going to do about Rachel?" He sounded panic-stricken.

"Did you have a nice day?"

"What am I going to say to the principal?"

Now Mina knew why Ted hadn't specialized in trial law. "Go into the office, act very contrite. Assure him that Rachel realizes her mistake and she will not shoot milk through a straw again. That's all he wants to hear."

"Rachel says she's going to beat up Deborah on the play-ground."

"Tell her that if she does, Mommy will be very mad at her. Very mad. And she knows what that means."

"What does it mean?"

"I don't know, Ted. I figure it out differently on each occasion."

"Mina, I wish you were here. Don't I have enough problems at the office? Oh, hell, I'm sorry. How's everything going?"

"I struck out with the Markses, though they look well. I'll tell you all about it when I see you. In about half an hour I'm going to drop in on the relatives."

"Take care of yourself."

"Don't worry."

"I do worry and I want you home. I love you."

"I love you, too, darling. I'll see you tomorrow night." She hung up. Poor Ted. Fatherhood came hard to men. She didn't know why. They just seemed incapable of handling life's little crises. She smiled. Rachel was such a warrior. Sam was smart and sweet. How could they both have come from her body? But look at the differ-ences among her mother's children. Did her mother ever lie in bed warmed by the thought of her children? Mina sat up. Her mother never lay in bed at all. Maria was so industrious. Did she ever have time to think, to wonder? Did she ever want time to do these things?

By 7:15 Mina had freshened up her make-up, combed her im-possible hair, straightened her dress, and left her motel room. Once in the car, she automatically drove to the street in Trenton that housed so many of her relatives, those old-timers who had not moved out of the city to join the younger crowd in the suburbs.

Uncle Jurek's house was like the house on either side of it. It was two-story and had a porch and maybe fifteen feet separating it from its neighbor. Without curtains, you could look into the neighbor's living room or bedroom. Mina parked in front of the house. She rang the doorbell and waited. Seven-thirty-five. There definitely should be someone home by this time.

Uncle Jurek opened the door. He didn't recognize her. He looked at her suspiciously, as if she were about to try to sell him something. "Hello, Uncle Jurek. I'm Mina Prychek." He recognized the name, but not her. "Maria Jankowski's daughter," she explained further. "I've come to see Aunt Basia." She supposed she should have said Great-aunt Basia. Or maybe the woman wasn't even her aunt, if her mother wasn't really Maria Prychek.

Uncle Jurek made no response at all, so Mina simply pushed past him. "She's watching her favorite game show," he called, as Mina followed the noise into the living room. There sat Aunt Basia, old, in a faded housedress. Her eyes were glued to the TV and she hadn't noticed that a stranger had entered her living room.

Mina went over to the television and turned it off. That quickly changed the focus of Aunt Basia's attention. Mina could hear Uncle Jurek dialing the telephone in the kitchen.

Mina pulled up a chair and sat right across from Aunt Basia, not even three feet away. "Aunt Basia, I'm here to talk to you about my mother, Maria Prychek."

"Maria Prychek's dead. She died during the war."

"How can you be so sure?"

"I was in Kowitz. I found out things."

"What did you find out?"

"Her mother, Maria's mother, my half-sister, had pneumonia. Maria nursed her. Her mother died. It was during the war, you know. Maria's husband was in the Home Army. After her mother died, Maria learned that her husband had been killed by the Germans. She caught the fever, and there was nothing anyone could do for her. She didn't want to live. Forty-two. She died in 1942."

"Are you sure you haven't confused things?"

Aunt Basia almost smiled. "I went to Kowitz to see where my family had come from. I told them the story of Maria Prychek, how she was now living somewhere in Chicago. They told me it must be a miracle. Maria must have risen from the dead. I remember you. Little frizzy-haired girl. You always stood silently by your mother's side. Maria Prychek was a plump brunette. Your mother was blond and thin, and the men loved her. She used to pretend she didn't notice how the men looked at her when she came to our house for dinner. But she did. I could tell."

"In other words, you didn't like my mother. So now's your chance to get even."

Aunt Basia shook her head. "No. Your mother was fine. Your mother was beautiful. Maria Prychek was pleasant. Not beautiful. Your mother was not Maria Prychek."

"Then who was she?"

Aunt Basis shrugged. "You should ask her who she is. Why are you coming here to bother an old lady?" Her eyes flickered back to the blank television screen.

"Did you go to Poland alone?" Mina asked.

"With a friend from the church. We've grown old together. She also came from Poland a long time ago. It was a good trip. I enjoyed it. They had buses that took us everywhere, so we didn't have to walk at all."

Mina shook her head. She stood up and turned the television back on. Then she returned the chair to its place. Aside from learning that the description of Maria Prychek did not match that of her mother, Mina had gained nothing from Aunt Basia.

She looked toward the foyer. While she had been talking to Aunt Basia, she vaguely heard the door open and close several times. Now she knew why. Assorted "relatives" of hers stood there like a pack of wolves, waiting for the right moment to attack. She walked toward the group, intent on walking through them. "What do you have to say for yourself?" one asked her.

The doorbell rang again. Peter and Doreen Novoveski must have raced from the suburbs to get there in time to see Mina. "I'm surprised that you had the nerve to show up here," Doreen said to her, before greeting the rest of her family.

"Why?"

"Because of the way your mother took advantage of our offer under false pretenses."

"My mother never did you any harm."

"She lied to us," Peter said. "She used us."

"To come over here to a better life? Can you blame her?"

"We were tricked into believing she was one of us."

"She *was* one of you. Only not by blood. But since you're all such good Catholics, and charity plays such a large part in your daily lives, I'm sure that such a simple matter as blood relationship would not have stopped you from extending a helping hand."

"Immigration should be notified," one of the relatives said.

"Don't bother," Mina replied. "And don't bother trying to contact Jerry or any of my family, ever again. We don't want to have anything to do with any of you."

"I can understand that," Doreen said.

"I don't think you can," Mina retorted. "My mother died on

the same day we received your poison-pen letter.'' She looked around her, trying to spot the murderer. They stood there open-mouthed with shock. "Vindictiveness is a sin, isn't it? Maybe someone has something to confess? And then you can do your penance and forget about it. But there will be some people on this earth who will always remember what you did. They will always remember that one of you killed Maria Prychek. And they will not be as forgiving as Our Lord and Saviour.''

No one tried to stop her when she left.

63

A MEDICAL REVELATION

MINA SLEPT WELL THAT NIGHT, DESPITE THE FACT THAT THE Holiday Inn was situated along a major highway. Somehow that night the rigs that rolled by didn't disturb her. Whether it was exhaustion or a triumph of sorts, she didn't know.

When she woke up the next morning, there was only one thing on her agenda. She checked her watch. Too early. She took a morning shower. That was one thing she enjoyed about staying in a motel. She showered both night and morning, something she wouldn't do at home, not with the water and heating bills being what they were. By the time she was dressed and had put on her make-up, it was 8:30. Someone should be in the office by this time.

Mina had a hard time getting through, but someone finally answered the phone. "Braunstein, Braunstein, and Bacon.''

Mina almost laughed. It seemed not quite kosher to have Bacon with Braunstein. But she said, "Hello. I'm an old patient of Dr. Braunstein's, and a problem has come up. I wonder if he could fit me in this morning.''

"Which Dr. Braunstein?''

"I'm sorry—''

"Father or son?''

"Father," Mina said.

"Well that makes it easier. Dr. Braunstein's not taking any new patients, so, yes, I can fit you in. Would you give me your name, please?''

"Maria Jankowski."

"Fine. And could you give me the date of your last visit to Dr. Braunstein, Mrs. Jankowski?"

"Oh. I really don't recall. It was quite some time ago."

"You mean over a year."

"Yes. Well over a year."

"Well, then, you'll need your regular checkup, won't you?"

"I'd really just like to consult with Dr. Braunstein about an old problem. If you could just have my records waiting, to refresh his memory."

"The doctor does like everyone to have an annual checkup."

"I'm sure he'll understand."

"Then if it's just for a consultation, perhaps you can come in at 10:30?"

"Great. Thanks so much."

Mina smiled as she put down the phone. Boy, would she hate to be in that woman's shoes when she looked for Maria Jankowski's records. Then Mina realized she would probably have to face that woman when she reached the doctor's office.

She gave herself enough time to check out of the motel and found a doughnut shop for her morning fix of refined sugar. After that, she drove past their old subdivision, past her old schools, not knowing if anyone from her youth still lived in the neighborhood. She wondered what it was like to be born, grow old, and die in the same place. She supposed if she had stayed in Kowitz, that's exactly what she would have done. But in America there weren't many people who stayed in one place for very long. Old friends were exchanged for new friends the way one casts off old clothes for new.

It took her two stops at two different gas stations, but by 10:15 she had found her way to Braunstein, Braunstein and Bacon. Dr. Braunstein no longer practiced out of his house. Now he was in a modern medical building, where everything was painted an antiseptic yellow and green.

With some trepidation, Mina made her way to the receptionist, who was closed off from the waiting room by a thick glass window. Was this a bank or the doctor's office, Mina wondered. The window slid open. "Maria Jankowski," Mina announced.

The receptionist smiled at her and checked her name off. This was obviously not the woman Mina had spoken to earlier.

By 10:50 Mina had exchanged stories with several women in the room and read all the magazines she wanted to read. The door opened. "Maria Jankowski?" This must be the woman who had taken her call. She looked stern and angry. Mina walked toward the door as the woman looked her over. "You didn't tell me that the last time you saw the doctor was over twenty years ago."

"I did tell you it had been quite some time," Mina pointed out.

The woman led her to an examination room. "Take everything off, please, and put on the robe."

"I'd like to talk to Dr. Braunstein, not be examined by him."

"But if you're having problems?"

"No."

The woman looked flustered. All patients came into the back, got undressed, lay on the cold table and waited. Why was this woman causing a problem? "Well, you have to go into one of the examination rooms."

"Fine. But I won't undress."

"You'll be wasting the doctor's time."

"But I'll pay him well for it, believe me."

She left in a huff, as if Mina had said something insulting by mentioning money.

It was 11:15 by the time Dr. Braunstein entered the examination room. He stared at her over his eyeglasses. Then he looked at the chart. "You're not Maria Jankowski."

"No," Mina agreed. "I'm her daughter."

"Then why did you claim to be Maria Jankowski?"

He still had the door open, and Mina was afraid he was going to leave. "Because I had to see you, and I heard you weren't taking any new patients," Mina lied.

He closed the door. "What did you want to see me about?"

"I wanted to talk to you about my mother." He was already shaking his head. "She's dead," Mina added quickly.

He turned his head to the side, looking surprised. "I'm sorry."

"Do you remember her at all?"

He glanced through her chart, then at Mina. "Why don't we go into my office?" he suggested.

She followed him to his office, giving the woman who had taken her to the examination room a look of triumph. The chairs in his office were comfortable, she noted, as she gratefully sank into one. "I know you're busy," she said before he could say anything, "so let me explain the circumstances of my visit to you. My mother, as you might recall, was a refugee from Poland. She and I came over to this country about a year after the war ended. Last summer, my stepfather received a letter from relatives here in Trenton. According to the letter, my mother was not who she claimed to be. One of the relatives had visited my mother's hometown and found that the woman she claimed to be, Maria Prychek, had died of a fever during the war. The same day my stepfather received that letter and confronted my mother with it, she died. Traffic accident. Yes, maybe it was suicide. But we prefer to think of it as an accident.''

"I'm terribly sorry to hear all this. But what can I do?''

"I want to find out who my mother was. Both Terry and Kristin, the two children you helped deliver, know who their mother was, if you see what I mean. She was no longer a refugee; she was married to my stepfather; they had a nice home. They could define their mother. Now, I don't even know my mother's name.'' Mina shrugged. "I know nothing about my father. I was told he was a member of the Polish army and was killed fighting the Germans. Who was he really? I know this is an ethical situation for you. I loved my mother very much. She was a good woman. I don't think you'll ever find anyone who would say differently. But I want to know who she was, so I can discover who I am.''

Dr. Braunstein sat back in his chair. "This isn't as unusual a circumstance as you might think,'' he said. "Of course, it usually comes in a different guise. Children who have been adopted come to this office trying to discover who their natural parents were. There's a process for handling this. A legal process.''

"So I must get a lawyer and have him—''

Dr. Braunstein leaned forward. "Your mother's dead, you say? How much do you want to know? Really? Consider that.''

"I want to know the truth.''

"You say your mother was a good woman. You loved her. Isn't that all that one needs in a mother?''

"I *will* find out the truth.''

"And if that isn't possible?''

"But you said there's a legal process and—''

Dr. Braunstein interrupted. "I can give you the information you want. But I don't think you're going to like it.''

Her lips parted slightly.

"Do you know what *primipara* means?''

"Um—I've heard it before.''

"Do you have children?''

"Two.'' She smiled. "They're beautiful.''

He smiled back at her. "Then that's where you probably heard the expression. When a woman gives birth to her first child, she's called a *primipara*.''

Mina nodded.

"When your mother came to me, she was a primipara.''

It took Mina a while to understand what the doctor had said to her. "But that's impossible!"

"I do remember your mother. She made me promise not to tell her husband. She didn't make me promise not to tell you, so maybe it's okay that I'm letting go of this secret now. She had not given birth to a child before her son was born."

"But I'm nine years older than Terry. She gave birth to me. Obviously, everything healed or whatever—"

"Mrs.—"

"Eisenberg."

"Mrs. Eisenberg, medical science is not exact on a lot of things, but doctors can tell whether a woman has had a child before. Good doctors can even tell how many. Your mother had never been pregnant before she showed up at this office, pregnant with her first-born."

"I can't believe it."

"You wanted to know."

Mina buried her face in her hands. "Oh, God."

"Was telling you a mistake?"

"But she was so good to me."

"Most adoptive parents are good to their children."

"Then how, I mean, who—"

He shook his head. "She never told me."

Mina leaned back in her chair. "Do you want some water?" Dr. Braunstein asked.

She stood up. "No. Thank you, Doctor. I really appreciate this. It just—is so incredible that all these years—" She gave a short laugh but found tears rolling down her cheeks. "To think that she cared for me so much, and I wasn't even hers."

"But, as you said, she loved you."

"Yes, she did, Dr. Braunstein. Thank you so much for telling me this. It confirms everything I've ever believed about her. She was truly a good woman."

"I'm sure she was."

When they left the office, his handmaiden was waiting. He handed her the slip for Mina's appointment. "No fee," he told her. The woman glared at Mina as she left.

Almost without thinking, Mina drove to Newark Airport. On the plane home she sat there amazed that someone would do such a thing for her. She must have been an orphan that this blond woman who called herself Maria Prychek had come across. But even so, why would Maria help her? What had saved Mina when so many others had been lost?

She got up suddenly and lurched to the back of the plane. In the lavatory she stared at herself in the mirror. Who was she? Gentile? Jew? Pole? Russian? German? Who was she, if not Maria Prychek's daughter?

She hit the rush-hour traffic on her return home to Cleveland. When she walked into the house, Ted was in the kitchen, making a mess, and the children were racing around the living room, teasing each other. They all jumped on her, the kids screaming their latest news. How annoying children can be! How annoying she must have been! And yet her mother never turned her back on her, never said, "This child isn't mine anyway; let her lie by the wayside."

She told Ted that night, after she'd listened to the agony of his confrontation with the principal. "It made me feel like a bad little boy again," he confessed.

"Were you ever a bad little boy?" she mocked.

Where he put his hands rather proved the point that he had been. Tired as she was, she appreciated his advances. It made her feel good. It made her feel like an adult. It made her feel like a woman, instead of somebody's daughter.

"No luck, eh?" Ted guessed, as he rested on her.

"As a matter of fact—"

"What!" Ted shot up. "Did you find out anything about who your mother actually was?"

"On the contrary, the mystery deepened."

"You look happy about it. The cat with the cream?"

"No. Just the wonders of human behavior. I'm not who you think I am."

"You mean you're not the loving, sexy woman I married, who bore me those two brats down the hall?"

"I'm not Mina Prychek."

His face became more serious. "What did you find out?"

"My mother is not only not Maria Prychek—she's not my mother. I saw her doctor. Terry was her first child."

"You're joking! Then who are you?"

"Spin the wheel."

"Mina!"

"Or whoever."

"But you have papers. You told me you found papers."

"In two names: Maria Prychek, Mina Prychek. Neither of us exists."

Ted flopped over on his back. "What a mess!"

"Why?"

"Legally."

"Don't be silly. I have all the papers. They're just false."

"Mina."

"Yes. I think I'll keep the name Mina. Do you mind? Or would you prefer something more flashy, like Gloria? Sybil?"

"It's not funny."

"No pedigrees. Even dogs have pedigrees."

"Mina the mutt."

"Ted!" She hit him. They both burst out laughing and tumbled on the bed together. "I have to call Jerry, you know. I promised him."

"This is going to be the first piece of news to make him happy since Maria's death, to know that you really were a stranger."

"God, did we have some fights," Mina recalled.

But Jerry was not exactly thrilled with the news. "Well, you always knew there was something wrong with me," she said. "And there were times when I felt I didn't fit in. Now we both know why."

"I can't believe it, because she would never let me say anything against you, even when you were driving her nuts, too," he said. "I thought, well, this is the child of someone she had really loved when she was young; and she was protecting you from everything, even your own stupidity. But now what should I think?"

"I don't know, Jerry. I don't know what either of us should think. I hope this doesn't mean you won't be my stepfather?"

"Why should you want me to be after what's happened?"

"Jerry, there's nothing we can do to change it. But we can find out more. Maybe."

"How?"

"I don't know yet. Let me absorb this blow, and then figure it out."

"Maybe it's not worth knowing more."

"For you, if that's what you believe. But for me, well, you should know I can't stop now."

64

FLYING BACKWARD

TED WAS UPSET WITH HER. HE CALLED IT "REGRESSING TO FEMInist tactics." All she had asked for was a week alone. But the week she wanted to herself was the week of Passover, and Ted felt she should stay with the family. The family in this case meant Ted, Sam, and Rachel. She knew the reason he was afraid of her going off by herself. Then the family would mean his family. As soon as Ted's family found out she was leaving, Ted and the children would be invited over there for meals, with much false sympathy about the deserting wife.

Mina couldn't blame Ted for the waves of dread that sometimes swept over him where his family was concerned. There was a definite tendency for each family affair to turn into a free-for-all. She liked to be on hand, not for the glee with which they afterward dissected his relatives, but merely to protect her own brood from any attempted criticism. She knew she would be in for it. She always had been, right from the start. A convert from Poland? And also she worked, instead of staying home and having children. When she had children, she had hired a housekeeper, Hispanic at that. What were her other faults? Well, she could count on hearing them enumerated each year at the seder.

Ted should appreciate the fact that she had carefully chosen to stay for the seder. Nor was she avoiding the second seder, the one they traditionally attended at the Friedan house, with Lydia's parents, Lydia's brother, Alan, his wife, Simone, and their child, Henriette. Rachel loved that seder because she was able to show Henriette, two years younger than she, the ropes. Mina was not too sure the Friedans appreciated Rachel's efforts.

This year the second seder eve would be different from many others in the past. Lydia was coming home. Ever since Mina had found out about her mother, or whatever Maria had been to her, she had sought out Lydia's expertise. Ted's advice was to turn the entire matter over to a private detective. Sometimes Ted annoyed her. He was a very careful person. When they were sleeping together in college, except for the first time, he always used condoms. She reminded him of that now, constantly, as if it were a guilty quirk. Now that she thought about it, she realized he kept all receipts, too. Everything had to be documented. Did Ted give way to passion only when he wanted her body? She asked him that one night when they were wrangling over the next step in her search. He had stalked out of their bedroom, slammed the door, gone downstairs to his study, and locked himself in. It was such a child-like performance, she had to laugh. "Why did you marry me?" he had asked later, when he had recovered his equilibrium.

"I married you because I loved you."

"You married me because I was safe, secure. I married you because you were different."

She was hurt. "How different?"

"More different than I knew."

Whether Ted was referring to her background or their life together since marriage she didn't know. And since he was intent on being so nasty, she didn't care. She would do what she thought was best, and what she thought was best was to call Lydia.

Lydia Friedan had never married. Her mother gave one of those brave little smiles whenever anyone asked. Naomi Friedan ached for Lydia's happiness. But her picture of happiness and Lydia's were entirely different. Lydia never gave any sign of regretting her choices; and now, in 1977, more and more women were making the same decision Lydia had made over a decade ago, when it was less popular, more of a disgrace. Still, Naomi Friedan didn't relish her daughter's role as a trailblazer.

Lydia had again changed careers. After working as a foreign correspondent for various news organizations over the last eight years or so, she had given up reporting and gone into public relations work in Washington. Her clients were foreign countries who sought to improve their image among government officials and the Washington press establishment. Lydia also handled foreign businesses who wanted to take advantage of the inflationary American economy without appearing to be greedy at the expense of the American public. Ted had benefited from Lydia's new career. She threw business in his direction. He was her lawyer for the heartland of America.

It was Lydia who had suggested that the only answer was for them to go to Kowitz. At first Mina thought Lydia meant Mina and Ted. But Lydia had meant Lydia and Mina. "When can you go?" she had asked.

Mina considered the months ahead of her. The rest of February,

March, April, May, and on into the summer were all heavy travel months. The only time she knew her office would not be totally bombarded was during Passover, when her main clientele had so much else to attend to. Lydia also could clear her calendar during Passover week, although she had to be home by the weekend.

"You and Lydia on the loose in Poland?" had been Ted's response.

The Eisenbergs kept up a united front at the second seder dinner with the Friedans. Ted gave no indication that he was not delighted that his wife and Lydia were flying off late that very night to be able to hop on the first plane out of New York in the morning. "We're taking the business special to Frankfurt. From there we'll make the spy's leap to Warsaw, then an internal flight to Cracow," Lydia explained.

"Why can't we go with you?" Rachel whined.

"Yeah," Sam agreed. "We want to see where you were born."

"So does your mother," Lydia said. "But it might take a bit of searching. Maybe someone took the stake out of the ground."

"Did they put stakes in the ground when someone over there was born?" Sam asked.

"Aunt Lydia's only joking," Ted informed his son. He could see from the excited looks that passed between his wife and her best friend that no matter what they found out, they were planning to have a good time.

By eleven o'clock the seder was over and the children were getting tired. "I've got to take them home," Ted told his wife.

"And we've got to get to the airport," Lydia added.

Mina walked to the car with Ted and her children. Ted got out her bags, put them on the curb for her, and watched while Mina gave each of the children a hug and a kiss. Then they stood together for a few minutes. "I don't really like your going into Poland, especially with Lydia."

"She has connections."

"But are they in her brain?"

"Ted, she has done pretty damn well for herself. So stop taking cheap shots."

"Poland is a Communist country. 'Civil liberties' is a term they don't understand. Just watch your step."

"I will."

"I hope you find what you're looking for. I hope you find an answer you can live with. But have you considered what you're going to do if you don't?"

"What do you mean?"

"What if you find something that you don't want to know?"

She wouldn't. There wasn't anything she didn't want to know. Not about her mother. "Take care of the kids?"

"Have I a choice?"

"Don't be mad at me."

"I'm not mad, Mina. I'm just not happy."

"Then don't leave me feeling guilty."

But that was too much of a sacrifice to ask for. He kissed her good-bye, and she clung to him until he pulled away.

Mina stood by her bags and watched Ted drive off. Lydia came down the steps, wrapping her coat around her. "A tender parting?"

Mina turned. "He doesn't want me to go."

"Unless an idea comes from a man himself, it doesn't have validity. You should know that by now. Here, bring me your bags. We'll put them in my trunk."

"How radical you sound," Mina chided.

"Darling, when I first gave up my glorious career in journalism, I joined a public relations firm already in existence. I was the only woman in the conference room, besides the secretary. I would say something, and it was as if they couldn't hear me. Not wouldn't—couldn't. Then half an hour or an hour later, one of the male partners would come up with the same idea and, bingo, how they celebrated. I left after two months, and, as you know, started my own firm, with a former television colleague. She and I are doing very well, thank you. The only man in our office is the janitor, and sometimes I think we could do better with a janitress. Come on. Let's go say good-bye to my family. We don't have much time left."

During their flight to New York and the wait for the plane to Frankfurt, they talked constantly, mainly about the new man in Lydia's life. "So how handsome is he?" Mina had to ask. Lydia took out her wallet and flipped it open. Mina studied the photograph of Lydia in a bathing suit—no cellulite, the bitch—standing next to a man in bathing trunks. He looked about five inches taller than Lydia, was bald, but still had a trim build. "Tom Knoble," Lydia explained. "He's a lawyer with the Justice Department. Since we've been living together for over a year now, we've decided it's a commitment. Now we have to decide whether it's enough of a commitment to have a child. A child ties you down, doesn't it?"

"Yes. There's no going back."

"That's what I'm afraid of."

"But there's also no stronger love than a mother for her child."

"I'm thirty-five."

"So am I."

Lydia sighed. "I have to decide. Soon." She looked at her friend. "Mother's love," she almost mocked. "Who do you think your real mother is?"

"That's what you're going to help me find out."

65

RETURN STEPS

THEY SLEPT FROM NEW YORK TO FRANKFURT. THEIR SYSTEMS WERE already off kilter. Travelling from Frankfurt to Warsaw they looked merely bedraggled; from Warsaw to Cracow they began to look wretched. In Cracow, they took a taxi to a hotel, booked rooms, enjoyed long hot baths, ate dinner, and slept.

When Mina awoke, she had no idea what hour it was. Her watch was still on Cleveland time, and she didn't know what the time difference was. She felt tired, but her mind was alert. She washed, got dressed, and gently knocked on Lydia's door. There was no answer, so she assumed Lydia was still asleep.

Mina took a cage elevator down to the ground floor of the hotel. Looking for the breakfast room, she walked past the main desk and was surprised to find Lydia standing there in deep conversation with a young man in a gray hotel uniform. Mina went up to them and found they were speaking a mixture of German and English. "Can I help?" Mina asked in Polish.

"Mina! You're up. About time," Lydia chastised. "I'm trying to find out how to get to Kowitz."

Lydia backed away and let Mina take over. Polish no longer came easily to Mina's lips, and she stumbled over many expressions, but the meaning was clear. She got instructions on how to reach Kowitz by bus, taxi, and private car. And she also found out that the breakfast room was closed, so she dragged Lydia to the café across the street, where they had an eye-opening cup of coffee. "Now I remember why I gave up this life," Lydia said.

"You mean the smell of the hunt no longer appeals to you?"

"No, it's the smell of myself after long-distance travel. So what shall we do?"

"Since money is no object, let's hire a private car."

"How much of your mother's money do you have left?"

"Let's hope it's enough to find the truth."

The hotel clerk told them he didn't know how soon he could arrange for a car; certainly today was out of the question. Twenty American dollars made him reconsider his assessment. By twelve o'clock, the private car was waiting outside the entrance to the hotel. The driver introduced himself as Emil and put himself totally at their service.

"We want to go to Kowitz," Mina explained.

"Why?" he asked.

"Can you take us there?"

"Certainly."

Lydia insisted that Mina sit in front with Emil so that she could get a clear view of where they were going. All during the drive she kept asking Mina, "Do you recognize any of this?"

"I was three when I left Poland," Mina reminded her.

Emil understood enough English to say, "So you are Polish then?"

"Do I look Polish?"

He stared at her and shrugged.

When they pulled into the town square of Kowitz, Mina did not recognize it. "There were no paved roads there," she said to Lydia.

"But there had to be, with farm equipment, tractors, and things," Lydia corrected her.

"There was no farm equipment. Except for animals."

Emil had been listening to their conversation. "Yes. You're right. Even now, animals are more reliable. On my cousin's farm there is a tractor that sits in the barn, because there are no spare parts. You must encourage your government to send spare parts to us. It's not fair to make our people suffer."

"Don't you get your farm equipment from Russia?" Lydia asked.

"Not if we can help it," he answered.

Mina turned slowly, gazing around the square. "It looks new."

"If you left in 1944 or 1945, of course there must have been changes," Lydia said.

"Who are you looking for? Relatives?" Emil asked.

"Yes. Relatives," Mina repeated.

"Then try the general store."

The suggestion seemed a logical one. She and Lydia went to the store and peered in. Mina shook her head. "I don't remember this at all. It's so large. No store was this large."

"Maybe it wasn't here when you were here," Lydia offered. "Let's go in and find out."

They entered the store and were immediately stared at by its customers. Lydia purposefully marched up to the counter where the cash register sat. "May I speak to the owner of the store?" she asked in English.

The English language brought an immediate response. A man stepped through a doorway leading to a stockroom and faced Lydia. "I speak little English," he told her.

Mina stepped forward. "It's all right. I speak Polish. I'm looking for some information. I believe I lived in this village as a very young child, and I'm looking for someone who might have known me and my mother. Have you lived here long?"

He smiled. "I've lived here all my life."

"What is your name?"

"Borek Wieczorek."

Mina expected a thunderbolt of recognition to hit her, but it did not. She said carefully, "I'm Mina Prychek."

"Prychek. Prychek. A year ago, or less, an American lady came here looking for the Prycheks. But they had all died during the war."

"You're sure?"

"I'm not sure. This is only what I heard. I was nine when the war ended. But this is what I understand from others who have better memories."

"Your parents?"

"I'm sorry. My parents are dead. But my Aunt Irena would remember. She never forgets a thing. She lives down the street, above the appliance shop, which her son-in-law owns. She'll be glad to have company and can tell you anything about Kowitz you wish to know. Mina Prychek," he repeated.

"Borek," she said thoughtfully.

"Mina? How old were you when you left Kowitz?"

"I think three."

"Then we never played together."

Mina smiled. "Probably not."

"Aunt Irena. She'll tell you everything."

Lydia wanted an exact translation of what Borek Wieczorek had said, but Mina was only halfway through when they reached the appliance store. "A fan, a radio," Lydia counted off the items in the window. "I guess no VCRs."

"Radios were forbidden," Mina said, though whether she recalled it or had simply read it, she didn't know.

They climbed the narrow steps to the apartment above the appliance shop. When they knocked, a young woman answered. "Yes?" she said.

"Borek Wieczorek sent us here to see his Aunt Irena," Mina explained. She studied the woman carefully, but this woman looked younger than Mina, so she probably hadn't known her.

"She's just finished her noontime meal. She usually sleeps for an hour or two after eating."

"Who is it, Katya?"

"Someone to see you. Borek sent them over."

"Then show the company in."

"I must go back to the store," Katya explained. "Please. She's in her room, to the left."

Mina and Lydia entered the bedroom. An old woman sat propped up by pillows, which gave her a good view of the street below. She might not be able to get out, but she still saw what was happening.

"Hello," Mina said, as she approached the bed. "I'm Mina." She dared not add her last name, since obviously she was not a Prychek.

"Mina!" the woman said. "Little Mina!"

Mina would not even glance at Lydia, lest Aunt Irena's concentration be broken. She pulled a chair close to the woman and sat down. "You recognize me then?" she asked.

"Oh, that hair of yours. How much trouble you gave your sister with it."

"My sister?" Mina repeated.

"We all chastised her for not taking better care of your hair. It looked like you had birds nesting in it. That's what we all used to say when you walked down the street, trailing after your sister. Such a scared little thing you were, though you had good reason. You looked like a little Jewish girl, with your dark hair and pale face. The boys used to tease you about it, threatening to tell the Germans about you when they came for their quotas. Then your sister would chase the boys with a stick. Hit them, too. She was a ferocious one, that Wanda."

"Wanda." The name lingered in Mina's mouth. Aunt Irena looked at her suspiciously. "Tell me about my sister," Mina said.

"Why?"

"We were separated from each other."

"Ay." She shook her head. "The war. Well, your sister, she was almost like a mother to you."

"What does that mean?"

"You must remember. She did the laundry for the village and— took care of other needs." Aunt Irena saw she wasn't making herself clear. "The men were very fond of Wanda."

"Men?"

"For money. She needed it, sure. After her mother deserted her, she had to live somehow. But even before she left her mother had started Wanda on the same road she had taken. Wanda was such a pretty girl. Well built, you know. The kind men like. Her mother, too, come to think of it."

"What was my mother's name?"

Aunt Irena pursed her lips together. "The questions you ask. Magda, of course. Magda Zbyszek. Though don't ask me your father's name. Or Wanda's father's name, for that matter. I don't believe even Magda could have told you that one."

"I don't think I remember my mother at all."

"Ay. Then Wanda couldn't find her."

"What do you mean?"

"After the war, Wanda left Kowitz, with you in tow, as usual. She was going to Cracow to look for her mother. We all warned her. We said that with the Russians swarming through the countryside, she'd better stay at home. But she was determined to go. One day she's here and content to wait for her mother to show up. The next day she's packed and she's off. But the Zbyszeks were like that. Take your appearance in the village. One day you weren't here; the next day you were. Your mother came in the night and dropped you off like a load of dirty laundry. Never saw the woman. She didn't even stop to say hello to old friends. What do you make of that? Your father was probably waiting for her. They probably couldn't get enough food for the three of you in the city. So they figured Wanda could take care of you until the war was over."

Mina, fumbling, slowly opened the envelope where she kept all the documents and pictures she had brought with her. She picked out one the Novoveskis had taken of her and Maria soon after their arrival in America. "Do you recognize anyone in this photo?" she asked Aunt Irena.

Irena reached over to her bedside table and put on her glasses. "Why, that's you, of course, and your sister, Wanda."

"Me and my sister," Mina repeated.

"So you weren't separated. I thought you said you were."

"Wanda died, just recently."

"Where did you two end up? Warsaw?"

"The United States."

"The United States! Wanda did well for herself. Probably slept her way through Europe to do it."

"No," Mina said. "She didn't. We found friends to sponsor us.

Thank you for your help," she added. "You've filled in a lot of blanks for me."

"That's what old people are for," Irena said. "Though no one seems to value our memory."

Mina left the apartment and walked woodenly down the stairs. "What did she say?" Lydia demanded to know as she followed her friend.

Mina couldn't speak. She wouldn't speak. On the street she walked back and forth until she spotted a man old enough perhaps to have slept with Wanda. She called to him in Polish, "Do you know where Wanda Zbyszek used to live?" He remembered very well. Perhaps he had found his way to her house many times at night.

Mina followed his directions, with Lydia, who, maddened by Mina's lack of communication, trailed along behind her. When the trees drew closer together, Mina knew she was headed in the right direction. She remembered the forest. She remembered gathering wood in the forest. She remembered—

The house still stood. It was dark and forbidding and surrounded by trodden earth. There were no people living in it now. Someone had turned it into a barn. Mina entered. Lydia followed. They both looked around at the lightless room, the wooden beams. "How oppressive!" Lydia said.

"I used to live here."

Once they got back to the village, Mina suggested a light lunch. "Only if you'll tell me what that woman said," Lydia bargained.

There was only one place to eat in town, a small café. Silently, Mina led the way to it. They took a table. Mina ordered a beer with her meal; Lydia settled for coffee. Once they were served, Mina looked around. In the back corner sat a group of old men, laughing and joking among themselves. "Excuse me a minute," she said to Lydia.

"Go where you want to. I'm just along for the ride."

Mina walked over to the men. They stopped talking and stared at her. She took a chair and sat down. "I'm Mina Zbyszek," she said, trying to grow used to another name. She took several photos from her envelope and laid them on the table. "Do any of you recognize these people?"

"Wanda and Mina," was the one-hundred-percent response. It was nice to be remembered. Mina checked out various points of Irena's story. The men verified them, up to and including the embarrassing fact that both Wanda and her mother, Magda, took in one-hour boarders.

So that was it. She was Wanda Zbyszek's/Maria Prychek's sister. Her mother was Magda Zbyszek, her father unknown. Somehow—and this Mina was afraid to ask about—Wanda had gotten her hands on the letter to an already dead Maria Prychek. Maybe she slept with the postman, and the postman said, ''Hey, there's this letter to Maria Prychek, who's dead,'' and Wanda wheedled it from him. However she'd done it, Wanda had got hold of that letter, changed her identity, and Mina's, and made her way to America. Did she ever look for her mother in Cracow? Or their mother?

Beyond the disappointment, Mina knew she should feel grateful. After all, Wanda could have abandoned her, left her in Kowitz to take in men and laundry for the rest of her life. But, instead, she'd taken Mina with her to America. She'd done everything for her. And she'd never let on to anyone that they were sisters, not mother and daughter.

''So when are you going to tell me?'' Lydia asked, after Mina had returned to the table.

''Lydia, you're my friend. As one friend to another, let's talk about something else. Baseball, football, life, love—anything else but this.''

''Okay.'' Lydia nodded. ''How do you think the Indians will do this year?''

''Who gives a shit!''

They ate in silence. At the back table, talk continued, though much quieter than before. Mina paid, overpaid, she decided, after they had finished. They left the café. Emil was waiting patiently by the car. Mina walked steadily over to it. ''Aren't you going to take one last look around?'' Lydia asked.

''I've seen enough to last a lifetime,'' Mina replied.

66

LECTURER

MINA LAY ON HER BED LOOKING OUT THE WINDOW. RAIN POURED down, splashing against the panes, drumming on the roof, giving her a feeling of security. If Ted were here with her—thank God he wasn't—he would be wondering about leaks. Did they need a new roof? Were the gutters clean of leaves and debris? Was it worth it to put a sump pump in the basement?

Ted was not a romantic. Rain couldn't be just rain. There had to be cause and effect. She wondered sometimes why she had married him. It was 1981. They had been married seventeen years. The great passion had died. Life's details had replaced the romance. If someone asked her what she felt for Ted, she wouldn't know what to say. What is a marriage made up of after seventeen years?

Lydia had married Tom Knoble two years ago. The commitment she had been so afraid of had finally been made. And now she was pregnant. All of life was starting for her, while Mina was on some endless treadmill of watching the years pass, fumbling around, with no peaks, no valleys.

In the darkness of this gloomy day, she could barely make out the picture that sat on her dresser. Her and her mother.

She flipped over and turned away from the window. What had she wanted from her trip to Kowitz four yeas ago? Perhaps romance. Not as in love, but as in searing adventure, passion, fantasy. Instead, she got the truth. She felt betrayed and empty.

It didn't help that, upon her return, Ted had had the bad sense to lecture her in his I-told-you-so mode. "My experience with these cases has shown me that—" "If you had listened to me, you would have—" Would have what? Avoided the truth? Would she have made up stories in her head to refurbish her past? Instead, she had found out her mother/sister was a whore, that she herself was illegitimate, that their real mother had deserted them. How sordid the whole thing was! Until that trip to Kowitz, she'd never thought that events connected with her life were anything but pure and miraculous.

How could she acknowledge the truth?

Ted's suggestion had been simply to accept what the facts had been before the trip to Kowitz. Maria/Wanda had been her mother. She had done everything for Mina that a mother should do, could do. Mina must honor her for that. Certainly, that was a reasonable alternative. But why had her mother never told her the truth? Why, when Mina had children of her own, a husband, a house, had Maria never come to her and said, "Now, there is something we must talk about?" How much easier that would have been than finding out about it the way she had, after her mother's death, when there was no way to resolve any issue by confrontation, by understanding, by forgiveness.

And now Maria's secret was Mina's secret. She knew, Ted knew,

Lydia knew. No one else. They had all sworn to keep silent about it.

Mina had spoken to Jerry, of course. She had told him his wife's real name and that she had been a laundress in Kowitz. Mina had also informed him that she herself was Wanda's sister, not her daughter. That had really been a shocker for Jerry. He simply couldn't believe it, not after all those years of martial defense Maria had put up in Mina's behalf. Mina reported that she couldn't find out anything about her and Wanda's mother except the woman's name. Magda Zbyszek had disappeared from Wanda's life before the war. She had gone home only once, and that was to drop Mina off, because the child was in the way in Cracow.

"At least you know now that she was not a Nazi war criminal," Mina consoled him a bit nastily.

"How could I have thought such a thing, even for a minute?" Jerry still rightfully berated himself.

"I wish she had lived, so that we could have heard the truth from her," Mina said. "But she's dead. So. What do they say? Let's remember the good things, the good times? We don't have much of a choice."

Jerry had remarried the year before. The woman, named Sylvie Conners, was a market analyst. Mina was ashamed of herself for resenting the marriage; yet she couldn't help but believe it was one betrayal too many on Jerry's part. If he had only confronted Maria in another way! But it was too late, much too late.

Jerry and Sylvie were living by the lake in a condominium he had bought for about the same price he sold the house for. Mina had been up to see it before Jerry remarried. It was absolutely gorgeous, luxurious, if a bit sterile. The second time she had visited, it wasn't sterile anymore. It had a feminine touch, as if someone had been giving Jerry advice on throw pillows and draperies. Sylvie, no doubt. And why should Mina expect Jerry to remain alone? Should that be the price he had to pay for his crime? She was being foolish. She had Ted and the children. Jerry had no one.

Ted and the children. She had heard of a disease people got when they grew older. They lost their sense of taste. Sometimes she felt she had lost hers. Her sense of taste, of smell, of touch. Could she feel anymore? Sometimes Ted looked at her as if he were looking through her. Was she no longer there?

She wasn't sure she was there. Perhaps she could admit to that. Only half of her functioned. She could cry, but only a little; she could laugh a bit at something really hilarious; she could love, but only so much. She was cheating her husband, her children. She was cheating herself. And yet she could not seem to overcome the depression that overwhelmed her.

Mina heard shouting downstairs. She turned over and checked the clock. Time to get up. Enough of a lazy Sunday. She stood and ran her fingers through her hair. As she did, her eyes again focused on the picture of her mother holding her small hand. Same mop of unmanageable hair. She almost smiled.

When she got downstairs, Ted caught sight of her. "They're creaming me in Monopoly," he told her.

"Daddy lost all his hotels," Rachel said happily.

She sat down on the couch and watched them. "Have a nice nap?" Ted asked her, without looking up.

"Fine. Just watching the rain, really."

"God. We have to get someone out here to check the roof."

She leaned back on the couch and tried not to look hostile. Ted glanced around at her but said nothing. A half hour later Rachel proclaimed victory, while Sam asked for a recount of the money. Both got up and left before putting the game away. Mina watched while Ted neatly stacked everything in place. "Ted, do you ever feel we're strangers?"

He didn't even bother looking at her. He simply said, "No."

"Sometimes I think we are."

"Well, sometimes I think you're crazy, but it's only a passing thought. Then I go back to seeing you as Ms. Industrious, successful businesswoman, mother, wife."

"I'm just going through the motions."

"Maybe we need a vacation."

"Taking vacations is my business."

"What do you want to do, Mina?"

The way he asked it made her realize he was annoyed with her. "You don't care, do you?" she asked. "You don't care if our touching has no meaning anymore."

"Maybe that's because it still has meaning for me." He stood up, clinging to the Monopoly game. "I don't know what to do for you. You're just drifting farther and farther away. Ever since—"

"Don't say Kowitz, okay?"

"I wasn't going to say that. I was going to say since your mother's death."

"She wasn't my mother."

"Mina, drop it. You act as if you were the only person in the world to ever experience a tragedy. So your past is a little convoluted. Look at what you have now. For God's sake, be thankful. Don't destroy love."

Ted turned and walked out of the living room. That's all he gave lately, advice. Sometimes she got sick of it.

She curled up with the Sunday Paper. *This Week*. Boring. Her eyes scanned the list of lectures Clevelanders could attend to improve their minds. Maybe Ted should work up his own series. There were pop psych lectures, support groups, religious events, computer classes, investment groups, archaeology. Her eyes stopped. Archaeology. Prof. Amihai Barak, of Tel Aviv University, speaking on the excavations at Tel Dan. She wondered if this was the same Amihai Barak who had shown her the Galilee all those years ago? Hmm. Probably not. She recalled that Ketura Travel used to receive greeting cards from Barak Enterprises for Rosh Hashanah and Christmas, but none had come in years. She had assumed they'd gone out of business.

She flipped through the fashion section. There were sales all this week in honor of dear old Christopher Columbus. Maybe a new dress would make her feel better. She would try that gambit tomorrow, if she had the time.

Tuesday's paper featured a picture of the archaeology lecturer. Under the photo was the name Amihai Barak. But did he look like her Amihai Barak? He was no longer young. It had been fourteen years since she last saw him, but he looked as if he had aged more than fourteen years. His face was lined, his eyes deeply set. He wore a mustache. The article said he was a visiting professor at McGill University in Montreal, and that he would be speaking on the latest excavations in northern Israel. The more she stared at the picture, the more she remembered her tour of the Galilee with him, his boyish enthusiasm, his worry about war, his love for his country.

He was speaking at Case-Western Reserve. That certainly was close enough to her office to make it possible for her to attend if she didn't plan on having dinner with the family. She liked to be home for dinner with the children and Ted. Or so she told herself. But one night away from them wouldn't be so terrible. Ted did it all the time, when he had to stay to prepare a case or meet a client who couldn't get away from work during the day.

She would not feel guilty. She called Mrs. Mendez and told her she would not be able to make it home for dinner.

There was already a good-sized crowd of young people in the hall when Mina arrived. They must have been graduate students, because the topic of his lecture was "The Use of Technology in the New Science of Archaeology." She hoped she would understand some of it.

Barak was introduced as a speaker who had been educated both in Israel, at Hebrew University, and in the United States, where he had received his Ph.D. He had returned to Tel Aviv University as a lecturer in archaeology and was busy applying high technology along with good old-fashioned guesswork to the excavations at Tel Dan. There was polite applause when he stood and stepped forward to the rostrum.

Mina took a good look at him. She barely recognized him. But he had to be the same person. She listened carefully. Yes. He was mentioning how his interest in archaeology had begun. How, as a youth, he had explored the Galilee, where it was easy to find signs of a more ancient civilization. She smiled as she remembered happier, less complex times.

Mina's concentration ebbed and flowed along with the intricacies of Ami's talk and the questions that followed it. She chided herself. She had once had an academic mind. Where had it gone? Should she have felt so grateful when the moderator announced that coffee would be served in Room 126 for those who would like to talk further with Professor Barak?

Mina didn't want coffee, but she did want the chance to speak with Ami, to remind him of their previous meeting and how she still remembered it with pleasure. There were several people surrounding him, types who looked terribly important, too important to be interrupted. She waited until some of the students edged in; then she went up and joined the group.

When there was a break, and many had trailed off toward the refreshments, she said, "Ami?"

He looked at her with the same impersonal smile he had used on the others.

"I'm sure you don't remember me, but when you were sixteen, you showed me around the Galilee."

His smile became broader.

"My name is Mina Eisenberg. I have a travel agency."

"Mina!" he said. Whether he remembered her or not she couldn't tell.

"I saw your name and picture in the newspaper and wasn't sure if it was the same person I had met or not. So I decided to come and see."

"I remember," he said more slowly, and this time it looked as if he did. "You had come to Israel just before the Six Day War. You were one of the few who braved it."

"Few and foolish."

"Not so foolish. We won that one."

"Professor Barak?" a student interrupted.

"Just one minute," he said kindly. "Can you stay afterward, so we can talk?" he asked Mina.

She shook her head. "I have to get home to the kids. I just wanted to see if you were the same person. I enjoyed your talk this evening."

"Thank you. What about tomorrow for breakfast, before I head to the airport? We can catch up on old times?"

She looked doubtful. "How early?"

"Eight-thirty."

She considered it. "Why not?"

"Love your enthusiasm." He took a piece of paper from his pocket and wrote down his motel and room number. Then he said good-bye and turned his attention to the student.

She felt happy when she left the room. She didn't know why. Maybe Ami reminded her of a different time, a time when everything was alive and exciting.

Ted was cleaning up the kitchen when she got home. "Hi," he said.

She went up to him and gave him a kiss. "Kids in bed?"

"In bed, yes. Asleep, no."

"I'll go up and give them a kiss." Along with the kiss, she pointed out that they should have been asleep hours ago.

Her parental duties fulfilled, she went downstairs. Ted had switched on the television. He picked up the newspaper, then glanced carefully over at her. "I called the office, but you weren't there."

"I know. I went out tonight."

"Oh? Mrs. Mendez said something about your being at the office."

"I went to hear a lecture at Case-Western."

"Really? On what?"

"Archaeology in Israel. It was quite interesting."

"I wish you had mentioned it to me, Mina. I would have arranged to go with you."

"Well, I didn't know if the lecture would be interesting. I recognized the name of the lecturer from one of my trips to Israel, and I wanted to see how he was."

"And how was he?"

"He looked much older, but he still had the same sweet temperament. I'm meeting him tomorrow for breakfast."

Ted put the paper down and stared at her. "What is this, Mina?"

She laughed at him. "He's a boy, Ted. He must be ten years younger than I am."

"You're at a dangerous age for a woman now, Mina."

She could not help smiling. "Thirty-nine? Darling, you're forty-three. That's a hell of a lot more dangerous than thirty-nine."

"If you don't stop meeting strange men at lectures, I'm going to take up divorce law again. Lots of available women there."

She realized that he was only half joking, so went over and sat on his lap. "Do you think this chair can hold us both?" she asked.

"It's your head that's fat, not your ass."

"Thanks, darling." She kissed his cheek, feeling the day's growth with her lips.

Ted's hands went around her body. "I love you, Mina," he told her.

"I know."

"Don't torment me. Especially not with other men."

"He's not another man. He's just a man."

Ted's hand reached up to turn off the light. He opened her blouse and brought her breasts to his lips. She slowly undid his pants and freed him so that her hands could caress him. Her skirt went up, and together they fought with her pantyhose. She sat on him and shuddered with pleasure as he entered her. Then she moved slowly around on him, feeling him inside her. She watched while his face strained at the agony/ecstasy of their lovemaking, until he exploded. She wished it could happen for her, but she felt nothing, not even frustration.

They sat there together, intimately sweaty. She traced his features with her finger. "Age has not withered you," she sweetly teased.

"I'll plumb any depths for a quotation from you," he returned. He studied his wife, then lay back in the chair, relaxed. "You do love me, don't you?"

"Of course," she answered automatically.

"Remember that at breakfast tomorrow."

Why was she so pleased that he was concerned about another man?

67

GREAT LISTENERS

"YOU'LL HAVE TO AGREE THAT BREAKFAST HERE IS NOT AS GOOD as Pension Bracha's," Ami said.

They were gorging on pancakes. Or Mina was gorging. Perhaps Ami ate them every day when he was in the States. "You know, it's funny," she said to him. "Each year I received a New Year's card from your father, and then all of a sudden they stopped coming. I guess your family's given up the tourism business?"

"In a way, yes," Ami said. "My father's become a corporation. He has sold off most of the hotels, because they were second-rate hotels on first-rate land. Like Pension Bracha. You wouldn't believe what he got for those two plots of land."

"But he was so attached to that hotel."

"Yes, it's what he started with, he and Mother. But then Mother lost interest completely, and my father didn't want to worry about managing the hotel. So Pension Bracha is gone. It's where I spent my early years. Now, it's been demolished and they're putting up a high rise. With the money he got for it, Father invested in more real estate."

"You must have disappointed him when you didn't go into the family business."

"No. He's always said, 'It's only money; it's not important.' "

"How untrue!"

Ami smiled. "You're right, his money has been important. It's allowed me to do what I wanted, study archaeology, come to the States, to California. I've led a privileged life, thanks to my father and mother."

"Tell me how you've spent the years since I last saw you," Mina insisted.

"Since you last saw me? How old was I? Sixteen, seventeen? Well, I finished high school. Passed my *bagrut*, which is our comprehensive exams. Then I was drafted, into the Golani Brigade. At the end of my three years, we had a nice leave-taking party. A month later we were back and, true to our name, fighting for the Golan."

"That was awful. I can't tell you how devastated we all were during that war. And afterward."

"Not as devastated as we were." His eyes saddened.

"But you survived the war all right."

"No. Not really," he corrected her. "I lost half of my leg on Mt. Hermon."

"Ami!"

"Does that sound to you as if it might be the title of an interesting song?"

"Don't joke. But you don't limp or anything."

"No. Israel's expertise in physical therapy cannot be equalled. Practice makes perfect. Unfortunately, I am one of the few who needs to wear long pants when I excavate. Especially when guests come. I don't want to shock them."

"Your parents must have been—"

"My brother died in the war."

"Oh, my God!"

"He was a paratrooper, killed in Egypt. The loss of my leg didn't seem so important. My mother's never really recovered from my brother's death. Let's see." He leaned back. "After the war, Hebrew University. That was fun. I met my wife there. She's a Canadian."

"So that's why you're in Montreal."

"Yes. Her family is there. Her name is Yehudit."

"Judith."

"Yes. Right. I call her Judy, but others stick to the Hebrew. We were married just before we left Israel for Berkeley. We made a lot of friends from all over the world. It was an exciting time for me. Then, after I got my degree, I thought about what I would do next. I seriously considered staying here in America. But so much exciting work is being done in my field in Israel. Professionally, advancement is quicker here. But I went back to Israel to become a lowly lecturer at Tel Aviv University. Although McGill very nicely made me assistant professor. So maybe I can use that to boost my standing at Tel Aviv."

"Do you have any children?"

"One. A boy. He was born a month before we returned to Israel. We named him Ron, after my brother."

"Are you staying in Montreal long?"

"No. We go back next Sunday. This was a very short visit, to try to work on some proposals and to give Judy a chance to visit with her parents, to let them see Ron. We have to be back in Israel for the holidays and for the new school year, which starts right after Yom Kippur.

"Now that I've given you a brief synopsis of my life, tell me what you've been doing."

"Nothing."

"Nothing? Let me see. I saw you in 1967. It's now 1981, and you've done nothing in fourteen years? You ought to be ashamed of yourself."

She laughed. "I had two children."

"See. You did do something."

"Sam's thirteen."

"And you didn't bring him to Israel for his bar mitzvah?"

She shook her head. "No. Rachel's eleven."

"So for her bat mitzvah you can bring her."

"I'm still married to Ted. I was married to him when I saw you last."

"Good. That's impressive in America."

She smiled. "My mother died." Her smile dropped.

"I'm sorry."

"She wasn't really my mother."

He shook his head, not understanding. "An archaeological puzzle?"

"Almost," she said. "I don't know if I told you I was born in Poland."

"I don't—yes! I do remember. Because my mother was born in Poland, too."

"Well, my mother—do you want to hear this story?"

"Sure."

"It's—well, it's become an obsession with me. But that's because I've lived it. Maybe other people find it boring."

"I'll let you know."

She smiled, then her smile faded. Her words tumbled out toward this relative stranger, all the hurt, all the anger, all the bewilderment. When she finished, she looked up into his sad, comforting eyes.

"I don't know what to say," he admitted.

She gave a short laugh. "Say what everyone else in America would say: 'You need professional counseling, Mina.' " She giggled; then, she became somber. "The thing is that, ever since my mother's, my sister's death, I haven't been able to live again. Ever since finding out 'the truth,' I've felt numb. Do you know what I mean? Food tastes bland; colors aren't as bright; my love for my husband and children doesn't seem as strong as it was in the past. Nothing is as good as it once was."

"I understand."

"Do you?"

"I understand because you sound like my mother. Ever since Ron's death, she hasn't lived either. Oh, she goes through the motions."

"Yes! I know that feeling."

"But nothing seems to bring her back to life. At first I tried. I tried to be the perfect son, to take the place of both Ron and the imperfect me. But she wasn't interested. She built a memorial to Ron in her mind, and nothing I did existed for her. It was as if neither of her sons had survived. When I graduated from Hebrew University, when I got married, when I brought home her first grandchild—nothing. I was a stranger, a passing acquaintance on the street."

"Stranger. That's what I say to my husband, that I feel like a stranger."

"Don't do that to him, Mina. Someday he may stop caring."

"You don't care anymore about your mother?"

"I care about her, sure." He shrugged. "She's my mother. But I don't depend on her for anything. She's living in a shell. I can't break it. Not even my father can reach her." Ami smiled. "I think that's why he's so successful in business, because he has nothing else."

"He has you."

"Yes, but I'm grown now. He and my mother should be having better times than this."

"I sometimes think of seeing a psychiatrist. The thing is, how can I grieve if I don't know whom I'm grieving for? My mother, my sister? I love and hate her at the same time. It drives me crazy that she never told me, that there will never be any resolution."

"Yes, and my mother says if only Ron hadn't been in Egypt, if only he hadn't been in the paratroops, if only—there's no way of calling life back, Mina. It happens. Don't let what's precious slip away. Your husband, your children. I've watched my mother. All I can do is watch her. No one can share her suffering. She won't let them."

When the waitress brought the bill, Mina picked it up. "I'm older," she told him. "Besides, this is a business breakfast. And my way of apologizing for ruining it with my problems."

He shook his head. "You didn't ruin it."

"I don't know why I told you," Mina said, suddenly shocked

by her own confession. "I've never told anyone before, not anyone.
Just my husband and my friend Lydia, but she was with me when
I went to Kowitz." She shook her head. "Do you always get con-
fessions from strange women in restaurants?" she said, trying to
make light of it.

Ami smiled at her compassionately and shrugged. "There's just
something about me that draws women," he teased. Then he said,
more seriously, "As a matter of fact, I'm glad we talked. You've
given me some insight into what my mother is going through. For
that, I'm grateful. Come to Israel, Mina. Bring your children. You'll
always be welcome."

Mina was feeling so guilty about dragging Ami down into her
own depths that she offered to drive him to the airport, an offer he
cheerfully accepted. When she got back to her office, she discovered it was a little before eleven. But no one seemed to have missed
her.

She tossed her messages aside and picked up the phone. She had
to go through Ted's receptionist and his secretary before she reached
him. "What's wrong?" he asked.

"Does something have to be wrong for me to call you?"

"No, but—"

She laughed. "Do you want to meet for lunch?"

"What's the occasion?"

"I just want to see you, to be with you for a while."

There was silence on the other end. He was probably figuring
how to get out of it, Mina thought. "I'd love to be with you for a
while, too, Mina. That's for a while on our way to forever. Twelve-
thirty?"

"Great."

"The Courtyard?"

"Only if you're paying."

He laughed. "See you then, my love."

Mina put down the phone and stretched back in her chair. At
twelve-thirty she would be meeting a handsome stranger for lunch.
She looked at herself. Ted had seen the suit before. She needed
something exciting to go with it, some eye-catching blouse that
would say "Here I am; take me," in the most subtle fashion. She
got up and grabbed her purse. She had enough time to buy something new before she saw him, her husband, her secret lover.

68

WRITING

Eliza Barak had made an office for herself in the dining room of the Barak villa on the outskirts of Tiberias. She had a desk, a comfortable office chair, several pencils and pads of paper. Her desk was right in front of the window, so that she could look out into the garden for inspiration. She cherished the flowers. She wept for them when they faded. She didn't weep much, though. The flowers would bloom again. But people died.

Yehuda stepped into the dining room and stood there. She was annoyed with him. He knew enough not to disturb her while she worked. These precious morning hours were hers, to think, to write, to remember. "What is it?" she asked sharply, not even bothering to turn.

"Eliza, come to the airport with me."

"I've told you, I can't waste the time."

Yehuda, with a sigh, sat down on one of the dining-room chairs. "Ami has been away for almost three months. I know he'd like to see you at the airport. Yehudit, too. And your grandchild. Do you realize how much he's probably changed? I bet he can speak now, a few words, and walk. Remember how crazily the boys used to walk when they first started?"

Eliza looked at her husband. He was old. That's what writing did for her. It made her concentrate on details. Yehuda was old. His face was lined, burned like a dried apricot by the Middle Eastern sun. His body, though not fat, was stocky around the middle, so that when she held him, her fingers could press into his flesh. His hair was thin. Balding? But he would be upset if she pointed that out to him.

What did she look like to him, she wondered. She had not really stared at herself in the mirror for a long time, in order not to give herself an honest evaluation. She knew that ever since Ron's death her hair had been gray. She combed it carefully. It was a sign of her suffering. She would never be happy again. To do so would be to betray her son. She would not feel what he could not.

"Eliza."

"Are you bringing them up here?"

"I'm sure they'll want to go to their apartment in Tel Aviv first."

"Well, if they don't want to come up here, why should I go down there?"

"Eliza, why are you twisting things? Of course, they'll want to come up here. They'll just want to get settled in their own apartment first."

"Yehuda, I have my work. I know you understand how important my work is to me. I'm sure Ami will, too."

"People can understand for only so long, Eliza."

She didn't hear him. "I'm afraid I'll die before this is finished."

"You're in perfectly good health."

"My heart."

"Eliza."·

Her head was bent over the paper once more, her fingers wrapped tightly around the pencil, as she thought of what she could write next. Yehuda grimaced, then got up and left her. She stopped writing and listened to the car pull away from the villa. Good. Now she would be uninterrupted for the entire day.

Where was she? Up to 1940. Her parents were alive in 1940, her sister, her sister's children. She would probably have to return to Poland sometime soon to see if her brother-in-law still lived in Cracow. That was a story in itself, his changing his name from Hershel to Jan. What had his disguise won him? She would try to find out.

She looked at the part of the manuscript that was finished. She had started out with a bang, she thought, her search for her daughter. Yes. It was nice to be able to turn her life into words. It gave it a distance she could not achieve within her heart. To her, loss was ever present, ever biting. First Mina. Now Ron. She had nothing left. Nothing except these words she wrote. For this she was grateful to Branek Weiss.

She had seen Branek maybe ten or twelve times the entire thirty-odd years they had both spent in Israel. She had heard of him, naturally, read about him in the papers, as he made his way through the political twists and turns of Israeli life until he became a member of the Knesset for the Herut party. When Likud had won, when labor had been defeated and Yitzhak Rabin's government gave way to Menachem Begin, she knew Branek would be in his glory. And she had seen him on television when Anwar Sadat came to Jerusalem. She had heard and read Branek's speeches about the impending peace with Egypt, the pullback from the Sinai. She had listened to his oratory on Judea and Samaria. He had done well for himself in Israel. A man like Branek had a need to be prominent.

She had assumed that with all his importance, Branek had forgotten about her. But she'd received a personal call from him, to let her know that the partisans were having a reunion in Tel Aviv, and he expected to see her there. No excuses!

She laughed now to think she had once been a soldier, and under Branek's command. Those years in the forest seemed so long ago. Memory was treacherous. She remembered so little, only the lovemaking with Adam Feuerstein, only the birth of her child, only the laughs and loves around the campfire. She had buried the fear, the horror, the filth, the death. Now Branek wanted to revive that?

Soldiers. Yehuda had been a soldier when she met him. She could even now feel his skin against her when he took her into the dark and made love to her. And then in the army camp, while she was training others and he was passing through, how beautiful he had looked.

If only—if only they could have continued the battle. If only they could have somehow not passed the fight down to their sons. Why, after what had happened to them, should their sons die?

She had gone to the reunion. Yehuda, too. When she first saw Branek, she'd told him he was fat. "And you're not gray?" he had responded. She'd laughed. She'd remembered the hostility, the love/hate she had felt for him all those years ago.

Branek's wife, Sophie, had not suffered in Israel, either. She looked fit and rich and happy. She had four children. The two youngest were girls. One was still in high school; the other attended Hebrew University. One son was a pilot; the other was in the navy. She was not too thrilled with them staying in Zahal, the Israel Defense Forces. There wasn't that much money in it. But she supposed the pilot would one day transfer to El Al, and the boy in the navy was specializing in computer systems, so there would be no lack of jobs for him, either, when he chose to become a civilian.

Sophie had asked after Ami, not Ron. Everyone knew that Ron was dead. Branek and Sophie had come to Ron's funeral. They had tried to console her with the fact that he had died for his country. She had never forgiven people who had said that to her. She hadn't wanted him to die for his country. She hadn't wanted Ron to die at all. But one had to go on pretending to be normal, so she had answered Sophie's questions about Ami. About his job, his wife, his child, how well he was doing, how happy she was that he had learned not to hobble around on his false leg. Yes, a son to be proud of, but Ron was dead. Her whole body screamed her grief, but with whom could she share it? It was, after all, eight years later. One is not supposed to grieve for eight years. It is unseemly.

She had gotten a grip on herself and circulated. And she really had enjoyed herself. At that one Tel Aviv meeting there were partisans who had come to the reunion from all over the world. There was even a contingent of Polish partisans that had joined them here in the Jewish state. These, she assumed, were the more tolerant ones, the ones who had not killed any Jew they had come across. And there were Jewish partisans who had not settled in Israel but came from the States, Canada, South America, New Zealand, Australia, even Hong Kong. It was incredible how strong they all seemed, as if fighting all those years ago had steeled them for the rest of life. She felt as if she were the only weak one.

A chance comment by one of the Americans had caught her attention. The woman had said, in Yiddish, "We have to write this down. All of us have to write something down. No one has told our story."

Yes, that was true. The survivors of the camps had borne witness. The escapees who went to Israel, to London, to wherever they could flee had published their accounts. But the partisans? Eliza had read nothing that covered her experience.

She decided that very evening that she would be the one to write about her life. She had so much to tell. She would write about her four years in the forest and the destruction she found when she emerged. Dust. Ashes. Smoke. Her parents, her family, her child, her life as Eliza Wolf of Cracow could not be recaptured. Except in writing.

"I really enjoyed that," Yehuda had said to her as they drove back the next day to Tiberias.

"We're going to make love when we get home," Eliza had told him.

"Oh, yes?"

"In celebration of the life you gave me."

"Really? Now our love-making is monumental?"

"And then I want to go shopping with you for furniture."

"An interesting combination," he'd said.

Yehuda didn't understand the desk or the chair or their location in the house. She explained to him that she would be writing every morning now and she didn't want to be disturbed.

She wasn't either. Yehuda spoke to her about being obsessed. First Ron, he pointed out, and now writing. He'd suggested gently that they take a year's vacation, a "sabbatical," as Ami called it, and go overseas, where she could receive treatment.

"Psychiatric treatment?" she had asked.

"I think it's time," he'd said with a gentle smile.

She could not get psychiatric treatment in Israel, because it would be too embarrassing for the family. It was simply not done for ordinary people to get help. There was too much shame attached to seeing a head doctor. That's because in Israel everyone was supposed to take care of himself, or herself. It was a nation built on the necessity for invincibility. It was a nation built on the blood of its sons, her son, her Ron.

She wrote. It was her salvation.

69

THE VISIT

YEHUDA WATCHED THROUGH THE GLASS PARTITION AS THE PASsengers from his son's plane disembarked and made their way through customs. Good, there they were, Ami and Judy and little Ron, slung on his mother's hip. Yehuda pushed through the waiting crowd and rapped on the glass. Then he shook his head, irritated. It was foolish to try to attract their attention that way. But he couldn't wait to see them.

The bags were slow in coming, as usual. Judy grew annoyed. While Ami patiently waited, she turned toward the glass, and Yehuda rapped again. She walked over and stood in front of him, pointing out his grandfather to little Ron and having him wave. Then she put him down and let Yehuda see the tricks he had learned. He could walk and fall, pick himself up and walk again. Yehuda clapped. "Cute kid," the man next to him commented.

"My grandchild," Yehuda said with pride.

Ami called his wife over. Judy gave a quick wave and dragged Ron off to collect the luggage that was now slowly circulating by. Yehuda moved away from the window and around to where his family would come out. Half an hour passed before a bedraggled Ami showed up with the first two bags. Judy hurried behind him, carrying an overnighter and Ron. Ami dropped the bags when he saw his father. They embraced. "Customs," Ami explained.

"Why didn't you go through the green line?"

"I did. They stopped me. We had to unload everything." He shook his head. "I didn't think we'd ever get things stuffed back in."

"How much did you have to pay?"

"Nothing. The appliances were all in Ron's diaper bag."

Yehuda nodded his head in approval. "I've raised you right." He grabbed one of the bags from his son. "I might have a heart attack before we make it to the car."

"Hey, that's only the clothes. You should carry this one."

After they loaded everything into the car, Yehuda slowly pulled out of the parking lot and drove past several checkpoints before he hit the expressway to Tel Aviv. "So, how was it? Judy, how were your parents?"

"Sorry to see us leave," she told him.

"I don't blame them. But I'm happy you came back."

"How's Mom?" Ami asked.

"She's fine. She couldn't come today, because—"

"Don't make excuses, Dad. I just asked how she was. Did you ever have a chance to check on our apartment?"

"Yes. It was left in good shape. I had it cleaned two days ago. No *hamseen*, so it shouldn't be all covered with dust."

"Good," Judy said. "I don't think I'm up to cleaning."

"You just take care of Ron. That's what's important."

"Yes, Grandpa."

He drove them to their apartment in a high rise in Ramat Aviv. It wouldn't have been his choice of a place to live; but it was close to the university, and he had promised his son any apartment he wanted for his wedding gift. This one had three bedrooms and a study, which Yehuda supposed could be made into a fourth bedroom if they had three children. He wouldn't plan ahead for them. He helped them with their suitcases, then left them for a quick trip to the supermarket to buy the bare essentials."

"Can you stay for a while?" Ami asked.

Ron was on the floor, whining. "You're tired," Yehuda pointed out.

"Not that tired."

Ron belied that with a scream of impatience for something Yehuda couldn't understand, but, fortunately, Judy could.

"You'll come for Rosh Hashanah?"

"Sure. Where else would we go?"

"Your mother will be happy to see you. And by that time you should be settled in and relaxed. More relaxed anyway."

"Let me get you your gifts."

"No," Yehuda forestalled him. "Bring them up when you come. See you in a few days."

Ami finished packing the car, then got into the driver's seat. "You know, we can spend our days at the beach, visit friends, check out the digs, see how they're being worked. It will go fast, I promise you."

"I think we should just go for Rosh Hashanah and come back," Judy said. She turned around to check on Ron, making sure he was well fastened in his car seat. Ami noted how his wife was finally returning to her shape before Ron, before nursing. Her breasts were small again, her waist trim, her hips inviting, her legs fit to pinch. She noticed him looking her over. "Letch," she castigated.

He ran his hand through her red hair, kissed her freckles. "You and I can have some time alone up there," he reminded her.

"I'm not the nature lover you are when it comes to love-making."

"But you can learn to like it, I promise you."

"Besides, whenever I'm at your parents' place, I always feel as if I'm in the way."

"My father loves having you."

"It's not your father, Ami."

"For my mother, everyone's in the way. You know that." He started the car. They headed for Derech Haifa and the trek north. They thought they had gotten an early start, but already the highway was filled with vacationers traveling north for the week's holiday. "When I was a kid, this used to be a very hectic time," Ami remembered. "The hotels would be full. Ron and I would stay out of the way when we were young, help as we got older. When we were teenagers, we used to have so much fun with those girls from Tel Aviv and Jerusalem. Did you know that women from Jerusalem have bigger tits than those from anywhere else in Israel?"

"No, dear, I didn't. That's fascinating."

He gave her a quick look, and they laughed. They made it half-way to Haifa before Ron woke up from his nap and started fidgeting and then screaming his protests at being tied down. By the time they reached Tiberias, the traffic was terrible, and Judy's nerves were totally frazzled.

Ami pulled off onto a side road outside the city and took its curves slowly until he reached his parents' villa. It was strange to think that years ago there had been nothing here, and now there was an entire community, a rich community.

His parents' villa was sheltered by eucalyptus trees and covered with bougainvillea. The gardener had encouraged both orange trees and lemon trees to grow in the backyard, and flowers sprang up year-round in the garden. Ami found it comforting to come here, and sometimes wished that he could live here instead of in the middle of Ramat Aviv, stuck between the university and the sea.

Judy unstrapped Ron and set him down. He raced into the yard and plopped into the dirt. He definitely would not make his best impression. Four o'clock. His mother should be here, Ami thought, unless she was still shopping.

The door opened. Eliza stood there in a pretty blouse and a new skirt. "Ami!" she said, as if she weren't expecting him.

"Surprise," he answered.

"How nice of you to come." She said it as if he were a stranger. Well, maybe he was.

"Judy and the baby. How wonderful! Do come in."

Maybe it had been a mistake to name their child Ron. His mother had yet to pronounce the name. But it was Ami's duty to remember his brother.

"How are things going, Mom?" he asked as he leaned down to kiss her. She allowed it.

"Well."

"Still writing?"

"Yes. Didn't your father tell you? I've really been making progress. I'm going back and forth in time, because that's the only way I can make sense of things. Your father's going to hire a typist for me. I wish I had learned how to type. I imagine you know how."

"Yes."

"I don't know why I never learned."

They heard a crash and rushed into the dining room. Ron had knocked a chair over and, trying to keep his balance, had pulled on the tablecloth. A candy dish had slid off and broken. Judy was scolding him, trying to pick up the pieces. Eliza grabbed the child and held him to her. "You have to watch out that he doesn't cut his fingers. Judy, leave that. I can get that later."

"Luckily, it broke into big pieces," Judy said, as she bent over the broken dish. Ami stooped to help her while Eliza carried Ron into the living room and sat down with him on her lap.

She was playing peek-a-boo with him when Ami and Judy rejoined her. "Everything's back to normal," Ami said.

Eliza placed Ron's hands on her cheeks. Then she played patty-cake with them. "Did you know that my child was almost exactly your baby's age when I lost her?"

Judy stared at Ami, then turned and walked into the kitchen.

"She was so cute," Eliza said, as her son took a seat across from her. "I'm remembering more and more about her as I write. She wasn't like your child, of course."

"Ron."

"Ron? No, she wasn't like Ron, either."

"Our child's name is Ron, Mom."

"Ron," Eliza managed carefully. "Your child has beautiful red hair. Just like Judy's. Like King David's, right?"

Ami smiled.

"My girl had black hair. Like her father's. Like Adam Feuerstein's. Did I ever tell you about Adam?"

"No."

"He was my first love. I know you think I couldn't possibly love anyone but your father. However, I didn't meet your father until I was old. How old? I'll have to check on that. I think twenty-eight, twenty-nine. Before I was thirty, I'm almost sure. It's hard writing the truth. Some people write lies to make themselves seem more important. But I want this book to be totally true."

"I'd like to read what you've written."

"Would you?" She seemed surprised. "I'd like that, too. I need critical comment, Ami. Your father reads what I write and pats me on the head. He thinks I'm crazy. Well, I suppose he's told you that."

"No. He hasn't said a thing, Mom."

"Guilty silence?" She smiled thinly at her son. "I think this book is helping me, Ami. I really do."

Ron slid down from her lap, to go exploring. "I suppose we should watch him. I should have put everything up high. I don't know where my head was. I certainly remember how much trouble you and your brother used to get into."

She stood. Ami noted how thin and gray she had become. He embraced her and could feel her heart beating. "I love you, Mom," he said to her.

She suffered his embrace, then broke away, putting her hand to his cheek. "I love you too, Ami. How's your leg?"

It's not there anymore, he wanted to tell her. But she didn't wait for an answer. She was off after Ron.

Yehuda came home from work at six. He carried two briefcases with him. "It's tough making money," he shouted to Ami, as he got out of the car. Ami was in the garden watching Ron try to uproot several plants. Yehuda stared at his grandson. "He's going to be a troublemaker, just like you boys were."

"You should see what he does to our apartment," Ami said.

"I wish you would let me buy you a house. Maybe in Afeka; that's close enough."

"Dad, Judy likes the apartment. She has friends there. They go out walking with their babies, go to the milk bar, have a snack. She's enjoying life. The apartment is fine."

Yehuda shrugged. "So how's everything?"

"Great. We're all settled again."

"And inside?"

"Judy and Mom are getting dinner ready."

"Is she better or worse, do you think?"

"You know, Dad, in Tel Aviv there's a support group."

"A what?"

"A group of people who have lost someone in the wars. They get together, share feelings, help each other over the bad spots."

Yehuda quickly shook his head. Then he asked, "Do you go?"

"No. But Judy has a friend from South Africa who does. Her whole family immigrated in 1966. The woman's brother was killed in 1973. They were twins. About ten people get together every few weeks to discuss things, how they're dealing with death, loss."

"Who are these people?"

"English-speaking immigrants mainly. If that's what you mean."

"You know that's what I meant. It's their way to talk things to death."

"Maybe it's the right way. Maybe it would be the right way for Mom."

"There's no group like that here in Tiberias."

"Maybe she can start one. I could have Judy's friends get in touch with her. Perhaps Mom would like to come down to Tel Aviv, to see what it's like."

"I'm sure your mother wouldn't be interested."

"I'll talk to her. Do you mind?" He could see his father hesitating. "You know, there's one thing I've learned from living with Judy, living in the States. They have an expression: Troubles shared are troubles halved. Something like that. Not everything has to be kept inside. You don't always have to be strong."

"Really?" Yehuda asked. "Well, if I'm not strong, how will I survive? How will I cope? With your mother? With Ron's death? With what happened to you?"

"I'm here. I'm whole. It's you and Mom whose lives have been torn apart."

"You have a son. When he goes into the army—" Yehuda sighed—"you'll die a little."

"If Ron knew what his death had wrought—"

"But he never will know, will he?"

A sharp wail cut short their conversation. Ami nodded sadly. "I think he's found the briar patch."

Judy hurried to the front door. "Ami! Haven't you been watching him? My God! Oh. Hi, Yehuda." She gave her father-in-law a kiss on the cheek. Ron toddled back into sight holding his bruised arm out. "Honestly!" Judy gave Ami a parting shot before she whisked Ron up and took him into the kitchen for first aid.

The Rosh Hashanah meal was a little noisier than usual. Last year Ron had been asleep in his carry-cot. This year he made sure everyone knew there was a new king at the table. What he didn't throw on the floor, he spilled; when others were talking, he gurgled his opinions. As the night grew longer, he seemed to become more wide awake.

"He's just overexcited," Eliza said, excusing her grandson.

"He's just being a pain," Judy corrected her.

They tried to put Ron to sleep in his room. But every time they closed the door, he let out an impatient wail. By eleven, they were all exhausted except Ron.

"Go to bed," Ami told the family. "This is the perfect time for me to start on Mom's book."

"Are you sure you want to do it tonight?" Eliza asked. "You need a clear head."

"I have a clear head. I'll sit in the rocker with Ron and read. Believe me, Mom, that's how I get through most of my scholarly journals."

"Well—if you're sure you can concentrate."

"If I can't, I'll put the pages down," he promised.

Ami was relieved when everyone retired. He liked being alone. He especially liked being alone with his son. "You are a deliberate troublemaker, aren't you?" he asked Ron.

The baby smiled. Maybe his eyes twinkled. Ami held his son, walked into the dining room, and picked up the bulk of his mother's manuscript. Then he pulled the rocker out onto the patio next to the living room. He dragged the lamp over so it would shine on the pages. But before he turned it on, he looked up at the stars. How he loved the stars, and being out in the open with nothing between himself and God. He smiled, then held Ron against his shoulder and began to read. Long after Ron had been rocked to sleep, Ami kept reading. Feeling shock and horror and recognition, he read through the night and into the dawn.

70

CONVERSATIONS

AMI SAT SLUMPED IN THE ROCKER AND WATCHED THE SUN COME up. He had long ago put Ron to bed; though with the lightening of the sky, he expected him to be up and running before long.

He had not stayed awake all night since the war. No, that wasn't entirely true. After the war, in the hospital, the pain had kept him awake. Even with painkillers he couldn't sleep. The most difficult period came when he heard about his brother. But after 1973, he had never had trouble sleeping, even on his wedding night. He remembered well his wife's comforting body alongside his.

The manuscript sat in his lap, and the pages made an occasional attempt to flutter down to the floor. He caught them with his hand.

What if he was wrong?

The sun rose. It would be a fair October day across the land of Israel.

Life cheated so many. It wasn't right to be born with expectations that could not be fulfilled. Life had cheated six million of his people. Even those who had survived had never got what they had earned by their suffering. In his mother's case, all she had received was more suffering.

He was still holding the manuscript and staring into the garden when his mother, on her way to the kitchen to start the coffee, noticed him. She crossed to the patio. "Still here? You haven't been here all night, have you?"

Ami looked up at her and smiled. "Yes."

"Why?"

"Reading."

"You could have read that anytime. You're going to be here a week, aren't you?"

"Once I got started, I couldn't stop."

"Why are you looking at me so strangely? I know. You can't believe I was ever young, can you?"

"It's interesting, Mom, what you have written."

"Thank you. But that's a rather limited critique."

379

"It's jumbled. The time is out of whack."

"I was trying to give it a stream-of-consciousness flavor. Was that a mistake?"

"It would make much more sense to go from year to year. That's the way the horror built, wasn't it?"

She took the manuscript from him. "I don't know. The horror built as I discovered things. Some of these events I didn't find out about until the war was over—such as, what happened to my family, how my daughter disappeared."

"Why did you never tell us much about her?"

"I told you about her when Eichmann was captured. I can distinctly remember telling you and Ron. I remarked to both of you how important it was that I never lose anybody again. But that didn't stop—anything, did it?"

"But you said she's alive. In this manuscript you say that when you and Dad went to Kowitz, the townspeople told you she had left with this Wanda Zbyszek."

"And they both promptly disappeared from the face of the earth. My dear, you obviously don't understand what conditions were like back then, how many displaced people there were."

"And you've never thought to search for her again." It was a statement.

"Search where?"

Ami nodded. "I'm tired."

"Night is for sleeping."

"Night is for nightmares, Mom. I'm going to drive down to the lake and go for a swim. Tell Judy when she gets up, will you?"

"You shouldn't go swimming alone. What if something happened?"

"Mom, Lake Kinneret is crawling with people. There are hundreds tenting on its shores. They are using the lake as a place to wash, their own private sewer. Believe me, I'm not going to drown."

By the time Ami got home from the lake, the family gathering was in full swing. Aunt Yael had come from Haifa with her daughter, Sarah, and her three grandchildren. Ami greeted the women, then went in search of his father. Finding no sign of him, he entered the kitchen, where his mother was fixing another round of drinks. "Where's Dad?" he asked.

"Out in the garden."

Ami found his father sitting on a chair near the gardening shed, reading. He shook his head. "What was it? The noise?"

His father looked up and smiled. "They're not missing me, are they?"

"Have you read Mom's book?"

"Yes. I hear you stayed up all night devouring it. I hope you said something pleasant about it."

"Dad?"

"Hmm?"

"Dad? Can I have the keys to your office?"

"My office? On Rosh Hashanah?"

"I want to make an overseas call. I'll pay you back."

"A business call?"

"Sort of."

"Well, you can do that from here, Ami. There's no sense in going into town today."

"Please, Dad. It's private."

"Private," Yehuda repeated. "My keys are in my top dresser drawer. You know which ones they are?"

"Yes."

"No one's going to be in on Rosh Hashanah."

"Maybe you're right." Ami turned to go. "Oh, by the way, guess who I met in Cleveland, Ohio."

"Who?"

"Mina Eisenberg. Do you remember her?"

"Mina Eisenberg." Yehuda thought for a minute. "No."

"Travel agent? She came up here touring before the 1967 war?"

"Oh, yes. Didn't she stop by the apartment after the war to check—"

"Yeah, to see if you had made it."

"Umm. I remember her vaguely. She told me my hotels were too European for American tourists. Yes, I remember that." He looked at his son, who continued to stare at him. Was Ami annoyed, puzzled, or what?

"You've read Mom's book," Ami said.

"Yes. I've already told you."

"Life makes no sense sometimes, does it?"

"You're too young to say that, Ami. Life should be making a lot of sense to you about now. It's when you get old that life betrays you."

"Really? Hey, thanks for the keys, Dad. I'll return them in a little while."

"Fine." His father had already dismissed him and was back to his reading.

When Ami got to his father's office, he found himself totally alone. No one worked on Rosh Hashanah in Israel, except maybe the telephone operators, who watched the circuits being loaded with calls between continents, between parents who had immigrated to Israel and children who had emigrated elsewhere.

It was early in Cleveland, Ohio, now. Seven-forty-five, if he'd figured the time zones right. He could probably still catch Mina Eisenberg at home. He remembered last night sneaking into the room where his wife and Ron were sleeping and frantically searching for his wallet in the dark. Back in the light, he'd hurried through the cards and papers he had collected during his visit to North America. Good times, fading conversations came to his mind as he went through the names one by one. "Mina Eisenberg." She had a nice embossed card, her name followed by all her certifications as a travel agent. Her office number was followed by another one, which had after it, in parentheses, *R*. Did *R* stand for residence? Her home number? An answering service?

He might never find out. It was impossible to get a long-distance line. He tried for half an hour. "We can get you a line now," some operator told him. Thanks a hell of a lot, he felt like saying. At eight-fifteen, Mina Eisenberg might have left her home.

"The circuits to Cleveland are all busy. Would you like us to keep trying?"

"Yes, please." Who else would call Cleveland? But now that he had an operator and she was actually connected to the States, he didn't want to let go.

All of a sudden, Ami heard a buzzing, the soft burr of a phone ringing someplace. He only hoped it wasn't one operator talking to another. "Hello?"

"Hello?" Ami said.

"Go ahead please," the operator said.

What did she think he was doing? "Thank you, operator. Hello, is this the Eisenberg residence?"

"The Eisenberg residence? Well, it's our house." The voice was that of a little girl. Ami smiled.

"Could you put your mother on the line, please?"

"I think she's still sleeping."

Ami loved good Jews who took Rosh Hashanah off. "This is *very* important. Could you please wake her up?"

"Okay. Hold on."

He held on and prayed that the connection wouldn't be broken. It was so hard to know, in Israel, when the next breakdown might occur.

"Hello." The voice sounded heavily drugged.

"Mina?"

"Yeah."

"This is Ami Barak."

"Who?"

"Is this Mina Eisenberg?"

"Oh, Ami. God, I'm sorry. It was a long night last night. I always have a hard time getting to sleep after visiting Ted's relatives."

"Who is it?" Ami heard another voice ask.

"Ami Barak," he heard Mina say. "The guy I met for breakfast. So how's Montreal?" she said into the mouthpiece. "Happy holidays, by the way."

"I'm not in Canada, Mina. I'm back in Israel."

"Oh. Then this is long long distance."

"Yes. Are you wide awake now?"

"Well, not wide, but I believe I'm in full control of my faculties."

"Do you remember our conversation in the restaurant?"

"Not word by word."

"You told me you had a picture of your mother and you taken just after you'd arrived in America."

"Yes. It was taken in 1946."

"Could you copy it and send it to me?"

"Why?"

"I don't know yet, but I want a copy."

"That's silly."

"What can I say to convince you? As a favor to me? For old time's sake? What are the magic words?"

"The magic word is 'please.' Didn't your mother ever teach you that?"

"Please, then. Do you have a pencil and paper there?" Ami asked.

"Yes."

"Okay. Write down my address." He gave it to her very slowly and then made sure she had taken it down correctly. "You'll do this as soon as possible? Even today?"

"I could do it today."

"Make sure you send it airmail."

"Of course. I know how to send things overseas."

"Thanks, Mina. I really appreciate this. It's *very* important to me."

"Ami?"

"Yes?"

"You know, you don't appear weird in person. It might be better for your career if you stay off the telephone."

"Thanks for the suggestion, Mina. I'm going to be waiting every day for that envelope from you. *Hag samayah?*"

Ami put down the phone and sat back with a smile. But then the smile dropped. How did one handle dynamite?

He didn't have to think of it right then and there, however. After all, with the holidays, the mail service would be exceedingly slow. If he was lucky, and Mina sent it right off, he might get it in two weeks—if he was lucky.

71

CONFRONTATIONS

IT TOOK THREE WEEKS FOR THE ENVELOPE TO ARRIVE. AMI PUT Judy on watch for it. She was to call him as soon as it was delivered. The day that it came, he rushed home from the university and slit the envelope open carefully. Out fell the picture. Judy stood behind him, looking over his shoulder. Ron was also hanging over him, almost perpetually attached to Judy's upper body. Ami snatched the photo away before Ron drooled on it. Ami looked up at his wife. "Doesn't he know yet how to eat cookies with his mouth closed?"

"I'm sorry, doctor. I just don't have the time to teach him, and you haven't been around much lately."

He swiveled to face his wife. "Sorry," he apologized.

Judy put Ron down and sat across from her husband. "Okay, who's in the photo? What's so important about it?"

"I can't tell you."

"Why not?"

"Because I might be making a fool of myself."

"Darling—"

"No cracks, please. I don't know how to go about using this photo."

"Well, why don't you confide in me? I might be able to help."

"No. This is something I've got to keep to myself for a while longer."

"You're always like this, you know."

"Like what?"

"When you make a discovery, you always like to keep it to yourself until you're sure what it is. The great detective at work. It's maddening."

"Well, you do maddening things, too."

"Like what?"

"Like walk around the bedroom naked."

"If that's what you've come home for—"

"Well?"

"Well—I suppose I could put Ron down early for his nap."

"He did look very tired."

"Drooling can be exhausting work." She smiled at her husband.

Ron was the only one unwilling to cooperate. They finally decided to put him in his playpen with a box of cookies and hope for the best, at least fifteen minutes of it.

They stripped in less than a minute, throwing their clothes in a heap on the floor. In the other room Ron giggled. "He's happy with something," Judy interpreted.

"Good. I'm happy with something, too." Ami placed his hands on his wife's back and drew her down to the bed on top of him.

"Ooh! You are happy."

"That's called big, not happy."

"And such a braggart." She kissed him on his lips and followed that with little kisses all the way down to his groin.

They heard Ron giggle again. "That was a wicked giggle. He's up to some mischief."

"Will we ever get a chance to fuck?" Ami complained.

They heard a crash. "Oh, God," Ami moaned. "Lock him in a closet. Please."

Judy threw on her robe and rushed into the living room. "No!" Ami heard her scold. "Mommy is angry! Now you stay there and keep quiet." By the time she returned to the bedroom, Ron was crying. Ami wasn't doing so well himself. "He catapulted out of the playpen," she explained.

"Judy, we used to have such fun in bed together."

"We can still have fun."

"When he's eighteen?"

"Come on, honey. Just lie back and relax."

"I've lost it."

"We'll get it back." She set her tongue to work on him. It was hard to ignore the crying child in the living room, but Ami's natural urges took over. Judy sat on him, placing him inside her. He watched her breasts jiggle in front of his face as he thrust deep into her. He closed his eyes and concentrated on his body, one area of his body in particular. He grabbed her hips tightly and released himself into her, moaning in satisfaction.

"Five minutes," she reported.

"Lie down with me. Let him cry."

"Can we do that to our own son?"

"Yes. If we try hard enough."

Judy lay down next to him, half on, half off his chest. "Ami?"

"Umm."

"Have you ever thought that now might be a good time to start another child?"

"Oh, God, no!"

"Oh."

"You're not pregnant, are you?"

"I'm not sure."

"Judy, don't ruin my day, please. Let's wait until Ron is ten or something. Then maybe we can adopt a twelve-year-old to play with him."

"It's just that, well, I felt nauseous this morning."

"Food poisoning."

"I missed my last period. I thought it might have been caused by our move from Canada."

"Probably that's it."

"Would you be terribly unhappy?"

"That would be an understatement."

"Ron's not as bad as all that."

"Why is it then that every other child knows how to sleep and he's still learning?"

"They say second children are sweeter, calmer."

"And then there's sibling rivalry. If he won't let us go into the bedroom for a fuck, what is he going to do if you present him with a rival? Remember what he did to his teddy bear?"

"He was teaching it how to swim, darling. Anyway, I do have one piece of good news for you."

"Thank God."

"That support group that Lillian goes to? It's meeting Thursday night."

Thursday night, Ami thought. Somehow he was going to get his mother to Tel Aviv for it.

Ami discovered it was really his father he had to convince. "I don't want to air our grief in public," Yehuda said when Ami confided in him.

"It's not public. It's about ten people, that's all."

"That's enough."

"So you're willing to let Mom go on the way she is."

"She's writing now."

"Great. And when she finishes writing, what will she do? Don't you want her to have an integrated life again?"

"Don't talk garbage to me, Ami. I wasn't educated in America."

"Okay. Let me put it to you this way: I hardly ever ask anything of you. I'm asking that you come down here Thursday night."

"You don't ask anything of me, because I'd gladly give you anything I have."

"So I'm asking for a little of your time."

"Your mother won't go for it."

"She will, because I won't tell her."

"I won't join her."

"I'll take her myself."

His father was silent, and Ami suspected he had won. "I'll be there about five, six at the latest," Yehuda conceded.

Ami was both pleased and worried. This tactic might not lead to victory. He would have to see how his mother reacted to the meeting. He called Judy, who promised to call Lillian and find out where the meeting would be held. Then he went back to work, almost. His mind could not help floating to the photo Mina Eisenberg had sent. By rights, he should have told his father about it. But how? He felt certain that Mina was his mother's child. He believed it with all his heart. But what if she weren't? Who knew how many children this Wanda What's-her-name took in? And what happened to those children?

Thursday night his parents arrived at the apartment. They looked grim, as if they were coming for something distasteful. Ami knew Yehuda didn't approve of this visit; he didn't know what was troubling his mother. She confessed immediately. "I hope this is important, Ami, because I'm missing a day's work."

Judy came out of the kitchen, stared at his parents, and went back in. Ami wished she had known them before Ron's death. Life had been so different then.

"How's the baby?" Eliza asked.

"Ron's fine, Mom." He wanted to ask her what she was going to call Ron when "baby" no longer fit.

He helped Judy with the final stages of getting supper ready while his parents kept Ron company. "This isn't going to work," Judy whispered.

"Either things will get better or they'll get worse," he said to her. "If they stay the same, I'll have to disassociate myself from them, and that wouldn't be right, would it?"

When they sat down and been served, Judy said, "I have an announcement to make." She smiled broadly. Eliza and Yehuda waited attentively. "I'm pregnant."

"Congratulations!" Yehuda said, mainly to his son.

"It wasn't planned," Ami confided.

"No one has an unplanned child nowadays," Eliza scolded.

"We managed."

"I'm rather happy about it," Judy confessed.

"Then maybe it was planned by you," Eliza said.

"I hadn't considered that." Ami gave his wife a look.

She laughed. "No. Sorry. I'm not that clever. But it will be nice. Ron's a beautiful fourteen months; and now, in seven months or so, we'll have another one."

"I can hardly wait," Ami mocked.

She reached over and put her hand on top of his. "I know you're joking. You're a terrific father." He sighed.

The meal went pleasantly after that, with talk of pregnancy and birth and how many of Judy's friends were also pregnant, what the doctors were like, how different it was to have a child here in Israel from the way it was in the States.

After the meal, Eliza insisted she was going to help Judy clean up, but Ami said. "You can't, Mom. We have to go to a meeting."

"Meeting?"

"Yes. Grab your sweater or something. It's probably colder than you think."

Yehuda said nothing to his son. Ami shrugged in response. Eliza came back, ready to go. "You're giving a lecture tonight, aren't you?" she said to her son.

"Let's go."

"Yehuda?"

"No, I'm staying here."

"But your son will be speaking."

"I'm staying here," Yehuda reiterated.

Ami and his mother left the apartment and waited in the hallway for the elevator. "He would probably be overwhelmed with tears; that's why he won't go," Eliza said, making excuses for her husband. "You know how emotional he gets. He was so proud when you became a professor. To hear you talk would be too much for him." They got into the elevator. "After Ron died—"

"Yes?"

"Your father used to lie awake at night and cry. He never reached out for me; he never even knew I was awake. But he cried night after night.''

Ami couldn't believe that his father didn't know his mother was also awake. Even when Judy woke up for a minute, he knew. ''Why didn't you reach out for him?'' he asked his mother.

''Eliza, the Nurturer? I had already nurtured enough, and look what it got me.''

She abruptly led the way to the car. ''Are we driving? Or shall we walk?''

''It's not far. Only two blocks.''

''Well then, we'll walk, of course. I like Ramat Aviv, even though it looks like a city now. I don't like cities much. You know, this used to be all sand, an annoyance that would blow across the road so you would end up on the shoulder up to your axle in a dune.'' She smiled. ''What changes have been made. Yet nothing has changed, has it? We're still encircled. We have no friends. It's like when the Germans came to Poland. We had no place to hide.''

''And yet someone took in your daughter?''

''I practically forced the woman. I turned away from her and left my daughter with her. Later that night I went back. I was going to kill the woman if Mina was not alive and inside, safe. I would have, too. I would have killed anyone to save my child. Now, I suppose, you're going to give me a lecture on sociobiology.''

Ami smiled at her. ''Not quite my field.''

''What are you talking about tonight?''

''It's going to be a seminar, Mom. Many people will be talking.''

''Oh. I was looking forward to hearing only you. I hope I won't be bored.''

''If you are—terribly bored—we can leave.''

They reached an apartment building that was two stories taller than Ami's. The lobby was carpeted. The elevator cranked upward, delivering them to the eleventh floor. Ami knocked on a door and was admitted by someone he didn't know. Lillian caught sight of him almost immediately and came over. ''Ami,'' she said. ''I'm so glad you're here. Judy told me the good news. And this is your mother?'' She turned to face the dark woman by Ami's side.

''Yes. Mom, this is Lillian—''

''We use only first names here,'' Lillian said, cutting him off. ''So I'm Lillian,'' she said to Ami's mother. ''An you're—?''

''Eliza.''

''Eliza. What a pretty name. Do you speak English, Eliza?''

''Yes.''

''I'm afraid most of us do, and we find it easier to express ourselves in our native tongue. I hope you don't mind. Please, help yourself to coffee and cake. We're just about to start. You're actually the last to arrive.''

Lillian guided them toward the dining-room table.

Ami held Lillian back while his mother went ahead. ''I haven't told her what this is or why we're here,'' he confessed. Lillian gave him a chiding look. ''I didn't want to have to bring her in irons. So let her just listen for a while.''

''Okay. But we like to introduce ourselves and say who we lost and where.''

''I'll do it. Don't press her.''

''No one is forced to say anything. Matter of fact, some times all we do is sit and cry. I guess it clears out the system, if nothing else. Let her get coffee and take her to a comfortable chair.''

Ami couldn't lead his mother to the most comfortable chair, because someone his father's age was already sitting in it. But he took her to the next best thing and sat in a kitchen chair next to her. ''Ami,'' she said, ''what kind of academic meeting is this?''

He smiled down at her, but said nothing.

Lillian started the meeting by thanking everyone for coming. They seemed quite comfortable with each other, even though their ages differed, from teenagers up to grandparents. ''Let's start by introducing ourselves, shall we? I'm Lillian. I lost my twin brother in the Sinai in 1973.''

''I'm Sondra. I lost my husband in a terrorist attack in 1979.''

''I'm Harry. I lost my granddaughter in a terrorist attack in 1980.''

And so it continued. ''I'm Ami. This is my mother, Eliza. I lost my brother, she lost her son, in Ismailia in 1973.''

Eyes rested briefly on Eliza. Ami stared straight ahead; Eliza looked down at her lap. They did not look at each other: Ami out of fear, Eliza out of anger.

Harry started the conversation by talking about doing civil-guard duty at his granddaughter's former high school, how he was torn between love for and resentment of the children he saw. How could they be so alive when his granddaughter was dead? Why her, he had to ask himself over and over again.

Michael, father of a soldier, asked himself why he had come to Israel in the first place. ''I thought I was doing the right thing for my children. And now I have no son. It would have been better if we had stayed in England.''

''Then why don't you go back to England?'' a woman asked him.

A MOTHER'S SECRET 391

"If we did, what would be the reason my son died?"

Sally, from Australia, pointed out that old friends still avoided her. They didn't invite her to the weddings of their children because they didn't want to remind her of her son, who would have no wedding. "Instead of being comforted by the community as a whole, I'm treated like a pariah. The only time I feel I'm being remembered by the state is on Memorial Day; and as soon as that's over, everyone is out on the street celebrating Independence Day, hitting each other with those ridiculous plastic hammers. How can I grieve for my son and go out and celebrate the next moment?"

"My problem is my mother," Melody remarked.

They all smiled at her. She was the group's only teenager that night. Probably they all remembered problems with their mothers during those harsh years.

"Nothing I do matters to her," Melody said, tears coming to her eyes. "I get high grades; I do public-service work. I won a commendation for my summer's work with the disadvantaged. I showed it to my mother, and she said, 'That's nice, dear.' It's like, now that my brother is dead, nothing I do counts for anything. She's forgotten me. She's forgotten that I'm her child and I need her, too. Sometimes I fantasize. Next year, when I go into the army, I dream that I'll be killed. Then maybe she'll remember who I am."

There was silence until everyone was sure Melody was through speaking. Then Ami said, "I've had the same experience, Melody. My younger brother died in the 1973 war. We all loved him very much. It was a lingering death. He was kept on life support until we could convince my mother to let him go. Ever since then, life has not gone on.

"I lost a leg in that war. Well, the part just below the knee. My mother never once asked after me, never once considered my pain. Instead of sharing grief with the rest of those who loved Ron, loved her, she seemed to savor it, as if it were her private affair. I said to myself that she was still in shock over Ron's death, that I was being selfish for wanting some of her attention.

"But the years passed. I went to Hebrew University and got my degree. I married a beautiful girl I met there. We went to the States, where I got my Ph.D., and we had a formidable son, whom I named after my brother. My mother has yet to call my son by his name.

"After getting my degree, I came back to Israel, not because I didn't have other opportunities, but because this was the country of my commitment. I'm a lecturer at Tel Aviv University. Nothing I have done since the war has mattered to my mother. Not the degrees, not the marriage, not the grandchild, not the position. I've distanced myself from the pain she has unwittingly inflicted on me. I no longer seek her approval. Now I simply worry about her, wonder is she is going to spend the rest of her life inside this cocoon of grief.

"What I guess I'm trying to say, Melody, is that you, too, must go on with your life. Don't wait for your mother, because she may never be there for you again."

Melody looked across at him. "Thank you, Ami. I always feel better coming to this group. I need advice like that. I'm sort of lost."

Eliza said nothing.

Several mothers responded to what both Ami and Melody had said by defending a mother's grief. One said, "It's hard to hold onto what you have when you know that what you've lost is so great and not recoverable in any measure."

The conversation turned to memorials and then government benefits and how to get them in this perilous economic age. Then Sondra, the woman who had lost her husband, said, "I'm seeing someone."

They all applauded her.

"He's not like my husband." She corrected their impression immediately. "He's from Argentina." She grimaced. "But he's nice and he seems interested. Interested in more than just a fling in bed," she added. "I must say that, as soon as men find out I'm a widow, they seem to think I'm dying for them to ravish me. It's been long enough since my husband died so that I do consider my own needs, but I have no intention of being promiscuous, which I think most Israeli men can't understand. My Argentinian has been very respectful."

"I hope not too respectful," Lillian said.

Everyone laughed, even Sondra. "My problem is," Sondra continued, "I can't help comparing everything he does with the way my husband did it. Even the way he holds his fork or chews when he's eating. It's as though my husband's ghost superimposes himself on Alex's body. It makes me believe that maybe I'm not capable of loving again. Has anyone had—well, not two lovers; I'm not asking that—but two men they would marry? How does one adjust?"

No one said anything for a long time. Then Eliza lifted her head. "During the war, in Poland, I had a man I loved. We were partisans together. He insisted I accompany him. He took me away from Cracow just in time. He was killed by the Germans. We had a child together.

"When I came here to Israel—well, it was different from your experience, of course. Times were different. I went from fighting in one place to fighting in a second place. But when I met my husband-to-be, here, I didn't compare him to my former lover. Not for long, anyway. I wasn't the same woman. I didn't have the same dreams I'd had as an innocent child. I wanted someone the second time who could be my partner in life. There was passion, yes, but the fire wasn't so fierce. It was more of a mutual compromise the second time. Maybe your Argentinian also has had someone else. Why don't you talk to him about it?''

"There was someone,'' Sondra said. "One of those who disappeared, I think.''

"It might be a good idea to find out about it and discuss your feelings with Alex,'' Lillian said. "Maybe he's also haunted by ghosts.''

The meeting broke up shortly after ten. Friday was a working day. Sondra confessed as she was leaving that she always felt exhausted after these meetings and could barely make it up the next day. "Thanks for your help,'' she said to Eliza. "I hope to see you again.''

Lillian assured Ami that even if his mother couldn't make it, he was welcome to join them.

It was quiet that night when Ami and Eliza reached the street, not many cars. The stores had all closed. It was silent and dark. They walked along together, mother and son, not saying anything to each other, maybe afraid to. Then Eliza put her arm through Ami's and held on tight. Ami felt her closeness. It was good. "You're a silly boy, Ami,'' she said finally.

"Why?''

"To say I stopped caring about you.''

"I only said what I felt.''

"Even so.''

He waited. "Even so, what?''

"I find it hard to call your child Ron because Ron was my child. When I see your child growing, it's like seeing Ron growing up all over again.''

"That was the point, Mom.''

"But Ron won't grow up all over again, Ami. Ron is dead.''

"My son is named after my brother so that Ron's name will be perpetuated. The Arabs will not have wiped it off of the face of this earth. If it makes you feel better, why don't you call him Ronnie, as Judy's parents do?''

"I'll call him Ron. If it pleases you.'' She kicked a stone in front of her. "I never meant to hurt you, Ami.''

"But you did."

"You were always independent."

"But I needed you. After the war, I needed you. I was hurting, too."

"I needed something, also."

"I would have given you anything."

"I needed my son alive again."

Ami sighed, but it turned out to be more of a sob. Eliza stopped and faced him. She reached out her arms. "My baby, my poor baby," she said.

He stood in the middle of the road with his mother hugging him and cried without restraint. Although he was bigger than Eliza, she managed to rock him back and forth and tell him that everything would be all right. When his sobs subsided, she took out a tissue, wiped his eyes, and told him to blow. Smiling, he took the tissue from her, and said, "I'm not a child, Mom."

They resumed walking, arm in arm. "I'm glad we went tonight," Eliza said. "You needed it."

"I needed it!" Ami shook his head. "I didn't go for myself. I went for you."

"Yes, you little stinker, that was a dirty trick. But, well, it might have been beneficial."

"I'm glad."

"I think that you and Judy—and Ron, of course—should come up to Tiberias tomorrow."

"Why?"

"Because, I think—yes, it's time to bury Ron properly. We can pray and cry together and celebrate the life remaining to us. Okay?"

He nodded shakily. "Okay."

72

THE PHOTOGRAPH

THEY WENT TO RON'S GRAVE ON SATURDAY. ELIZA AND JUDY BOTH carried bouquets of flowers. It was a bright day, though the wind whipped through the cypress trees, giving a hint of the winter to come. Together Ami and Yehuda recited *Kaddish*. Ami was surprised that his mother did not cry. She looked surprisingly at peace. When their little ceremony was over, she took her grandson's hand and said, "Come on, Ron. It's time to go home."

Ami looked at his father. Yehuda shrugged. "It's over," he said. "You were right, Ami. I was wrong. Maybe that's why you're working at the university."

"Are you happy?"

"Yes. I will be." Yehuda put his arm around his son's shoulder, and together they walked from the cemetery to Yehuda's car.

A storm in the afternoon kept the family inside. It would have been a cozy occasion if Ron could have found someone or something with which to occupy himself. Finally he settled on throwing a ball back and forth with his grandfather.

Ami sat there with the photograph of Mina Eisenberg and Wanda Zbyszek in his pocket. Why should he bring it up now? Everything was fine with his mother, or would be. Life would be as it had been. This photo might mean nothing. Or it might mean everything. How would his mother react?

He should have told his father. Ami realized that. And yet he hadn't. Was he a child, that he had to keep his surprises to himself? Or was he afraid of what his father would say?

"What are you thinking of, Ami?" Eliza asked.

He smiled.

"Does your leg hurt when it's damp like this?"

Surprised, Judy looked at her husband.

"Sometimes," Ami admitted.

"Sometimes he takes it off and stomps around the house on one leg," Judy reported.

"Don't you lose your balance?" Eliza asked.

"I keep a crutch in the closet."

"I didn't know you still used a crutch. Did you, Yehuda?"

Yehuda shook his head. "I thought you weren't supposed to."

"The doctor says I'm not supposed to, but the doctor doesn't live with an artificial leg."

"Well, you've adjusted very well," Eliza complimented him.

"How's the book going?" he asked her.

She looked up thoughtfully. "I'm trying to put things in chronological order now, since that's what you suggested. I don't like it as much as skipping back and forth, but you might have a point."

"I have an illustration you might be able to use. Would you like to see it?"

"Certainly. Is it from one of the archives?"

"No. It's from a private source." He took the photo out of his shirt pocket and passed it to his father for transmittal. Yehuda stared at it and gave his son a quizzical look. Then he handed it to Eliza.

Eliza put down her knitting, took it from her husband's hand, and pushed her glasses higher on her nose. She stared at the photograph for what seemed like a very long time. Then she raised her face to her son. "Tell me!" she demanded.

"Do you recognize them?"

"Don't you know that I recognize them?" she almost screamed.

"Who?" Yehuda wanted to know. "Eliza, are you all right?"

"Wanda Zbyszek and Mom's daughter," Ami said.

"What!"

"Ami!" Judy added.

"Your daughter's alive, Mom. I found her. Or, she found me."

"You're lying."

"I'm not lying, Mom. Look at the picture."

"But this was taken—"

"Is it really your daughter?" Yehuda asked. "Look hard. Don't make a mistake."

"The hair."

"It's still rather wild," Ami said, smiling.

Eliza glared. "You bastard! Tell me everything."

He laughed. "I've wanted to tell you everything for over a week now."

"You've kept this from me for over a week?"

"I wanted to tell you that night after the meeting, but I thought you, we, had been through enough. You said you wanted your son back. I wished to God I could have brought you Ron. But Ron is dead. Mina is not. She's alive and well, and lives in Cleveland, Ohio. She has a husband and two children."

"My God, Ami! How?"

"What an archaeologist you turned out to be," Yehuda said.

"I'll tell you everything if you'll only listen and stop interrupting me. And may I say, Mom, that you probably needed glasses in 1967. Because she sat right in the same apartment with you, after Dad got back from the front."

"I don't believe you. I would have known."

"The travel agent. She was with her friend, a reporter, and that guy from the army."

"I don't remember! I don't remember! How could I not recognize my own daughter? Sixty-seven, and now it's 1981. All those years wasted."

"Forget the wasted years for a moment," Yehuda said. "Let's

let Ami tell us how he found all this out. I assume you're talking about Mina Eisenberg."

"Yes."

"You know her, too?" Eliza said.

"I did some business with her back then."

"Did you have any inkling?"

Yehuda shook his head.

Ami continued. "I remember her telling me she was from Poland, and I told her my mother was from Poland, that I felt close to her because my mother had a daughter named Mina, but she was lost during the war."

"You didn't know she was your sister?"

"No. I knew only after I read your book. You see, Mom, when I was in Cleveland giving a lecture, Mina came to see me, just to say hello. We met for breakfast the next morning, and she told me this crazy story about finding out that her mother wasn't her mother, but her sister."

"Her sister?"

"Wanda must have told the people in Kowitz that Mina was her sister. Anyway, after the war—and this is the reason you couldn't find her—Wanda somehow got hold of a letter to another villager, Maria Prychek, inviting Maria to come to America. So Wanda procured new identity cards for herself and Mina, and off they went to the United States.

"A few years ago, one of the Prychek relatives went on a sentimental journey to dear old Kowitz and found that the real Maria Prychek had died in 1942.

"Mina's mother—no one knew who she was at the time—either committed suicide or died accidentally the same day her husband discovered the hoax. Mina searched in Poland, and what she found was Wanda Zbyszek and herself as Wanda's sister.

"I guess since then she hasn't known for whom to mourn, her mother or her sister."

"All those years," Eliza said, almost as a sigh. "I dreamed many lives for her, but not that one. It was a good choice I made, wasn't it, to leave her with this woman."

"She survived," Yehuda said.

"Not many of us survived. Not many in Poland."

"Not many throughout Europe made it," Ami added.

"There were so few who would take us in. I asked for nothing for myself. But for my daughter, I asked for life."

"Well, she's got it, in spades. And you have two more grandchildren."

Eliza smiled. "I'll go to her, of course."

"When?" Yehuda asked.

"Now. On the first flight to New York."

"Can we wait a week, Eliza, until I clear my desk of pending business?"

She looked at her husband, surprised. "I must go alone, Yehuda."

"What do you mean?"

"I want to see my daughter alone. First. Then, of course, she'll be part of the family. But first there are things we must settle between us."

"You can't go alone, Mom. You've never been any place alone," Ami objected.

"I've been in the forests of Poland alone; I've walked through Nazi-held territory alone! Alone I guarded Kfar Hannah from the watchtower. Alone I had you."

"I think Eliza should go alone," Judy added. "What's so difficult about traveling? It's not as if Eliza doesn't speak English. And to wait even a week, now that she knows her daughter is alive, seems to me to be asking too much of any woman." Both men stared at her. "I'm not keeping out of it," she told them.

"As soon as Shabbat is over, you'll make arrangements, Yehuda?" Eliza said.

What could he say except yes?

73

SEEING YOUR FACE

ELIZA HAD NOT REALIZED THE FLIGHT TO THE UNITED STATES took so long. Somehow she had thought it was a short hop, because so many people did it, but there was no flight without a stop. Maybe that was good. It gave her a chance to think, to plan. Planning had been necessary to get her on a plane, to obtain a visa to enter the United States; there were so many in line. But Ami did it for her through Tel Aviv University, where one person's entire employment was devoted to standing in line for visas for the professors.

She smiled as she thought of the farewell she had had at the airport. All those instructions aimed at her—she was shot through with them—but she remembered none very clearly. She had a whole list of emergency numbers and strict orders to call as soon as she was safely in Cleveland.

The flight Yehuda had arranged for her was to land in Chicago. From there it would be a short hop to Cleveland, the airline had assured her.

The only thing she took with her on the plane, aside from several gossipy magazines Judy had thrust into her hands at the last minute, was the picture of Mina with Wanda Zbyszek. It was carefully placed in an envelope and in her purse. Every now and then she got it out and smiled down at it. How? How was she to approach Mina and say to her, "I am your mother"?

She had so many questions to ask her child. How many pictures did Mina have of herself growing up? Did she have an easy adolescence or did she fight with her mother? Eliza could remember arguing with her mother when she was in her teens. During the war, how she wished she could take back those angry words. Did her mother know that love was all there was between them? Dear Lord, let her not think back, but think forward. Mina was alive!

Eisenberg was a Jewish name, wasn't it? Or was it German? Did Wanda raise Mina as a Jew? Impossible, Eliza thought. Was Wanda a good mother? She must have been if Mina had searched for her origins after her death.

Questions with no answers kept Eliza awake the entire trip. She would look old and exhausted before she ever reached Cleveland.

At a little before five in the afternoon, a taxi pulled up in front of the Sheraton Hotel. Ami had stayed there only a few months before, and he had assured her it was a nice, respectable place, giving easy access to all of Cleveland. She checked in and was handed the key to her room. It was good that her suitcase was light, because there was no one to help her carry it. Maybe that was for the best, because, as much as she knew of American money from her days in the hotel trade, she still wasn't sure how much to tip.

Her room was lovely. It was bright and modern with a TV and radio and so many different lighting combinations that she had to wonder who could use them all.

She sat down on the bed and stared across at herself in the mirror. She looked—she had to admit it—gray and sallow. Right then and there she decided she would not see Mina when she looked like this. Not for the first time, certainly. Instead, she would sleep through the night. The next morning, she would take a taxi to the travel agency where Mina worked. And then?

Eliza showered and put on a dress that was supposedly wrinkle-free. It looked respectable enough, maybe. Then she went down to the lobby and used a pay phone with push buttons to call home, to let Yehuda know that she had arrived safely and was about to have dinner. He asked her all sorts of questions: Had she filled out the forms correctly? Did she have enough money? Did she feel she could handle things? Why did he treat her like a child? And yet hadn't she benefited from his protection over the years? From his goodness? His love?

After dinner, Eliza returned to her room, undressed, and slipped on her nightgown. She hadn't slept in more than twenty-four hours, except for catnapping on the plane. She would lie in this luxurious bed. She had her choice of two of them! It was hard to believe such luxury.

She slept. When she woke, it was 6:00, Tiberias time. She had the whole night still to go. She warned herself not to start thinking, and slept again. When she woke again, it was 7:30, American time. When did business open in America? In Israel they would be open by 8:00. She called the desk. Either 9:30 or 10:00, she was told. So there was plenty of time to dress and have breakfast.

She did everything in slow motion, as if it were an act of avoidance. Was she afraid of seeing her daughter? At 9:30 she took a taxi to the address on Mina's business card.

Ketura Travel was in a neighborhood of office buildings, with several small cafés, boutiques, and copy services at street level. People passed by her as she stood on the sidewalk outside the window of Ketura Travel, seemingly studying the pictures of suntanned men and women frolicking on sandy white beaches. Again Eliza chided herself. What was she waiting for?

She opened the door and stepped in. "May I help you?" someone asked almost immediately. Eliza turned too quickly toward the girl, stared at her, saw blond hair, a thin figure, youth. This was not Mina. "I'd like to look around," she said.

"Surely. If you need any help, I'm Jane."

Eliza surveyed the agency. It was filled with racks of brochures and several desks, similar to a consulting room. Others like Jane were behind the desks, either writing or talking on the phone or looking through thick digests of information. Eliza studied each in turn. None of them was Mina. Of that she was sure.

"Are you looking for someone in particular?" Jane asked. "Has one of us helped you before?"

Eliza was about to say something, but she saw a halo of dark hair moving from a back office toward the front. The woman wore a beige suit with a pleated skirt and low heels. Eliza tried but could not get a view of her face. It was bent low, as the woman talked to one of the consultants. Then she was gone, back into the office.

"Ma'am?" Jane said to her. But Eliza moved past the desks toward the office. She knocked.

"Yes?" a voice called from inside. What kind of voice was it? Eliza tried to decide. But it had been one word, an ordinary tone, an ordinary expression.

Eliza opened the door. The woman behind the desk looked up at her. It suddenly struck Eliza that she knew this face. "You look almost exactly like Paula Feuerstein," she said before she could stop herself.

"Paula Feuerstein?" Mina repeated. This strange woman came closer and slowly sank into the seat opposite her. Jane stood in the doorway making all kinds of signs, shrugs and telephone dialing. Mina waved her off. But for safety's sake Jane left the door open.

"Paula Feuerstein. She was your aunt," the woman explained.

"I'm sorry," Mina said. "Have we met?"

Eliza laughed. "Do you remember going hunting with me? In the woods? We'd bring home the day's catch. We were good at it, you and I. You were always so silent, like a hunter."

Okay, first nut case of the day, Mina thought. "Forgive me, but I—" She watched as the woman opened her purse. Mina was sure there was a gun in there and this was her last day on earth. Instead, the woman drew forth an envelope. From the envelope came a photograph, which the woman lay before Mina on the desk.

Mina looked down at the frozen forms of herself as a little girl and Wanda Zbyszek. "Where did you get this?" she asked.

"From Ami Barak."

"Ami? Look, I don't understand any of this."

"He said you wanted to know. I can tell you. You were born in the woods, deep in the woods. I can remember the pains and looking up into the trees, praying to God, hoping you would come soon. It was a summer's night, July 7, 1942. Three women who had had children before were there to help me, while your father sat with the other men by the fire, waiting, wondering at our nerve, to bring a child into the world at such a time. You were beautiful. But maybe you looked like the Feuersteins from the very beginning. You had a dark head of hair at birth. Your father was pleased. We called you Mina after my grandmother.

"I breast-fed you, of course. I was always afraid you weren't getting enough milk. It was summer then, so it was easy to forage for food. I hadn't gone hungry. I was determined that you wouldn't, either. In the winter it wasn't so easy. I worried about keeping you warm. I fought for the coat of a man who had died. I cut it down for you and made a bunting of wool for you to keep out the wind. It was horrible keeping you dry, but you survived that winter and into spring.

"All that time, we were on the move, fighting the Germans, evading them, trying to survive. We knew what was happening. We knew about the death camps, the labor camps. We knew that our people were being wiped from the face of the earth. You were the symbol of our survival, you and the other children of the partisans.

"Your father was killed fighting the Germans. And I was afraid. Not for myself, but for you." Eliza smiled a sad smile of remembrance. "With Adam alive, the world still had some order. But with his death, there was only me and there was only you. I didn't want to lose you." Eliza looked up into her daughter's face and almost laughed. "That seems funny now, doesn't it, after all these years?" She reached her hand across the desk and gently laid her fingers on top of Mina's. She remembered with the sharpness of pain how small Mina's hands were the last time she had seen her.

"Wanda Zbyszek was a woman I had met before the war. How I met her, that doesn't really matter. But I thought that there in Kowitz, with that woman, you would be safe. No matter what happened to me.

"Near the end of the war, we partisans joined forces with the Russian army. I almost made it back to Cracow, where our family is from. But I got typhoid; I was mad, delirious. By the time I recovered and reached Kowitz, you were gone. So was Wanda. I went crazy trying to find you. I stayed in Cracow over a year, hoping for some sign of you. Nothing.

"So I emigrated to Israel. I arrived the day partition was declared. There was another war to fight. During the war I met my husband, Yehuda Barak. Yes, you know him. We—you and I—even met right after the 1967 war, or so Ami said. Why didn't I see you then as I see you now?"

Mina sat across from this woman, her mouth hanging open. What should she say?

Eliza smiled. "It is so late in our lives. I know you don't need a mother, especially a mother who is a stranger to you. But I still need my daughter. I still need you, Mina. Will you allow me into your life?"

Mina rose, and Eliza did, too. They were the same height. Maybe they had the same eyes. Mina stared, finally, into the face of her mother.

"Feuerstein? That was the name of my father?"

"Adam Feuerstein. You would have liked him. I loved him."

Mina smiled. "I've had to get used to so many names lately. It's hard to know who I really am."

"The names don't make a difference. You are who you are. I see a very beautiful woman before me."

Mina came around the desk, holding her mother's hand. With the other hand she touched her mother's face. She leaned her cheek against her mother's; she kissed it. "Would you like to come home with me?" she asked. "There's so much I want to show you."

"There's so much I want to know," Eliza agreed.

Together, hands holding as if they could never be parted, Eliza and Mina left the travel agency and headed home.

74

FAMILIES

WHEN TED RETURNED HOME FROM WORK THAT NIGHT, THERE WAS a strange woman in the living room talking to his children. His wife looked guiltily up at him, and he knew what had happened almost immediately. Somehow Mrs. Mendez had finally wised up and quit her job as housekeeper. Or Mrs. Mendez and Mina had had a little tiff, and the result was Mrs. Mendez's departure. This woman was obviously here to take the housekeeper's place. He wasn't ready for this, not after a house-closing fight that had consisted of a pitched battle over the curtains and the broiler pan in the oven.

Mina stood up. She glanced down at Eliza, at her children, then back to her husband, who was poised at the threshold to the living room. Eliza sat on the couch looking from one to the other. Obviously, Mina was going to be allowed to handle the whole thing. "Ted. I don't know how to tell you this."

Ted nodded knowingly. Mrs. Mendez was gone.

"I should have called your office, but I was selfish. I wanted to experience everything before I shared it."

Experience everything before she shared it? Okay. Now he was lost.

"Ted, this is for real. This is my mother."

"Your mother?" he mouthed silently.

Eliza stood up. "Hello, Ted. I've seen so many pictures of you that I feel I know you already. I'm Eliza Barak. Mina is the daughter I lost so many years ago in Poland."

They ordered pizza. It was the only sensible thing to do. Ted sat on the couch while Mina and Eliza shot different aspects of the story at him. He was stunned. "I wish I had as many pictures of my family as you have of yours," Eliza concluded sadly. "I would have liked to have had just one of Adam, so that Mina could have seen what he looked like. But I will tell you that he had a cousin who left for Palestine before Hitler's rise to power. When I return home, I'll ask if he'll let me look through his photo albums. Maybe there's one of Adam as a boy, as a teenager."

Mina put her arm around her mother. "We've spent all day looking at photographs."

"I must have time, time to see everything." Eliza was worried. "Mina was kind enough to take me out to lunch, and then we bought presents for the grandchildren. What beautiful children you have! They are so healthy, so alive. So safe. And I called my husband. I hope you don't mind."

Ted was still in shock. "Please. Call him as often as you like. I just can't believe, after all these years, that you found each other."

"I hope over the winter holidays you can come to Israel. I would very much like to show Mina off to all my friends and the rest of her family, on Yehuda's side. And maybe your children can meet my other grandchild. He's not yet two, and already he's a real terror. I hope—I hope we can be a family."

"We will be," Mina assured her. "And there's so much you have to tell me."

"You, too. I want to hear about your life day by day."

"Maybe year by year," Ted suggested. "Otherwise, you're not going to have a chance to do anything else."

"What is it?" Mina asked, noting Ted's expression.

"I wonder what my family is going to say when they find out you're Jewish, after all."

Mina laughed. "I haven't told Mother about your family yet."

"I'd love to meet them," Eliza said.

"No, you wouldn't."

"Relations, any relation is precious," Eliza told them. "There are so many of us who have no one left. But now, there is you," she told Mina. Eliza touched her daughter's hair again, kissed her cheek.

"Now I know why my mother, Maria, never objected to my converting," Mina said.

"What is Lydia going to say?" Ted asked.

"Lydia! I have to call her. You remember, Mother. I told you about how Lydia went with me to search for answers in Poland."

"Yes, of course."

Mina jumped up. "I'll call her. Ted, talk to my mother."

Ted talked. Eliza opened her wallet to show him photos of her husband, Ami and Ron, Ami and Judy, her grandchild Ron. By the time they had both admired the new wing to the family, Mina was back, looking a trifle annoyed. "Lydia never changes. She wants to write a book proposal for this and see if she can get some money for our story. God, that woman! All she does is hustle."

Eliza stayed in Cleveland for two weeks. Mina took as much time off from work as she could. When Mina wasn't at home, Eliza walked in the neighborhood, restudied all the photographs Mina had left with her, and waited for her grandchildren to come home from school. She then talked to Sam and Rachel—when they weren't on the phone with their friends. They asked her about the war, as if she were from another planet. She supposed, for them, she was. And that was a very good thing.

On the second weekend of her stay with Mina, she told her daughter she must get back home.

Mina protested, claimed it was unfair. But Eliza pointed out that she had other commitments, like that to her husband. Her daughter unhappily relented. "Before you go," Mina suggested, "we should see Jerry."

"Wanda's husband."

"Maria's husband, my stepfather. We had our differences, a lot of them, but he has been good to me, in his own way. He should know the truth. Not about Wanda the prostitute, but the rest of it. I feel funny, you know, calling Maria my mother and you my mother."

"But we are your mothers," Eliza assured her.

"So, will you go with me to see Jerry?"

Eliza nodded.

Mina had not seen Jerry for more than two years. She called him on holidays and on his birthday. But since he had remarried, she didn't feel any desperate need to keep their contact close. She supposed she still resented him for remarrying, especially after what had happened to Maria. But maybe she should be a stronger believer in life going on.

When she called Jerry and asked to see him, all he said was "Trouble." She laughed. "Not really," she told him.

"In other words, yes."

Jerry wasn't used to trouble anymore. Terry was doing well in his practice and had presented Jerry with three grandchildren, not to mention two granddogs. Kristin was working in Silicon Valley, as a packaging expert. Jerry was near retirement and looked forward to traveling with Sylvie. He had told Mina the last time she'd called that he wouldn't miss work at all, and she believed him. He was thinking of moving out of Chicago, to someplace warmer.

She had arranged to arrive at Jerry's condo on Lake Shore Drive after he'd had time to digest his dinner. She didn't know if what Eliza had to say would upset him or please him. Maybe both.

When Jerry opened the door and saw the two women, he again said, "Trouble."

"Hi, Jerry," Mina said. She leaned forward, and they kissed. Then he opened the door wide for them to come in. Sylvie came and took their coats: She was soft and sweet and twenty years younger than Jerry. Mina tried to swallow her hostility. She told Sylvie how marvelous she looked, what lovely things she had done with the condo. She put great effort into being polite. Mina wondered how Terry handled the situation. He saw his father and Sylvie much more often than any of the rest of them.

Jerry led them into his sunken living room, done up in rose, which must have been Sylvie's choice. Mina sat down, and Eliza sat very close to her. "Would you like coffee? Tea?" Sylvie asked.

Eliza looked at Mina and shook her head. "Nothing for us, thank you, Sylvie," Mina said.

"Bring me a beer," Jerry yelled. "I think I'm going to need it."

Mina laughed. "Why do you always fear the worst when I'm around, Jerry?"

"Habit?"

Sylvie brought the beer and was going to join them. Jerry noticed Mina stiffen. "Didn't you want to watch that television show?" he asked his wife.

Well, no, she didn't want to watch it, but Sylvie was nothing if not gracious. She stood, smiled at them, and left.

"It's about Mom," Mina said when Sylvie was safely tucked out of sight.

Jerry looked from Mina to the strange woman and back again. "Why open that up again, Mina? It brings nothing but pain."

"Do you want to know the truth? Or not?"

"What is the truth, Mina? What did the truth ever bring us? Your mother died because of the truth. Or your sister? Whatever?"

"She was neither my mother nor my sister, Jerry. This is Eliza Barak. She's originally from Cracow, but now lives in Israel. She has something to tell you."

Startled, Jerry looked at the woman. "You know my wife?"

"Yes. I knew Wanda Zbyszek as someone I could turn to when there was no one else," Eliza said.

"What is that supposed to mean?" Jerry asked.

"You see, Mr. Jankowski, I am Mina's mother. Both Mina's father and I are Jewish. We were being hunted as you hunt boar in the forest. Adam, Mina's father, was caught and slaughtered. Wanda took Mina in so the same thing would not happen to her."

Jerry stared at her. "You're telling me that my wife took in a Jewish baby during World War II?"

"Oh, yes. And, yes, if anyone had ever found out, Wanda would have been killed along with the baby."

"But why?"

"I don't know why."

"Why didn't she tell me?" Jerry asked.

"Oh, Jerry, you've always been so prejudiced," Mina said off-handedly.

"Not to the extent of wanting to kill Jews or see them killed. What, are you crazy, Mina?"

"I don't know why she didn't tell you," Eliza said to Jerry. "I don't know how she changed from Wanda Zbyszek to Maria Prychek. But everyone wanted a better life. If Wanda saw her chance and took it, why should you blame her?"

Jerry looked gray. "When I confronted her with the letter, why didn't she simply sit down with me and say, 'Look, Jerry, this is what happened?' Am I so inhuman that I couldn't have understood? And you, Mina? Why didn't she tell you, for instance, when you were converting?"

"Don't you think those questions have been circling in my mind constantly?" Mina shot back.

"She was secure as Maria Prychek Jankowski," Eliza said. "There wasn't much security in the world she came from. Should she destroy what she had gained?"

"But why, when faced with the truth, did she let it destroy her?" Jerry asked.

Mina shrugged. "Who knows what was in her mind that day, Jerry? If only we could call her back to us."

"If only we could forgive ourselves," Jerry added. He put his face into his hands and cried. Mina moved quickly around to him and put her arm on his shoulder. "It's over with, Jerry. It was all so long ago."

75

THE FACE OF LOVE

THE GRAVEYARD WAS A QUIET PLACE, WINDSWEPT AND BLEAK, BUT not unfriendly. Both women carried bouquets. "I haven't been here in so many years," Mina confessed. "I think about her at least once or twice a day, but I haven't been to her grave in a long time."

"The last graveyard I was in was the one that held my son's body," Eliza confided. "We had a memorial service for him. It was very nice. But whatever we do, we carry the dead around with us."

"I can't remember," Mina said, looking puzzled. "Oh, yes. Over there. By that angel. It's not her angel. It's too gaudy for me. I insisted that we get a simple headstone, and Jerry wasn't in any mood to argue."

They reached the grave of Maria Jankowski, Beloved Wife and Mother. It lay simply, in a row with others. Together they placed their bouquets gently on the earth. Then Eliza backed away, looking around her for something. "What are you looking for?" Mina asked.

"A stone. Here's one. Here, for you, too." She handed Mina a stone. Then she placed hers on the headstone, urging Mina to do likewise. "For remembrance," Eliza told her. "It's a Jewish custom. Didn't you learn that? You must come to Israel." She smiled wanly. "We have a lot of experience with death."

Eliza sighed and looked down at the grave. "I had hoped to see Wanda alive one day. To take you from her and thank her with all my heart. Now I must thank this empty earth and hope that she hears."

Mina shook her head, trying to clear it. "Was it really so horrible during the war? Was there no refuge?"

Eliza looked at her, puzzled, almost angry. "Haven't you read your history? Don't you know? We can't sit for hours in my house, Mina, looking at photographs. There are none. All is ashes.''

"And yet you remember.''

"And now you must, too.''

"What made it happen? How did people let it happen?''

Eliza almost smiled. "The new Passover Haggadah for the Jews of our age. Why was this time different from the others? Why this time were we all destroyed and not just a few here and there? The answer is simple, isn't it? There were too few good people. If one person steps forward and says, 'This is wrong,' she can be silenced. But if all had come forward and said, 'No! There will be no Slaughter of the Innocents,' it would have stopped immediately. If neighbor had protected neighbor—but what is the use? It happened. There's no calling it back. And we must take comfort in the fact that there were men and women who risked everything they had to protect those in danger. Wanda risked her life to save you.''

"Why? I wish I knew why.''

Eliza shrugged. "Why? Maybe she felt she was an outsider anyway, that it wouldn't matter to people, whatever she did. Maybe she just didn't believe that little children should be gassed to death. Maybe she held fast to the sanctity of human life.''

Mina was struck by the strength of Maria Prychek's image as it guided her through life. "She cherished me. She was my mother.''

"She was a true Christian.''

"A righteous Gentile.''

Having said their benediction, they slowly walked away from the grave. The Midwestern wind swept against their backs, but left the stones on the grave's marker untouched.

ABOUT THE AUTHOR

CAROLYN HADDAD is the author of six earlier novels, among them OPERATION APRICOT, THE ACADEMIC FACTOR, and FLOWERS OF THE DESERT. She lives in Atlanta, Georgia.